Mind-slave Of The Serpent Queen

Zelia lay on her side, coiled in a position no human could have emulated, her torso bent sharply backward so that her head was pillowed on one calf. She had a lean, muscled body that was soft and round in just the right places. Arvin noted that her scales gave way to a soft fuzz of red hair at her groin and that her breasts were smooth and pink, quite human in appearance. He found himself imagining what it would feel like to have Zelia's body coiled around his—to feel the contrasting textures of rough, scaly skin and smooth breasts—then realized that Zelia had lifted her head to glance sleepily at him. Arvin, still on his knees, his head level with the ledge on which Zelia lay, dropped his gaze. He concentrated on the floor and waited for her to bid him to speak. The air seemed even hotter and drier than it had been a moment ago; Arvin found himself wetting his lips, just as the yuan-ti around him were doing.

Zelia chuckled, as if at some private joke. "You've been hunting sewer rats?" she asked, eyes still half-hooded with sleep. Her tongue tasted the air. "Yet you smell sweet."

Enter the House of Serpents

House of Serpents
Lisa Smedman

Book I
Venom's Taste

Book II
Viper's Kiss

March 2005

Book III
Vanity's Brood

March 2006

Also by Lisa Smedman

R.A. Salvatore's War of the Spider Queen, Book IV
Extinction

Sembia
Heirs of Prophecy

VENOM'S TASTE

HOUSE OF SERPENTS

BOOK 1

LISA SMEDMAN

VENOM'S TASTE
House of Serpents, Book I
©2004 Wizards of the Coast, Inc.

Distributed in the United States by Holtzbrinck Publishing. Distributed in Canada by Fenn Ltd.

Distributed to the hobby, toy, and comic trade in the United States and Canada by regional distributors.

Distributed worldwide by Wizards of the Coast, Inc. and regional distributors.

Cover art by Terese Nielsen
Map by Dennis Kauth
First Printing: March 2004
Library of Congress Catalog Card Number: 2003111907

9 8 7 6 5 4 3 2 1

US ISBN: 0-7869-3166-3
UK ISBN: 0-7869-3167-1
620- 96529-001-EN

U.S., CANADA,
ASIA, PACIFIC, & LATIN AMERICA
Wizards of the Coast, Inc.
P.O. Box 707
Renton, WA 98057-0707
+1-800-324-6496

EUROPEAN HEADQUARTERS
Wizards of the Coast, Belgium
T Hofveld 6d
1702 Groot-Bijgaarden
Belgium
+322 467 3360

Visit our web site at **www.wizards.com**

The Vilhon
Reach →

Cathedral of Emerald Scales

The Solarium

Zelia's Tower

House Extaminos

The Mortal Coil

Arvin's Warehouse

N

HLONDETH

PROLOGUE

23 Kythorn, Darkmorning

So this is to be my coffin, Arvin thought.

Had he been capable of it, he would have groaned in despair.

He was sprawled on his back inside a leaky rowboat, too weak to lift himself out of the cold, filthy water in which he lay. Even blinking was beyond him. With eyes too dry for tears, he stared at the bricks that drifted past a short distance above him—the arched ceiling of the sewage tunnel. Water sloshed against him as the boat nudged against a wall with a dull thud. Then the lazy current scuffed the boat away from the wall again and dragged it relentlessly onward.

It was not so much the knowledge that he was dying that filled Arvin with impotent grief—even though twenty-six was far too young for any life to end—it was the thought that his soul would begin its journey to the gods fouled with this intolerable stink. The sewage tunnel was slimed not just with centuries of human waste, but also with the pungent excretions of the serpent folk. The stench of the water eddying back and forth across Arvin's hands, plucking wetly at his hair and wicking up through his clothes, was unbearable; it brought back childhood memories of being unable to get clean, of tauntings and humiliation. Even Bane, god of crushing despair, could not have dreamed up a more perfect torment for Arvin's final moments.

He felt no pain, unlike those whose screams he could still hear echoing distantly from farther up the tunnel. There was just a dull heaviness that dragged him further toward unconsciousness with each passing moment, gradually slowing his thoughts to a trickle. Body and mind seemed to have become detached from each other, the one lying limp and unresponsive in the boat while the other spun in slow spirals, like water going down a drain. Pain would have been welcome; it might have blotted out the thoughts that were turning slow circles inside his mind.

Why? he asked himself, thinking back to the events of only a short time ago, of his meeting with Naulg in the tavern. Why was I ... so careless? That woman....

The thought drifted away as consciousness fled.

 **CHAPTER 1**

Arvin reached into his mug and fished a small, speckled egg out of his ale. He set it on the wooden table in front of him and, with a quick flick of his forefinger, sent it rolling. The egg wobbled to the edge, teetered, and fell, joining the sticky mess that littered the sawdust on the tavern floor.

He sighed as he raised the mug to his lips. Eggs. Why did the barkeep bother? Some humans had a taste for them—or rather, a taste for pretending to be something they were not—but Arvin despised the gagging, slippery feel of raw egg sliding down his throat. Next thing you knew, the Mortal Coil would be offering half-and-hares—ale mixed with rabbit blood.

The ale was surprisingly drinkable this evening; the barkeep had either forgotten to water it, or he'd washed the mugs. Arvin sipped it slowly, hoping he wouldn't have to wait all night. The pipe smoke drifting in blue swirls against the low ceiling was already thick enough to make his eyes water. The twine in his breast pocket didn't like the smoke much, either. Arvin could feel it twitching within its tightly stitched leather pouch. But at least the air was cool, a welcome relief from the muggy heat of a summer evening.

The Mortal Coil occupied the cavernous, circular basement of one of the warehouses that lined the Hlondeth waterfront. The tavern had been named for its ceiling, carved to resemble an enormous coil of rope. At high tide the room's southern wall sweated seawater. Arvin, seated on a bench that curved along that wall, sat stiffly erect at his table, loath to let his shirt brush against the damp stone behind him. The sooner Naulg arrived, the sooner Arvin could get out of this crowd, with their tarred hair and unwashed clothes that smelled of tendays at sea.

It was late at night and the tavern was crowded—despite rumors that the waterfront had become more dangerous of late, with more than the usual number of disappearances from the area around the docks. Sailors jostled each other, tilting back mugs and blowing loud, ale-frothed kisses at doxies who'd come in from the stroll. One noisy group—a crew, judging by their linked arms—sang a boisterous song about hoisting the yard, complete with lewd actions that made the double meaning of the chorus clear. On the other side of the room, another crew had shoved the tables aside and were lined up for a game of toss-knife. A dagger suddenly spun through the air between the two lines of men, zigzagging back and forth across the gap as each man caught and tossed it as rapidly as he could. Halfway down the line, one man suddenly howled and yanked his hand back against his chest, letting the dagger fall behind him. Blood dribbled from his clenched fingers as the others pounded him on the back, laughing at his misfortune at having to buy their next round of drinks. The wounded sailor, staggering under the thumps of mock congratulation, slowly opened his hand and stared, blinking and suddenly sober, at a fingertip that dangled from a thin thread of flesh.

Arvin winced. A dull ache flared in his finger as he involuntarily clenched his left hand. He opened his fingers and rubbed the smallest one, massaging it through the soft black leather of his glove. Years had passed since the Guild had cut off the last segment of that finger as retribution for intruding on their turf, yet the stub still smarted, especially if the weather was about to change. The wad of felt stuffed into the fingertip of Arvin's glove provided some padding for the lumpy scar tissue but not enough.

Waiting, sipping his ale, he smiled grimly at the irony. Back when Arvin was a teenager, living on the few coins he was able to filch from unguarded pockets and purses, the Guild had come close to depriving him of what was to become his livelihood. Thank the gods they'd found the rope he'd made and recognized his talent before they cut off the rest of his fingertips. Now, years later, they valued his skills highly—so highly they wouldn't let him go. They'd arranged for him to rent a warehouse at a ridiculously low price and saw to it that he was able to acquire whatever exotic and expensive materials he needed in return for the right to be his only "customers"—and the right to a steep discount.

Speaking of customers, where was Naulg?

Arvin glanced around the room but saw no sign of the rogue. His eyes darted to the entrance as someone in yellow—a color Naulg often wore—came down the ramp, but it turned out to be a woman in a yellow dress. A yuan-ti, human in overall appearance, with long red hair, but with skin covered in a sheen of green scales that thinned to a freckle of green on her face and hands. She moved with a grace that contrasted with the rolling gait of the sailors and the pouting slouch of the doxies. Despite the fact that she was female and wearing a dress that hugged the sensual curve of her hips like a second skin, the sailors kept their hands to themselves. Several scrambled out of her way, automatically dropping their glance to the ground and touching their foreheads in a subservient gesture that their ships' yuan-ti masters had ingrained in them, one painful lash at a time.

Arvin watched the woman out of the corner of his eye as she settled at a table two down from his, her back to the wall. When she flicked a finger impatiently for ale, the barkeep hurried to her side, setting a mug in front of her. He took her coin quickly, jerking his hand back as she reached for the mug, then bowed and backed away. The woman lifted the mug to her lips, tipping it until the egg inside the ale slid into her mouth, then swallowed it, shell and all, with one quick gulp. A forked tongue flickered as she licked her lips appreciatively.

As she glanced in Arvin's direction, he noticed her eyes. They were sea-green flecked with yellow. As they met Arvin's they emitted a flash of silver, momentarily reflecting the lantern light like those of a cat. Aware that she was staring at him, Arvin hastily averted his eyes. Yuan-ti often slummed at the Coil, but when they did, they came in groups and looked down haughtily on the "lesser races" who frequented the place. What was this woman doing in the tavern on her own, quietly sipping an ale? She, like Arvin, seemed to be waiting for someone.

If she'd been human—and wearing even a scrap of green—Arvin might have worried that he was the object of her search. The druids of the Emerald Enclave usually stuck to the wilderness, but were known to occasionally enter a city to sniff out wizardry—and Arvin's craft required him to work with wizards on a regular basis. He did so only at arm's length, through a middler, but the druids would hardly believe that if they discovered the ensorcelled twine in his shirt pocket.

This woman, however, seemed to have no interest in Arvin. After her brief scrutiny of him, she no longer glanced in his direction. She was obviously looking for someone else.

A second glimpse of yellow attracted Arvin's attention to the tavern entrance—Naulg. Small and dark-haired, Naulg had eyebrows that formed an unbroken line over his squared-off nose. He had a big grin on his face—and one arm firmly around the waist of a doxy who snuggled tightly against his side. With his free hand, he reached up and rubbed first the inside corner of his right eye, then the outside corner—the sign that he was looking for somebody. It was an unnecessary formality, since he and Arvin had known each other for years, but Arvin played along. Placing an elbow on the table, he rested his chin on his fist and raised his little finger so that it touched his lips. *I'm your man.*

Naulg shoved his way through the crowd, dragging the doxy with him. He found an empty chair at a nearby table, dragged it over, and sat in it, pulling the woman down into his lap. As they settled themselves, Naulg waved for two ales, one for himself and one for Arvin. He insisted Arvin join him in a drink. The doxy looked impatiently around as if she'd rather complete her business with Naulg and move on to the next tumble.

Despite the perpetual frown his heavy eyebrows gave him, Naulg was a likable fellow, with his easy grin, boldly colored shirt that drew the eye, and generous nature. He and Arvin had met when both were boys at the orphanage, during Arvin's first year there. Naulg had shared his meal with Arvin after a larger boy had "accidentally" knocked Arvin's trencher out of his hand. He'd been the only one to show friendship toward Arvin without wanting something else in return. They'd developed a close bond immediately and cemented it by twining their little fingers together like snakes.

Naulg had run away from the orphanage a year later—and had never been caught. His escape had been an inspiration to Arvin through the years that followed, and Arvin had always wondered to where Naulg had fled. After Arvin's own escape, he'd at last learned the answer. It was ironic that both men had wound up under the thumb of another, even more repressive organization—though Naulg didn't seem to see the Guild that way. To him it was a game, an adventure. To Arvin, the Guild was a rope around his wrist—one that kept him as bound to Hlondeth as a slave was to his master.

The doxy's shrill laughter jerked Arvin sharply back to the present. Staring at her, he decided that she would make a better rogue than Naulg. She was pretty, with fluttering eyelashes and long dark hair that coiled in soft waves around a milk-white face, but there was something about the hard glint in her eye that told Arvin she could hold her own. He disliked her immediately—perhaps because of the faint odor that clung to her—a ripe smell that reminded Arvin of spoiled meat. Of course, the smell might have been coming from Naulg, who was scratching absently at the back of his neck, revealing a large sweat stain in the armpit of his shirt.

"It's finished, then?" Naulg asked, ignoring the distraction of the doxy nuzzling his ear.

Arvin reached into the breast pocket of his shirt and pulled out a leather pouch that had been sewn shut with small, tight stitches. Keeping it hidden under his palm, he slid it across the table, leaving it beside Naulg's mug.

Naulg prodded the pouch with a finger and watched it bulge as the coil of twine inside it twitched. "Are there words that need to be spoken?"

Arvin shook his head. "Just cut the stitches and slip the pouch into a pocket. It'll do the job."

The doxy whispered something in Naulg's ear. Naulg laughed and shook his head.

"Be patient, woman. We'll be alone soon enough." Then, to Arvin, "Good. The middler already has your coin. You can collect it any time. I'm sure the goods will perform as promised."

"When will you be . . . using it?"

"Tonight,"—his grin broadened and he winked at the doxy—"much later tonight."

He picked up his ale and raised his mug to salute Arvin; his wide, sweeping gestures suggested he'd already had one too many.

Arvin nodded. He could guess what the twine would be used for—assassin vine almost always went for the throat—but maybe Naulg had something else in mind. Maybe he just meant to use it to bind someone's wrists.

Arvin twitched his mouth into a grin and covered his discomfort with a hearty joke. "Just be sure you don't let pleasure get in the way of business."

Naulg laughed. "'Idle hands make merry,'" he quipped.

Arvin smiled. "You mean 'mischief,'" he said, correcting the motto that had been drummed into them at the orphanage. Then he *tsked*. "Brother Pauvey would weep for you."

"Yes, he would," Naulg said, suddenly serious. "He

would indeed." He paused then added, "Can we talk later?"

Arvin nodded. "I'd like that."

Naulg shifted the doxy from his lap and rose to his feet, slipping the pouch into a trouser pocket. The doxy staggered slightly, as if she'd had too much to drink, but Arvin noted the quick, sharp glance she gave the pocket where Naulg had stored the pouch. If she was a rogue, as Arvin suspected, one quick stroke of her hand would see it gone, especially if Naulg was ... distracted.

Arvin had labored for two full tendays to make the twine—and he'd spent good coin on the spell that kept the tendrils of assassin vine fresh after their harvesting. Braiding them had been like working with writhing snakes; if he'd let one go even for a moment, it would have coiled around his throat. If the twine disappeared, would Naulg demand a replacement?

As Naulg headed for the door, doxy in tow, Arvin decided to protect his investment. At least, that was what he told himself he was doing. He waited until the pair were halfway up the ramp then rose to his feet.

Hlondeth by night was a city of whispers. Its cobblestoned streets had been worn smooth by the endless slither of the serpent folk. High above, the ramps that spiraled up the outside of buildings to join viaducts that arched across the street were alive with the slide of scales on stone. Soft hisses of conversation whispered out of round doorways and windows. From the harbor, a few hundred paces away, came the crash and sigh of waves breaking against the seawall, rhythmic as breathing.

The streets alternately widened and narrowed as they curved between the city's circular, dome-roofed buildings, continuously branching into the Y-shaped intersections that were unique to Hlondeth. Cloaks rustled against walls as people squeezed against buildings in the narrower portions of the street, making room for Naulg and his doxy to pass.

The buildings on either side of the street they were walking along glowed with a faint green light—a residual glow left by the magics used to quarry the emerald-colored stone from which Hlondeth had been built. Its light, not quite bright enough to see by, gave a sickly, greenish pallor to the doxy's skin, making her look even less appealing than she had in the Coil.

Arvin had been keeping a careful distance behind Naulg and his doxy. He lost sight of them momentarily as the street took yet another sinuous twist then spotted them a few paces later as they entered one of the small, circular courtyards that dotted the city. At its center was a lightpost, wrought in iron in the shape of a rearing cobra. The cobra's mouth held an egg-shaped globe, which should have been glowing brightly, flooding the courtyard with light, but this one had dimmed, leaving the courtyard in near darkness. Arvin saw at once why the globe had remained untended. The residence whose walls formed the courtyard had windows that were boarded over and dark lines of soot smudged the walls above each window. Its main entrance was in shadow, but even so, he could still make out the yellow hand that had been painted on the door. Clerics had cleansed the building with magical fire more than fifty years ago, but like so many other buildings in Hlondeth that had been subjected to a similar fate, the residence remained vacant. The fear of plague was just too strong.

Arvin watched as the doxy steered Naulg toward the darkened doorway. Naulg either didn't notice the faded symbol on the door—or was too engrossed in the woman to care. Judging by the way he was fumbling at the woman's skirts, it looked as though they were going to complete their transaction then and there. Arvin waited just outside the courtyard, watching and wishing he were somewhere else. If he'd been wrong, it would just be a short while—Naulg's bragging notwithstanding—before the doxy would be on her way again.

Arvin stiffened, realizing he could no longer hear the rustling noises. Something was wrong; Naulg was no longer moving. Then Naulg's body fell out of the doorway to land with a thud on the cobbles. He lay, stiff as a statue—paralyzed. Nothing moved except his eyes, which rolled wildly in their sockets.

Arvin would have to be careful; the doxy obviously had magic at her disposal. He touched the clay bead he wore on a thong around his neck. The unglazed bead, about the size of a hen's egg and carved with circles representing a pupil and iris, was a cheap copy of the good luck charms known as cat's eyes. It was the last gift his mother had ever given him. "Nine lives," he whispered to himself, echoing the words she'd spoken that day.

As the doxy bent down over Naulg, Arvin reached under his jacket with his left hand and drew the dagger that was sheathed horizontally across the small of his back. He turned it in his gloved hand, ready for throwing, then whispered the command that activated the glove's magic. The dagger disappeared.

Arvin walked boldly into the courtyard, hands apparently empty at his sides. Out of the corner of his eye, he searched the shadows on either side, alert for any accomplice the woman might have.

"Get away from him," he ordered. "Leave now, and I'll forget I ever saw this."

He expected the doxy to startle, but instead she looked up boldly. Arvin saw with a shock that her face had changed. Instead of being smooth, her skin was pocked with dozens of overlapping scars. So, too, were the hands that gripped Naulg's trousers. Arvin jerked to an abrupt halt, heart hammering in his chest as he recognized the scars for what they were—the hallmarks of disease.

In the moment that he stood, rooted to the ground with surprise, the doxy sprang into action. One of her hands rose and she began to chant. Arvin reacted a heartbeat later, speaking the glove's command word as he raised his hand. But even as the dagger point became solid between his fingers, the doxy completed her spell. Blindness fell over Arvin like a heavy curtain, leaving him blinking.

He threw the dagger—only to hear it thud into the door behind her. At a word, the magic weapon unstuck itself and flew back to his hand; even blinded, Arvin had only to grasp the air in front of him to catch it by the hilt. Now the doxy was whispering a second spell—and approaching him. Afraid of catching her contagion, Arvin jumped sideways, sweeping the air in front of him with the dagger to keep her at bay. The tip of his dagger caught and sliced through something—her clothing?—but then his foot caught on a loose cobblestone and he tripped. He landed hard, cracking his cheek against the cobblestones.

He started to rise, all the while slashing blindly with the dagger, but then a hand shoved against his back. He sprawled forward into a tight space that must have been the doorway, and an instant later felt something hard smack into his face. Dazed, he realized it had been the door opening.

He tried to get up again, but a foot slammed into his back, forcing him back to the ground. Strong hands wrenched at his arm then banged his hand against the ground in an attempt to loosen his grip on the dagger. Frightened now, realizing he might lose the magic weapon, Arvin spoke the command that made it vanish into his glove. With luck, the doxy and her accomplice would simply take the coin in his pocket and run, leaving Arvin to recover from her spell.

But it seemed Tymora did not favor him this night. Instead of patting him down, the doxy's accomplice wrenched Arvin's hands behind his back and lashed his wrists tightly together. Then Arvin felt the hands shift to his ankles. He kicked violently but to no avail; whoever the doxy's accomplice was, he was strong. He trussed Arvin up neatly, like a swine ready for slaughter. He said something in a low voice to the doxy, and they both chuckled. Arvin thought he caught a name: Missim.

"Take what you like and leave," Arvin yelled—in a voice that was tight with fear. "I'll keep my mouth shut. Neither the militia nor the Guild will—"

The jerk of being hoisted into the air cut off the rest of Arvin's plea. As he landed across the accomplice's shoulders, he swallowed nervously, suddenly aware that words wouldn't save him. This was no ordinary bait and jump.

What in the Nine Hells had he blundered into?

22 Kythorn, Middark

Arvin tensed as the accomplice shrugged him off his shoulders and let him fall. Tensing was the wrong thing to do; Arvin hit the ground hard, cracking his head against stone. When the sparkles cleared from his blinded eyes, he tried to lever himself into a sitting position, but the ground was too slippery. He succeeded only in fouling his face and clothes with muck before falling back down again.

Judging by the smell, he was in the sewers. The stench was overwhelming; it filled his nostrils and throat, making him gag. The feel of sewer muck on his clothes and skin was worse than being covered in crawling spiders and renewed his determination to escape. He thrashed even more frantically, half expecting a blow from his captors at any moment, and eventually managed to sit up—albeit awkwardly, with his wrists tied firmly behind his back and his ankles lashed together.

If he could only see, he might conjure his dagger back into his hand and start to cut himself free, but blind as he was, he had no way of knowing where his captors were. One of them might have been standing right behind him, ready to pluck the dagger out of his hand.

Then he heard chanting. Men's and women's voices together, perhaps a half-dozen of them. He tilted his head, listening. It sounded like they were close—no more than a pace or two away—and all together in the same spot. He turned so his hands were away from them and considered calling his dagger back into his glove. Should he risk it?

Suddenly his sight returned. Arvin saw that he was sitting inside a circle of yellow lantern light on an island of stone at the center of a large, water-filled chamber. The island itself was perhaps a dozen paces wide and no more than a handspan above the surface of the water that filled the chamber; in the shadowy distance he could just make out brick walls and a half-dozen arched tunnels leading away from this place.

Five figures—three men and two women, all dressed in grayish green robes with frayed hems and sleeves—were kneeling in a circle around a small wooden statue a couple of paces away. One was the doxy who had rolled Naulg. All had skin that was heavily pocked with thumbprint-sized scars. One of the men had a face so disfigured with disease that his eyes were mere squints; another—a hulking giant of a man—had hair that grew only in patches between the scars.

Turning his head, Arvin saw Naulg—no longer stiff with paralysis, but bound hand and foot as Arvin was. They were not the only captives. Three other unfortunates lay on the stone nearby: an older sailor with tarred hair pulled back in a tight bun; a boy of about twelve who was crying with soft, hiccuping sobs; and a woman Arvin remembered seeing inside the Coil earlier that evening, soliciting the sailors. She was struggling fiercely against her bonds, her hands white as the cord bit deep into her wrists, but the sailor appeared to have given up. He lay with eyes closed, whispering a prayer to Silvanus.

Arvin caught Naulg's eye then jerked his head backward to draw Naulg's attention to his hands. *Which way is out?* he signed in finger-speech.

Naulg glanced from one tunnel to the other and then shrugged. *Can't swim. Drown.*

Arvin ground his teeth. They lived in a port city, and Naulg couldn't swim? He glanced around, seeking other options. Just beyond the spot where their captors chanted, a rowboat was tied up. It seemed to be riding low in the water; its gunwales could barely be seen above the lip of the stone island.

Boat, Arvin signed back.

Naulg glanced at it out of the corner of his eye and shook his head. *Too far*, his fingers replied.

Arvin winked. *Wait. I signal. You. . . .* He stared purposefully at the lantern and twitched one foot. Their captors had set the lantern down halfway between themselves and their captives, close enough that Naulg could kick it if he wriggled just a little closer.

Arvin wiggled his fingers to draw Naulg's attention to his gloved left hand. *"Shivis,"* he whispered, calling the dagger into it. Turning the weapon, he carefully positioned its edge against the cord that bound his wrists.

Naulg grinned and shifted—slowly, and without making any sound—just a little closer to the lantern.

The female captive, having followed their hand signals avidly—though presumably without understanding them—edged closer to Arvin. She turned her bound hands toward him and gave him a pleading look.

Arvin ignored her and continued his work with the dagger. His hands were numb from being bound, his fingers fumbling as he sawed at the cord. The dagger slipped, slicing into his wrist, and he nearly dropped it.

The chanting stopped. The pockmarked people rose to their feet and turned toward the captives, each holding a small metal flask with ridged sides that was shaped like the rattle of a snake. Arvin jerked the blade frantically up and down against the cord that held his wrists, heedless of the jolts of pain as its point jabbed into his forearm. He felt the cord start to part. But then the larger man with patchy hair kicked Arvin in the chest, knocking him onto his back. Arvin gasped as the blade sliced a hot line across the small of his back and lost his grip on it. He wrenched with all of his might against the cord, but though it gave slightly, it refused to break.

Arvin squirmed, trying to find the dagger again, but now the larger man was kneeling on his chest. Thick fingers pried at Arvin's lips, forcing his mouth open. Arvin tried to bite him—then immediately thought better of it, not wanting to sink his teeth into the man's pockmarked flesh, which exuded the same tainted-meat smell the doxy's had. Realizing this, the larger man laughed. He shoved Arvin's head to the side, forcing his cheek against the stone, and held him there while he popped the cork out of the flask with a thumb. Then he jammed the flask into Arvin's mouth. A vile-tasting liquid rushed out of it, making Arvin gag. He tried to wrench his head away and spit, but the larger man forced his jaw shut. The bitter liquid slid down Arvin's throat like a snake finding its hole.

"Embrace him," the pockmarked man chanted. "Enfold him, endure him."

The man's four companions were also chanting. Above the drone of their voices, Arvin heard the female captive shouting violent curses and the boy screaming. The larger man released Arvin suddenly and clambered to his feet then reached down for Arvin's ankles. Instead of wasting time kicking, Arvin fumbled for the dagger that still lay under his back and at last managed to close his fingers around it. He tried to saw at his bonds as the large man dragged him across the island toward the statue, but the dagger was nearly ripped out of his hand as it grated against the stone. Just before it left his fingers he spat out the command word that made it vanish. He'd try again in a moment, but first, a distraction.

"Naulg," he shouted, "now!"

Then a wave of agony gripped him. It felt as though a hand were reaching into his guts, twisting them. Arvin's skin suddenly went ice cold and violent trembles raced through his limbs. His jaw clenched and his neck spasmed, jerking his chin down against his chest.

The larger man dropped Arvin's ankles and grabbed his hair, forcing his face closer to the statue. Arvin was trembling so violently he could barely see the thing. It looked like the statue of a woman, but the wood was so rotted and worm-eaten it was impossible to make out more detail than that. Still holding Arvin's hair, the larger man coughed into his free hand and smeared his phlegmy palm against first Arvin's forehead, then that of the statue. "Mother of Death, take him, torment him, teach him."

All of the other captives were screaming now as they too were dragged toward the statue; Arvin could hear Naulg's voice among them. Then he heard a loud clatter. Flashes of light spun across the ceiling as the lantern rolled. It hit the water with a loud sizzle, and the chamber was plunged into darkness. Immediately, Arvin called the dagger back to his gloved hand. This time, despite the violent shaking of his hands—or perhaps aided by it—he was able to saw through the cord. His hands sprung apart. One arm clutching the ferocious ache in his belly, he spun around and plunged the dagger into the pockmarked man behind him. He wrenched himself away, leaving the man gasping, and slit the cord that bound his ankles. Then he began crawling toward the sound of Naulg's screams.

Someone was in his way—Arvin's outstretched hand encountered the soggy hem of a frayed robe and a pair of legs. He thrust his knife into one of them and heard a grunt of pain. Then the person whirled. A woman's voice began chanting; Arvin recognized it as that of the woman who had posed as a doxy. She was casting a spell. Arvin, already doubled over with pain, felt its magic strike his mind like a gong. Over the ringing in his ears came a single, shouted command: "Retreat!"

Compelled by its power, he scrambled backward across the slippery stone. He was barely able to crawl, so fiercely was he trembling; the pain caused by whatever they'd forced him to drink was almost overwhelming now. Suddenly there was nothing under his hand—he'd been driven all the way back to the lip of the island. He tumbled off the edge, twisting as he fell. Instead of splashing into water, he landed sprawled inside something that rocked back and forth as he landed in it—the rowboat. Cold, stinking water slopped inside, soaking his shirt and pants as he lay on his back. Arvin heard a wet tearing noise as the line that moored the boat to the island parted as easily as rotted cloth. Then the boat, nudged by the current, began to float away.

Naulg and the other captives were still screaming. Arvin, however, only dully felt the agony that had gripped his body a few moments before. It had been replaced with an overwhelming weakness. He tried to sit up, but found he could not; his body no longer responded, not even so much as a finger twitch. Dully, he tried to make sense of what was happening, but his thoughts were as frayed as the pockmarked peoples' robes.

Dying, he thought. I'm dying. I thought I could escape, but all I was did was crawl into my coffin.

23 Kythorn, Darkmorning

Arvin's eyes sprang open as a sharp hissing noise filled his ears. Where was he? Had he been dreaming? No. He was wet, and shivering, and surrounded by the overpowering stench of sewage. He could feel its slime on his skin; inside his wet, clinging clothing; in his hair. And he could feel something more—something heavy lying on his chest. A moment later it shifted, revealing the source of the hissing noise he'd heard a moment ago. It was a snake twice the length of his arm and as thick as his wrist.

Two unblinking eyes stared into his.

Startled, Arvin sat up—only to crack his head against a low ceiling. He fell back into whatever he was sitting in, and it rocked to one side, nearly spilling him out. He saw that he was lying in a decrepit-looking rowboat, its gunwales almost touching the brickwork overhead. Worried it would sink, he kept as still as he could. The snake, meanwhile, turned and slithered across Arvin's body, down toward his feet.

Arvin turned his head to the right and looked through the space between the boat and the ceiling. He saw that the side of the boat was butted up against vertical iron bars that were rusted with age. Beyond these he could see the harbor, crowded with ships. From somewhere outside and above, he heard the voices and footsteps of sailors walking along the seawall that lined the waterfront. Turning his head to the left, he saw a darkened, water-filled tunnel. From some distant point inside it, he heard what sounded like falling water.

After a moment's confusion, Arvin realized where he was—and remembered what had happened. Despite having been fed what he could only assume was poison by those crazed, pockmarked people, he'd survived. The pain and trembling—and the lethargy that had followed—were gone. Some time while he lay unconscious, his body must have conquered the toxin. He was alive and healthy—and covered in a stench that made his skin crawl. Somehow the rowboat he'd fallen into had made it, without swamping, down the series of spillways that carried Hlondeth's sewage to the sea.

"Nine lives," he whispered, touching the bead at his throat.

Was Naulg still alive? How much time had passed? The gods only knew how long Arvin had lain unconscious in this boat. The only thing he knew was that it was still night. He listened, straining his ears to catch the sound of distant screams, but heard only the low gurgle of water and the *plop-splash* of what was probably a rat dropping into the sewage.

The snake, meanwhile, slithered across his ankles and up over the edge of the boat and began to coil up one of the bars. Was it just an animal, or a yuan-ti in serpent form? And what was it doing in the boat with him? Arvin touched its scaly body with his fingertips. "Who are you?" he asked. "What—"

The snake paused and turned to look at Arvin. Light from the harbor glittered off its green scales. A slender blue tongue flickered in and out of its mouth as it tasted the air. Its eyes remained locked on Arvin's for several long seconds, as if taking his measure.

Then it drew back and slithered up the bar toward the seawall above. In another moment it was gone.

Quickly, Arvin took stock. The ensorcelled glove was still on his left hand, and—he spoke the glove's command word twice and the dagger appeared in his hand then disappeared again—he hadn't lost his dagger. Nor had his captors taken the braided leather bracelet that encircled his right wrist. All three of his magical devices were still with him.

He'd need them if he was going to rescue Naulg.

The chamber with the island of stone would be farther up the sewer line. If Arvin remained flat on his back and pushed with his hands against the ceiling, he could send the rowboat back up the tunnel. Carefully, not wanting to swamp the boat, Arvin placed his hands flat on the ceiling above.

Then he paused. Would he really be able to find his way back? The sewers were said to be as much of a maze as the streets above them, with more twists and turns than a nest of coiled snakes. By the time he found Naulg—assuming he did—Naulg could very well be dead.

Then there was the prospect of facing the pock-marked people again. Plague had always terrified Arvin; he didn't want to expose himself to it in what was likely to be a lost cause. And really, Arvin didn't owe Naulg anything. When Naulg had escaped from the orphanage, he hadn't come back for Arvin. He hadn't even sent word. Instead, he'd forgotten Arvin— until fate threw them together a second time. If it had been Naulg who had escaped, Arvin wouldn't have counted on the rogue to rescue him; he'd have expected to be on his own.

Just as he had been in the orphanage.

Except for that brief time when Naulg had befriended him.

But those screams. . . . Could Arvin really turn his

back on Naulg and not expect to hear them echoing in his memory for the rest of his life?

Arvin had to rescue Naulg. That was who he was. Foolish and loyal, just like his mother.

He just hoped he didn't wind up dead, as she had, because of it.

He started to guide the rowboat back up the tunnel, but after moving it only a short distance, he noticed something. The gap between the gunwales and the brickwork above was getting smaller. The tide was rising, backing up the water in the sewage tunnel. It would be only a matter of moments now before the gunwales were touching the ceiling. Then the boat would fill with water and sink.

That was it, then. The tide had decided for him. In a few moments this tunnel would be flooded and there would be no way for Arvin to make it back to the chamber where Naulg was—not until low tide, by which time it would probably be too late, anyway.

Arvin wasn't going to be able to find that chamber again....

Unless, of course, the pockmarked people returned to the Coil for more victims. And there was a slim chance that they might, since at least two of the victims—Naulg and the woman who had implored Arvin to cut her bonds—had been plucked from there. With luck, they'd assume Arvin was dead. If he could spot one of them at the Coil, he might be able to follow him back to the chamber.

The ceiling grated against the gunwales, shutting out the harbor lights like a coffin lid closing. The water in the tunnel was nearly at ceiling height now and streaming into the boat. Time to get out of here.

Arvin rocked to his right, deliberately swamping the boat, and grabbed for one of the bars as he was spilled into cold, stinking water. The bars were spaced far enough apart that he might just squeeze through them, especially with sewage lubricating his skin. Clinging to the bar to keep his head above the rapidly rising water, he jammed his shoulder through the gap between two bars. By turning his head and exhaling, he was just able to squeeze through.

He climbed the brickwork of the seawall, levered himself up over the edge, and stood up, looking around to get his bearings. Then he set out, dripping stink in puddles around his feet, in the direction of the Mortal Coil.

CHAPTER 2

23 Kythorn, Darkmorning

As Arvin walked along the seawall toward the Mortal Coil, suspiciously eyeing everyone who passed under the streetlights, four sailors staggered toward him. He stepped to one side, intending to allow the group to pass, but as they drew nearer, one of them took a long, bleary look at Arvin then loudly guffawed. His two companions all turned to see what the joke was; an instant later they sniffed and pinched their noses. They began shouting drunken oaths at Arvin, telling him to haul his stink downwind.

Arvin felt his cheeks grow hot and red. Suddenly he was a boy again, enduring the taunts of the other children in the orphanage as they made fun of the punishment he'd been subjected to—the touch of a wand that had made his skin stink worse than a ghoul's. The punishment was a favorite one of the priests and had been inspired by the martyrdom of one of Ilmater's innumerable, interminably suffering saints. Arvin had tried to scrub the magical stink off, scraping his skin raw with a pumice stone and standing under the tap until he was shivering and wrinkled, but still it had persisted, filling his nose with a sharp reek, even lingering on his tongue until he wanted to gag. Even shaving his hair off hadn't helped—the other kids had only incorporated his shaved head into their taunts, pointing at the stubble and calling him "rotten egg."

A dribble of filthy water trickled down Arvin's temple. He flicked his wet hair back and felt the dribble transfer to the back of his neck. At least, this time, the smell would wash off.

And he was no longer a cringing child.

Grabbing the largest sailor by the shirtfront with his bare hand, Arvin summoned his dagger into his glove and jammed the blade up the man's nostril. As the point pierced flesh, a trickle of red dribbled out of the nostril onto the man's upper lip. "Shall I cut your nose off, then?" Arvin said through gritted teeth. "Would that alleviate the smell? Or would you and your friends prefer to take your insults somewhere else?"

The man's eyes widened. He started to shake his head then thought better of it. "Easy mate," he gasped. "We'll ship off."

Arvin stepped back, removing his dagger. The sailors staggered away, the bloody-nosed one muttering curses under his breath.

Arvin stood for a moment in silence, watching other late-night revelers stagger along the seawall, wondering if any might be hiding pockmarks under a cloak of magic. The taunts of the sailors had made him realize one thing, at least. The only way he was going to locate any of the pockmarked people was by using his nose to pick out their sour, sick odor. Enfolded in sewer stink, he didn't have a hope of doing that.

Sighing, he strode away to find a bathhouse.

A short time later, Arvin felt human again. The bathhouse—a circular stone chamber where patrons basked lazily in hot, swirling steam while slaves soaped and scrubbed them—had been worth the delay. Arvin—scrubbed pink and smelling of good, clean soap—and dressed in a fresh change of clothes felt ready to face any challenge.

Even a descent back into the sewers to find Naulg.

He returned to his only starting point: the Mortal Coil. It was still some time before dawn, and business at the Coil was slow, most of the sailors having staggered back to their ships to sleep off their revels. No more than a dozen patrons sat at tables. One of them Arvin recognized immediately: the yuan-ti woman with red hair who had been drinking there last night.

The woman, who had changed into a dress made from a shimmering green fabric a few shades lighter than her scales, looked up as Arvin entered the tavern. He didn't think she'd recognize him from yesterday evening—he'd gotten his hair cut short at the bathhouse. Even had his hair still been shoulder length, odds were she wouldn't remember seeing him. Arvin's average build and pleasant, "anyman" face gave him a natural talent for disappearing into a crowd. It was a godsend in his line of work—though with it came the annoyance of people frequently mistaking him for someone else.

The woman was still staring at him. Arvin crossed the first two fingers of his right hand while holding it discreetly at his side. *Guild?*

The woman made no response. Instead, she turned away.

A thought occurred to Arvin. Last night, the woman had seemed to be searching the crowd for someone. Had she, too, lost a friend to a pockmarked abductor? Was that why she'd returned to the Coil? If so, she might be willing to join in the search for Naulg. At the very least, she might have noticed something that Arvin had missed.

Arvin crossed to her table and bowed deeply, waiting for her to bid him rise. When she did, he gave her his most winning smile and indicated the empty chair opposite her. "May I join you?" A familiar prickling sensation tickled the base of his scalp—a feeling that always boded well in this sort of situation. She would invite him to sit down. He was certain of it.

The yuan-ti tilted her head as if listening to something—another good sign—but didn't speak. For a moment, Arvin was worried she'd dismiss him out of hand—yuan-ti were prone to doing that, with humans. But then she nodded and gestured for him to sit. A faint smile twitched her lips, as if she'd just found something amusing. Then it disappeared.

Arvin sat. "You were here last night," he began.

She waited, not blinking. Arvin had grown up in Hlondeth and was used to the stares of the yuan-ti. If she was trying to unnerve him, she was failing.

"Do you remember the man I was sitting with—the one in the yellow shirt?"

She nodded.

"The woman who was sitting on his lap, the doxy, have you seen her since then?"

"The pockmarked woman?" Her voice was soft and sibilant; like all yuan-ti, she hissed softly as she spoke.

Arvin raised his eyebrows. "You saw her sores?"

"I saw through the spell she'd cast to disguise herself," the yuan-ti answered. "From the moment she entered the tavern, I recognized her for what she was."

Arvin was appalled. "You knew she was diseased? Why didn't you warn us—or call the militia?"

The woman shrugged, a slow, rolling motion of her shoulders. "There was nothing to fear. Plague had touched her then moved on, leaving only scars behind."

"But her touch—"

"Was harmless," the yuan-ti interrupted. "Her sores had scarred over. Had they been open and weeping, it would have been another matter entirely."

"What about her spittle?" Arvin asked.

The yuan-ti stared at him. "You kissed her?"

"My friend did. Or rather...." He thought back to the phelgm that had been smeared on his brow. "The doxy kissed him on his forehead. Would that pass the plague to him?" He waited, breath held, for her reply. Had he fought off the poison he'd been forced to drink, only to be condemned to death by disease?

The yuan-ti gave a faint hiss that might have been laughter. "No. Tell your friend not to worry. The plague that left the pockmarks was long gone from her body. From *all* parts of her body."

She said it with such certainty, Arvin believed her. Relief washed through him. Knowing that he'd been touched by people who themselves had been touched by plague had filled him with dread. He wasn't old enough to have witnessed the last plague that swept through the Vilhon Reach; the "dragonscale plague" had been eradicated thirty years before he was born. Like most people, though, he feared to even speak of it. The disease, thought to be magical in origin, had caused the skin of those it touched to flake off in huge chunks, like scales, leaving bloody, weeping holes.

Shuddering, he ordered an ale from the serving girl who approached their table; then he turned back to the yuan-ti. "You seem to know quite a lot about disease."

"In recent months I've made a study of it."

Arvin's eyes narrowed. "Is that so?" A suspicion was starting to form in his mind—that it was the "doxy" this woman had been looking for last night, or one of her pockmarked companions.

"Did you follow us after we left the tavern?" Arvin asked bluntly. He waited tensely for her answer; perhaps she could describe the place where the pockmarked people had entered the sewer system. If he knew that, he might be able to find the chamber where—

"There was no need. I had a ... hunch that I'd see you again this morning and hear your story." Her eyes bored into his. "Tell me what happened last night after you and your friend left the Mortal Coil."

Arvin stared at her, appalled by her indifference. She'd sat and watched as Naulg was led away by a dangerous, diseased woman—and done nothing. At the very least she might have warned Arvin not to follow them. Instead she'd let events unfold, content to question the survivors afterward.

"Some 'study of disease,'" Arvin muttered under his breath. Then, meeting the yuan-ti's unblinking eyes, he asked, "Who are you?"

"Zelia."

Arvin supposed that must be her name.

"Who do you work for?"

Zelia gave a hiss of laughter. "Myself."

Arvin stared at her, frowning. When it was clear she wasn't going to add anything more, he made a quick decision. He had little to lose by telling her his story—and everything to gain. Perhaps she might pick out some clue in his tale that would help him find Naulg. She seemed to know more—much more—than she was letting on, but then, yuan-ti tended to give that impression.

Omitting any mention of his transaction with Naulg, Arvin reiterated the events that had taken place a short time ago: his fight with the doxy and her accomplice, finding himself in the sewage chamber, being force-fed the poison, the terrible anguish it had produced, and escaping in the rowboat. He watched Zelia closely as he told his tale, but her expression didn't change. She listened most attentively as he described the chamber where the force-feeding had taken place, stopping him more than once to ask for more detail, including full descriptions of the people who had abducted him. She made him describe each person's appearance and exactly what had been said. Arvin concluded with a description of the statue. "The wood was rotted, but it was definitely a statue of a woman. The hands were raised, as if reaching—"

"Talona."

"Is that a name?" Arvin asked. He'd never heard it before.

"Lady of Poison, Mistress of Disease, Mother of Death," Zelia intoned.

Arvin shuddered. "Yes. That's what they called her."

"Goddess of sickness and disease," Zelia continued, "a lesser-known goddess, not commonly worshiped in the Vilhon Reach. Her followers only recently surfaced in Hlondeth."

"Last night was a sacrifice, then," Arvin said.

"Yes. It is how they appease their goddess. They appeal to Talona to take another life, so she will continue to spare their own."

"That's why they fed us the poison."

"Yes," Zelia said. "Sometimes they use poison and sometimes plague. Usually, a mix of both."

Arvin felt his face grow pale. "Plague," he said in a hoarse voice. Had there been plague mixed with the poison they'd forced him to drink? He gripped the edge of the table and stared at his hands, wondering if his skin would suddenly erupt into terrible, weeping blisters.

Just at that moment, his ale arrived. The serving girl set it on the table then stood, waiting. Arvin stared at the mug. He suddenly didn't feel thirsty any-more. Realizing that the serving girl was still waiting, he fumbled a coin out of his pocket and tossed it onto her tray. He'd probably just paid her too much, judging by the speed with which she palmed it, but he didn't care. His thoughts were still filled with images of plague: his lungs filling with fluid, his body burning with coal-hot fever, his hair falling out of his scalp, his skin flaking away in chunks....

"Will Talona claim me still?" he croaked.

Zelia smiled. "You feel healthy, don't you?" She waved a hand disparagingly. "If there was plague mixed in with the poison, it's been held at bay by the strength of your own constitution. You slipped out of the goddess's grasp. Talona has lost her hold on you."

Arvin nodded, trying to reassure himself. He did feel healthy—and strong. Refreshed and alert, despite having had no sleep last night. If he had been exposed to plague, he was showing no signs of it—yet.

A question occurred to him. "Why are you so inter-ested in this cult?" he asked.

"They're killing people."

"They're killing humans," Arvin pointed out. "Why should a yuan-ti care about that?"

All he got in reply was a cold, unblinking stare. For a moment, he worried he'd gone too far. Did he honestly care why Zelia was "making a study" of disease, or on whose behalf? Really, it was none of his business. He quickly got back to the matter at hand—trying to learn something that would help him find Naulg.

"Does this cult have a name?" he asked.

Zelia gave a slight, supple nod. "They call them-selves the Pox."

"Can you tell me anything else about them? How I can find them again, for example?"

Zelia smiled. "What would you do if you found them?"

"Rescue my friend."

Zelia frowned. "Rushing in will only alert the Pox to the fact that someone is watching them," she told him. "And it would serve no purpose. Your friend is already dead."

When Arvin began to protest, she held up a hand. "As would you be, if you hadn't proved stronger than the rest. But there is a way for you to avenge your friend's death. Would you like to hear what it is?"

Arvin's eyes narrowed. He could tell when he was being manipulated. How did this woman know for certain that Naulg was dead? Like Arvin, he might have fought off the draught of plague. He might still be alive—and a captive. Arvin nodded.

"I want to know more about the Pox—things that only a human can uncover," she continued. "I'd be willing to pay for that information, providing the human was smart and knew how not to tip his hand."

Arvin feigned only a passing interest by crossing his arms and leaning back in his chair. "How much?"

Zelia took a sip of her ale—not quite quickly enough to hide her smile. Her teeth were human—square and flat, rather than the slender, curved fangs some yuan-ti had. "Enough."

It was Arvin's turn to stare. "Why do you need a human?" he asked at last.

"The cultists won't accept any other race into their ranks."

Arvin wrinkled his nose in disgust as he realized what she was asking him to do. "You want me to join their cult? To worship that foul abomination of a goddess? Never!"

Zelia's expression tightened. Too late, Arvin realized what he'd just said. "Abomination" was the word that humans elsewhere in the Vilhon Reach used to describe the yuan-ti who had the most snakelike characteristics. It was an insult that no human of

Hlondeth ever dared use. It commonly provoked a sharp, swift—and fatal—bite in return, or a slow constriction.

Arvin swallowed nervously and half-closed his gloved hand, ready to call the dagger to it, but Zelia let the insult pass.

"To *pretend* to join their cult," she said.

Arvin shook his head. "The answer is still no."

"Is it because of your faith you refuse?" she asked.

For one unsettling moment Arvin wondered if she was referring to Ilmater, if she knew about his time in the orphanage and the endless attempts by the clerics to instill in the children under their care a sense of "eternal thankfulness for the mercy of our lord the Crying God." Then he realized that Zelia was simply asking a general question. "I don't worship any particular deity," he told her. "I toss the occasional coin in Tymora's cup for good fortune, but that's all."

"Then why do you refuse?"

Arvin sighed. "I'm a simple merchant. I import ropes and nets. For this job, you need an actor—or a rogue."

Zelia's eyes narrowed. "It's you I want. You survived the disease the Pox infected you with. In their eyes, that makes you blessed."

"I see." He decided to see how badly she wanted these cultists. "I lost one thousand gold pieces last night. Would you be willing to pay that much for me to spy on them?"

Zelia gave a dismissive wave of her hand, as if the figure he'd just named were pocket change. "Certainly."

"Five thousand?"

"Yes."

"Ten?"

Zelia gave him a tight smile. "If you produce the desired results, yes—and if you follow orders."

With difficulty, Arvin kept his expression neutral. As he collected his thoughts, he sipped his ale and considered her offer. Ten thousand gold pieces was a lot of coin—enough to get him out of Hlondeth and free him from the Guild's clutches forever. But he wondered for whom Zelia was working. Someone with deep pockets, obviously—perhaps someone with access to the royal coffers. Unless she was lying about the coin, and didn't intend to pay anything, which was more likely when you came right down to it. A classic bait and jump—offer the victim anything he asks for then give him more than he bargained for.

"Well?" Zelia asked. "Will you do it?"

Arvin shuddered, remembering the terrible pockmarks on the cultists' skin. Was that how his mother had looked as she lay dying? He decided he couldn't bear the foul touch of their fingers again, even if they carried no taint. Even for ten thousand gold pieces.

"No," he answered. "Not for all the coin in the Extaminos treasury. Find someone else." He set his ale down and started to rise from the table.

Surprisingly, Zelia didn't protest. Instead, she took a long swallow of the ale in front of her, gulping down the egg inside it. When she was finished, she licked her lips with a tongue that was longer than the average human's, with a slight fork at the end of it . . .

A blue tongue.

Arvin felt his eyes widen. He sank back into his seat. "You were the snake in the rowboat."

"Yes."

"You neutralized the poison?"

Zelia nodded.

"Why?"

"I wanted you alive."

"Knowing—thanks to your 'hunch'—that I'd return to the Coil, and I'd tell you my story," Arvin said.

"Yes."

Anger rose inside Arvin, flushing his face. "You used me."

Zelia stared at him. "I saved your life."

"The answer's still no. I won't join the cult."

"Yes you will," Zelia said slowly. "Seven days from now, you will."

She said it with such certainty that it gave Arvin pause. "What do you mean?" he asked slowly.

"After I neutralized the poison, I planted a 'seed' in your mind," Zelia said. "A seed that takes seven days to germinate. At the end of those seven days, your mind will no longer be your own. Your body will be mine—to do with as I will." She leaned across the table and lightly stroked his temple with her fingertips then sat back, smiling.

Arvin stared at her, horrified. She was bluffing, he told himself. But it didn't *feel* like a bluff. Her smile was too confident, too self-satisfied—that of a gambler who knows he holds the winning hand. And now that she'd drawn his attention to it, Arvin could feel a faint throbbing in his temple, like the beginning of a headache. Was it the "seed" spell she had cast on him, putting down roots?

"What if I agree to join the cult?" he asked. "If I do that, will you negate the spell?"

Zelia hissed softly. "You've changed your mind?" Her lips parted to add something more, but just then, from somewhere behind Arvin, there came a shout of dismay and the sound of chairs being scuffed hurriedly back—and the clink of chain mail.

Turning on his chair—slowly, so as not to attract attention to himself—Arvin saw a dozen men in armor descending the ramp: Hlondeth's human militia. Each wore a helmet that was flared to resemble the hood of a cobra, with a slit-eyed visor that hid the face from the nose up. The bronze rings of their chain mail shimmered like scales as they marched into the tavern. They were armed with strangely shaped crossbows. Arvin observed how these worked a moment later, when a boy in his teens leaped from his chair and tried to run to a door that led to the tavern's stockroom. At a gesture from their sergeant—a large man with a jutting chin and the emblem of two twined serpents embossed on the breastplate he wore—one of the militia pulled the trigger of his crossbow. A pair of lead weights linked by a fine wire exploded from the weapon, whirling around one another as they flew through the air. The wire caught the youth around his ankles, sending him crashing into a table.

The silence that followed was broken only by the sound of a mug rolling across the table and falling with a soft thud into the sawdust below. Then, as the man who had shot the crossbow strode across the room to apprehend the runaway, the sergeant spoke.

"By order of Lady Extaminos, I am commanded to find crew for a galley," he announced. "Those who have previously served in the militia are exempt. Roll up your sleeves and account for yourselves."

A handful of men in the tavern dutifully began to roll up their sleeves, exposing the chevrons magically branded into their left forearms by battle clerics—chevrons that recorded the four years of service required of every human male in Hlondeth. Arvin, meanwhile, glanced around the tavern, his heart pounding. A galley? Their crews had even less expectation of coming home again than the men who were sent to the Cloven Mountains to fight goblins. Arvin wasn't so foolish as to get up and run; he'd get no farther than the bare-armed youth who was being hustled toward the exit. The one avenue of escape—the wide, sloping ramp that led up to the seawall above—was blocked by militia, who were only letting men with chevrons leave the tavern.

More worrisome still was the man who stood beside the sergeant. He wore neither helmet nor armor, and carried no weapon other than the dagger sheathed at his hip. He had strange eyes with a curious fold to the eyelid—Arvin's mother had described the peoples of the East as having eyes like that. Judging by his gray hair and the deep creases at either side of his mouth, he was too old to be a regular militiaman. He stood with one hand thrust into a pocket—closed around a concealed magical device, perhaps—as he scrutinized the faces of the men in the tavern, one by one.

This was no press gang. The militiamen were searching for someone.

Arvin swallowed nervously and felt the bead he wore shift against his throat. "Nine lives," he whispered. Reaching down, he began to unfasten his shirt cuff. As he pretended to fumble with the laces, he turned to Zelia.

"I won't be able to spy for you if I'm aboard a galley," he whispered. "If you have any pull with the militia, use it now."

Zelia's lips twitched into a slit of a smile. "You accept my offer?"

Arvin nodded vigorously as a member of the militia approached their table.

"Too late." With a supple, flowing motion, she rose from her chair. Cocking her head in Arvin's direction, she spoke to the man approaching their table. "Here's one for you." Then she strode away.

As the man's visored eyes locked on him, Arvin felt the hair at the back of his neck rise. His hand froze on his shirt cuff. Even if the press gang was a sham, the fact remained that he'd never served his time with the militia. In order to keep up the pretense of the press gang, they'd have to arrest him. They'd toss him in jail, where, in seven days' time, Zelia's spell would take effect.

Arvin couldn't allow that to happen. The only way he could find out whatever Zelia wanted to know about the Pox, and save himself, was to remain a free man.

The militiaman raised his crossbow. "Roll up your sleeve."

Arvin forced his lips into a smile. "There's been a mistake," he began, rising to his feet. "I served my four years, and they branded me, but a year ago I contracted an illness that"—his mind raced as he tried to think up a story the man would actually believe—"that left me terribly pockmarked." He dropped his voice to a confiding whisper. "I think it was plague."

Arvin widened his eyes in mock alarm, but it didn't have the expected result. The militiaman stood firm and unflinching. He'd obviously heard similar excuses before.

Arvin pressed on hurriedly. "Only recently did I earn enough coin for a tithe. The cleric who healed me did a wonderful job—he actually restored my skin to an unblemished condition. But in the process, he erased my chevrons. See?"

Rolling up his sleeve, Arvin showed the man his bare arm. As the militiaman looked at it, Arvin felt the base of his scalp begin to prickle. Quickly, he caught the militiaman's eye and gave him a friendly grin. "Listen, friend, it's true that I haven't served," Arvin said. "But you could let me go this time—right? Since this isn't really a press gang and I'm not the man you're looking for."

Slowly, the militiaman's expression changed, until his smile mirrored Arvin's own. "Don't worry," he whispered back. "I won't tell them about you."

"Thanks," Arvin said, rolling down his sleeve. "I knew I could count on you, friend." He turned then and began walking toward the ramp, as if the militiaman had granted him leave to go. Zelia was just exiting; the militiamen blocking the ramp parted to let her pass, leaving a gap in their ranks. Arvin lengthened his stride, but then the gray-haired man turned his full attention in Arvin's direction. Arvin saw the man's strangely shaped eyes narrow slightly as he glanced down at Arvin's gloved hand then up at his face again. His expression hardened.

He's recognized me as Guild, Arvin thought, fighting down panic. Or he's mistaken me for whoever the militia are looking for. Either way, I'm in trouble. If only I could distract him for just an instant....

The prickling sensation he'd felt at the base of his scalp a moment ago, when he'd charmed the militiaman, returned—this time deep in Arvin's throat. Within heartbeats it became so strong that Arvin began to hum involuntarily. A low droning filled the air—a sound like that of a bow being drawn against the low bass string of a musical instrument. The militiamen and their sergeant all glanced around as if trying to find its source, but its effect on the gray-haired fellow was even more dramatic. He suddenly lost interest in Arvin and stared at the far wall, a far-off look in his eyes, as if he were completely engrossed in it.

Now! Arvin thought. Seizing his chance, he bolted. He sprinted through the gap in the ranks, and, as one militiaman lunged out to grab him, made the most of the man's mistake by grabbing the fellow's hand and using the man's own momentum to tumble him into the fellow behind him. He heard the *snap-whiz* of a crossbow being fired—and a sharp exhalation just behind him, followed by curses, as the wire-linked weights wrapped around the man he'd just tumbled. Zelia, farther up the ramp, turned to see what the commotion was. As Arvin sprinted past her, he saw her eyes widen. Then Arvin was around a bend in the ramp and running up it as fast as his pumping legs would carry him.

He emerged onto a seawall limned red by the rising sun—the start of another hot, muggy day. He ducked left into a narrow street, and as soon as he was a few paces down it, leaped headlong at a wall. Fingers splayed, he activated the magic of the leather cord knotted around his wrist. His fingers and boot toes found cracks in the stonework that ordinarily would have offered no purchase, allowing him to scramble up the building like a cat climbing a tree.

Below and to his left, two militiamen emerged onto the seawall. Arvin froze, not wanting to betray his position with movement. One of the men stopped, crossbow at the ready, to stare down the narrow street Arvin had entered, but Arvin was already level with the building's third story—well above where anyone would reasonably expect him to be. The militiaman looked away.

"Nine lives," Arvin panted, grinning.

Then the gray-haired man stepped into sight beside the militiaman. He held an unusual object in his hand—three finger-sized crystals, bound together with silver wire and pulsing with a faint purple glow. Arvin had never seen anything like it before. The militiamen heeded the call of one of their fellows, ran farther up the seawall, and ran off, but the gray-haired man stood, still staring at the crystals. Then, slowly, he looked up.

Right into Arvin's eyes.

"There he is!" he shouted, pointing.

Arvin cursed and resumed his climb up the wall. The top of the building was just above him—one quick scramble and he was on the roof, a spot where the crossbows wouldn't be able to take him down. He ran lightly along the slate tiles, in a direction they wouldn't expect—back toward the seawall. From below, he could hear the gray-haired man shouting directions.

With a sinking heart, Arvin realized the man had guessed the direction in which he was headed. Arvin abruptly changed direction—and heard the man below shout that the quarry was going *this* way, not *that* way. Cursing, Arvin changed direction again, sending a tile skittering down the rooftop, but that telltale sign was the least of his worries.

The gray-haired man below had magic that could track Arvin, whichever direction he ran. Arvin's only hope was to somehow get out of its range.

CHAPTER 3

23 Kythorn, Sunrise

Arvin ran toward the rear of the warehouse, his feet slipping on the tiles. The rooftop was domed, forcing him to run with one leg slightly cocked and his other against the metal gutter that ringed the roof, his arms extended for balance. He made for the rear of the warehouse, toward the point where the curve of the building across the street forced the street to narrow. A split-second glance told him he was in luck; the ramp that spiraled up the outside of that building was one story lower than the warehouse rooftop.

He sprinted the final few steps and hurled himself into the air. He landed on his feet on the ramp of the building opposite, but momentum carried him forward, sending him crashing into the wall. Hot sparks of pain exploded in his nose as his face slammed into the smooth, hard stone. As he staggered down the ramp, nose dripping blood, he startled two men in tattered trousers and sweat-stained shirts who were hauling a two-wheeled handcart up the ramp. Each man had several days' growth of stubble—not quite enough to hide the *S* that had been branded into his left cheek.

Shouts came from the street below. A quick glance over the edge of the ramp told Arvin the militia had rounded both sides of the warehouse and were almost in a position to shoot up at him. Arvin had to get off the ramp—and quickly.

He ran headlong at the two slaves, shouting, "Out of my way!" Shoving his way between them, he leaped onto the handcart. He'd intended only to scramble over it and continue running down the ramp, but the force of his landing jerked the poles out of the slaves' hands. Suddenly the cart was rolling down the slope, poles scraping the stone behind it. Arvin teetered on top of its load, sacks of grain from the Golden Plains. His eyes widened as it careened toward the edge, but before he could jump, one wheel thumped against the low, outside lip of the ramp. The jolt staggered Arvin, nearly spilling him from the cart.

Guided by the scrape of its outside wheel against this barrier, the cart changed direction slightly, its path curving as it followed the ramp. The cart picked up speed, its outside wheel grinding like a millstone against the rock, and Arvin smelled friction-scorched wood. Barely able to keep his balance, arms flailing, he rode the cart down the ramp like a man standing on a galloping horse.

Wire-linked weights shot past over his head as one of the militiamen below loosed a crossbow in his direction. Then he was around the curve of the building, and the bottom of the ramp came into sight.

At its base were two more slaves, just turning a second handcart onto the ramp. Near them stood an overseer who Arvin assumed was human until he opened his mouth to hiss in surprise, baring curved fangs. The two slaves, eyes wide at the sight of the runaway cart, dived to one side, abandoning their own cart. Arvin could see it was time to do the same. He crouched and leaped off the back of his cart. As he landed, skinning the palms of his hands and tearing one trouser knee, he heard the sound of splintering wood followed by the soft hiss of spilling grain.

Arvin leaped to his feet and sprinted past the slaves, who were cringing under a venomous spray of curses from their overseer. Another pair of wire-linked weights crashed against the wall next to Arvin, spurring him onward. He could hear shouted orders and running feet behind him as he pelted through an intersection, choosing a route that led away from the harbor. He turned up one side street, then another. At the next intersection, he changed course yet again, this time heading back toward the harbor. A few more twists and turns and he'd lose them. But somehow, the militia didn't seem to be falling behind. Then he heard the shouts of the gray-haired man, telling the militia which way Arvin had gone. Cursing—he still wasn't out of range of the fellow's magic, it seemed—Arvin ran on.

Up ahead was a wider intersection from which came the smells of overripe fruit and goat dung. In it, street merchants were setting up their wares. Women shook out dusty blankets and laid them on the cobblestones, claiming their selling space for the day. Heavily laden goats stood with heads lowered, picking at the scraps of rind and peel left behind from the previous day, while older children unloaded produce from bulging sacks on the goats' backs, setting it out in neat piles on the blankets their mothers had spread.

All of this Arvin took in at a glance as he pounded toward the Y-shaped intersection. He also noted the buildings that framed the intersection: a sprawling pottery factory with smoking chimneys jutting out of its roof, a slaughterhouse with freshly skinned rabbits hanging from its eaves, a tinsmith's factory from which came the din of hammers pounding on metal, and a narrow two-story tower housing a business Arvin recognized—a spice shop.

Its owner was Guild—a man who, like Arvin, sold products other than those on display. Viro had olive skin and dark, thinning hair with traces of yellow powder in it. He was just unlocking the curved wooden shutters that fronted the spice shop when he heard Arvin running toward him and glanced back over his shoulder.

Arvin's fingers flicked quick signs in the Guild's silent language. *Need to hide. Distract?*

Pretend back door, Viro signed back. *Stay inside. Loft.*

Arvin panted his thanks and ran into the shop.

The interior was only dimly lit; Viro had yet to open its shutters to let in the dawn's light. The smell of freshly extinguished candles drifted through the dusty air, together with the sweet scent of cinnamon and the sharp tang of ground coriander. The spices were held in enormous, open-mouthed clay pots that had scoop handles sticking out the tops; Arvin deliberately snagged one of these as he ran by, sending it clattering to the floor amidst a scatter of black pepper. He hoped the pepper wasn't too exotic or expensive; he'd have to pay Viro for it later.

He ran to the back door and flung it open. Then he doubled back and clambered up a rope ladder that led to a wooden platform—the loft where sacks of unground spices were stored.

Outside the shop, he could hear Viro shouting protests at the militia. "No! There's valuable merchandise in there. You can't run through there! Stop!"

The militia, urged on by a babble of voices as street merchants pointed out which doorway Arvin had run into, ignored Viro. A heartbeat after Arvin had pulled the last rung of the ladder up into the loft and flung himself down, out of sight, they burst into the shop.

"The back door!" one shouted. "He must have gone that way."

Peering down through a knothole, thankful that blood was no longer dribbling from his injured nose, Arvin watched as two militiamen ran out the back door. The third man—their sergeant—held back, eyeing the thigh-high jars of spice as if trying to decide whether they were big enough to hold a man. Spotting the scoop that had fallen, he drew his sword and thrust it into the pepper inside the jar, stirring up the black powder. Suddenly he began blinking rapidly, and gave an enormous sneeze. He yanked his sword out and kicked the jar instead, knocking it over. Pepper cascaded onto the floor.

Arvin silently groaned; the cost of his freedom had just gone up significantly. But at the same time he smiled at the man's discomfort; the sergeant was sneezing violently. Arvin knew just how that felt. One of the times he'd run away from the orphanage he'd hidden inside a bakery and accidentally wound up pulling an entire sack of flour down from a shelf he'd tried to climb. The rupture of the sack over his head had set off a sneezing attack. As a result, the bakers had discovered Arvin, but the spilled flour had been a blessing in disguise. It had coated him from hair to heel, hiding the ink on his wrists that identified him as belonging to the orphanage. Unfortunately, he'd been recognized for what he was when he stepped outside into the rain and the flour washed off.

Below Arvin, the sergeant turned as someone walked in through the front door. Arvin's heart sank as he saw it was the gray-haired man. Behind him came Viro, wringing his hands.

"That's pepper!" Viro wailed, staring at the toppled jar. "Ten silver pieces an ounce!" The protest sounded genuine—and probably was. Viro glared at the back door of his shop, as if trying to spot Arvin. "When you catch that rogue, drag him back here. He's got to pay for what he's spilled."

The sergeant ignored him. "Where did he go, Tanju?"

The gray-haired man—Tanju, his name must be, though the word sounded foreign—closed his eyes and raised the wire-bound crystals to his ear as if listening to them. A faint sound, like that of chimes tinkling together in the wind, filled the air. Arvin wondered just who in the Nine Hells he'd been mistaken for. Whoever it was, the men below certainly wanted to find him. Arvin glanced frantically around the loft, looking for an escape route. Morning sunlight slanted in through the shutters of a small window a few paces away. Rising to his hands and knees, he began a slow, silent crawl across the spice sacks toward it.

In the room below, the purple glow of the crystals intensified. Then, just as Arvin reached the window and began turning its latch—praying all the while it wouldn't squeak—the purple glow dimmed.

Arvin heard Tanju's voice drop to a low whisper. Viro immediately began a loud protest. "Where are you going? He's not up—"

Viro's protest ended in a sharp grunt. Arvin winced, realizing the fellow had probably just been punched in the gut. An instant later, the creak of boards and the slight clink of chain mail completed the warning Viro had begun. The sergeant was climbing toward Arvin's hiding place. Someone else—probably Tanju—was striding toward the back door, presumably to call back the other militiamen.

The time for stealth was long gone. Leaping to his feet, Arvin booted the shutter open and dived head-long through the window. He landed in a controlled tumble on the flat, soot-encrusted rooftop of the pottery factory and sprang once more to his feet, this time smudged with black. He glanced behind him—just in time to see the sergeant lean out the window with a crossbow—and threw himself behind a chimney a heartbeat before a crossbow bolt shattered the roof tiles where he had been standing. The sergeant wasn't carrying one of the immobilizing crossbows. He was shooting to kill.

Arvin touched the bead that hung around his neck for reassurance and glanced across the rooftop, estimating how far he'd have to run. The militia had obviously given up on merely capturing him. They meant to kill him instead. "Nine lives," he whispered, dropping his hand, but it was more of a question, this time. Had his luck finally run out? He heard the creak of sinews tightening and the winding of a crank. The sergeant was reloading his crossbow.

Breaking from cover, Arvin sprinted across the roof. There were chimneys every few paces, emitting thin, hot smoke laden with glowing sparks that settled on his hair and skin. Ignoring these pinpricks of pain, he zigzagged from one chimney to another, all the while making for the center of the building, which was open to the sky. The open area was a circular courtyard filled with stacks of newly made pots and firewood for the kilns. No one was in it at the moment.

This courtyard looked like a dead end—but Arvin knew it must have doors leading out of it. He could always double back through the factory and escape onto the street again.

As he ran toward the lip of the roof, Arvin scanned the courtyard below, looking for a place to jump down. There: that pile of straw looked soft enough.

Just as he started to jump, something *whooshed* past his head and the sharp edge of a fletch scraped his ear. The crossbow bolt sailed on across the courtyard, but its close passage unnerved Arvin and threw him off his stride. He tripped over a lip of decorative tile that undulated around the inner edge of the rooftop and fell headlong into the courtyard.

He crashed down onto the lid of an enormous clay pot. It stood inside the courtyard—most of it underneath the overhang of the roof, but with just enough of it protruding that Arvin had landed on it. The wooden lid Arvin had fallen onto was as wide as a feast table. He'd landed facedown on top of it with his head, one arm, and one leg dangling over the edge of the pot. He'd heard something crack when he landed and felt pain flare in his collarbone, but it wasn't sharp enough for the bone to be broken. Dazed, he rolled onto his back and found himself looking up at the underside of the rooftop. Above, someone was making his way cautiously across the roof, coming in his direction—the sergeant.

Arvin rolled over a second time—farther into the shadow of the overhang—then rose to his elbows and knees, his back brushing the rooftop above him. He glanced quickly around the courtyard. A few paces away from the pot on which he was perched were double doors leading into the factory. These doors were just starting to open—but whether it would be a factory worker or a militiaman who came through them would be a coin toss. Arvin spoke his glove's command word and his dagger appeared in his left hand. He dropped flat onto his stomach, hoping they wouldn't spot him.

Suddenly, the lid tilted underneath him. Arvin grabbed for the rim of the pot but missed. Flailing, he tumbled down into its darkened interior and landed in something wet, soft, and squishy. The lid struck the underside of the overhanging roof with a dull thud, teetered an instant, and then fell back into place. It had closed—but not completely. A thin crescent of morning light shone down into the otherwise dark interior of the pot.

Arvin lay in what felt like soft, wet earth. The smell of wet clay surrounded him. The squelch of it between the fingers of his bare hand and inside his trouser legs as he sat up reminded him of the sewers, and he shuddered. For the second time that morning, he was covered in muck. But at least the clay didn't stink. Instead it had a pleasant, earthy smell.

The running footsteps reached the edge of the overhanging roof then stopped.

"Do you see him?" the sergeant shouted down.

"No," another man's voice shouted back—the person who came through the door had been a militiaman, after all. "But he's got to be hiding here somewhere. Tanju will sniff him out. We'll soon have that rebel in our grasp."

"Just remember the bounty that goes to whoever takes him down," the sergeant called back. "And keep your eyes sharp."

"For ten thousand in gold, you bet I will."

Ten thousand gold pieces? Arvin whistled under his breath. That was some bounty. As he slowly sank into the clay in which he sat, he wondered again who they'd mistaken him for. He didn't dare stand up; the sucking noise of his legs pulling out of the clay would betray his location. And he was starting to wonder if he would ever be able to climb out of the pot. Its walls were concave and thickly coated with clay. It had partially dried to a crumbly consistency, but underneath this skin was a damp, slippery layer. And the pot was enormous; even standing, Arvin wouldn't be able to reach its rim. A jump would allow him to catch hold of it—assuming his feet and legs didn't become so deeply mired in clay that jumping became impossible.

His dagger had landed point-down in the clay beside him. Slowly, wary of squelching the clay, he drew it out. Armed again, he felt better, but only slightly. With his ungloved hand, he reached up to touch his bead—and found it rough to the touch.

Superstitious dread washed through him as he realized what must have happened. When he'd struck the edge of the pot, the bead had cracked. Holding it at the end of its thong, he stared down at it. He couldn't see much in this dim light, but the front of the cat's eye appeared to have a deep, jagged line running across it. The damage could be temporarily mended—all Arvin had to do was fill the crack with some of the clay he was sitting in—but the timing of it frightened him. His mother had said the bead was a good luck charm—that as long as Arvin kept it close, it would provide him with the nine lives of a cat.

Had he just used up his last one?

He could hear the murmur of voices—both men's and women's. They had to be those of the potters, emerging into the courtyard to find out what was happening. One voice rose above the rest—Tanju, calling up to the sergeant, asking him exactly where he'd last seen the man they'd been pursuing.

"He jumped down from here," came the answer from above. "And I can guess where he's hiding. You there—fetch a ladder so we can look inside the pot."

Arvin gritted his teeth. In another moment the lid would open and the militia would lean over the edge to feather him with crossbow bolts. Readying his dagger for throwing, Arvin vowed to take at least one of them with him. He waited, heart racing, almost forgetting to breathe.

He heard running footsteps—and a breathless voice, announcing that a ladder could not be found.

Arvin opened his mouth to whisper a prayer to Tymora for favoring him—then halted as he noticed the light filtering down into the pot through the crack where the lid was askew. The light had a distinctive purple glow.

"Is he inside?" the sergeant asked from close above.

The purple glow came nearer; as it did Arvin heard a low humming noise. It must have been Tanju, humming to himself as he worked his magic. Above it, Arvin heard the clink of mail; the militiamen must be standing just outside the pot, waiting for Tanju's pronouncement.

The humming stopped. "No," Tanju called back. "All I see is darkness. The pot is empty. He must have escaped from the courtyard."

The purple glow dimmed.

Arvin felt his eyes widen as the sergeant shouted down at his men, ordering them to search the factory. Despite his magic, Tanju hadn't been able to find Arvin, this time. Something had saved him—but what?

Arvin stared at the clay caked onto the walls of the pot and the inside of its wooden lid. The clay had a peculiar undertone to its smell, one that he was at last able to place. It was heavy and metallic—lead.

Suddenly, Arvin understood. He'd heard that lead would block certain magics; the spells Tanju was casting must have been among these.

Breathing a sigh of relief, Arvin touched the bead at his throat. His mother's blessing still held; he hadn't used up his last life, after all . . . yet.

Whispering the two words that had become his personal prayer, Arvin started to rise to his feet but then thought better of it. Though the militiamen had jogged away, for all Arvin knew, the sergeant might still be waiting on the rooftop above, watching to see if the man he'd been pursuing would emerge from some other, hitherto unspotted hiding place. No, Arvin would wait until he was certain everyone was gone.

Which would give him plenty of time to think about a few things. He thought about Naulg—who probably *was* dead already, since a yuan-ti hadn't conveniently taken an interest in him and neutralized the poison in his body. And he thought about Zelia and whether she'd been lying about the spell that would allow her to take over Arvin's body in seven days' time. There was a slim chance she'd been bluffing—but Arvin wasn't willing to bet his life on it. No, the only safe course was to find out everything he could about the Pox, report his findings to Zelia, and pray that she'd show him mercy. Or rather, since Zelia didn't seem like someone inclined toward mercy, to pray that she'd recognize Arvin's worth and spare him, just as the Guild had.

In the meantime, there was this little matter of being hunted by the militia—and their tracker. That was going to complicate things.

Arvin settled back into the wet clay with a sigh, waiting for the silence that would be his signal to scramble out of the pot.

CHAPTER 4

Arvin stood in his workshop in front of a half-completed net that was suspended from a row of hooks in a rafter. Beside him on the floor was a ball of twine spun from yellow-brown dog hair. He worked with a length of it, knotting the silky stuff into row after row of loops. One end of the twine was threaded through a double-eyed wooden needle, which Arvin passed through, around, and over a loop, forming a knot. With a quick jerk, he tightened the knot then went on to the next.

He worked swiftly, unhampered by his abbreviated little finger. Knotting nets and braiding ropes was a craft he'd honed over twenty years, at first under duress in the orphanage then later because it was what he did best—and because it was what the Guild wanted him to do. His hands were much larger than they'd been when he started, but his fingers were no less nimble than when he had been a child. They seemed to remember the repetitive motions of net knotting of their own accord, allowing his mind to wander.

His thoughts kept looping back to the events of last night. To Naulg—dead, he was certain—and his own fortunate escapes. Tymora had smiled upon him not once, but twice. Eluding the militia had been equally as miraculous as his escape from the Pox.

He'd waited in the clay storage pot for some time, until he was certain the militia were gone and none of the factory workers were about. Then he'd scrambled out of the pot, quickly washed off most of the clay with water from a barrel in the courtyard, and crept back to his warehouse. He'd changed for the second time that morning into fresh, dry clothes then prowled the city, peering down stormwater grates, looking for some clue that would lead him to the Pox. He'd hoped to lift one of the grates and slip into the sewers, but every time he found a likely looking one, a militia patrol happened by, and he was forced to skulk away.

His search was further frustrated by the fact that he didn't dare go anywhere near the sewage tunnels that emptied into the harbor—or anywhere else in the vicinity of the Coil—not for some time, at least. Zelia might be there, or worse yet, the militia sergeant and Tanju. The former looked like a man with a long memory and a short temper, and the latter was a frighteningly efficient tracker. Arvin didn't want to repeat the morning's chase and narrow escape.

Realizing that he wasn't going to find the Pox on his own, he'd turned, reluctantly, to the Guild. He'd made the rounds of his usual contacts, dropping a silver piece here, a gold piece there, putting out the word that he was looking for information on newcomers to the city—

newcomers who were heavily scarred with pockmarks. Then he'd retired to the workshop he'd built between the false ceiling and rooftop of the warehouse the Guild had rented for him. Exhausted, he'd fallen into a deep sleep. When he woke up, it was long past Highsun; the air felt heavy and hot. Deciding that he might as well continue with his work, he'd soon lost himself in the soothing, repetitive steps of netmaking.

The net he was working on suddenly vanished. Arvin waited patiently, keeping his fingers in exactly the positions they had been when the twine blinked into the Ethereal Plane. A few heartbeats later, the twine reappeared and he continued at his task.

In its raw form, the blink dog hair was unstable, shifting unpredictably back and forth between the Ethereal and Prime Material Planes, but when the net was complete, a wizard would attune it to a command word. This done, the net would then blink only when its command word was uttered. Then Arvin would deliver it and collect his coin.

Arvin had no idea who had commissioned the net. The order had been passed along by a middler who already had the coin in hand and who would take delivery of the net when it was done. Arvin would never know if the product would be used for good or ill—for restraining a dangerous monster or for ensnaring a kidnap victim—nor did he want to know.

When Arvin had first begun working for the Guild, nearly twelve long years ago, he'd quickly realized that the magical twines and ropes and nets he had a hand in creating were used in crimes ranging from theft to kidnapping to outright murder. Not wanting blood on his hands—even at one remove—he'd begun to include deliberate flaws in his work.

Those flaws had been discovered, and an ultimatum delivered. Arvin could continue to produce product for the Guild—*quality* product—or he could go under the knife again. It wouldn't be a fingertip he'd be losing this time, but an eye. Perhaps both eyes, if the flaw caused a "serious difficulty" like the last one had.

Arvin had nodded and gone back to his work. He kept smiling as he passed the finished goods to his customers—even when he knew they were destined to be used to kill. In the meantime, he'd begun padding his orders for material, setting some aside for himself. A slightly longer section of trollgut here, a larger pouch of sylph hair there. The extra material was used to create additional magical items that he'd cached in hiding places all over the city. One day, when he had enough of these collected, he'd gather them all up and leave Hlondeth for good. In the meantime, he continued to serve the Guild.

At least this time, with the net he was weaving, he wouldn't have to meet the customer face to face. It was better not to get to know people, to keep them at a distance, even old friends like Naulg. Trying to help Naulg had only gotten him into trouble. Arvin should have heeded the painful lessons he'd learned in the orphanage.

He'd been only six when he'd been sent there as a "temporary measure"—a temporary measure that had lasted eight long years. Before leaving on the expedition that had turned out to be her last, Arvin's mother had arranged for Arvin to stay with her brother, a man Arvin had met only twice before. This uncle, a wealthy lumber merchant, had cared for Arvin for two months after his sister's death. Then he'd set out on a business trip across the Reach to Chondath. He'd placed Arvin with the orphanage "just for a tenday or two," but when he returned from this trip, he hadn't come back to collect Arvin.

At first Arvin had assumed that he'd done something wrong, that he'd angered his uncle in some way. But after running away from the orphanage, he had learned the truth. His uncle wasn't angry, just indifferent. Arvin had arrived at his uncle's home with fingers blistered from net knotting and tears of relief in his eyes—only to have his uncle pinch his ear and sternly march him back to the place again, refusing to listen to Arvin's pleas.

That was the first time Arvin had been subjected to the ghoul-stench spell. It wasn't the last. After Naulg's escape, Arvin had attempted one escape after another. Some failed due to the orphanage's reward system, which encouraged the children to spy on each other. Later, when Arvin learned to avoid making friends, even with the newly arrived children, his escapes had failed due to poor planning or bad luck. Prayers to Tymora had averted some of the latter, and an increasing maturity helped with the former. Over time, Arvin learned to wait and prepare, and his escape plans grew more cunning and complex. So, too, did his skill at knotting, weaving, and braiding, until he was almost never punished for being too slow, or for mistying a knot.

Arvin continued working on the net, letting his painful memories drift away in the repetitive thread-loop-loop-tie of netmaking. After a time, his emotions quieted.

Then he saw something out of the corner of his eye—a movement where there should have been none. He whirled around, left hand reflexively coming up to a throwing position until he realized his glove was lying on a nearby table. His eyes scanned the low-ceilinged workshop. Had the length of trollgut on the workbench across the room suddenly flexed? No, both ends of the gut were securely held in place by ensorcelled nails.

Through a round, slatted vent that was the workshop's only ventilation he heard a cooing and the flutter of wings. Striding over to the vent, he peered out and saw a pigeon on the ledge below. That must have been the motion his eye had caught—the bird flying past the slats. Three stories below was the street; none of the people walking along it were so much as looking up. Above—Arvin craned his neck to look up through the slats—was only the bare eave of the rooftop, curving out of sight to either side of the hidden room that housed his workshop. Satisfied there was no cause for alarm, he wiped sweat from his forehead with a sleeve and returned to his work. He picked up his netmaker's needle and rethreaded it with a fresh piece of dog-hair twine then began to loop and tie, loop and tie.

"So you escaped."

Arvin whirled a second time. "Zelia!" he exclaimed.

The yuan-ti was standing against the far wall, her scale-freckled face partially hidden by a coil of rope that hung from one of the rafters. She stepped out from behind it and stared at Arvin with unblinking eyes, her blue tongue flickering in and out of her mouth.

Arvin darted a glance at the spot on the floor where the hidden trapdoor was; it hadn't been opened, nor should it have been. Arvin was the only one who knew about the three hinged boards in the net loft ceiling, adjacent to a "roof" support post, that opened into his workshop.

"How did you find me?" he asked.

Zelia smiled, revealing perfect human teeth. "Your blood was on the ramp. Fortunately for you, I collected it before anyone else did."

"And you used it in a spell to find me," Arvin guessed. But how had she gotten into his workshop? More to the point, had she brought the militia with her? Were they waiting in the streets below?

Zelia's eyes flashed silver as they reflected the light from the lantern that hung from a nearby rafter. She gave a breathy hiss of laughter that somehow over-lapped her words. "I've decided against having the militia arrest you," she said.

Arvin startled. Had she read his thoughts? No, it was an easy thing to have guessed.

"I'm going to take you up on your offer," she contin-ued. "Find out what I want to know—without alerting the Pox—and I'll remove the mind seed."

"What do you want to know?"

"What the Pox are up to—over and above the obvi-ous, which is poisoning people. What is their goal? Who is behind them? Who is really pulling the strings?"

"You don't think they're acting on their own?"

Zelia shook her head. "They never could have estab-lished themselves in Hlondeth without help."

"Where do I begin?" Arvin asked. "How do I find them?"

"When I locate the chamber you described, I'll contact you," Zelia said. "In the meantime, there are re-sources you have that others don't. Put them to work."

"Use my ... connections you mean?" Arvin asked.

"No," Zelia said, her eyes blazing. "Say nothing to the Guild."

"Then what—"

"You have a talent that others don't."

Arvin shrugged then gestured at the nets and ropes and delicately braided twines that hung from the raf-ters and from pegs, leaving not one blank spot on the wall. "If it's an enchanted rope you want, I can—"

Zelia moved closer, her body swaying sinuously as she made her way around the hanging clutter. "You're a psion."

Arvin felt the blood drain from his face. "No." He shook his head. "No, I'm not."

Zelia's eyes bored into his. For once, the unblinking stare of a yuan-ti was getting to him.

"Yes you are. In the tavern, when we first met, you tried to charm me. And later, you used psionics to distract the militia."

A cold feeling settled in the pit of Arvin's stomach. He opened his mouth but found himself unable to deny Zelia's blunt observation. For years, he'd told himself that his ability to simply crack a smile and have people suddenly warm up to him was due solely to his good looks and natural charisma, but deep down, he'd known the truth. What had happened this morning—when Tanju had been distracted in the tavern—had confirmed it.

Arvin's mother had been right about him all along. He had the talent.

"The Mortal Coil," he began in a faltering voice. "That droning noise. . . ."

"Yes."

Arvin closed his eyes, thinking back to the day he'd finally succeeded in running away from the orphanage. He'd been in his teens by then—hair had begun to grow under his arms and at his groin, and the first wisps of a beard had begun on his chin. His mother had always warned him that "something strange" might start to happen when he reached puberty. Arvin, surrounded by the rough company of children "rescued" from the gutters by the clerics of Ilmater, had developed his own crude ideas of what she'd been referring to—until that fateful day, just after his fourteenth birthday, when he'd found out what she'd really meant.

It had happened at the end of the month, on the day the clerics renewed the children's marks. The children had been summoned from their beds, and Arvin contrived to place himself last in line—an easy thing to do, since those at the end of the line had to wait longest to return to their beds. As the cleric who was applying red ink to the children's wrists worked his way down the line, staining the symbol of Ilmater onto the wrists of each child with quick strokes of his brush, Arvin stood with fingers crossed, wishing and wishing and wishing that somehow, this time, he might be overlooked.

One by one, the children were painted and dismissed, until only Arvin remained. Then, just as the cleric turned toward Arvin, brush dripping, something strange happened. It started with a tickling sensation at the back of Arvin's throat. Then a low droning filled the air—the same droning that had filled the tavern this morning.

Suddenly, the cleric had glanced away. He stared at the far wall, frowning, as if trying to remember something.

Arvin seized his chance. He stuffed his hands into his pockets, deep enough to hide his wrists, and turned away. Then he began to walk out of the room, as if dismissed. From behind him came not the shout he'd expected, but the sound of a brush being tapped against a jar. The cleric was cleaning his brush and preparing to leave.

Later that night, when he was certain the other children in his room were asleep, Arvin had climbed down from a third-floor window using the finger-thin rope he'd secretly braided over the previous months. After four days of hiding in a basement, what remained of the previous month's mark had faded enough for him to venture out onto the streets. He was free, and he remained that way for several tendays ... until the Guild caught him thieving on their turf.

Thank the gods he'd still been carrying his escape rope at the time. The rope appeared ordinary, but woven into it were threads that Arvin had plucked from a magical robe owned by one of the orphanage's clerics. The resulting rope had chameleonlike properties and magically blended with its surroundings—allowing it to dangle against a wall, undetected, until the moment it was needed. One of the rogues who had captured Arvin had tripped over it—and cursed the "bloody near invisible" rope. The other rogue had paused, dagger poised to chop off another of Arvin's fingertips, then slowly lowered his dagger.

"Where did you get that rope, boy?" he'd asked.

Arvin's answer—"I made it"—had saved him.

In the years since his escape from the orphanage, Arvin had deliberately avoided thinking about what had happened to the cleric that night. He'd hadn't been willing to face the truth. He hadn't wanted to wind up like his mother, frightened by her own dreams—and dead, despite her talent for catching glimpses of the future.

Arvin opened his eyes and acknowledged Zelia. He could no longer deny the obvious—even to himself. "I do have the talent," he admitted.

Zelia smiled. "I could tell that by your secondary displays—by the ringing in my ears when you tried to charm me, and later, by the droning noise. Beginners often give themselves away."

"That's the thing," Arvin hastily added. "I'm not even a beginner. I haven't had any training at all."

"I'm not surprised," Zelia said. "Psions are extremely rare, especially in this corner of the world. Their talent often goes unrecognized. Even when a high-level power is manifested, it is usually attributed to some other magical effect."

"High-level power?" Arvin echoed. He shook his head. "All I can do is make people like me. I have no control over it. Sometimes it works ... and sometimes it doesn't. And once, no, twice ever in my life, I was able to distract—"

"You could learn more. If I taught you—which I would, if you prove that you're worth the time and effort."

That startled him. Zelia was a psion? Arvin had always assumed his mother had been the only one in Hlondeth—maybe in all of the Vilhon Reach. But here, it seemed, was another.

That surprise aside, did he *want* to be trained? He had dim memories of his mother talking about the lamasery, far to the east in Kara Tur, that she had been sent to in the year her woman's blood began. The discipline and physical regimen she'd been subjected to there had sounded every bit as strenuous as that imposed by the orphanage, but strangely, she'd spoken fondly of the place. At the lamasery, she learned the discipline of clairsentience—an art she'd used in later life during her work as a guide in the wild lands at the edges of the Vilhon Reach. She'd been in great demand in the years before Arvin was born.

Yet her talent had come with a price. Some of Arvin's earliest memories were of being startled awake by a sharp scream and trying to comfort his mother as she sat bolt upright in the bed they shared, eyes wide and staring. She'd muttered frightening things about war and fire and children drowning. After a moment or two she'd always come back to herself. She would pat Arvin's hair and hug him close, reassuring him that it was "just a bad dream." But he'd known the truth. His mother could see into the future. And it scared her. So much so that she'd stopped using her psionics around the time that Arvin was born and had spoken only infrequently about them. Yet despite this, her nightmares had continued.

"I don't know if I want to learn," he told Zelia.

"You're afraid."

"Yes."

"Why?"

"I don't want to see my own death," Arvin answered.

Zelia's lips twitched. "What makes you think you will?"

"My mother did—though a lot of good it did her. She thought the vision would help her to avoid dying. She was—"

"Clairsentient?" Zelia interrupted.

Arvin paused. That wasn't what he'd been about to say. He had been about to tell Zelia that his mother had been wrong in her belief that even the most dire consequences could be avoided, if one were forewarned. He'd been about to tell Zelia about that final night with his mother—about seeing her toss and turn in her bed and being able to make out only one of the words in her uneasy mutters: plague. The next morning, when he'd nervously asked her about it, she'd tousled his hair and told him the nightmare wasn't something to be feared—that it would help keep her safe. She'd given him his cat's-eye bead and left on the expedition she'd only reluctantly agreed to guide. Later Arvin had learned what this expedition had entailed—guiding a group of adventurers who wanted to find a cure for the plague that still lay dormant in the ruins of Mussum. They hadn't entered the ancient city, but its contagion had found them nonetheless.

Just as her dream had foretold.

"The talents of mother and child do not always manifest in the same way," Zelia said, breaking into his silent musings as she moved closer to him. "You may turn out to be a savant or a shaper or even a telepath. Their talents lie in glimpsing and shaping the present, not the future. Would that be so frightening?"

Arvin had never heard of savants, shapers, or telepaths before, but understood the gist of what she was saying. Not all psionic talents came with the terrible visions that had plagued his mother. "I suppose that wouldn't be so bad," he conceded.

"I can also see to it that you receive your chevrons. You'll never have to run from the militia again."

"Those chevrons are impossible to fake," Arvin answered. "You must have powerful connections."

Zelia smiled, but her eyes remained cold and unblinking.

"Why the sudden change?" Arvin asked. "Why promise me so much—when before you were content to threaten me?"

Zelia moved closer. "I find that it's most effective to use both the stick"—she brushed his cheek with her fingertips—"and the carrot. At the same time."

Arvin's skin tingled where she'd just touched it. Zelia was an attractive woman, for a yuan-ti. A very attractive woman. Not only that, she was powerful—and well connected. But if his guess was right about her serving House Extaminos, he had little reason to trust her. The expression "deceitful as a snake" hadn't come from nowhere. Humans in the service of the ruling family had to watch their backs constantly, never knowing when a fang might strike. And because they were working for the royal family—whose members could do no wrong—their poisonings were always "accidental."

No, working for Zelia was going to be just as demanding—and nerve-wracking—as working for the Guild. Arvin wanted to escape Hlondeth, not mire himself even deeper in it.

"You're not going to remove the mind seed, are you?" he asked.

Zelia shook her head. "Not until I get what I want."

"Where can I find you if I learn anything?" Arvin asked.

"Ask for me at the Solarium," she said. Then, bending gracefully, she inserted a finger into a knothole in the floor and pulled the hidden trapdoor open. She straightened, stepped through the hole, and fell out of sight. Arvin rushed to the trapdoor in alarm, and saw that she had assumed her serpent form. She was hissing loudly—and falling as slowly as a feather. Her sinuous green body lightly touched the floor, and she slithered away between the dusty coils of rope and spools of twine stacked in the warehouse below.

Arvin started to close the trapdoor then had second thoughts. Until he heard back from the Guild, he had nothing to go on, no way of locating the Pox. Sand was slipping through the hourglass. In less than seven days, Zelia's spell would activate.

No, he corrected himself, not a spell, a power—a psionic power. But psionic powers were like spells, weren't they? They could be negated.

But how? Arvin ground his teeth. Despite the fact that his mother had possessed the talent, psionics was something about which he knew very little. Maybe, by following Zelia and observing her, he could learn more.

Arvin scooped up his glove from the workbench and yanked it onto his hand. Then he clambered through the trapdoor and slid down a rope. He ran across the warehouse floor, toward the door that was slowly swinging shut.

CHAPTER 5

Arvin pulled open the front door of the warehouse and stepped out into the humid summer heat. He glanced anxiously back and forth but saw no sign of Zelia, in either yuan-ti or serpent form. The street was filled with people, most of them human. One of the Learned, his ability to read and write proudly displayed by the two red dots on his forehead, swept past in a silken cloak, nose in the air. A stonemason, hammer and chisel hanging at the belt of his leather trousers, shouted at a brace of four slaves yoked to a rumbling cart bearing a snake-headed statue carved from cream-colored alabaster—one of the many statues that had been carved for the restoration of the oldest part of the city. Women returning from the public fountain in the plaza just down the street to Arvin's right swayed across the cobblestones, pots of water balanced on their heads, while children lugged smaller vessels along beside them.

Across the street, young Kolim, the seven-year-old son of the woman who owned the bakery up the road, was pressing his palm against the stonework of the building opposite. When he removed it, the stone's magical glow, triggered by the momentary darkness, was revealed. Spotting Arvin, Kolim hurried across the street, pulling from his pocket a loop of string with a bead on it.

"Hey, Arvin!" he called, threading it over his fingers as he ran. "I can do that string puzzle you showed me. Hey, Arvin, watch!"

"Later, Kolim," Arvin told the boy, gently patting him on the head. "I'm a little busy just now."

The section of city the yuan-ti preferred to live in lay to the left, uphill from the harbor. Arvin closed the door behind him and strode in that direction. He spotted a woman with green scales coming toward him and, for a heartbeat or two, thought it was Zelia returning to the warehouse, but it turned out to be another yuan-ti, this one with darker hair and a snakelike tail emerging through a slit in the back of her skirt. Wrapped around her neck like a piece of living jewelry was a tiny bronze-and-black-banded serpent with leathery wings, one of the flying snakes imported from the jungle lands far to the south. As if sensing Arvin staring at it, the winged snake flapped its wings and hissed as its mistress walked by.

Zelia was nowhere in sight—she'd probably maintained her serpent form and slithered away. Either that or she'd gone in the opposite direction. Sighing, Arvin slowed his pace.

He was just turning to go back to the warehouse when he heard a man standing in a nearby doorway give a low, phlegmy cough. Arvin glanced in the fellow's direction, expecting to see someone aged, but the man who had just cleared his throat was even younger than he. And not a human, either, but a yuan-ti—albeit one with a fair amount of human blood in him. The fellow had olive skin, black hair, and a heavy growth of beard that nearly hid his mouth. Arvin could see the small patches of silver-gray scales dotting his forehead, arms, and hands. He wore black trousers and a white silk shirt with lace around the cuffs and neckline. Arvin walked past him, automatically lowering his eyes in the yuan-ti's presence—and suddenly caught a whiff of something he recognized: a sour, sick odor.

The smell that lingered on the skin of members of the Pox.

Arvin had worked among rogues long enough to instantly stifle his startle. He continued walking past the "yuan-ti," deliberately not looking at him. Arvin's escape of the night before had not gone unnoticed. The Pox were looking for him. And they'd found him.

"Lady Luck, favor me just one more time," Arvin whispered under his breath. "I'll fill your cup to the brim, I promise." He continued to walk steadily down the street toward the front door of his warehouse, shoulders crawling as he imagined the cultist behind him, about to reach out and touch his shoulder with filthy, plague-ridden hands. . . .

As Arvin approached the door, he suddenly realized something. The cultist wasn't behind him. Risking a glance back, he saw that the man was still lounging in the doorway down the street. He wasn't even looking at Arvin. Instead his attention seemed to be focused on the women who were drawing water from the public fountain.

Arvin paused, considering. Was the cultist's presence outside the warehouse mere coincidence?

He decided not to take any chances.

Arvin stepped inside the warehouse and scooped up a coil of rope. Then, with the rope looped over his left forearm, he walked up the street toward the cultist. The man paid no attention to Arvin's approach. Either the cultist's presence here truly was coincidence—or he was as good at hiding his emotions as any rogue. He glanced at Arvin only at the last moment, as Arvin stepped into the doorway with him.

"Hello, Shev," Arvin said in a hearty voice, greeting the fellow with what was a common name among the yuan-ti of Hlondeth. "So good to see you! The thousandweight of rope you ordered has just come in with the shipment from *shivis*."

As Arvin spoke the glove's command word, the dagger appeared in his hand. He jabbed the point of the weapon into the man's side and let the rope looped over his forearm slide down to hide it. "Let's go to the warehouse," Arvin continued in his falsely hearty voice. "I'll show it to you."

The cultist startled then flinched in realization that Arvin meant business. He allowed himself to be marched down the street, toward the warehouse door. Not until he'd stepped inside did he suddenly spring away. Arvin, however, had been expecting something similar. He had, accordingly, steered the cultist slightly to the left as he marched him through the door. As the man jumped, he barked out a command word. A coil of what appeared to be ordinary hemp rope lashed out toward the cultist, spiraling around him like a constricting snake. Confined in its coils, the cultist toppled like a felled tree and landed in a patch of sunlight that slanted in from one of the barred windows above. He immediately opened his mouth to cry out for help; in response Arvin threw his dagger at the man. The blade sliced open the cultist's ear and thudded into the wooden flooring behind him; at a whispered command, it flew back to Arvin's hand again.

"Be silent," Arvin growled as he closed the door behind him. "And I might let you live."

The cultist did a credible job of imitating a yuan-ti. "Release me," he spat arrogantly, glaring as he blinked away the blood that was trickling into his right eye. "And I might let *you* live."

Arvin chuckled. "I know what you are," he told the man. "You might as well drop your disguise. I can see—and smell—Talona's foul touch all over you."

The cultist hissed in anger, still trying to convince Arvin that he was really a yuan-ti then gave up. The magical disguise in which he'd cloaked himself dissipated, revealing a young man whose mouth was so disfigured by scars that his lips would not close. A faded gray-green robe with frayed cuffs and a torn neck covered all but his hands and feet, which were covered in pockmarks. Arvin made a mental note not to touch the magical rope that entangled the fellow; perhaps even to burn it, despite the expense that had gone into its manufacture. He bent over a burlap sack and carefully wiped the cultist's blood from his dagger.

The cultist strained against the rope for a moment but only succeeded in causing it to constrict further. He glared up at Arvin. "What do you want?" he said in a slurred voice.

"I'll ask the questions," Arvin countered. "For starters, why were you watching me?"

"Watching you?" The cultist seemed genuinely puzzled. He tried to purse his disfigured lips together, but they formed an uneven, ragged line. Staring down at the fellow, Arvin suddenly felt sorry for him. This man had been handsome, once, but those lips would never again know the soft caress of a woman's kiss.

Surprisingly, the cultist laughed. "You pity me?" he slurred. "Don't. I *sought* the embrace of the goddess."

Arvin felt a chill run through him. "You did that to yourself deliberately?" he asked. He'd given little thought to the motivations of the Pox. He'd assumed they were driven to worship Talona after illness claimed them in the hope that she would free them from their afflictions. He'd never dreamed that anyone would afflict himself with plague on purpose. Yet that was what this fellow seemed to be saying.

He thought of the liquid they'd forced him to drink. "The liquid in the metal flasks," he said, thinking out loud as he stared at the terrible pockmarks on the cultist's skin. "Is this what it's supposed to do to people? Make their skin . . . like that?" He resisted the urge to touch his own skin to make sure it was still smooth.

The cultist started to speak then gave another of his phlegmy coughs. He glanced around as if about to spit. Without intending to, Arvin backed up a pace.

The cultist gave him a penetrating look. "You've seen something, haven't you? Something you shouldn't have." He paused for a moment, and his expression turned smug. "It doesn't matter. Cry all the warnings you like—it won't help you. Talona will soon purge this city, sweeping it clean for the faithful. We will rise from the ashes to claim it."

Arvin shivered, suddenly realizing what the Pox must be up to. Last night's ritual hadn't been an isolated sacrifice. Thinking back to the rash of disappearances that had taken place in recent tendays around the waterfront, Arvin realized that he and Naulg weren't the first to be subjected to the Pox's vile ministrations. Nor would they be the last. The Pox meant to spread plague throughout the entire city.

But if that was their goal, why hadn't their victims been turned out into the streets, where they would spread their contagion to others? Perhaps, Arvin thought, because they had all died. But if they had, why weren't the cultists dumping their bodies in the streets instead?

Maybe the cultists were saving them up, intending to scatter them throughout the city like seeds when they had enough of them.

As Arvin stood, these dark thoughts tumbling through his mind, he became dimly aware of noises from the street outside—the chatter of voices, the *rumble-squeak* of carts, the voices of women returning from the fountain.

The public fountain, one of dozens from which Hlondeth's citizens drew their daily drinking water.

The one the cultist had been watching when Arvin spotted him.

Arvin suddenly realized the answer. If the Pox wanted to spread contagion, what better way to do it than by tainting the city's water supply? All they had to do was carry to each fountain a little of whatever was in the flasks and tip it into the fountain under the pretense of filling their vessels. But would this work—or would the volume of water in the fountain dilute the plague, rendering it ineffective? How much did a person have to ingest for it to kill?

Perhaps that was what the Pox were trying to find out.

As Arvin stared down at the cultist, his expression hardened. If the Pox had their way, forty-five thousand people would die—perhaps more, if plague spread beyond Hlondeth into the rest of the Vilhon Reach. The gods had just placed what might be the key to preventing these people's deaths in Arvin's hands. All he had to do was find out where the Pox were and report that to Zelia. She would take care of the rest.

"Where are the other cultists?" he asked. "Where do you meet?"

The man gave a phlegmy laugh. "In the Ninth Hell."

Arvin hefted his dagger, wondering if pain would prompt the truth. Probably not. Anyone who deliberately disfigured himself like this had little consideration for his own flesh.

The cultist's disfigured mouth twisted into a lopsided grimace. "Go ahead," he countered. "Cut me again with your fancy dagger. Perhaps a little of the blood will spray on you, this time, and you'll know Talona's embrace. Throw!"

As the cultist mocked him, Arvin's mind exploded with rage. He whipped up his dagger and nearly threw it, only stopping himself at the last moment. His temper suddenly cooled, and he realized what the cultist had just attempted. He'd cast a spell on Arvin, compelling him to throw his dagger. Only by force of will had Arvin been able to avoid fulfilling the cultist's wish to be silenced.

Slowly he lowered the dagger. That had been a narrow escape, but it reminded him of something. Perhaps there was another way, other than threats, to get the man to talk—by charming him.

Arvin had felt the first sputters of this power—which, until his conversation with Zelia a short time ago, he hadn't admitted was psionic—back when he was a boy. Back when his mother was still alive. She'd discovered him cutting one of her maps into parchment animals and had raised her hand to strike him. Frightened, he'd summoned up a false smile and pleaded in the most winsome voice a five-year-old could summon—and had felt the strange sensation prickle across the base of his scalp for the first time. His mother's expression had suddenly softened, and she'd lowered her hand. Then she'd blinked and shaken her head. She'd tousled Arvin's hair and told him he'd very nearly charmed himself out of a punishment—that he showed "great promise." Then she'd taken his favorite wooden soldier and tossed it into the fireplace, to teach him how bad it felt when another person damaged something that was yours.

He hadn't been able to manifest that power again until he reached puberty. He'd charmed people in the years since then, but his talent was unreliable. Sometimes it worked ... sometimes it didn't. But that time with his mother, it had arisen spontaneously.

Why?

Suddenly, Arvin realized the answer. Strong emotion. Like a rising tide, it had forced his psionic talent to bubble to the surface.

Standing over his captive, Arvin tried to summon up an emotion equally as strong as the one he'd felt that day. Then, he'd been motivated by fear; this time, he let frustration carry him almost to the edge. He embraced the emotion and combined its rawness with the urge to get the man to talk to him. Why couldn't he get the cultist to speak? The fellow was his *friend*. He should *trust* Arvin. The prickling began at the base of his scalp, encouraging him.

Arvin squatted on the floor next to the man. Deliberately he let his frown smooth and his voice soften. "Listen, friend," he told the cultist. "You can trust me. I drank from the flask and survived. Like you, I am blessed by the goddess. But I don't know how to find the others. I need to find them, to talk to them, to understand. I yearn to feel Talona's...." He nearly lost his concentration as he spoke the goddess's name then found his calm center again. "I need to feel Talona's embrace again. Help me. Tell me where I can find the others. Please?"

When Arvin began his plea, the cultist's eyes had been filled with scorn and derision. As his expression softened, a thrill of excitement rushed through Arvin. Untrained he might be, but he was doing it! He was using psionics to mold this man to his will!

The excitement was his undoing; it broke his concentration. The cultist jerked his head aside and broke away from Arvin's gaze then began blinking rapidly. He heaved himself into a sitting position, fingers straining between the coils of rope as he reached for Arvin, who jumped back just in time. Then the cultist's eyes rolled back in his head.

"Talona take me!" he cried. "Enfold me in your sweet embrace. Consume my flesh, my breath, my very soul!"

Though Arvin was certain the cultist was not crying, three amber tears suddenly trickled down the man's pockmarked cheek. With each wheezing exhalation, the cultist's lungs pumped out a terrible smell, worse than that of a charnel house stacked with decaying corpses. Arvin staggered back, afraid to breathe but unable to run. He stared in terrified fascination as the sores on the cultist's body suddenly burst open and began to weep. Violent trembling shook the cultist and his robe was suddenly drenched in sweat. Even from two paces away, Arvin could feel the heat radiating off the man's body. With horrid certainty, he realized what the cultist had just done—called down a magical contagion upon himself. Had Arvin been crouched just a little closer, and had the man succeeded in touching him, it would have been Arvin lying on the floor, dying.

The cultist's body was swelling like a corpse left in the sun. In another moment his stomach would expand past the breaking point; already Arvin could hear the creak of flesh preparing to rupture ...

And he was just standing there, staring.

Arvin flung open the warehouse door. As he slammed it behind him, he heard a sound like wet cloth tearing and the splatter of something against the inside of the door. He breathed a sigh of relief at yet another narrow escape, and touched the bead at his throat.

"Nine lives," he whispered.

He stood for a moment with his back against the door, staring at the people in the street. If the cultist's boasting was true, their days were numbered. Did Arvin really care if they died of plague? He had hundreds of acquaintances in this city but no friends, now that Naulg was gone. He had no family, either, aside from the uncle who had consigned him to the orphanage.

The sensible thing to do was report what he'd just found out to Zelia and see if she would remove the "seed" from his mind. Whether she did or didn't, he'd clear out of the city as quickly as possible, since staying only meant dying.

If Zelia had been bluffing, Arvin would be safe—assuming that the plague the Pox were about to unleash stayed confined within Hlondeth's walls. Even if it didn't, clerics would stop the spread of the disease eventually—they always had, each time plague swept the Vilhon Reach. Maybe they'd lose Hlondeth before they were able to halt the plague entirely, but that wasn't Arvin's problem.

Then he spotted Kolim, sitting on the curb across the street. The boy had his string looped back and forth between his outstretched fingers in the complicated pattern Arvin had taught him. He was trying—without much success and with a frown of intense concentration on his face—to free the bead "fly" from its "web."

Arvin sighed. He couldn't just walk away and let Kolim die.

Nor could he walk away from something that might produce orphans for generations to come. He thought of his mother, of the trip that had taken her to the area around Mussum. That city had been abandoned nine hundred years ago, but the plague that had been its ruin lingered in the lands around it still.

If Mussum's plague had been prevented, Arvin's mother might never have died. Had there been one man, all those centuries ago, who had held the key to the city's survival in his hand—only to throw it away?

Arvin realized he really didn't have a choice. If he left without doing as much as he could, and plague claimed Hlondeth, the ghosts of its people—and everyone who ventured near it and died in the years that followed this—would haunt him until the end of his days.

Including the ghost of little Kolim.

Sighing, he trudged up the street to find Zelia.

CHAPTER 6

23 Kythorn, Fullday

Arvin strode across one of the stone viaducts that arched over Hlondeth's streets, glad he didn't have to shoulder his way through the throng of people below. The narrow, open-sided viaduct didn't bother him the way it did some humans. He was agile enough to feel sure-footed, even when forced to squeeze to the very edge to let a yuan-ti pass.

Ahead lay the Solarium, an enormous circular building of green stone topped with a dome of thousands of triangular panes of glass in a metal frame that was reputedly strengthened by magic. The sun struck the west side of the dome, causing it to flare a brilliant orange.

The viaduct led to a round opening in the side of the Solarium. The human slave sitting on a stool just inside it rose to her feet as Arvin approached. She had curly, graying hair and wore, in her left ear, a gold earring in the shape of a serpent consuming its own tail. It helped distract the eye, a little, from the faded *S* brand on her cheek. She held up a plump, uncalloused hand to stop Arvin as he stepped inside the cool shade of the doorway.

"Where do you think you're going?" she demanded.

Arvin peered past her, down the curved corridor that led to the heart of the building. Side tunnels with rounded ceilings branched off from it, leading to rooms where the yuan-ti shed their clothing. The air was drier than the sticky summer heat outdoors and was spiced with the pungent odor of snake. He was surprised to find no one but this woman watching the entrance; he'd expected at least one militiaman to keep out the rabble.

"A yuan-ti asked me to meet her here," Arvin told the slave. "Her name is Zelia."

The slave sniffed. "Humans aren't allowed to use this entry. You'll have to wait at the servant's entrance with the others."

Behind her, within the Solarium, a yuan-ti that was all snake save for a humanlike head slithered out of a side tunnel. It turned to stare at the humans with slit eyes, tongue flickering as it drank in their scent, then slid away down the corridor in the opposite direction, scales hissing softly against the stone.

Arvin stared down at the slave. She might be twice his age, but he was a head taller. "I'm on state business," he told her firmly. "Zelia will want to see me at once. If you won't let me in, then go and find her. Tell her I'm here."

The slave returned his glare with one of her own. "The Solarium is a place of repose," she told him. "You can't expect me to burst in and wake our patrons from their slumber, looking for some woman who may or may not exist."

Arvin fought down his impatience. Slave this woman might be, but she'd been at her job long enough to consider herself mistress of all who entered the doorway, be they slave or free folk.

"Zelia has red hair and green scales," Arvin continued. "That should narrow down your search. Tell her Arvin is here to see her with an urgent message about...." He paused. How to word it...? "About diseased rats in the sewers." He folded his arms across his chest and stood firm, making it clear he wasn't going anywhere until his message was delivered.

The slave tried to stare him down, but her resolve at last wavered. She turned away and snapped her fingers. "Boy!" she shouted.

From a side tunnel came the patter of footsteps. A boy about eight or nine years old, carrying a glass decanter containing pink-tinged water, emerged in response to the doorkeeper's call. He was barefoot and dressed only in faded gray trousers that had been hacked off at the thigh; his knees and the tops of his feet were rough, as if he'd scraped them repeatedly. His hair was damp with sweat and the *S* brand on his cheek was still fresh and red.

"This man claims to have been summoned here by one of our patrons," the doorkeeper told the boy, placing emphasis on the word "summoned," perhaps to remind Arvin that, while he might be a free man, he was ultimately at the beck and call of the yuan-ti. "Find the yuan-ti Zelia and deliver this message to her." She relayed Arvin's message. "Return with her reply."

The boy ran off down the main tunnel. Arvin waited, stepping to the side and dropping his gaze as two yuan-ti entered the Solarium and were greeted with low bows by the doorkeeper—who all the while kept one eye on Arvin, as if expecting him to dart into the Solarium at any moment. The boy came running back, this time without the decanter.

"Mistress Zelia says to bring the man to her," the boy panted.

The doorkeeper was busy directing the yuan-ti who had just entered to one of the side rooms, but Arvin saw her eyebrows rise at the news that Zelia would see him. As the yuan-ti departed down a side corridor, she glared at the boy. "Take him to her, then," she snapped, "and be quick about it." She aimed a cuff at the back of the boy's head, but the boy ducked it easily.

"This way," he told Arvin.

Arvin followed him down the corridor. The farther along it they went, the hotter and drier—and muskier—the air became. Arvin couldn't imagine having to spend his whole life working in this snake-stink. It was already making his temples pound. "Here," he said, fishing a silver piece out of a pocket and holding it out to the boy. "Keep this somewhere safe, where the others won't find it. Maybe you'll have enough to buy your freedom, one day."

The boy eyed the coin in Arvin's hand suspiciously.

"Nothing is expected of you," Arvin reassured him. "It's just a gift."

The boy plucked the coin from Arvin's hand and tucked it into his own pocket then grinned. As they reached a point where sunlight flooded into the corridor from the large room beyond, he dropped to his knees, tugging on Arvin's shirt as he did so. "We're not allowed to stand," he whispered.

Arvin wasn't sure if this rule applied to free men, but he complied. Dropping into a kneel, he followed the boy into the main room of the Solarium, trouser knees scuffing against the floor.

The sunning room of the Solarium was even larger than he'd imagined. The enormous circular chamber, capped by its high dome of glass, was bathed in hot, bright sunlight. Perhaps a hundred or more yuan-ti lounged on a series of low stone platforms on the floor, while snakes of every color and size—either more yuan-ti or their pets—hung from the delicate framework of wooden arches that connected one platform to the next. Some of the yuan-ti could pass for human at a distance while others had obvious serpent tails, heads, or torsos. They lay naked in the bright sunlight, men and women together, in some cases coiled in what Arvin would have assumed were sexual unions were it not for the slow, sleepy languor that pervaded the place. Human slaves—most of them young children— moved between the platforms on their knees, offering the yuan-ti sips of blood-tinged water or thumb-sized locusts, impaled on skewers and still twitching.

The boy led Arvin toward a platform near the center of the room where Zelia lounged with three other yuan-ti who looked almost human. The boy then backed away. Zelia lay on her side, coiled in a position no human could have emulated, her torso bent sharply backward so that her head was pillowed on one calf. She had a lean, muscled body that was soft and round in just the right places. Arvin noted that her scales gave way to a soft fuzz of red hair at her groin and that her breasts were smooth and pink, quite human in appearance. He found himself imagining what it would feel like to have Zelia's body coiled around his—to feel the contrasting textures of rough, scaly skin and smooth breasts—then realized that Zelia had lifted her head to glance sleepily at him. Arvin, still on his knees, his head level with the ledge on which Zelia lay, dropped his gaze. He concentrated on the floor and waited for her to bid him to speak. The air seemed even hotter and drier than it had been a moment ago; Arvin found himself wetting his lips, just as the yuan-ti around him were doing.

Zelia chuckled, as if at some private joke. "You've been hunting sewer rats?" she asked, eyes still half-hooded with sleep. Her tongue tasted the air. "Yet you smell sweet."

"One of the rats came out of the sewers," Arvin said. "I caught him."

Zelia sat up swiftly, her eyes glittering. "Where is he?" The three yuan-ti behind her stirred in their repose, disturbed by her sudden motion. One of them—a man who might have been handsome, save for the hollow fangs that curved down over his lower lip—rolled over and laid an arm across Zelia's thigh. She slid her leg out from under it.

"The rat is dead," Arvin answered.

Zelia gave an angry hiss.

"But not by my hand," he swiftly added. "His . . . mistress claimed him. But before he died, I managed to learn what he and the others plan to—"

"Not here," Zelia cut him off with a fierce whisper. She glanced pointedly at the three other yuan-ti who shared the platform with her. "Follow me and keep silent."

She slid off the platform in a flowing motion and moved toward the exit—walking at an apparently unhurried pace and nodding her goodbyes to those she passed, but hissing softly under her breath as she went. Arvin followed on his knees, which were already sore despite the trousers that padded them. He wondered how the slave children could stand it, scuffing about on bare knees all day long. He supposed they got used to it, just as he'd gotten used to cramped and blistered fingers when he was a child.

When they reached the corridor, Zelia quickened her pace. Arvin leaped to his feet and trotted after her then waited while she pulled on sandals and a dress scaled with tiny, overlapping ovals of silver. After she had dressed, she led him down a ramp and out onto the street.

They walked uphill for some time past enormous mansions. Human servants and slaves hurried through the streets, intent upon their masters' business, but parted quickly to make way for Zelia when they saw her coming. The yuan-ti who lived in this part of Hlondeth strolled leisurely along the viaducts that arched above, enjoying the view out over the city walls and the harbor.

As he jostled his way through the crowd that quickly closed in Zelia's wake, Arvin wondered why she had chosen the street-level, more crowded route. Perhaps because she wanted to avoid having to stop and chat with other yuan-ti, or perhaps because she didn't want any of those above getting a close look at the human who was accompanying her.

Zelia at last turned off the street and ascended a narrow ramp that spiraled up the side of a tower that was several stories tall. Arvin followed her. The roof of the tower turned out to be flat. It was surrounded by a wrought-iron railing covered in flowering vines. Bees droned lazily among tiny blue flowers. Arvin wondered if the tower was Zelia's home—if so, she certainly came from a wealthy family. She paused at the top of the ramp to unlock a gate with a key taken from a belt purse at her hip. The gate squeaked open under her touch.

Arvin followed her through the gate into what turned out to be a rooftop garden. On the rooftop were several enormous clay pots, planted with shrubs that had been carefully clipped into shapes reminiscent of coiled serpents. The bushes had obviously been grafted together from several different plants; the colors of the flowers changed abruptly at several points along the length of each coil, mimicking the banded pattern of a snake.

At the center of the rooftop was a fountain. Its gentle splashes filled the air with a cool mist. Arvin wet his dry lips, wishing he could take a sip of the water. Perhaps that would help the headache that was still throbbing in his temples. This was probably one fountain the Pox wouldn't be able to get to, but still. . . .

Zelia closed the gate behind them. "We'll have privacy here," she said.

Arvin nodded uneasily as the gate's lock clicked shut. Despite the vines that screened the railing, he'd noted the intricate pattern of its metalwork. The wrought iron formed an inscription, which, judging by the one character Arvin could make out, was written in Draconic. Arvin couldn't read Draconic but had once painstakingly memorized a handful of its characters so that he could include them in his knotwork. It was a language well suited for sorcery. He hoped—and this hope was reinforced by Zelia's assurance of privacy— that whatever magic the rail worked was designed to keep people out, rather than in.

Zelia turned to him and spoke without preamble. "Tell me what happened."

Arvin did, describing how he'd spotted the cultist in the street, and then he told her everything that had followed from there. He expected Zelia to raise her eyebrows when he told her his conclusions about what the Pox were up to—tainting Hlondeth's water supply—but she merely nodded. If anything, she seemed slightly disappointed by what he'd just told her.

"The cultist said Talona would purge the city 'soon,'" Arvin noted. "I don't think he'd have gloated that way if they planned to taint the water supply months from now. It sounded as though they were going to put their plan into action within a tenday, at most. I hope that will give you time to—"

Zelia held up a hand, interrupting him. "Your conclusions are . . . interesting," she said. "I suppose time will prove whether they're correct."

Arvin frowned, not understanding Zelia's apparent lack of concern. "Humans aren't the only ones who drink from the public fountains," he told her. "Not all yuan-ti live in mansions with private wells. Some are sure to quench their thirst at the fountains, and though they may be immune to poison, they can still die of plague—and spread it to others. Unless. . . ." He paused, as a thought suddenly occurred to him. Did Zelia know something that he didn't? Did yuan-ti have a natural immunity to plague, as well as poison?

Even if they did, a city with ninety-five percent of its population ill or dying wouldn't serve their interests.

When Arvin reminded her of this fact, Zelia gave him a cold smile. "I am well aware of the role humans play in Hlondeth," she told him. "And I agree. The cultists must be stopped."

Arvin nodded, relieved. It was out of his hands. He could step back and let Zelia—and the powerful people who backed her—deal with the crisis from here on in.

"I suppose it will be a simple matter of stationing militia at every public drinking fountain and arresting the cultists as they appear," he said, thinking out loud. "Or are you going to try to capture them before they make their move?"

"Capturing them will only solve part of the problem," Zelia said. "The cultists are just one playing piece in a much larger game. I still need to find out who is behind them."

Arvin frowned. "If you stop them, will it matter?"

"Someone wants to upset the balance of power," Zelia said. "My job is to discover who. Find that out—and you'll earn your freedom. And all that I promised you earlier."

Arvin nodded. He'd expected her to say that. Why remove the mind seed when it was such an effective tool? "I have an idea that might help me to infiltrate the Pox—once we find them," he told her. "The cultist who died today in my warehouse used magic to alter his appearance, but I got a good look at his face after he dropped the spell. If I described him to you, perhaps you could use your psionics to alter my appearance. I could pass myself off as him and—"

"You would never be able to carry it off," Zelia said. "One false gesture or word, and the Pox would use their magic to see you as you truly are. You will have to present yourself as you are—or rather, as how they want to see you: someone who survived their draught of plague and now wants to join their cult."

Arvin grimaced. He'd been afraid she'd say that. "Won't they also have magic that will allow them to see through my lies?" he asked, thinking back to the spells the clerics at the orphanage had used.

"If you choose your words carefully, you won't have to lie," Zelia told him. "A cleverly worded half-truth—plus a little charm—will carry you a long way."

Arvin nodded. That much, at least, was true. "Have you been able to locate the chamber I told you about?"

"I think so," Zelia told him. "Or at least, I've located a chamber in the sewers that matches the description you gave."

Arvin wet his lips nervously. Finally he would be able to find out whether Naulg was alive—or dead. "Did you see my friend there, or . . . his body?"

"The chamber was empty. But the cultists may return to it at Middark, the time they seem to prefer for their sacrifices."

Arvin nodded. "Where is it?"

Zelia ignored his question. "Until then, you will wait here with me. As Middark approaches, I will begin observing the chamber. As soon as I see any activity, you can set out."

Arvin chafed, wishing he could just get this over with—but he could see that Zelia wasn't going to tell him where the chamber was until she was good and ready. In the meantime, he needed to prepare. He hadn't exactly gone to the Solarium ready for an excursion into the sewers. If he was going to confront the Pox, he'd need to equip himself.

"There're some items I'll need," he told Zelia. "If I promise to meet you back here at Sunset, can I go and get them?"

Zelia stared at him for several long moments, hissing softly to herself. Silver flashed in her eyes as they caught the sun. "Go," she told him, unlocking the gate. "Purchase your potions, but don't be late."

Arvin was halfway down the ramp before what she'd just said sank in.

He hadn't told her he intended to buy potions . . .

Not out loud, anyway.

23 Kythorn, Sunset

Arvin sat cross-legged in the rooftop garden, watching Zelia exercise. She was naked, with her hair bound in a loose knot at the back of her neck, but she didn't seem to mind him watching her; yuan-ti didn't have the same concept of modesty that humans did. He'd never seen anything quite like the convolutions she was putting her body through—a series of poses that bent her torso, arms, and legs into positions he was certain no human could ever achieve. She held each pose for several moments, muscles quivering from the strain and sweat beading at her temples, then suddenly her body flowed into the next position in one smooth and supple motion. One moment her ankles were wrapped around her neck tighter than a knot as she balanced on her palms, seemingly sitting in midair, the next she was in a handstand, her body straight as an arrow. Down she swept to hover at the horizontal a palm's width above the ground, balancing her rigid body on her hands, then up went her head and feet to meet in an arch over her back.

Arvin expected her to be exhausted when she finished, but instead she seemed invigorated. Her eyes sparkled and her cheeks were flushed a healthy pink, enhanced by the light of the setting sun.

"Those exercises," Arvin said. "They remind me of an acrobat I saw once—though he was nowhere near as graceful."

"They're called *asanas*," Zelia answered.

"Do you do them every day?"

"At Sunset, without fail," Zelia said, slipping on her dress. "They focus the mind."

"My mother meditated each morning at sunrise," Arvin said. "These—*asanas*—are for the same purpose, aren't they? To aid your psionic powers?"

"They restore my ability to manifest my powers," Zelia answered, "much like a cleric praying or a wizard reading his spellbooks."

"I see," Arvin said. During her routine, Zelia had gone through a *lot* of different poses. She must have had quite a number of psionic powers at her disposal. If he wanted to learn how to master his psionics—to do more than merely charm and distract people—Zelia would be an invaluable instructor. "You said you'd teach me to use my talent," he reminded her. "Do you think you could teach me one of those *asanas?*"

Zelia untied the thong that had held back her hair and shook out her long red tresses. "It takes years of practice to learn to do them properly," she answered. "You need to master not only the movements of the *asana* itself, but also the mental focus that goes with each pose. You might be able to crudely mimic one of the simpler *asanas*, but—"

"Will you teach me a simple one, then?" Arvin asked. He rubbed his temples. It hadn't been his imagination, earlier; his head was throbbing. He really could feel the mind seed putting in roots. "At the very least, it'll give me something to ... distract me."

Zelia stared back at him, and for a moment Arvin wondered if she was going to dismiss his request as ridiculous and impossible. Then her lips twitched into a smile. "Why not?" she said at last. "It might prove amusing. An interesting test of your potential. I'll teach you the *bhujanga asana*. Take off your clothes."

Arvin blushed. "It that absolutely necessary?"

Zelia's eyes narrowed. "Do you want to learn—or are you wasting my time?"

"I want to learn," Arvin hurriedly assured her. "But my bracelet and amulet stay on."

Zelia raised an eyebrow. "Everyone draws the line somewhere," she said. "But your glove must come off."

Arvin fumbled at the buttons of his shirt then peeled it over his head. He unfastened the belt that held his sheathed dagger and set the weapon to the side then sat and pulled off his boots and his glove. Finally he unfastened the laces of his trousers, let them fall in a heap at his feet, and stepped out of them. He stood with hands cupped in front of himself, hiding his nakedness. Zelia seemed oblivious to it, however. Her eyes never strayed from his.

"Lie down," she instructed, "on your stomach."

Arvin did, gratefully. The stone of the rooftop was warm against his bare skin.

"Place your hands, palms down, under your shoulders," Zelia continued.

Arvin did. Zelia walked behind him and nudged one of his ankles, adjusting his legs. Arvin's ankle tingled where her bare foot had touched it. "Feet together, and point your toes," Zelia said. "Now arch your back—slowly—and tilt your head back until you are looking straight up at the sky."

Arvin did as he was instructed, arching until his stomach and throat were taut. He stared up at the rapidly darkening sky, wondering how long he'd have to maintain this position.

"Continue to hold the pose," Zelia said.

Arvin did. Above him, the first glimmers of star-light became visible as Sunset slid into Evening. Slowly the sky darkened, changing from purple to a velvety black. Arvin held the pose, expecting further instruction, but Zelia merely strode around him, adjusting his pose with a nudge here, a pressing down of her palm there. Each time she touched him he felt a flush go through his body, making it difficult to concentrate on the pose. His mind wandered to the stories he'd heard about the delights and terrors of sleeping with yuan-ti women. About their sensual, twining embraces, their reputed ability to coax a man on past his limits—and their rumored tendency to, in the heat of passion, inflict a fatal bite. Legend had it that, in the convulsions of death, the man experienced a release unlike anything he'd ever—

"Concentrate on the pose," Zelia hissed. "Keep your mind in the present."

Obediently, Arvin tore his mind away from fantasy.

Zelia stood, arms folded, staring down at him in silence.

As the evening continued to lengthen, Arvin began to wonder if Zelia was toying with him. Was she ever going to tell him what to do next, or just leave him frozen in this pose until he collapsed? The muscles in Arvin's lower back were starting to bunch with strain and his stiffly extended arms had begun to tremble. The human body wasn't built to hold a pose like this for so long. But at least it took his mind off the throbbing in his head that had been pestering him most of the day. Compared to this new pain, the headache was inconsequential.

"Hold the *asana*," Zelia droned. "Feel the energy in your lower back—in your *muladhara*. That's where the energy lies, coiled tight like a serpent."

Arvin concentrated on his lower back but could feel

only the tension in his muscles, which were starting to burn. It wasn't working. Already it must be halfway between Sunset and Middark—surely this had gone on long enough. He let his arms bend, just a little, to ease the strain.

"Maintain the pose!" Zelia snapped, her voice like a whip.

Arvin straightened his arms at once. He could do this, he told himself. It was just like climbing a wall—a very high wall. You climbed so far, until your muscles were burning and you thought you couldn't support yourself a moment longer; then you looked down and realized how far you'd fall if you let go. And you kept going.

He refused to give up. He could do this. He had to. He was physically stronger than Zelia and determined to succeed. He wasn't about to fail at something she'd made look so easy.

More time passed. His arms began to tremble. His muscles had gone beyond burning, to the point where they felt like water.

"Move through the pain—send your mind to a place beyond it," Zelia instructed. "Send it deep, to the base of your spine. Search there for your *muladhara*. Find it."

Gritting his teeth, Arvin did as he was told. Rallying his flagging will, he blotted out the agony of his muscles and turned his mind inward. He sent his awareness sliding down his spine, to a place in the small of his back and concentrated on it, refusing to acknowledge anything else. He pushed himself through the pain ... and suddenly was beyond it.

There. Was that it? He felt, in the small of his back, a hot, tight sensation that reminded him of the prickling he felt in his scalp when he manifested his charm. It was coiled around the base of his spine, a focused energy waiting to be unleashed.

"You've found your *muladhara?*" Zelia asked. "Good. Now let the energy uncoil."

Arvin continued to stare up at the sky, which blurred as his vision became unfocused. Then suddenly, the knot of energy that was coiled at the base of his spine sprang open. A wave of energy surged through his body like a flash of wildfire. It was a feeling that came close to sexual release—except that the energy stayed within his body, tingling deep within every pore and hair.

Arvin laughed out loud, delighted. "I've done it!"

Zelia let out a slow, surprised hiss as Arvin sat up. "With a single *asana*," she said softly. "Incredible."

"Teach me more," Arvin said, flush with the energy that was coursing through his body.

"Very well," Zelia said, sounding edgy. It was as if Arvin's success had irritated her somehow. "Let's see if you can learn one of the simpler powers—the Far Hand. Hold the position and send the energy you've summoned to a point on your forehead, between your eyes."

Arvin did as instructed, mentally guiding the energy up his spine. It seemed to find a resting point all on its own, coiling just inside his forehead, between his eyes.

Zelia stepped in front of him, holding something: his magical glove. Seeing it in her hand, he nearly lost his concentration.

"Maintain your focus!" Zelia snapped. "Keep the energy tightly coiled, until it's time to use it."

Realizing that she had chosen a valuable possession deliberately, to test him, Arvin gritted his teeth and found his focus again.

"Good. Now reach out with the energy; direct its energy with your gaze. Take the glove from my hand."

Arvin tried but could not. "I . . . don't think I can," he gasped.

Zelia's lips curved into a tight smile.

Prodded by anger—she didn't *want* him to succeed—Arvin tried harder and felt the energy in his forehead loosen . . . just a little.

Zelia backed away from him, retreating until she was up against the vine-covered rail that surrounded the rooftop. She continued to hold the glove in front of her. "Give up?" she smirked.

Arvin shook his head and continued to concentrate. Once again, the energy loosened—but not enough. The glove in Zelia's hands twitched then lay still.

Zelia's eyes widened. "Try again," she said, serious once more. "Send the energy out all at once . . . now!" As she spoke, she tossed the glove over the edge of the rooftop.

"No," Arvin gasped.

The energy that had been spiraling between his eyes suddenly rushed out through them. He saw a bright streak of silver flash out toward the glove. His vision filled with sparkling light. When it cleared, the line of light was gone. The glove, however, was hovering above the rail. Tentatively, with slow jerks, he drew the invisible energy back toward him, reeling it back into his mind. The glove was tugged along with it and moved through the air toward him with short, choppy movements then fell onto the ground in front of him.

"You can relax now."

Arvin sagged onto the ground and let the tension flow from his muscles. Sitting up, he tilted his head to stretch his neck. "I did it," he said. "I learned a new power."

"Yes." Zelia stared at him with a thoughtful expression, as if his success had surprised her. "That's enough for one night," she said curtly. "It's almost Middark. I must see if the cultists have returned to the chamber."

Arvin nodded, suddenly exhausted. Trembling slightly, he pulled his clothes back on. He'd expected the invigorating rush of energy to continue, but all he wanted to do was sleep. He hoped the headache would let him. When he'd finished dressing, he sat again, his back against one of the potted plants. He found himself fighting to keep his eyes open. Even his curiosity about what Zelia was doing—sinking into a cross-legged position with the soles of her feet uppermost, just as his mother had done when she meditated—couldn't keep him awake.

As Zelia stared off into the night sky, hissing as she summoned up the psionic power that would let her peer into the sewer chamber, he fell asleep . . .

And into the strangest dream.

CHAPTER 7

Arvin lay on his side, knees drawn up to his chest and arms coiled around his legs. He was midway between sleep and wakefulness—aware that he lay on a rooftop, his breaths slow and even as they hissed in and out of his mouth, yet with his mind entangled in the strands of a dream. It was a strange sensation, almost as if he were awake and observing the dream from a distance—a dream that was as vivid as waking.

In the dream he was a child—a serpent child. He was slithering down a corridor as fast as he could, contractions rippling through his body as he pushed with his scales against the smooth green stone of the floor. Behind him loomed a human child of about five years of age—two years younger than Arvin—with braided hair and a slave brand on her cheek. She was laughing as she chased Arvin into a carpeted dining hall, her eyes glittering with excitement. Arvin, hissing with delight at having eluded the lumbering human, heaved the front half of his torso upright and began to slither up onto a table. Too late. The slave girl bent down and yanked the carpet, sending Arvin tumbling. Then she leaped forward and slapped his tail with her palm.

"Tag the tail!" she shrilled. "Tag the tail and you're it!"

Arvin felt rage course through him. No. It wasn't fair—the slave had cheated. She hadn't given him enough of a start. His body drew back into a coil; then he lashed out. His fangs sank into the girl's arm, and he tasted the sweet, hot tang of blood.

The slave girl gave a strangled gasp and staggered backward, staring at the twin beads of blood on her forearm, then collapsed onto the floor. "I thought ... " she gasped, her tongue already thickening in her mouth. "We ... friends. ..." Then her eyes glazed.

Arvin's tongue flickered in and out of his mouth. The slave girl lay still on the floor, no longer breathing. Dead.

Regret trickled through him. Perhaps he shouldn't have been so hasty. Who was he going to play with, now?

Arvin shifted, turning over in his sleep. The night air was growing cooler, less muggy. He squirmed over to a section of rooftop that retained a little of the day's warmth; his body drank it in. A part of him realized that he had moved like a snake, undulating hips and shoulders in order to shift himself. ...

The dream shifted. Now Arvin was kneeling on a low stone platform in the middle of a room richer than any he had ever seen. It had a high, domed ceiling held up by gilded columns, windows draped with silk curtains that fluttered in the evening breeze, and walls painted with *Origin* frescos—a series of images showing the World Serpent looking down upon the snakes, lizards, and other reptilian races issuing from Her cloaca.

Arvin was weary with the exhaustion that follows an intense rage. His hands were raw from having pounded his fists repeatedly against his sleeping platform, and his skin was moist and itching from the acidic sweat that had oozed out between his scales. He'd hissed until his jaw ached, thrown his dinner against the door—splatters of egg and shell clung to its polished wood—and still his mother hadn't relented. He was *not* going to be given another slave with whom to play. Not until he learned to coil his temper. Until he learned to master his emotions. Until he stopped acting so *human*.

That had punctured his pride. Humans were stupid, blundering creatures. Look how the yuan-ti manipulated and dominated them, just as humans and the other lesser races dominated animals. It was the natural order of things. It—

The door opened. Arvin looked up at the strangest human he'd ever seen. The man was short, dark skinned, and bald—and so wrinkled his face looked as though it had shrunk beneath its skin. Yet he was lean and well muscled. His only article of clothing was a loincloth, nearly as dark as he was. Around one wrist was coiled a finger-thin turquoise serpent with translucent yellow wings: a flying snake from the jungles of Chult. Arvin stared at it, transfixed, as it raised its head and hissed. He'd *wanted* one of those for *so long*. . . .

The bald man moved his hand up and down, causing the flying snake to flutter its wings. All the while, he stared at Arvin, not speaking.

In a distant part of the family manse, Arvin heard

a wind chime tinkling. Yet the breeze that had been ruffling his curtains had stopped. The clouds must have cleared; sunlight was shining in through the window now.

"Desire," the bald man said in a deep voice that was at odds with his thin frame. "I can feel it radiating from you, like heat from a sun-warmed rock. Your emotions run deep and swift—very unusual, in a yuan-ti."

Arvin stared at the impudent human, wondering when he was going to hand over the flying snake—perhaps he should just take it from the man, instead. The pet was obviously an apology from his mother for her overreaction about the slave girl.

The bald man raised his free hand and flicked a fingertip against the snake's nose. The tiny serpent recoiled, hissing. He flicked its nose again, and this time the snake bared its fangs. Arvin stared, appalled, as the man gave the snake's nose another flick, sending it lashing back and forth. He flicked his finger at it again, and again, and again, until Arvin was certain the snake would sink its fangs into the offending human at any moment. Yet, though the snake hissed its fury, mouth wide and venom dripping from its fangs, it did not strike.

The bald man gave a toss of his hand, sending the snake fluttering into the air. Arvin raced across the room, hoping to catch it, but the snake was too quick. It flew out the window. Arvin turned to glare at the human, teeth bared.

The bald man held up an admonishing finger. "Control," he said.

Now Arvin understood. The bald man was yet another tutor, come to drill him in moderation and self-restraint. A *human* tutor, this time, to further humiliate him. "The flying snake held its temper," Arvin hissed back at the man. "So what?"

The bald man chuckled. "You misunderstood my demonstration," he said. "I held the snake's temper. With mind magic. But before I could do that, I had to learn to control my own." He stared for several long moments at Arvin without speaking then asked, "Is this something you would like to learn?"

"Yes," Arvin hissed, speaking aloud in his sleep. "I want to learn."

Suddenly the dream became more chaotic. He was no longer a yuan-ti child, but himself—Arvin—an adult human. Yet strangely, his skin was covered in serpent scales. They were as brown as the bald man's skin had been, and crisscrossed with bands of reddish brown. No, that wasn't a scale pattern on his arms but a series of red thongs, looped around his body and slowly tightening. Zelia, dressed in a gray robe and skullcap, like the ones the priests at the orphanage had worn, was holding one end of the cord and slowly pulling it toward herself, coiling the cord around one wrist as she hauled it in. She stood on the ball of one foot, her other leg twisted up against her chest, the ankle tucked behind her neck. "Control," she said, the word somehow coming out as a hiss. Her jaws opened wide. Hot, stinging venom dripped onto Arvin's temple as she leaned over him, mouth opened, fangs bared—

Arvin's eyes sprang open. Suddenly he was wide awake. Someone was leaning over him, touching his shoulder. A dark silhouette in the moonlight with long, loose hair.

Throwing himself to the side, he called his dagger into his glove. In an instant he was on his feet—and then he recognized Zelia. "By the gods," he gasped, holding his weapon between them. "What did you just do to me?" He rubbed his temple and winced. The headache was still with him.

Zelia remained kneeling, hands on her knees. "What do you mean?"

Arvin blinked, trying to clear his head of the disturbing images. "That dream. I was. . . ."

"Someone else?" Zelia asked, rising slowly to her feet.

Arvin nodded. "A yuan-ti. A child. A . . . girl." The latter was something he'd only just realized—that he'd been female in both of the dreams.

"Sometimes when a psion sleeps, a power manifests spontaneously," Zelia told him. "You obviously manifested a telepathic power that allowed you to peer into another person's mind and listen in on her thoughts. That it was a yuan-ti is hardly surprising in a city with more than two thousand of us. Your mind tried to make sense of what the power showed you and turned it into a dream."

Arvin stood, considering. Was that what he'd just been doing? Looking in on another person's thoughts and knotting them into his dreams? It hadn't *felt* like a dream. Not until the last, chaotic part that had woken him in a cold sweat. That last segment was easy to explain—it was a jumble of his old memories and fears, combined with fragments of what had happened earlier today, including the headache that just wouldn't go away. But the first part had felt like . . . a memory.

Arvin stared at Zelia. "It wasn't just any yuan-ti," he said slowly. "It was someone trained in 'mind magic.' That girl was you—wasn't it?"

Zelia smiled. "I must have been thinking about my childhood." Her smile abruptly vanished. "The Pox have returned to the sewer chamber."

"They have?" Arvin asked, all thoughts of the dream driven instantly from his mind. He looked up at the sky and saw that it was past Middark. "Was my friend with them?"

"I saw two men. Neither was your friend. It looked as though they were waiting for something—or for someone."

She gave him directions to the sewer entrance he would use. It was just a short distance away, inside a slaughterhouse—one that had recently been shut down by the militia after its owners were caught butchering cattle that had succumbed to the rotting hoof disease and passing it off as quality meat.

"How appropriate," Arvin muttered. He slid his dagger into the sheath at the small of his back and picked up his backpack. He pulled out one of the potions he'd purchased earlier, a clear liquid with a sweet scent that lingered in the air even though the tiny bottle that held it was stoppered. The rogue who had sold it to him had assured Arvin it would purge any disease from his body, even ailments that were the result of clerical magic.

Arvin transferred the bottle to his gloved hand and whispered the word that made it disappear into an extra-dimensional space where it could neither be seen nor smelled. The last thing he needed was for one of the Pox to spot the bottle and recognize what it held.

He put on the backpack and nodded at Zelia. "Tymora be with me, I'll have some answers for you soon," he said. Then he realized something. "How will I get a message to you?" he asked. "Do I meet you back here?"

"No," Zelia replied. She opened her belt pouch and pulled from it a stone that glittered in the moonlight. It was dark blue, flecked with gold, about the size and shape of a thumbnail, and flat on one side. Arvin nodded, recognizing it by its distinctive color: lapis lazuli, with inclusions of pyrite. He extended his right hand, palm up, for the chip of stone.

Then he stiffened in surprise. He was no gem cutter. How in the Nine Hells had he known what type of stone it was?

Zelia tipped it into his palm. Arvin used a finger to flip it over. Its rounded surface was cool and smooth, but the flat surface was warm.

"When you have something to report, this will allow you to manifest a sending," Zelia said.

Arvin gave her a puzzled look. "What's a sending?"

"A psionic power—one the stone will allow you to manifest, even though you haven't learned it yet," she continued. "You can send a brief message to me—no more than two dozen words, and only once per day—and I can reply to you, in turn. The distance separating us is not a factor; your message will reach me, no matter where I might be."

"And no matter where I might be?" Arvin asked.

Zelia nodded.

"I see," he said. "It's a contingency plan. In case something happens to . . . prevent me from returning."

Zelia's answer was blunt. "Yes. In order to use the stone, you must place it over your third eye."

"My what?"

"You used it earlier tonight, when you manifested your telekinetic power. Place the flat surface of the stone here"—she touched a finger to a spot between her eyes, just above her nose—"and it will adhere."

Arvin stared at the lapis lazuli, wondering if there was more to it than Zelia was telling him. "Can I put it on later?" he asked. "If the Pox see it—"

"They won't know what it is. Only another psion would recognize it. But put it on and take it off as you wish. You need only think the command word—*atmiya*—and it will adhere or release. Just don't lose it."

"Why? Is it expensive?"

Zelia's lips twitched in what might have been a smile. "Yes."

Arvin stared at the stone. If he did run into trouble—if he wound up a captive, bound hand and foot and without his dagger to cut himself free—having the stone already in place on his forehead would allow him to call for help.

The question was would Zelia answer?

"All right," he said. "I'll use it—but I won't put it on until I need to contact you." He slipped the stone into his shirt pocket, tucking it safely inside a false seam.

24 Kythorn, Darkmorning

Arvin eased himself through a window and drew the shutter closed behind him. He stood a moment, letting his eyes adjust to the gloom and his nose adjust to the smell. The slaughterhouse stank of old blood, animal excrement, and spoiled meat. The stench was so overwhelming he nearly turned to leave, but he steeled himself by thinking of what would happen in less than seven days and pressed on.

He made his way toward the center of the building, avoiding the stained hooks that hung from the ceiling. As he stepped over one of the troughs used to catch the slaughtered animals' blood, his foot bumped against something in the darkness. Flies rose into the air with a soft buzzing noise. Looking down, he saw it was a cow's head, its tongue purple and protruding and both eyes missing. The putrid smell rising from it made his eyes water.

The troughs all led to the same place—a grate in the floor near the center of the building. The spaces between its rusted bars were nearly clotted shut with chunks of decaying flesh, but the crust of blood that had sealed the edges of the grate was broken. Someone had lifted the grate since the slaughterhouse had been shut down.

He removed a hooked tool from his belt and used it to lift one side of the grate. Grabbing the edge of it with his gloved hand, he moved it aside—carefully, so it wouldn't clank against the stone floor—then stared down into the shaft that led to the sewers. He could smell and hear water gurgling somewhere below, but the shaft was as black as a snake's heart.

Wetting his lips, he shrugged off his backpack and set it on the ground beside him then rummaged inside it for the second potion he'd purchased. It was in a vial made from glass of such a deep purple it appeared almost black. Arvin pried out the wax that sealed it and sniffed the vial's contents. It took him a moment to place the scent: night-blooming flowers, underlaid with a hint of something earthy—a root of some sort.

He tipped the potion into his mouth and swallowed. It tasted honey-sweet, with an aftertaste of loam. A heartbeat later, the room seemed to lighten. Murky shadows became distinct objects. A vertical line of darkness was revealed as a chain hanging from the ceiling, and a dark mound in one corner resolved itself into a fly-speckled tangle of cow's legs, minus the hooves. As the darkvision potion took its full effect, the room seemed to become as bright as day—except that everything was devoid of color. The hooks in the ceiling were a dull gray, crusted with blood that was a flat black. Looking down at his own hands, Arvin saw that his skin appeared gray—a lighter gray than his shirt.

This, he mused, must be how dwarves see the world most of the time. Only when they ventured out of their underground strongholds into sunlight would they see color. No wonder they were such a dour race.

But this was no time for idle thought. The potion would only last so long.

The shaft the grate had covered was square, barely wider than his shoulders. It descended some distance to a horizontal tunnel through which foul-looking water flowed. There was a gap between the murky surface of the water and the ceiling of the tunnel—quite a bit of a gap, almost as much space as Arvin was tall. The tunnel must be one of the main sewage lines.

A hook in the slaughterhouse ceiling, just over the shaft, told the story of how the cultists had descended to the tunnel below. The curved bottom of the hook was free of blood; the cultists had obviously tied a rope to it.

Arvin decided to do the same. His bracelet would have allowed him to climb down, but he didn't relish the thought of clinging to a wall so grimed with dried gore. He pulled from his backpack a trollgut rope he'd retrieved from its hiding place earlier that night, when he'd gone to buy the potions. It was rubbery and slightly warm to the touch. He tied the unknotted end to the hook and slipped the rest of its coiled length over his shoulder. Gripping the rope just under the hook with one hand, he transferred his weight to it. With his other hand, he lifted the grate and stood it at an angle on the floor, next to the opening. Then he spoke the rope's command word.

The magical rope lengthened, sending Arvin into a descent down the shaft. He let the grate close above him; its edge pinched the rope as it closed. He descended for a few heartbeats more; then, as soon as the soles of his boots touched the water, he spoke the rope's command word a second time, halting its magical growth.

He hung there a moment, looking around as he twisted on the rope. He immediately spotted what he'd expected to see—a convenient ledge that ran along one wall of the tunnel. He clambered onto it then used his dagger to cut the rope back to its original length. The freshly grown section of rope immediately began to rot; in a short time, it would fall off the hook, away from the spot where the grate pinched it, and all traces of Arvin's entrance would be gone. The original section of rope was still intact and could be used again another day. Arvin carefully stored it in his backpack and set off down the ledge, bending over slightly to avoid banging his head against the rounded ceiling.

After a short distance, the tunnel curved. As Arvin crept around the bend, he spotted the chamber to which he and Naulg had been taken. He'd expected to see the two cultists Zelia had just spotted, but the island of stone at the center of the chamber was bare, devoid even of the hideous wooden statue. Where had the two cultists gone? There was no sign or sound of anyone inside any of the other five tunnels that radiated away from the circular chamber, and this tunnel was the only one with a ledge to walk along. Had he arrived just a little too late? Had the cultists left through the tunnel Arvin stood in, passing beneath the grate even as he crept into the slaughterhouse?

He crouched and examined the ledge, but it held no clues. The sewage that mired its surface held no footprints but his.

Deciding he would wade out to the island, Arvin fished out of his pocket a spool of thread with a lead weight tied to one end. He walked to the mouth of the tunnel and lowered the weight into the water until it hit bottom then grasped the thread just above the point where it entered the water. Lifting it, he measured the depth of the water. It was well over his head.

That gave him pause for thought. How had the cultists who had captured them reached the island of stone that lay in the middle of the chamber, especially hauling captives along with them? They hadn't swum—their robes had been dry, as had the clothes of Arvin and the other captives. And they hadn't rowed there in the boat in which Arvin had escaped. It had been neither big enough, nor sound enough. It had obviously been tied up in the chamber, quietly rotting, for years. The hems of their robes had been wet however, as if they'd dragged in water. Had the cultists *walked* across the water to the island, using magic? If so, the two cultists Zelia had spotted might have strolled away down any of the tunnels, whether they had ledges or not. But which?

As if in answer, a low groan echoed out of the tunnel immediately to the right of the one in which Arvin stood. He tensed, recognizing the sound of a man in pain. Naulg?

He had to find out.

The wall between the tunnels was brickwork, its crumbling mortar offering numerous finger- and toeholds. Activating the magic of his leather bracelet, he began climbing along the wall, glancing over his shoulder frequently. All he needed now was for the cultists to show up. He could hardly claim to have come to join the Pox if he were found skulking around.

Reaching the mouth of the other tunnel, he slipped around the bend and continued into it, still climbing horizontally along the wall. A short distance ahead was a small, square door, up near the ceiling of the tunnel. As Arvin neared it, he saw that the door was open slightly; it gave access to a low-ceilinged corridor. The door was made of wood but was faced with bricks; when closed, it would blend with the wall of the sewage tunnel and be nearly impossible to spot.

Like the sewage tunnels, the secret corridor beyond the door curved; Arvin could see only a few paces inside it. The floor just inside the corridor was smeared with sludge; someone with sewage on his clothes had entered it recently. Arvin paused, clinging to the wall next to the door. Was this corridor where the groan had originated?

He climbed into it, making as little noise as he could. Once on his hands and knees, he drew his dagger. Weapon in hand, he crept up to the bend—and hissed in alarm as he came face to face with a body.

The man lay on his side, unmoving, eyes closed. He was older, with tarred hair pulled back in a tight bun and a face that was vaguely familiar. Only as Arvin reached out to touch the man's stubbled cheek—which was still warm—did he remember where he'd seen the fellow before. He'd been one of the five captives the Pox had taken last night. Like Arvin, he'd been forced to drink from one of the flasks.

Arvin jerked his fingers away from the corpse. Had the old sailor died of plague? Arvin's heart raced at the thought of sharing this narrow tunnel with a diseased corpse. He was breathing the same air the man had just groaned from his lungs—breathing in disease and death and. . . .

Control, he told himself sternly. Where is your control?

The self-admonishment steadied him, that and Zelia's reassurances that he was immune to the plague in the flasks, his body having already fought it off once. Or had it? His headache had dulled, a little, but it still nagged at him. Perhaps it wasn't the mind seed after all but the start of a fever. And he did feel a little light-headed—though that might have been due to the sewer stench.

Forcing himself to touch his amulet with the fingers that had just touched the dead man's cheek, he uttered the words that had always given him courage in the past: "Nine lives."

Then he noticed something—a smear of blood on the floor of the tunnel, just beyond the corpse. Curious, Arvin shifted position so he could see the sailor's back and spotted the fletched end of a crossbow bolt protruding from a spot just below the right shoulder. Had the old man tried to escape and the cultists shot him in the back?

Oddly enough, the thought fueled Arvin's hopes. If the old sailor had remained alive for this long—and had felt well enough to attempt escape—perhaps Naulg was still alive, too.

Arvin had just started to crawl past the body when he heard a groan issue from the man's lips. He froze, half-way over the sailor, as the man's eyes flickered open.

"It hurts," the sailor whispered.

Arvin's eyes flickered to the crossbow bolt. "You've been shot," he told the old man. "I don't think...." He didn't have the heart to say the rest—that he doubted the fellow would live much longer.

The old man stared at the wall, not seeing Arvin. "My stomach. It hurts," he whispered again in a voice as faint as death. "Gods curse them ... for doing this to me. I just want ... the pain ... to end."

"It will, old man. It will." Arvin wanted to pat the shoulder of the sailor, to console him, but was afraid to.

The old man was whispering again—fainter, this time, than before. "Silvanus forgive me for...."

Arvin could have leaned closer and heard the rest, but he was fearful of getting too close to the man's plague-tainted breath. Instead he drew back, holding his own breath.

A moment later, he realized the old man had also stopped breathing.

From somewhere up ahead, Arvin heard the metallic hiss of a sword being drawn from its sheath. Worried that Naulg might be the next to die, he crawled past the corpse and on up the corridor as quickly as he could.

CHAPTER 8

As Arvin hurried down the corridor on his hands and knees, the stench increased. It wasn't just the odor of the sewers that was clogging his nostrils, but something far worse—the reek of putrefying flesh, vomit, and sweat. Bile rose in his throat. He fought it down. He hurried on, blinking away a drop of sweat that had trickled into one eye. It wasn't just the exertion of crawling rapidly through a low-ceilinged corridor that had caused him to break out in a sweat. The air was definitely getting warmer, more humid. Up ahead, he could see the glow of lantern light. It turned the brick walls of the corridor from gray to dusky red.

There had been silence for some time after the sound of the sword being drawn, but now he could hear retching noises. Then a woman's voice, tense and low. "Something's coming, Urus. Hurry! Get up!"

Just a few paces ahead, the corridor gave access to a large chamber. Arvin saw a man, down on his hands and knees, vomiting. A woman was bent over him, tugging on the back of his shirt with one hand. Both wore high boots slicked with sewage to the knee. Judging by the crossbow that lay on the ground next to the man's knee, they were the ones who had shot the sailor.

He hadn't been their only victim.

A bull's-eye lantern lay on the ground beside the kneeling man, its light painting a bright circle on a cultist in faded gray robes who was slumped in a heap against one wall, his chest bloody. Judging by the slit in his robe, he'd been killed by a sword slash. A large basket lay on the floor beside the cultist. Freshly butchered chunks of meat had spilled out of it. One of them was recognizable as a human foot.

The man on his hands and knees was middle-aged and broad shouldered with dark, curly hair and a full beard. The woman was younger—in her early twenties—and slender, with a narrow face framed with waist-length hair that hung straight as a plumb line. She wore a man's trousers tucked into her boots and held a bloody sword. She tugged frantically on the man's shirt with her other hand, trying to drag him back to the corridor in which Arvin had halted, but without success. Her eyes were locked on the chamber's only other entrance: an archway that led into a darkened corridor tall enough for a human to walk upright. From it came a slurping sound, as if something large and wet were being dragged across the floor.

Arvin peered through the archway. His darkvision revealed what looked like a grayish mound, moving slowly toward the chamber. It hunched and sagged as it moved, sections of it bulging out like bubbles trying to burst through thick oil then sinking flat in a fold of flesh as the rest of the mass surged over them. As the thing drew closer to the lantern light, colors were revealed. Gray resolved into greenish yellow, the color of diseased flesh. Red pustules dotted the body of the thing, as did molelike tufts sprouting wiry black hair. The creature had no eyes, no mouth. Here and there, a bone jabbed momentarily out of the flesh like a thrusting sword, causing a dribble of pus-tinged blood, then was drawn back into the mass with a wet sucking sound as the mound surged forward.

"Torm shield us," the woman croaked as the thing bulged out of the archway. "What is *that?*"

The man glanced up as the fleshy mound squeezed its bulk through the archway and tumbled into the room with a sound like a bag of wet entrails hitting the floor. The mound hesitated, pulsing first in the direction of the two living humans, then toward the cultist's corpse. The kneeling man tried to climb to his feet but was only able to rise partway before clutching at his stomach and doubling over again. His back heaved as he gave in to nausea, retching over and over again. One hand gestured weakly, urging the woman to leave him.

The young woman, gagging in the overpowering stench that filled the chamber, at last let go of his shirt. But instead of turning and running, as Arvin expected, she stepped between her companion and the mound, readying her sword.

"You fool," Arvin whispered to himself. "Get out of there!" He'd already started backing down the corridor through which he'd crawled, though he could not tear his eyes away from the horrific creature that was only a pace or two away from the woman. The stench of the thing was terrific; Arvin's eyes watered as he fought to keep himself from vomiting. Control, he told himself fiercely. You can control—

No he couldn't. His stomach was twisted by a wave of nausea that felt like a dagger stabbing into his gut.

He vomited onto the floor, splattering his hands and knees.

The woman was shouting something. Suddenly, Arvin felt the humid air around him grow slightly cooler. As he fought down the next wave of nausea and managed to look up, he saw her leap forward, thrusting with her sword. The blade plunged into part of the mound that had been bulging toward her. An ice-white burst of magical energy erupted from the sword, instantly freezing the flesh around it. The creature's skin cracked like a frozen puddle that had been stomped on. Then the woman yanked her sword free, sending a scattering of frozen blood tinkling onto the floor.

The mound hesitated, sucking its wounded flesh back into itself. Then it exploded into motion. It surged forward, driving the woman back. Her companion had just enough time to glance up at the thing that was towering over him like a pulsating wall— and the mound collapsed on top of him, suffocating his scream.

"Urus!" the woman screamed in a strangled voice. "No!" She leaped forward, thrusting her sword into the side of the mound a second time. A blast of magical cold radiated through the creature's flesh, causing a section of it to expand and crack apart as it froze. But despite this new wound—and a third, and a fourth—the fleshy mound refused to retreat. It remained firmly on top of the spot where her companion had been crouched, its bulk filling the far half of the chamber. From beneath it came a muffled tearing noise, punctuated by the sharp crackle of breaking bone.

The sound drove the woman into a frenzy. She flung herself at the mound, thrusting with her sword. The weapon plunged to the hilt into the pulsating wall of flesh—and the pustule it had entered exploded, spraying her with pus. The mound pulsed forward in the same instant, engulfing her hand just as the magical cold erupted from the sword. She gasped as the flesh that surrounded her hand froze.

Arvin, meanwhile, fought his own battle against the nausea that was cramping his stomach. Move through the pain, he told himself, staring at the vomit-splattered brick between his hands. A part of his mind noted that the floor was gray again; the lantern must have been engulfed by the mound. Forcing the stray thought away, he concentrated on blotting out the cramps in his stomach. The mind is master of the body, he told himself, repeating the phrase his tutor had drilled into him. It is in control. Gritting his teeth, he tried to force his mind past the nausea ...

And found himself vomiting—this time, on his glove.

Staring at it, he remembered the potion that was hidden inside its extra-dimensional space. The potion was designed to remove disease—would it also cure nausea? It was worth a try.

Summoning the vial to his hand, Arvin ripped the cork out with his teeth. He drank the potion in one swallow, welcoming its honey-sweet taste ...

And suddenly, the nausea was gone.

Hissing in relief, he looked up. The lantern had indeed gone out; he viewed the chamber with darkvision alone. The woman had lost her sword and stood flexing frostbitten fingers, trying to make them work again. The mound had engulfed the cultist's corpse and was consuming it, giving her a brief reprieve. But even as Arvin watched, it began to slide toward her with a slow, certain malevolence. The woman retreated, backing toward the corridor Arvin occupied, her undamaged hand extended behind her as if she were feeling her way. Arvin wondered why she didn't just turn and run then realized that, unlike him, she couldn't see. She didn't have a chance.

Unless he helped her. Which would mean abandoning what might be his one chance to slip around the mound and into the corridor at the far end of the chamber—a corridor that might lead him to Naulg.

Or to a dead end, with a flesh-eating monster at his back.

"This way!" Arvin shouted to the woman, crawling forward as quickly as he could. He sprang out of the corridor and grabbed her, forcing her down into a crouch, then shoved her into the low corridor. "Move!" he barked. "Get out of here."

She did.

Out of the corner of his eye, Arvin saw the mound looming above him. He leaped out of the way an instant before it toppled onto the spot where he'd just stood—then cursed, realizing the mound had forced him into a corner, away from the exit. His only hope was to somehow drive the thing back, to force it to draw away from the mouth of the corridor that led back to the sewers. He slashed with his dagger at the bulge and felt the blade slice through soft, quivering flesh. But the mound was undeterred by the wound. It reared up until it touched the ceiling, towering above Arvin. As it did, the wound Arvin had just inflicted upon it gaped open. Staring into the depths of the creature, Arvin saw a gore-streaked ball of bone with two dark pits where the eyes had been—a partially digested head—and a rounded shaft of metal, wrapped with leather.

The grip of a sword hilt.

And not just any weapon, but the one that inflicted magical cold. He started to reach for it then realized it was buried deep inside diseased flesh and yanked his hand back.

Instead he sent his consciousness deep into himself and found his third eye—and the energy that lay coiled there—and flung that energy outward. A bright line of sparkling silver light burst from his eyes and coiled itself around the sword hilt then yanked it free. Grabbing the hilt with his gloved hand, he stabbed the blade into the bulge that blocked the corridor mouth.

Thankfully, the weapon's magic was still working: a burst of cold erupted from the blade, instantly freezing the protuberance. Arvin twisted the sword, using it like a lever, and the frozen bulge of flesh snapped off, revealing the exit. Unfortunately, the sword broke, as well. Dropping it, Arvin dived into the tunnel headfirst. Just in time—as he did, he heard the heavy slap of flesh hitting the wall behind him. A bulge of flesh forced its way into the corridor and brushed against one of his feet. Soft, squishy flesh engulfed his boot, nearly reaching his ankle before he could yank his foot free.

Spurred on by fear, Arvin crawled away as quickly as he could. Behind him, he heard bones cracking as the mound tried to force its bulk into the narrow corridor. As he retreated, the sounds of the creature slapping itself against the walls fell farther and farther behind—it couldn't fit into so small a corridor, Tymora be praised.

Up ahead, around a curve of the tunnel, Arvin could hear a scuffing noise and the rasp of a scabbard dragging on brick. He caught sight of the woman he'd just saved as she was crawling past the body of the old sailor. Leaving it behind, she rounded the bend in the corridor. In another moment she would reach its end.

"Wait!" Arvin shouted as he eased his way past the corpse, loath to touch it. "You're going to fall into—"

A splash told him his warning was too late. Reaching the end of the corridor himself, he looked down into the tunnel and saw the woman thrashing about in the sewage, her long hair plastered to her body. "I'm up here," he called out, reaching down to her. "Take hold of my hand." She startled at the sound of his voice, but accepted his hand readily enough when he grabbed hers and used it to lever herself up into a standing position. The sewage turned out to be no more than knee-deep.

She let go of his hand and clawed away the wet hair that was plastered to her face then spat several times, a disgusted expression on her face. Then she fumbled at the pouch on her belt, lifting its flap and tipping sewer water out of it. From out of the pouch, she pulled a small metal flask, its sides ridged like the rattles of a snake—the same kind of flask the Pox had used to force-feed Arvin plague-tainted water. She ran her fingers across the top of it, checking the cork that sealed it.

"Where did you get that?" Arvin asked.

His tone must have been sharper than he'd intended. The woman squinted up in his general direction, a wary look in her eyes. She took a step back, her free hand brushing her scabbard—she stiffened as she found it empty. "Who are you?" she asked, suspicion thickening her voice.

Arvin summoned up a smile, even though she couldn't see it. He needed to keep her talking. She might have seen other cultists—or even Naulg. A warm prickling began at the base of his scalp. "I'm a friend," he told her. "I followed you and Urus. I thought you could use some help."

Arvin saw her head tilt as if she were listening to something—a good sign. An instant later, her expression softened. "Thank the gods you came after us," she gasped. "I *told* Gonthril that sending just two of us was a bad idea, but he wouldn't listen." She tucked the flask back into her pouch and tied it shut.

"I'm glad I found you in time," Arvin said. Seeing her wet clothes clinging to her almost hipless body and noting that the belt that held her scabbard was much too large for her, he revised his estimate of her age to late teens. She was awfully young to be adventuring down in the sewers. Even with a chaperone.

"I'm glad you found us, too," she said. Then she shuddered. "Poor Urus. That *thing. . . .*"

"I've never seen anything like it," Arvin said. "Have you?"

"No. Whatever it was, I think the cleric was on his way to feed it," the woman said, a grimace on her face. "If I hadn't had my father's sword. . . ." She shuddered again then stared blindly up in Arvin's general direction. "Have we met?" she asked. "Or are you in a different arm of the Secession?"

Arvin made a mental note of the word—it sounded like the name of an organization, but it was one he'd never heard of before. "We haven't met," he answered honestly. "My name's Arvin."

"I'm Kayla." She glanced around, squinting as she tried to penetrate the absolute darkness. "I can't see anything—can you?"

"Yes."

"Good. Then you can help me find my way out of these gods-cursed sewers. I need to get back to Gonthril and make my report. He'll be glad to hear we were right about the clerics being down here."

"Good work," Arvin said, playing along. Gonthril was, presumably, the leader of whatever group this woman belonged to, and he seemed to be interested in the Pox—interested enough to send people into the sewers to search for them. Why was anyone's guess.

"Gonthril asked me to keep an eye out for someone while I was down here," Arvin told Kayla. "A dark-haired man whose eyebrows join above his nose. Have you seen him?"

"Who is he?"

"Someone who might be able to help us," Arvin said, keeping his answer deliberately vague.

Kayla shook her head. "I haven't seen him."

"How long have you been down here?"

"Since Sunset. We tried to enter the sewers earlier, but the militia were everywhere."

Arvin nodded. She'd been in the sewers quite some time, then. "Did you see any other clerics besides the one with the basket?"

"No."

"How did you know where to find him?"

"We didn't," Kayla said. "It was just Tymora's luck. We were snooping around in the sewers—we'd seen one of Talona's clerics come down here earlier. When we spotted the opening that led to the hidden corridor, we decided to follow it."

"I see," Arvin said, disappointed. Though Kayla had been forthcoming, she hadn't told him anything about the cultists that he didn't already know. Perhaps others in her organization would know more.

One thing was bothering Arvin. "That second fellow—the old sailor—why did Urus shoot him?"

The mention of her companion's name started the woman's lip trembling. "He attacked us."

Arvin frowned. "Are you sure the old man wasn't just trying to escape—to get by you?"

Kayla shook her head. "He was *with* the cleric. When Urus and I surprised them in the chamber, the cleric shouted at the old man to attack us and started casting a spell. I was able to stop him before his prayer was complete, but the old man managed to bite my arm before Urus could shoot him. He ran off while Urus was reloading . . . and that *thing* showed up."

Arvin frowned. "The old man *bit* you?" he said.

"You don't believe me?" Kayla shoved up her sleeve. "Look."

Arvin stared at the crescent-shaped bite mark on her wrist.

"His bite was venomous," Kayla continued. "He must have been yuan-ti—one that could pass for human in lantern light. If it weren't for this, I'd be dead." She touched something that hung from a silver chain around her neck—a pendant made from a black gem. That it was ensorcelled to ward off poison, Arvin had no doubt. But had the old man's bite truly been poisonous?

He gave the bite on her wrist a closer scrutiny. The wound lacked the distinctive puncture marks that hollow, venom-filled fangs would leave. "The old man was diseased, you mean," he corrected.

Kayla shook her head. "It wasn't disease—the effects were too quick. As soon as his teeth broke the skin, my entire arm felt as though it were on fire."

Arvin nodded, losing interest. The real question was whether the old sailor had joined Talona's cult or been magically compelled by the cleric to attack. Whichever it was, he must have been one of the two men Zelia had spied earlier on the stone island. She'd assumed that both were cultists even though only one was wearing robes. The old man obviously hadn't been acting like a prisoner—and he certainly hadn't been bound.

"We should get moving," Kayla said.

Arvin nodded. "Is there an exit nearby?"

Kayla found the wall of the tunnel by touch and ran her palm up it to locate the edge of the corridor in which Arvin crouched. Then she pointed up the sewage tunnel, away from the chamber with the stone island. "That way. There's a shaft that gives access to the street, about four hundred paces up the tunnel. It's at the base of the next spillway."

Arvin glanced down at the water, the surface of which was dotted with half-dissolved lumps that drifted gently with the current. The sewage was deeper than his ankle-high boots; he grimaced at the thought of climbing down into it. "I'm going to climb along the wall," he told her. "You can hold onto my shirt and follow me. All right?"

Kayla nodded.

They set out, Arvin making his way slowly along the wall, Kayla holding on to his shirt. Several times she slipped and nearly pulled Arvin into the sewage with her, but his bracelet allowed him to stick tight to the wall.

As he led her up the sewage tunnel, he considered his options. He could wait near the stone island to see if any other cultists showed up, could slog around in the sewers in the hope of stumbling into some of them—or he could leave with Kayla. The charm he'd placed on her would be effective for some time, and she could probably be talked into taking him along with her when she reported to her leader. This Gonthril fellow must know more than Kayla did. If Arvin could charm *him* into sharing what he knew, perhaps two knots could be tied with a single twist. Arvin might learn the answers to Zelia's questions *and* might gain some insight into where Naulg was ...

Without having to face the cultists.

24 Kythorn, Darkmorning

Arvin lifted the grate a finger's width and peered up and down the darkened street. They were inside the yuan-ti section of the city; mansion walls towered on either side. A slave was sweeping dust from an elaborate, column-fronted entryway to the right. A second slave with a handcart was picking up garbage from the street.

Arvin tipped the grate sideways and passed it down to Kayla, who had braced herself inside the narrow shaft with her back against one wall, her feet against the other. Arvin was just above her, in the same position, his backpack turned so that it hung against his chest. When both slaves had their backs to the opening, he clambered out of the shaft, took the grate from Kayla, and helped her up after him. A moment later the grate was back in place, and they were strolling in the opposite direction from the slaves, just two people out for a walk in the darkness that preceded dawn.

As they passed a light standard, Kayla glanced at Arvin. Seeing her eyes widen, he worried that she might have realized that he wasn't a member of her group after all.

"Amazing," she said. "You could be Gonthril's brother." She paused then added, "Are you?"

"No," Arvin said, not wanting to get caught up in a lie that would quickly unravel on him. "The resemblance is coincidental. I'm always getting mistaken for—" He paused, suddenly realizing something. *That* was who the militia had thought Arvin was that morning: Gonthril. A "rebel," the sergeant had called him. . . .

A rebel with a ten thousand gold piece bounty on his head. And Kayla was about to lead Arvin straight to the man. The next little while could prove interesting—and possibly lucrative.

He nudged Kayla into a walk again. "Let's keep moving. If anyone sees you like that. . . ."

Kayla nodded. "There's a fountain up ahead. I can wash up a little."

They quickened their pace, taking a side street to the fountain. Arvin stood watch as Kayla rinsed the worst of the sewage off herself by ducking into the spray, and they set off again. Arvin expected a lengthy, downhill walk, but Kayla instead led him uphill, deeper into the yuan-ti section of town. Several times they saw militia out on patrol and had to turn up a side street to avoid them. Once, while doing this, they blundered into a group of slaves. Arvin stuck his chin in the air haughtily and hissed at them, giving the impression that he was a yuan-ti. They touched their foreheads and turned aside, discretely ignoring the squelching sound Kayla's wet boots made and the odor that lingered in her wake.

"Not bad," Kayla commented. "You've even got the sway in your walk."

Did he? After she'd called his attention to it, Arvin realized she was right. He'd been swaying his shoulders and hips back and forth as he walked, without intending to. The realization that this must be the mind seed at work sent a chill through him. He rubbed his temple, feeling the ache that lurked just under the skin.

Kayla led him ever upward, into one of the oldest parts of the city, navigating by its most conspicuous landmark—the enormous, fountain-topped dome of the Cathedral of Emerald Scales. Eventually they passed under one end of an ancient, monumental arch that stretched from this street to the next—an arch that was undergoing restoration. Kayla stopped near the pillar that supported this end of the arch. It was surrounded by wooden scaffolding that in turn was sheeted with cloth. She glanced around then lifted a flap of the cloth and tilted her head, indicating that Arvin should slip behind it. He did, and saw that the pillar's decorative scalework was being rechiseled. The cloth must have been hung to prevent dust and stone chips from littering the street below.

Arvin ran a hand over the rough, half-finished carving. The arch was a snake in the process of shedding its skin. Then Kayla ducked behind the cloth with him. She winked at him, one hand on a bar of the scaffolding. They were obviously about to climb it. "Ironic, isn't it?" she whispered. "That scaly bitch is looking all over for the man who's treading on her tail, and he's hiding under her belly all the while. It's one of Gonthril's favorite tricks—hiding in the places she'd least suspect."

Arvin grinned back at her, pretending that he knew what Kayla was talking about. As he followed her up the scaffolding, however, he started to get an inkling. The higher they climbed, the more he could see of the surrounding area through gaps in the cloth draping. He found himself looking down on one of the private gardens of the Extaminos family, now closed for renovations. Its age-pitted walls dated back more than eight centuries, to the time of Lord Shevron, the man who had beaten back the kobold hordes that had besieged the city in 527. This act had ensured House Extaminos's standing for centuries to come. Indeed, for the past three centuries, all of Hlondeth's rulers had been members of House Extaminos, right up to Lady Dediana, the city's current ruler . . .

Who, like most of her predecessors, was yuan-ti.

Arvin understood who the "rebels" were. He'd heard rumors of a group of men and women who wanted to restore the city to human rule. They wanted to turn back the centuries to a time before Lord Shevron had made his pact with the scaly folk. They might as well try to turn the sun back on its course in the sky or cause lava to flow *into* Mount Ugruth. But they'd certainly stirred up the militia with their efforts.

Kayla reached the top of the scaffolding and clambered into one of the gaping serpent mouths that fronted the arch. She turned to help Arvin inside. When he climbed in after her, he was surprised to see that the arch was hollow—to help reduce the weight of so much stone, he supposed. He crawled along behind her through its corridorlike interior, hissing with pain each time he banged a knee against the uneven floor. More than once, his backpack caught on the rough stone ceiling and had to be yanked free. His darkvision was gone; the potion had worn off during the walk here. The only light came from the gaping serpent mouth behind them and a similar opening up ahead. He followed Kayla—who seemed quite familiar with the route—as she led the way through along the darkened passage.

When they reached the second serpent mouth, Kayla stopped. Arvin peered past her and saw they were directly over the private garden, which was illuminated only by moonlight. Its walls, like the monumental arch, were surrounded by scaffolding— part of the massive restoration project that had been undertaken by Dmetrio Extaminos, eldest prince of the royal family, in recent months. Rumor had it Dmetrio had already spent more than a million gold pieces on the project, which seemed destined to tear apart and remortar every building in the old section of the city, stone by stone.

Kayla leaned out of the mouth of the stone serpent head and whistled a tune. A moment later, an answering whistle came from below. The end of a rope rose into view outside the serpent's mouth. Recognizing it, Arvin cracked a wry smile. He'd woven it from sylph hair, a little more than two years ago.

At least one of his customers, it seemed, hadn't been Guild. Or if they were Guild, they were also working the other side of the coin.

Kayla motioned for Arvin to grab the rope. Instead, he took a cautious glance down. Only one person stood in the garden below—the man who held the other end of the rope. The fellow looked harmless enough, with a balding head and ale belly, but appearances could be deceiving. For all Arvin knew, the staff the man had propped against a bush next to him could be a magical weapon of some sort. Getting past him would be the first challenge on the way to meeting Gonthril. Arvin would need a backup, if he were unable to charm the fellow.

"Sorry," Arvin told Kayla with an apologetic smile. "Heights make me nervous." As he spoke, he slipped a hand behind his back and grasped the hilt of his dagger. At a whisper, the dagger disappeared into his glove.

"Go on," Kayla urged. "It isn't far."

Arvin winced, still pretending to be nervous, then grasped the rope. He swung out onto it and clambered down. Kayla followed.

As soon as they were both on the ground, the balding man ordered the rope down. As it looped itself neatly over his outstretched arm, he frowned at Arvin and picked up his staff. "Who's this, Kayla? And where's Urus?"

Kayla's lip began to tremble again. "Dead," she said in a quavering voice. "I'd be dead, too, Chorl, if Arvin hadn't come along when he did."

"I've come to speak to Gonthril," Arvin said. The familiar prickle at the base of his scalp began, and he smiled. "I'm not with the Secession, but I have similar interests—and some information I'm sure Gonthril will want to hear." Seeing a skeptical narrowing of the balding man's eyes, he quickly added, "Information about Talona's clerics—and what they're up to. Kayla managed to get her hands on a flask that one of them was carrying."

The man's eyebrows rose. "Did she?" He glanced at Kayla, who nodded eagerly. "Well done. Well, come on, then."

Arvin let out a soft hiss of relief. His charm had worked. Or had it? As he followed Kayla through the garden, he noticed that Chorl fell into step behind him. The balding man was keeping a close watch on Arvin—closer than Arvin liked.

The garden was laid out in a formal pattern. A path, bordered by flowering shrubs, spiraled in from the main gate to the center of the garden. Bordering this path were slabs of volcanic stone, their many niches providing shelter for the tiny serpents that called the garden home. At the center of the garden was a gazebo, its glass-paned roof reminiscent of the Solarium. The gazebo's wrought-iron supports, like the light standards in the street, took the form of rearing serpents, except that the globes in their mouths hadn't glowed in centuries. Its floor was a mosaic, made from age-dulled tiles. It was covered with what Arvin at first took to be sticks. As he drew closer, though, he saw that they were tiny, finger-thin snakes, curled around one another in sleep. The snakes obscured part of the mosaic, but Arvin could still make out the crest of House Extaminos: a mason's chisel and a ship, separated by a wavy red line.

Chorl stepped forward and used the end of his staff to flick away the tiny snakes. He was needlessly rough with them, injuring several with his harsh jabs, and Arvin found his anger rising. He balled his fists at his sides, forcing himself to hold his emotions in check as the tiny snakes were flung aside.

Chorl stepped up onto the spot the snakes had just been evicted from and pulled from his pocket a hollow metal tube. Squatting, he rapped it once against the tiled floor. The rod emitted a bright *ting*, and the air above the floor rippled. Then a portion of the floor—the section of the mosaic depicting the ship—sank down out of sight. Arvin peered into the hole and saw a ramp leading down into darkness.

Kayla stepped to the edge of the hole. "I always enjoy this part," she told Arvin. She sat on the lip of the hole then pushed off, disappearing into it. The sound of her wet clothes sliding on stone faded quickly.

Chorl nudged Arvin forward with the end of his staff. "Down you go," he ordered. Arvin hissed at the man and angrily knocked the staff aside. Who did this fellow think he was, to order him about?

Chorl was swifter than Arvin had thought. He whipped the staff around, smacking it into Arvin's head. A burst of magical energy flared from the tip of the staff, exploding through Arvin's mind like a thunderclap and leaving him reeling. Eyes rolled up in his head, unable to see, Arvin felt the staff smack against his legs, knocking them out from under him. He tumbled forward, landing in a heap on the tiled floor.

Arvin's backpack was yanked from his shoulders. He felt the end of the staff force its way under his chest, levering him over onto his back. He tried to speak the command that would make the dagger appear in his glove, but his lips wouldn't form the word. The staff thrust inside the collar of Arvin's shirt and shoved, sending him sliding toward the hole. He found himself at an angle, head and shoulders lower than his hips and legs.

Chorl leaned over him. "You may have charmed Kayla, you scaly bastard, but it didn't work on me." Another shove and Arvin was sliding headlong down a ramp.

Up above, he heard Chorl's shout—"Snake in the hole!"—and the sound of stone sliding on stone as the trapdoor slid shut.

He hurtled along headfirst through darkness, unable to stop his slide down what turned out to be a spiraling tunnel with walls and floor of smooth stone. At the bottom was a small, brick-walled room, illuminated by a lantern that hung from the ceiling; Arvin skidded to a halt on its floor. The room's only exit, other than the tunnel he'd just slid out of, was blocked by a wrought-iron gate that had just clanged shut. Still lying on his back, Arvin craned his neck to peer through it and saw Kayla being hurried away down a corridor by two men. She glanced back at Arvin, her face twisted with confusion, as they hustled her around a corner.

Arvin sat up, gingerly feeling the back of his head. A lump was rising there. It burned with the fierce, hot tingle of residual magical energy.

"Stand up," a man's voice commanded.

Turning, Arvin saw a man standing behind the wrought-iron gate. He was Arvin's height and build, had short brown hair, and was no more than a handful of years older than Arvin. His resemblance to Arvin, now that Arvin's hair was also cut short, was uncanny—so much so that Arvin could understand why Kayla had taken them for brothers. The only difference was that this fellow's eyes were a pale blue, instead of brown, and shone with such intensity that Arvin felt as if the man were peering into his very soul.

"Gonthril?" Arvin guessed.

The man nodded. The sleeves of his white shirt were rolled up, revealing bare forearms. He, too, had avoided service with the militia. He patted the lock on the gate with his left hand. Rings glittered on every finger of it. No wonder Tanju had mistaken Arvin for Gonthril in the Mortal Coil; he must have assumed the glove was hiding those rings.

"The gate is locked," Gonthril told Arvin. "You can't escape."

Arvin held out his hands. "I have no intention of escaping," he told Gonthril. "I'm a friend. I came here to ask you about—"

"Don't try to twist my mind with your words," Gonthril barked. "I'm protected against your magic. And just in case you're thinking of slithering out of there...." Letting the threat dangle, he drew a dagger from a sheath at his hip and turned it so it caught the lantern light. The blade glistened as if wet, and was covered with a pattern of wavy lines.

If Gonthril expected a reaction, Arvin must have disappointed him. He stared at the dagger, perplexed. "Am I supposed to know what that is?"

"Go ahead and assume serpent form," Gonthril said in a low voice. "You'll find out, soon enough, what the blade does."

"Serpent form?" Arvin repeated. Then he realized what was going on. Chorl—and now Gonthril—had mistaken him for a yuan-ti.

And they hated yuan-ti.

"You've made a mistake," Arvin told the rebel leader, wetting his lips nervously. "I'm as human as you are."

"Prove it."

Gonthril, standing just a few short paces away, must be able to see that Arvin had round pupils, but obviously believed that Arvin's clothes hid patches of snake skin or a tail. Realizing what he had to do, Arvin slowly began shedding his clothing. He started with the belt that held his empty sheath, letting it fall to the ground, then kicked off his boots. Shedding his shirt and trousers and at last tugging off his glove, he stood naked. Arms raised, he turned in a slow circle, letting Gonthril inspect him. He finished by briefly sticking out his tongue, to show that it was not forked.

"Satisfied?" he asked.

"I see you've had a run-in with the Guild," Gonthril observed.

"Fortunately, only one," Arvin said, picking up his glove and pulling it back on. Gonthril seemed to be finished with his inspection, so Arvin continued to dress.

When Arvin was done, Gonthril pulled something from his pocket and tossed it into the room—a ring. It tinkled as it hit the floor near Arvin's feet.

"Put it on," Gonthril instructed.

Arvin stared at it. The ring was a wide band of silver set with deep blue stones. He recognized them as sapphires—something he shouldn't have been able to do, since he didn't know one gemstone from another. "What does the ring do?" he asked.

"Put it on."

Arvin wet his lips. He could guess that the ring was magical and was reluctant to touch it, even though Gonthril had just done so. Still, what choice did he have? He needed to convince Gonthril that he was a friend—or at least that he was neutral—if he ever wanted to get any information out of him. He bent down to pick up the ring. No sooner did his fingertips brush its cool metal than it blinked into place on his forefinger. Startled, he tried to yank it off, but the ring wouldn't budge.

Gonthril smiled. "Now then," he said. "What were you doing in the sewers?"

Arvin found his mouth answering for him. "Looking for Naulg."

"Who is Naulg?"

Arvin was unable to stop the words that came out in short, jerky gulps. "A friend. We met years ago. When we were both boys. At the orphanage."

"What was *he* doing in the sewers?"

"He was captured. By the Pox. The clerics with the flasks. They made him drink from one. As a sacrifice to their god. They made me drink from one, too."

"Did they?" Gonthril's eyes glittered.

"Yes," Arvin gulped, forced by the ring to answer the question, even though it had obviously been rhetorical.

"What happened after you swallowed the contents of the flask?"

In short, jerky sentences, Arvin told Gonthril about the agonizing pain the liquid had produced, being dragged before the statue of Talona, fighting his way free, falling into the rowboat and escaping, losing consciousness—and coming to again, only to realize he'd left Naulg behind. He started to talk about going back to the Mortal Coil, but Gonthril cut him off with a curt, "That's enough." He stared at Arvin for several moments before speaking again.

"Are you human?" he asked at last.

"Yes."

The first two fingers of Gonthril's right hand crossed in a silent question: *Guild?*

"Yes." The ring jerked a further admission out of him: "But I don't want to be."

That made Gonthril smile. He nodded at Arvin's gloved hand. "Given the way they treat their people, I don't blame you." Then came another question: "Who are you working for now?"

Arvin could feel his lips and tongue starting to produce a *z* sound, but somehow the answer—Zelia—got stuck in his throat. "Myself," he told Gonthril. "I work for myself."

"Are you a member of House Extaminos?"

"No."

"How do you feel about the yuan-ti?"

Arvin didn't need the ring to answer that one honestly. "I don't like them much, either."

That made Gonthril smile a second time. "Why did you come here?"

"I wanted to talk to you. To learn more about the cultists. I thought you might be able to tell me something. Something that would help me save my friend. Like where I can find the cultists."

Gonthril shrugged. "On that point, your guess is as good as mine." He reached into his pocket and pulled out a small metal flask—either the one Kayla had recovered from the cultist, or one exactly like it. "Do you know what's inside this?" he asked.

Arvin shuddered. "Yes. Poison. Mixed with plague."

"You drank it, and it didn't kill you?"

Arvin found himself paraphrasing what Zelia had told him. "I have a strong constitution. The plague was driven out of my body. Talona was unable to claim me."

Gonthril stared at Arvin, a speculative look on his face. "Interesting," he said. "You called her clerics by a name—the Pox. Tell me what you know about them."

Arvin summed up what little information he had, concluding with, "They're a cult. Of Talona. They want to kill everyone in the city."

"How?"

"By tainting the public fountains. With what's in those flasks."

"When?"

"I don't know. Soon, I think."

"What do you know about House Extaminos?" Gonthril asked.

Arvin frowned, confused by the sudden turn the conversation had taken. His mouth, however, answered of its own accord. "They rule Hlondeth. They've lived here for centuries. Most of them are yuan-ti. Lady Dediana—"

"I didn't ask for a history lesson," Gonthril said, holding up a hand to stem the flow of words. "I meant to ask if you knew what their role is in all of this."

"What do you mean?" Arvin asked.

"A member of the royal family was observed meeting with Talona's clerics. They turned over several captives to him. Human captives. Including one of our members. Do you know anything about that?"

"No," Arvin answered honestly. He mulled this new information over in his mind. Zelia had been certain that the Pox weren't acting on their own, that someone was backing them. Could it really be House Extaminos? Why would the ruling house want to spread plague in its own city? Unless there was a coup in the works.

"Which member of the royal family?" Arvin asked.

Gonthril's eyes narrowed. "Why would you want to know that?"

"I suspect a yuan-ti might be behind the Pox. I want to know who it is."

"Why?"

"Because I need...." Arvin's voice trailed off as a fierce throbbing gripped his temples. Compelled by the ring, he'd started to answer honestly—to tell Gonthril that he needed to report this information to Zelia—but another answer was also trying to force itself out through his lips at the same time. That he needed to know if *Sibyl* was involved. Who that was, he had no idea—the name had just popped into his head. He knew where it had come from—the mind seed. Already, just a day and a half into the transformation, it was starting to take over his mind in subtle ways, to force his thoughts along channels that were foreign to him. And dangerous. The instant the Secession found out about his link with Zelia, Arvin would be a dead man.

With an effort that caused sweat to break out on his forehead, he forced himself to give an answer that would satisfy both himself and the mind seed. "I want to learn which yuan-ti are involved because it will help me stop the Pox," he told Gonthril. "Are you sure it was a member of House Extaminos?"

"We're sure. We observed him passing a dozen flasks—identical to this one—to one of Talona's clerics, in exchange for the captives. But given what you've just told me, I'm confused. Delivering plague to clerics who can call down disease with a simple prayer makes no sense. It would be like carrying fire to Mount Ugruth." He stared at Arvin, one eyebrow raised. "Would you like to know what's *really* inside the flask?"

"Yes," Arvin said, his answer uncompelled by the ring. "I would."

"So would I." Gonthril lowered the flask. "Two final questions. If I let you out of that room—let you move freely among us—will you attack us?"

"No."

"Will you betray us to the militia?"

Arvin smiled. "The ten thousand gold piece bounty is tempting," he answered honestly. "But no, I won't give you away. Not while you have information that can help me find my friend."

That made Gonthril smile. He gestured, and the ring was suddenly loose on Arvin's finger. "Take the ring off, and come with me."

24 Kythorn, Sunrise

Arvin sat on a low bench inside a room a short distance down the corridor from the one Gonthril had used to question him. He was flanked by two members of the Secession—Chorl, with his magical staff, and a younger man named Mortin, who had a day's growth of beard on his chin. Gonthril stood nearby, arms folded across his chest as he watched a wizard lay out his equipment. Gonthril didn't seem to regard Arvin as a threat—he had his back to Arvin—but Mortin had drawn his sword and Chorl held his staff ready. Neither of them took their eyes off Arvin.

Arvin stared at the wizard. He'd never met one face to face, but this fellow looked just as he would have imagined. He was an older man with wispy gray hair, thick eyebrows waxed into points, and a narrow face that was clean-shaven save for a goatlike tuft of white on his chin. The hand that stroked it had fingernails that were trimmed short, save for the little finger; that nail was nearly half as long as the finger itself. His shirt was large and hung loose over his trousers, giving it the appearance of a robe, and was fastened at the throat by an intricately wrought silver pin. The worn leather slippers on his feet had turned-up toes.

The table on which he was setting up his equipment took up most of the room. On it, the wizard had already set out a small pouch of soft leather, a bottle of wine, a feather, a mortar and pestle, and a pair of silver scissors. He opened the lid of a well-padded box and pulled from it a chalice with a bowl the size of a man's fist. He set it carefully at the center of the table then lifted the lantern down from its metal hook on the ceiling and set it next to the chalice. He closed the lantern's rear and side shutters, leaving a single beam. It shone on the chalice, illuminating the clear glass.

The wizard held out a hand. "The flask," he said.

Gonthril handed it over. Holding it in one hand, the wizard began to chant in a language Arvin didn't recognize—a lilting tongue in which soft-spoken words seemed to spill over one another with the fluidity of a tumbling brook. As he spoke, he held his free hand over the flask and made a pinching motion with fingers and thumb. Arvin heard a soft pop as the cork jerked out of the flask and rose into the air. Directing it with his fingers, the wizard sent it drifting away from him. Mortin drew back slightly as the cork moved toward him then relaxed again as it settled onto the table. Gonthril, meanwhile, watched closely as the wizard poured the contents of the flask into the chalice.

Arvin recognized the bitter odor of the liquid. He grimaced, remembering how it had been forced down his throat. As it trickled into the chalice, it was as clear as water, but as it filled the vessel, it changed color, becoming an inky black.

"Ah," the wizard said as he peered down at it. "Poison." He squatted, peering through the chalice toward the lantern, then nodded. "And a strong one, too. The light is almost entirely blocked."

"What about plague?" Arvin asked nervously. "Is there any plague in—"

"Shhh!" The wizard held up a hand, silencing him. His eyes, however, never left the chalice. The color of the liquid inside it was changing, turning from black to a murky red. In a few moments, it was as bright as freshly spilled blood. The wizard peered through the side of the chalice, his eyebrows raised.

Gonthril leaned forward. "Well, Hazzan?"

The wizard straightened. "The liquid contains no plague," he answered. He stared thoughtfully down at the chalice. "This is a potion ... one that contains poison. The poison must be a component."

Arvin hissed in relief. No plague. That was good news—one less thing to worry about. Meanwhile, his head continued its dull throbbing. He resisted the urge to rub his forehead.

"Can you identify the potion?" Gonthril asked the wizard.

"We shall see," Hazzan answered. He picked up the pouch, untied it, and tipped its contents into his palm. A handful of pearls spilled out. He chose one and placed it inside the ceramic vessel then put the rest back into the pouch. With smooth strokes of the pestle, he ground the pearl he'd chosen into a fine powder. Into this he poured wine. He stirred the mixture with the feather, using its shaft like a stick. Then he laid the feather down and picked up the mortar. He raised it to his lips and drank.

When he lowered it, his pupils were so large they seemed to have swallowed the irises whole. Staring at a spot somewhere over Arvin's head, Hazzan located the chalice by feel. He gripped it with one hand and dipped the tip of his overly long fingernail into the liquid. Then he began to chant in the same melodious, lilting language he'd used before. When the chant was finished, he stood for several moments, his lips pursed in thought.

Abruptly, his pupils returned to normal. He raised his fingernail from the liquid and snipped the end of it off with the scissors, letting the clipping fall into the potion.

Gonthril leaned forward, an anxious expression on his face. Mortin mirrored his leader's pose, barely breathing as he waited for Hazzan to speak. Chorl, meanwhile, kept his eyes on Arvin.

"It's a transformative potion," the wizard said at last. "With a hint of compulsive enchantment about it. But predominantly transformative."

"A potion of polymorphing?" Gonthril asked.

Hazzan shook his head. "Nothing so general. Its properties are highly focused. The potion is designed to transform the imbiber into a specific creature, though I can't identify which. But I can tell you this. Whoever drank this potion would be dead long before the transformation occurred. One of its components is a highly toxic venom." He looked up from the chalice to stare at Gonthril. "Yuan-ti venom."

Gonthril pointed at Arvin. "This man drank an identical potion—and lived."

Hazzan turned to Arvin. "Are you a cleric?"

"No," Arvin answered. "I'm not."

"Did a cleric lay healing hands on you?"

Arvin wet his lips. He was glad he wasn't wearing Gonthril's truth ring anymore—though perhaps he could have avoided giving the game away, since Zelia was a psion, rather than a cleric. "No."

"Are you wearing any device that would neutralize poison?"

Arvin thought of Kayla—of the periapt she wore around her neck. He touched the cat's-eye bead that hung at his throat for reassurance.

Hazzan noticed the gesture immediately. "The bead is magical?"

Arvin shrugged.

Hazzan cast a quick spell and pointed a finger at the bead. Then he shook his head. "It's ordinary clay. A worthless trinket." He lowered his hand. "It is possible that the potion you were forced to drink was different from the rest. Perhaps it lacked the venom."

"The flask was identical to this one," Arvin said. "The potion smelled like this one, too. And it certainly *felt* like I'd been poisoned. The pain was excruciating.

It felt as though I'd swallowed broken glass."

"Yet your body fought off the venom," Hazzan mused. "Interesting." He turned to Gonthril. "He could be yuan-ti. They're naturally resistant to their own venom."

"I knew it," Chorl growled. He shifted his staff.

Arvin hissed in alarm.

"Chorl, wait," Gonthril said. He placed a hand on Chorl's staff. "It's possible, sometimes, for humans to survive yuan-ti venom. And to all appearances, this man is human—despite his strange mannerisms."

Chorl glared at Arvin. "So what? He's still a danger to us. He knows where we—"

"He's an innocent caught up in all of this," Gonthril countered. "The ring confirmed his story."

Chorl's eyes narrowed. "Why does he hiss like that, then, and lick his lips? He even moves like a yuan-ti."

Arvin glared at the man. Chorl's constant hectoring was starting to annoy him. "I *am* human," he spat back. "As human as you."

Chorl's lip curled. "I doubt it."

Hazzan suddenly snapped his fingers. "The potion," he exclaimed. "So that's what it does—it transforms humans into yuan-ti."

Arvin felt his eyes widen. "No," he whispered. He started to wet his lips nervously then realized what he was doing and gulped back his tongue. Then a thought occurred to him. Maybe Zelia *had* been bluffing. Maybe there was no mind seed. She might have guessed what the potion did, realized it would work this transformation on Arvin, and tried to claim credit for it. If it was the potion that was causing the hissing and the lip licking, what would be next? Would Arvin's spittle suddenly turn poisonous, like that of the old sailor he'd found dying in the tunnel?

Realizing he was starting to panic, he forced himself to calm down. Would it really be so bad to turn into a yuan-ti? They were the rulers and nobles of Hlondeth; Arvin would certainly move up the social ladder if he became one. And in addition to their venom—handy, in a close-quarters fight—yuan-ti could assume serpent form at will. And they had magical abilities. They could enshroud themselves in darkness, use their unblinking stares to terrify others into fleeing, and compel others to do their bidding—a more powerful version of the simple charm that Arvin liked to use. They could entrance both animals and plants, causing the former to lose themselves in a swaying trance and the latter to tangle themselves about creatures or objects. And, as Zelia had demonstrated, they could neutralize poison with a simple laying-on of hands.

That thought led him to a realization. If the potion was intended to turn humans into yuan-ti, it would be useless if everyone who drank it died from the venom it contained. Which they didn't. The old sailor had survived. Had Naulg?

Maybe.

And if Naulg was still alive and slowly transforming into a yuan-ti, would he wind up embracing Talona's faith, as the old sailor had? Or ... had the sailor really become a convert? Thinking back to the old man's final words, Arvin concluded that was not the case. The sailor had invoked Silvanus's name as he lay dying—hardly something someone who had embraced Talona would do. No, the old man had probably been magically compelled by the cultist—for some time, probably, since the cultist no longer felt the need to keep him bound hand and foot.

A thought suddenly occurred to Arvin—one that sent a shiver through him. He caught the wizard's eye. "You called the potion something else, a 'compulsive enchantment,'" he said. "What does that mean?"

"A compulsive enchantment allows a wizard to dominate his victim," Hazzan answered.

Gonthril was quickest to catch on. "That bastard," he gritted. "He doesn't just want to turn us into serpent folk. He wants to turn us into his slaves."

Chorl's grip on his staff tightened. "This man might already be in Osran's power," he said, gesturing at Arvin. "All the more reason to—"

Gonthril silenced him with an angry glare. As Chorl flushed suddenly, Arvin realized what had just happened. In his anger, Chorl had let slip something he shouldn't have—the name of the yuan-ti who had been seen meeting with the Pox.

Osran Extaminos, youngest brother of Lady Dediana.

Arvin pretended not to have noticed the slip. "Can you dispel the potion's magic?" he asked Hazzan. He curled the fingers of his gloved hand, readying it for his dagger, as he waited for the wizard's reply. If the answer was no, he'd have to fight his way out.

Hazzan stroked his beard. "Possibly."

Gonthril took a deep breath. "For the sake of Hlondeth's true people, Talona grant it be so," he whispered. Then, to the wizard, he said, "Try."

Hazzan rolled up his sleeves then extended his right hand toward Arvin, pointing. Staring intently into Arvin's eyes, he began casting a spell. The incantation took only a moment; the final word was a shout. As it erupted from his wizard's lips Hazzan flicked his forefinger and Arvin felt a wave of magical energy punch into his chest. It coursed through his body like an electric shock, making his fingers and toes tingle and the hair rise on the back of his neck. Then it was gone.

Gonthril peered at Arvin. "Did it work?"

"Let's find out." Hazzan picked up the chalice and tipped the potion out of it, pouring it into the mortar. Then he pulled a scrap of cloth out of a pocket and wiped the inside of the chalice clean. He then held out a hand. "Give me your hand," he told Arvin, picking up the scissors.

Arvin drew back, unpleasant memories of the Guild filling his thoughts. "What are you going to do?"

"He needs a sample of your blood," Gonthril told Arvin. "To see if the potion is still in it."

"All right." Arvin answered reluctantly, placing his hand in Hazzan's. "As long as it doesn't cost me another fingertip."

Gonthril chuckled.

"A small incision should do," Hazzan reassured him. "I just need a few drops of blood, enough to cover the bottom of the chalice."

He winced as Hazzan sliced into his finger with the blade of the scissors—deliberate cuts always hurt more, it seemed, than those inflicted in a fight—but kept his hand steady over the chalice. A few drops of blood leaked into it, splattering against the clear glass.

"That's enough," Hazzan said.

Arvin pressed against the cut in his finger, staunching the blood. He sat back down and stared at the bowl of the chalice. Strangely, though the blood had been red as it had dripped into the bowl, now it looked clear as water—so clear that for a moment he thought the blood had disappeared. He leaned forward, peering down into the mouth of the chalice again, and saw that it was indeed drizzled with bright red blood. Surprised, he started to let out an involuntary hiss—and saw Chorl's frown deepen.

Hazzan—once again peering through the side of the chalice at the lantern—nodded. "The spell worked," he told Gonthril. "The potion has been neutralized."

Chorl stared at Arvin. "Why's he still hissing, then?"

Gonthril stared at Arvin thoughtfully. "I don't know."

Arvin did. It was the mind seed. Zelia hadn't been bluffing, after all.

"I still say we should get rid of him," Chorl urged.

The rebel leader shook his head. "Arvin will stay with us, for the time being. There may be ways in which he can aid our cause. But keep a close eye on him, Chorl, and let me know if he does anything suspicious. If he takes any hostile action against us, or attempts to escape, I leave his punishment to your discretion."

Arvin matched glares with Chorl, and for a moment actually considered summoning his dagger into his hand and plunging it into the man's heart. But this done, the odds of Arvin being the next one to die would be very high indeed. Mortin held his sword at the ready, the wizard could blast him with magic, and the gods only knew what the rings on Gonthril's fingers were capable of doing.

No, there were other, better ways to deal with the situation. Arvin relaxed his grimace into a smile and tried to summon up the familiar prickle of psionic energy. None came. And for good reason, he suddenly realized. He was exhausted, on the verge of collapsing on his feet. Only rarely had he been able to charm anyone under these conditions.

No matter. He could always do it later, when the odds of escape were better.

"Don't worry," he assured Gonthril. "I'll behave."

"Do I have your word you won't try to escape?" Gonthril asked.

Arvin smiled to himself; he wasn't bound by the ring any longer. "You have my word," he said solemnly.

CHAPTER 10

In his dream, Arvin moved through a crowd of laughing people who stood in a vineyard outside the city, their faces painted a ruddy orange by a bonfire that sent sparks spinning up into the night. Some stood and watched, tipping back bottles of wine, while others danced, arms linked as they moved in giddy circles around the bonfire. Several held small rectangles of wood, painted red and inscribed with a single word: "Chondath." These they threw into the fire, together with spoiled fruits and limp, moldy vegetables. The air was filled with smoke, sparks, and the hissing noise of food being blackened by flame.

The humans called it the Rotting Dance. It was a celebration of the defeat of Chondath in the Rotting War of 902, of the rise of the city-states of the Vilhon Reach. Hlondeth had gained its independence nearly three centuries before necromantic magic laid waste to the empire's armies on the Fields of Nun, and its people had suffered the aftermath of that battle—a plague that spread through the Vilhon Reach, afflicting those it touched with a disease that caused even the smallest of cuts to turn gangrenous. But its citizens celebrated the Rotting Dance just the same. Humans needed very little excuse for frivolity. Emotion was just one of their many weaknesses.

Arvin weaved his way through the humans, his tongue flickering in and out of his mouth as he tasted the excitement that laced the night air. Whenever he saw a man that caught his eye—one who was strong and well muscled, with lean hips and a glint in his eye that showed he was of a better stock than the average human—he worked his magic on him. "Come," he whispered, staring intently into the man's eyes. "Mate with me."

One of the men Arvin selected already had a mate picked out for the evening—a human a few years older than Arvin, and prettier, by human standards. No matter. When she protested, Arvin merely stared at her. She began to tremble then, with a small shriek, dropped the man's arm, surrendering him to Arvin, and fled into the night.

A part of Arvin's mind, observing the dream from a distance, recoiled at the thought of propositioning men. But to his dreaming mind, the act felt as natural as his own skin. He swayed through the crowd, the five men he had chosen trailing in his wake, each of them yearning to stroke his scales, to touch his newly budding breasts, and to press themselves against his curved hips. Flicking his tongue, tasting their desire, he felt a surge of power. He might be just fourteen years old and in his first flush of sexuality, but he was in control. He owned these men, as surely as a master owns slaves.

He led the men to a secluded spot in a nearby field and, as they converged on him, unfastened the pin at his throat and let his dress fall around his ankles, shedding it like an old skin. As the men stepped forward eagerly, pressing themselves against him and tearing at their clothes, he drew a curtain of darkness around them. Then he pulled the men to the ground, where they formed a mating ball with Arvin at its center. A hard body pressed against his and was wrenched away, only to be replaced by another—and another—as the men wrestled with each other in an attempt to mate with Arvin. The smell of their sweat and of crushed grapes and torn earth filled Arvin's nostrils as he slithered through the tangle of bodies, coiling around first one man, then another, taking each of them in turn. Acidic sweat erupted on his own body, soaking his hair and lubricating his scales—and burning the thin, sensitive skin of the humans who twined and fought and thrust against him. As ecstasy surged through Arvin again ... and again ... and again ... he gave vent to his passion, screaming and throwing his head back then lashing forward to sink his fangs into throats and thighs and chests. One by one the men coiled around him abruptly gasped, stiffened, and fell limp as poison usurped passion.

When it was done, Arvin lay on his back on warm, sweat-soaked soil, his forked tongue savoring the taste of blood on his lips. He smiled, satisfied that there would be no one to tell his guilty secret—that he felt an unnatural attraction toward an inferior race. A heavy body lay across him; he shoved it to the side. Then he assumed snake form and slithered off into the night, leaving the tangled remains of his lovemaking cooling on the ground behind him.

Arvin's eyes sprang open as he was wakened by

the urgency in his loins. He found himself lying on a straw pallet in a dimly lit room. A pace or two away, Mortin sat with his back against the wall, eyes closed, his sword on the floor beside him. For a moment, as Arvin stared at the handsome young man, dream and waking seemed to blend. Had he really just mated with Mortin and killed him? No... Mortin was still breathing; he'd merely fallen asleep. He was a member of the Secession, not a reveler, and he was guarding Arvin—though he was doing a poor job of it.

Arvin sat up, rubbing his temples. The headache that had been plaguing him was back again, despite his sleep. Doing his best to ignore it—and the unsettling dream—he forced his mind to the here and now. He was human, he told himself—and male—not a lustful yuan-ti female, as he'd been in the dream.

A yuan-ti female with the power to work magic with a mere thought.

Zelia.

Arvin cursed softly. Had the mind seed caused him to listen in on her thoughts again in his sleep? It seemed strange that, once again, he had picked up her memories, rather than her thoughts about more pressing matters, but maybe that was the way yuan-ti minds worked. Maybe all that lazy basking in the sun prompted them to dwell on the past, rather than the current moment.

Speaking of which, what time of day was it? Arvin's visit to the wizard had been around Sunrise. Afterward, Gonthril had given him a meal and some wine to wash it down. He'd even returned Arvin's backpack—after a thorough inspection of its contents by Hazzan, who seemed fascinated by Arvin's trollgut rope. Then Arvin had curled up to sleep, alone in the room except for Mortin, who had remained behind to keep a watch on him.

It must have been well into Fullday. The need Arvin

felt to relieve himself told him that he'd slept a long, long time. As he yawned, a suspicion started to dawn in his mind, fueled by the grogginess he felt. He'd been drugged. Maybe that was why only Mortin had been left to watch him—Gonthril had expected Arvin to sleep much longer than he did. If it weren't for the wild dream that had jolted him into wakefulness, Arvin might have slumbered for some time still.

As he sat on his pallet, thinking, he noticed he was swaying back and forth. Not only that, but he was wetting his lips again. His tongue felt shorter and thicker than it should have been . . . no, than it had been during the dream, he corrected himself. The stray thought alarmed him. The mind seed was still firmly rooted, despite the fact that Hazzan had cast a dispelling on him. Was there no way to get the gods-cursed thing out of his head?

He hissed as anger frothed inside him. Anger at the Pox for what they'd done to Naulg and their other victims. Anger at Osran Extaminos for inviting the cultists into the city. And, most especially, anger at Zelia for what she'd done to him.

If he was ever going to free himself of the mind seed, he needed to get going.

Arvin stood and put on his backpack. Thankfully, Mortin was still asleep. Moving silently past him, Arvin crept to the door. Not only was it unlocked, but the hinges of the door didn't creak when he slowly pulled it open. And—Tymora be praised—the hallway beyond it was empty.

Arvin closed the door behind him and let his eyes adjust to the hallway's gloom. Slipping out of the room had been too easy. Perhaps the Secession were toying with Arvin. Chorl might be just around the bend, happy to have an excuse to kill him.

Wandering the corridors unescorted seemed like an excellent excuse to Arvin.

He summoned his dagger into his gloved hand and crept down the hallway.

The first room he came to was a smaller version of the one he'd just left; through its open door Arvin could see sleeping pallets on the floor. Those in Arvin's field of view were empty, but the sound of a man's voice came from inside. It sounded as though he was singing a low, dirgelike hymn.

A lantern in this room was burning brightly, flooding the corridor with light. The doorway reached from floor to ceiling. There was no way for Arvin to sneak past it and not be seen by whoever was inside the room. Unless he had his back to him, of course.

Crouching, he held his dagger just above the floor and moved the blade slowly into the doorway. By tilting it, he could see a reflection of the inside of the room—a narrow, blurry reflection, but one that told him that Tymora's luck was still with him. The man's back was indeed to the door. He was bent over someone in a pallet; a moment later Arvin heard a woman's faint groan. Curious, he risked a peek.

It was Kayla on the pallet. Her face was flushed, her hair damp and tangled. She lay on her back, turning her head back and forth, groaning softly.

The sight sent a chill through Arvin's blood. Had Kayla succumbed to the disease that had pockmarked the cultists—or some other, even more terrible illness? The fleshy mound she'd fought had been one enormous, pus-filled bag of disease, and she'd been splattered with its fluids—perhaps that was what had laid her low.

Whatever the cause, at least a cleric was tending to her—the man who had his back to Arvin. If the fellow was wearing clerical vestments, however, they were of a faith that Arvin didn't recognize. They included a black shirt and long gray kilt that was belted with a red sash. Black leather gloves lay on the floor beside him. The cleric's dark brown hair was plaited in a single braid that hung against his back. One of his hands held Kayla's; the other was raised above his head. His sleeves were rolled up, revealing a patchwork of blotchy scars, faded to a dull white, on his forearms. They looked like old burn marks.

"Lord of the Three Thunders," he chanted, lowering his hand to touch Kayla on the forehead. "Free this woman from fever's grip. Heal her so she may live to carry out your divine justice."

The healing spell was almost finished. Any moment the cleric might turn around and see Arvin peering into the room. Arvin slipped past the doorway and continued down the corridor.

The rest of the doors he passed were closed. It was only a short distance to the spiraling tunnel that led back to the surface. Arvin wasn't sure how he was going to get the trapdoor in the gazebo floor open, but he'd deal with that problem when it presented itself.

As he drew near the room where the wizard had analyzed the potion, he heard voices coming from behind its closed door. One was unmistakable: Gonthril's. He was giving instructions on how the Secession would sneak into a building. Arvin paused to listen, excitement making his heart race. There was a good chance the Secession were planning a raid on wherever the Pox were holed up—Arvin might at last be able to learn where the cultists were hiding. But try as he might, Arvin couldn't puzzle out which building they were talking about. The only clear detail was that they were going to strike during the very heart of the evening—at Middark.

No matter. Arvin could always wait in the garden above then follow them. Assuming he got that far.

He tiptoed past the door to the wrought-iron gate, which was closed. The room beyond it was in near darkness; the lantern that hung from the ceiling had its wick trimmed low. Arvin gently pulled on the gate.

It was indeed locked, as he'd expected. He vanished his dagger into his glove then unfastened his belt. Digging a fingernail into a slot in the tongue of the buckle, he pulled out a hook that clicked into place. Inserting his pick into the hole in the lock plate, he twisted until he felt one pin click back ... then a second ... then a third. ...

He grinned as the bolt sprang open. He tried to open the gate. ...

He couldn't move.

Not a muscle. His eyes continued to blink and his chest rose and fell—albeit only in short, shallow breaths—and his heart thudded in his chest. But the rest of his body was as still as a statue. Realizing he must have fallen victim to a spell, he strained against it until sweat blossomed on his temples and trickled down his cheeks, but still he couldn't move.

Stupid. He'd been stupid to think they'd simply let him walk away. He should have paid attention to the warning voice that had told him it was all too easy.

Meanwhile, the voices continued from behind the door. It sounded as though Gonthril was wrapping up the meeting. At any moment, the door would open—and Chorl would have all the excuse he needed to kill Arvin.

Arvin could hear Chorl's voice coming from behind the door. "I'm in favor," Chorl growled. "It will send a message to that scaly bitch—that she's not safe anywhere."

Another voice—one Arvin didn't recognize—raised an objection. "I still think we should ambush him in the street."

"He'll be on his guard there," Gonthril answered. "Especially after what happened to the overseer."

"That was just thieves, trying to steal whatever it was the work crews found in the old tower," someone else protested.

"Those thieves killed a yuan-ti—one who served the royal family," Gonthril said. He sighed; Arvin pictured him shaking his head. "The only place he'll let down his guard now is within the walls of his own home."

"It's suicide," the other man grumbled. "We'll never get inside."

"Yes we will," Gonthril said in a confident voice. "One sip of this and we'll be able to slip right past the guard. They won't suspect a thing. They'll think we're his little pets, out for a Middark soar. We'll even have the right markings."

Suddenly a voice whispered in Arvin's ear. "I think you've heard enough."

Had Arvin been capable of it, he would have jumped at the touch of a hand on his shoulder. Held frozen by magic, all he could do was wonder who in the Nine Hells had crept up so silently behind him.

He heard a whispered chant, felt momentarily dizzy, and was standing in a room—a brightly illuminated room, next to the pallet on which Kayla lay. Her eyes were closed and her chest rose and fell smoothly. The flush of fever was gone from her face.

Arvin, still unable to move, could feel a hand on his shoulder—that of the person who had just teleported him. He could guess who it was. The cleric. The fellow spoke in a normal tone, no longer whispering. "That was poetic justice, don't you think?"

The hand fell away from Arvin's shoulder. Suddenly able to move, Arvin whirled to face the cleric. The green eyes that stared back at him were filled with mirth.

"What do you mean?" Arvin asked.

The cleric tipped his head in the direction of the hallway. As he did, an earring dangling from his left ear flashed in the light; the three silver lightning bolts hanging from it tinkled together. "By unlocking that gate, you locked your own body."

Understanding dawned on Arvin. "There was a glyph on the gate, wasn't there?"

The cleric nodded.

Arvin slid a wary glance toward the door to the room and saw that it was shut. It had no visible lock, but he was willing to bet its handle bore a glyph that was similar to the one on the gate he'd just tried. His imagination came up with unpleasant possibilities—turn the handle and have your head turned completely around. Until your neck snapped.

"What happens now?" he asked the cleric.

"We wait."

"Until . . . ?"

"Until Gonthril and the others have finished their night's work," the cleric calmly replied.

"Where are they going?" Arvin asked.

"To scotch the snake."

Arvin stared at the cleric, suddenly understanding. It wasn't the Pox the Secession were going after, but the yuan-ti who had supplied them with the potions, Osran Extaminos. And it wasn't just any building Gonthril had been talking about infiltrating, but the palace. The man who had been objecting to this scheme had been right. A plan to kill a prince inside the royal palace was indeed suicide. A desperate gamble. Yet it was a risk, apparently, Gonthril was willing to take. He must have been hoping that Osran's murder would cut off the source of the potion and save the city.

And he might just be right about that. Though Arvin couldn't help but wonder if the old adage would prove true. Scotch the snake, and watch another two crawl out of the hole. "Backers," Zelia had said. Plural.

Then there was the question of the cultists and why they had hooked up with a yuan-ti. As Gonthril had pointed out, why carry fire to a volcano? The cultists were perfectly capable of creating disease on their own, as the man who had killed himself in Arvin's warehouse had so aptly demonstrated. Why then, would they feel the need to obtain "plague" from an outside source?

Suddenly, Arvin realized the answer. That name he'd heard one of his attackers use, just before he'd been bundled off to the sewers, wasn't a person's name, after all. It wasn't "Missim" that he'd heard, but "Mussum." The city that fell victim, nine centuries ago, to a plague so virulent that to this day it continued to claim lives.

That was what the cultists believed was in the vials. The most potent plague in all of Faerûn—one that even they, in their most fervent prayers, would be hard-pressed to duplicate. They hoped to unleash it on Hlondeth, reducing it to a city of corpses. Instead they were being tricked into emptying a potion into its water system—one that would turn every human in Hlondeth into a yuan-ti, making it truly a "city of serpents."

A city of slaves.

Realizing the cleric was standing in silence, watching him, Arvin decided to play on the man's sympathies. "A friend of mine is in trouble," he began. "The Pox fed him the potion that turns humans into yuan-ti. He's the reason I was down in the sewers and"—he gestured at the sleeping Kayla—"the reason I was there to save Kayla's life. He's also the reason I was trying to leave, just now. I need to find him, before it's too late."

"A noble endeavor," the cleric said, nodding. "But I can't let you go. Too many other lives are at stake."

"Please," Arvin said, feeling the familiar prickle of psionic energy at the base of his skull. He gave the cleric his most pleading look. "I'm Naulg's only hope."

The cleric's expression softened. "I. . . ." Then he shook his head, like a man suddenly awakening from a dream. A smile quirked the corner of his lips. "A psion," he said. "That's quite rare." He folded his arms across his chest. "I'm sorry, but the answer is still no. And don't try to charm me again."

Arvin fumed. Just who in the Nine Hells did this human think he was?

Arvin hissed then leaped forward with the speed of a striking snake, intending to sink his teeth into the man's throat. The cleric, however, was quicker. He barked out a one-word incantation and whipped one of his scarred hands up in front of his body, palm outward. Arvin crashed face-first into a glowing wall of magical energy that rattled his teeth in their sockets.

Suddenly sobered, he staggered away, rubbing his aching jaw. The anger that had boiled in him a moment ago was gone. Mutely, he glanced at the glove on his left hand, wondering why he hadn't tried to summon his dagger to it.

Of course. The mind seed. He had reacted as Zelia might have done.

The cleric slowly lowered his hand. With a faint crackling, the magical shield around him disappeared. "Now that you've come to your senses, let's pass the time like civilized men," he told Arvin. "Gonthril told me part of your story; I'd like to hear the rest. But here's a warning. If you try to attack me again, you'll spend the rest of the day as a statue."

Arvin didn't bother to ask whether the cleric meant that literally—whether he was threatening to turn Arvin to stone—or whether he was simply promising to reimpose the spell that had held Arvin motionless earlier. Either way, Arvin didn't really want to find out. He spread his hands in a peace gesture.

"Fine," he said. "Let's talk."

CHAPTER 11

24 Kythorn, Evening

Arvin paced back and forth like an animal in a cage. He'd been trapped in this room for ages with a man he could neither charm nor fight his way past. He wanted to be out *doing* something. Only two days had passed since Zelia planted the mind seed, but already Arvin was starting to lose control. If he didn't do something soon he might make another dangerous—possibly fatal—mistake. And there was a chance, it seemed, that Naulg might still be alive. But all Arvin could do was weave his way back and forth, back and forth, across the floor.

He and the cleric—Nicco, his name was—were alone in the room now. Kayla had awakened some time ago, as refreshed as if she'd never succumbed to fever at all. She'd been summoned from the room by Gonthril, presumably to join the suicidal raid on the royal palace. Arvin supposed that was the last he'd ever see of her.

Arvin had passed the time by telling Nicco his story—omitting any mention of Zelia, since the news that he was gathering information for a yuan-ti was hardly going to endear him to the rebels. Thinking of her—and the mind seed—made him wonder. Hazzan's dispelling hadn't broken its hold over Arvin, but perhaps clerical magic might succeed where wizardry had failed.

"I've been thinking about the potion," Arvin began. "Hazzan's dispelling doesn't seem to have worked. I still seem to be turning into a yuan-ti. In mind, if not in body."

Nicco nodded grimly. "You do seem to be under some sort of magical compulsion—from time to time. Right now, I'd say you were your own man. But when you attacked me earlier...."

"I'm sorry about that," Arvin repeated. "I wasn't... in my right mind."

"Apology accepted."

"You recognized me as a psion earlier," Arvin said. "How?"

"You cast a charm spell without using either a holy symbol or hand gestures. Some wizards and sorcerers can cast spells with stilled hands or silenced lips, but the faint ringing sound I heard when you tried to charm me confirmed my guess. You're a psion."

Arvin's hopes rose. "Not many people know what a psion is."

Nicco shrugged. "I'm widely traveled."

"Have you dispelled psionic powers before?"

"Yes... why?"

Arvin smiled. Maybe Nicco *could* help him. "I've been wondering if the potion I was forced to drink might have contained a component that was psionic, rather than sorcerous," Arvin said. "If it did, Hazzan might have overlooked it. I was wondering if prayer might succeed where wizardry failed."

"It might," Nicco said slowly. "If it is the Doombringer's will."

"The Doombringer? Is that the name of your god?"

"In my country he is known as Assuran, Lord of the Three Thunders, but here they call him Hoar."

"I . . . think I've heard of him," Arvin said.

"He is the righter of wrongs," Nicco said with a grim smile. "I heard you whisper Tymora's name earlier. Like that goddess, Hoar is a bringer of luck—bad luck, but only to those who have called it down upon themselves by their own actions. He seals their doom—and in the process, saves those who are doomed."

"That's how I feel, right now," Arvin said somberly. "Doomed."

"Talona's clerics did wrong you," Nicco agreed. "The Doombringer will surely be moved to set matters right."

Arvin let out a long, slow hiss of relief. The sooner Zelia's mind seed was out of his head, the better.

Nicco stared at him. "Hoar's blessings come with a price."

Arvin gave the cleric a wry smile. "Nice of you to be up front about it. What is it?" He pictured a healthy tithe, or several tendays of fasting, self-flagellation, and prayer. The clerics who ran the orphanage had been big on flagellation.

"You must do everything you can to bring those who have wronged you to justice. And it must be in as . . . appropriate a manner as you are able. 'Blood for blood'—that is Hoar's creed."

Arvin nodded. It was easy to come up with a suitable punishment for the cultists. Slipping into their water a potion that would polymorph them into sewer rats, for example. But if Nicco's prayer succeeded in purging the mind seed, would Arvin be expected to also enact vengeance upon Zelia? What could Arvin—an untrained psion—possibly do to someone so powerful? For that matter, did he even want to take revenge on her? She'd saved his life by neutralizing the poison that had nearly killed him, after all. And she had offered to train him in psionics and ensure that the militia would never claim him, in return for information on who was backing the Pox—information Arvin now had.

"I'll do what I can," he told Nicco.

That seemed to satisfy the cleric. "Sit," Nicco instructed. "Hold in your mind the thoughts of vengeance you just imagined."

Arvin did as instructed, seating himself on one of the pallets and picturing the cultists turning into rats. Nicco knelt in front of him and rested three fingertips on Arvin's chest. Then he began to pray. "Lord of the Three Thunders, hear my plea. A great wrong has been done to this man. Set it right. Dispel the magic that is transforming him. Drive it from his body by the might of your thundering hand!"

The cleric closed his eyes then, dropping into silent prayer. Arvin heard a crackling sound—and a tiny spark erupted from each of Nicco's fingertips and shot through the fabric of Arvin's shirt. Arvin jerked back as they stung his chest.

Nicco smiled and dropped his hand. "The Doombringer has answered."

Arvin pulled his shirt away from his chest and saw, with relief, that his skin was still intact. He let out a long, slow hiss—then realized what he'd just done. His headache wasn't gone either. "I don't think your prayer worked," he told Nicco. "I feel . . . the same."

Nicco scowled. "Impossible. You felt Hoar's power at work. Whatever remained of the potion will be neutralized, now."

Arvin nodded. The potion indeed might be neutralized,

but the mind seed was still in place. Zelia's psionics must be more powerful than either Hazzan's spells or Nicco's prayers.

He eyed the door, wondering when the rebels were going to return. He wanted to be well on his way before Chorl came back. Could Arvin convince Nicco that he posed no threat to the Secession, that he should be allowed to leave? Perhaps ... if Nicco could be persuaded that he was an ally, a friend. But that would be difficult, without charming Nicco. Instead, Arvin would be forced to rely upon more conventional means. Conversation.

Fortunately, there was always one sure way to get a cleric talking.

"Tell me more about your faith," he told Nicco. "How did you come to worship Hoar?"

Nicco gave Arvin a searching look. Then he shrugged and sat down on a pallet next to the one on which Arvin was sitting. "In Chessenta, slaves are not branded," he began. "The only mark of their servitude is a thread around the wrist."

Arvin had no idea what this had to do with Nicco's religion, but his interest was piqued at once. "A magical thread?" he asked.

Nicco smiled. "No. An ordinary thread."

"But what's to stop the slave from breaking it?"

"Nothing," Nicco said.

Arvin frowned, puzzled.

"Slavery isn't a cruelty, as it is here, but a retribution," Nicco continued. "Here, innocent men and women are forced into servitude against their will and work until the day they die. In Chessenta, the term of slavery is fixed. It is imposed, following a public trial and a finding of guilt, as punishment for breaking the law. The criminal is a slave until his sentence is up then becomes a free man once more. The work slaves are set to can be hard and dangerous, but sometimes, if a slave performs well, his master may negate his sentence by breaking the thread." He paused, and the glower returned. "Of course, that is how it is supposed to work."

"Ah, I understand now," Arvin said. "You worship Hoar because you were once a judge."

"Not a judge," Nicco said, "a criminal."

Arvin tactfully avoided asking what crime Nicco had committed. Years of dealing with the Guild had taught him the value of silence at such moments—and a sympathetic nod, which he gave Nicco now. "You were unjustly accused," he ventured. "That's why you turned to Hoar."

Nicco shook his head, causing the lightning bolts in his earring to tinkle. "I was unfairly *treated*," he corrected. "I worked hard and well at the glass-blowing factory, and yet the overseer, instead of breaking my thread, falsely accused me of vandalism. Every time a piece of glassware broke due to some flaw—and there were plenty, since the iron, tin, and cobalt powders he purchased to color the glass were cheap and filled with impurities—I was punished. When I dared challenge him, he further insulted me by chaining me to my furnace, as if I were not a man of my word. So short was my chain that he shaved my head, to prevent my hair from being singed."

Nicco paused to toss his head angrily, setting his long braid to dancing against his back. Arvin, meanwhile, stared at the cleric's arms, understanding now where the patchwork of scars had come from. They were old and faded. This had happened long ago.

"I, too, was a slave·... of a sort," Arvin said. "When I was a boy, I wound up in what was supposedly an orphanage, but was in reality a workhouse. They worked us from dawn until dusk, weaving nets and braiding ropes. Every night when I went to sleep, my hands ached. It felt as though each of my knuckles were a knot, yanked too tight." He paused and rubbed his joints, remembering. He'd never discussed his years at the orphanage before, but telling Nicco was proving surprisingly easy.

"My term of servitude was supposed to end when I reached 'manhood,'" Arvin continued. "But no age was ever specified. My voice broke and began to deepen, and still I wasn't a man. My chest broadened and hair grew at my groin, but I was still a 'child.'" He held up his fingers, flexing them. "They weren't going to let me go. I was too good at what I did. I knew I had to escape, instead."

Nicco's eyes, which had dulled to a smolder, were blazing again. "I, too, was eventually forced to take that road," he said. "When it was clear that my overseer would never treat me fairly, I began to pray to Assuran—to Hoar. I prayed for justice, for divine retribution. And one day, my prayers were answered."

"What happened?" Arvin asked, curious.

"The overseer tripped. At least, that's what the other slaves saw. I was the only one to see Hoar's hand in it. Or rather, to hear it—to realize what it meant. The overseer fell headfirst into the furnace next to mine—just as thunder rumbled above. Varga, the slave working at that furnace, pulled the overseer out, but by the time he did the man's face was burned away. Despite the intervention of a cleric, he died later that day."

Nicco bowed his head. "It was Hoar's will."

"Did things get better after the overseer's death?" Arvin asked.

The scowl returned. "They became worse. Varga was accused of having pushed the overseer into the furnace. The evidence given was that Varga did not immediately help the man—that he waited until the overseer was burned beyond help. In fact, it was surprise and shock that caused Varga to stand gaping, not malice. I testified to this at his trial. And I told them the truth—that it was I who had killed the overseer."

"What happened then?"

Nicco sighed. "The judge didn't believe me. He misunderstood. He thought I meant that I had pushed the overseer—and noted that my chain was too short for me to have reached the man, even using my glassblowing pipe. I tried to explain that I had killed him with prayer, but the judge wouldn't listen. I had taken no clerical vows—I had never once set foot in the temple. The judge decided that I was lying to spare the life of the accused.

"When I saw that the judge remained unconvinced, I tried to explain to my master what had happened. He believed me—but he said I was too valuable a worker, whereas Varga was 'dispensable.' And *someone* had to be punished for the crime."

Arvin shifted uncomfortably, guessing what was coming next. "The other slave was found guilty?"

"He was—and of the murder of an overseer, a capital offense. Varga was put to death the next day. According to law, our master chose the form of execution. He chose drowning. He might have left it at that, but he was as cruel a man as the overseer. He ordered it done in the factory, in front of all of the other slaves, in a quenching bucket—mine."

Nicco stared at one of the walls, his green eyes ablaze with rekindled fury. "That night I prayed. I begged Hoar to give me the means to avenge Varga's death. I swore I would devote my life to Hoar's service, if only he would give me a sign. The next morning, the Lord of the Three Thunders answered. The padlock on my chain clicked shut as the new overseer closed it— then fell open a moment later, just as thunder rumbled overhead. Then there came a second thunderclap, and a third—the sound of Hoar calling me to his service."

Arvin wet his lips. "And you answered?"

Nicco nodded. "I did the unthinkable. I broke my vow of servitude and ran away. Hoar guided my steps to Archendale, to a temple in the Arch Wood."

Arvin nodded his encouragement. "You didn't run away. You ran *to* something." As he spoke, jealousy stirred. If only *he'd* had something to run to, after escaping the orphanage. How different his life might have been. Instead he'd run straight into the clutches of the Guild—from the fat into the fire.

"That's true," Nicco agreed. "It helps to think of it like that." He paused then continued his tale. "I spent the next two years in prayer. During that time, Hoar provided me with a vision of vengeance. The idea came to me during a thunderstorm, when I was caught in a torrential rain. I created a magical item—a blown-glass decanter that I crafted myself, exquisitely shaped and colored. I returned to Chessenta, disguised by magic, and spread the rumor that I had something rare and wonderful for sale—a decanter of unknown but extremely powerful magical properties. I made sure my former master heard of it. The price he offered was ridiculously low, but after putting up a show of haggling, I accepted it. I delivered the decanter to his home. As I left him in his study—a windowless room—I used a spell to lock the door behind me. When he removed the stopper, expecting a jinni to emerge and grant his every wish, all that came out was water."

Arvin leaned forward, caught up in the story. "What happened then?"

Nicco gave a grim smile. "Once removed, the stopper could not be replaced. The water filled the room. He drowned. Blood for blood—or in this case, a drowning for a drowning. Justice."

Arvin found himself nodding in agreement, which surprised him. He wasn't the sort of man to dwell on the past, to let it fester as Nicco had. The thought of devoting two years of his life to a scheme of revenge was utterly foreign to him. Despite his treatment at the orphanage, he'd never once had thoughts of exacting revenge upon the clerics who had humiliated him—not serious thoughts, anyway. Instead he'd avoided that part of the city. Best to let sleeping snakes lie. But now he found himself caught up in Nicco's tale, wetting his lips as he savored the taste of revenge secondhand . . .

. . . which scared him. Arvin didn't want to answer the call of such a grim and vengeful god. Part of him, however, enjoyed the cruel, poetic justice Hoar meted out.

The part that was thinking like Zelia. But it gave him an idea.

"Nicco," he asked slowly, pretending to be thinking out loud, "does your god ever forgive?"

The cleric folded his arms across his chest. "Never."

"So . . . if I sit here and do nothing to rescue Naulg—a friend since my days at the orphanage—a friend who was as grievously wronged by the Pox as I was. . . ." He paused and wet his lips nervously. "I can expect Hoar's retribution?"

Nicco was smart enough to see exactly where Arvin was going. "I can't let you leave."

"I won't betray the Secession," Arvin said. "I give you my solemn oath on that—my personal word of honor. You can trust me. I won't break my 'thread.' All I want to do is save my friend." And myself, he added silently.

Seeing a flicker of indecision in Nicco's eyes, Arvin pressed his emotional thrust to the hilt. "Chorl doesn't trust me—he wants me dead. He's just looking for an excuse to punish me for a crime I haven't even committed—and nothing either you or Gonthril will say will persuade him that I'm innocent."

Nicco held up an admonishing finger. "Don't you think Gonthril knows that?" he asked. "Why do you think Mortin was assigned to guard you? Unfortunately, you awakened early. You weren't supposed to 'escape' until Middark."

"I get it," Arvin said slowly. "I was to be a distraction, to draw the militia away from ... wherever it is Gonthril and the others have gone." He thought a moment. "I take it you're abandoning this hiding place?"

Nicco smiled. "We already have. You and I are the last ones here."

"So what happens now?" Arvin asked. "Do we sit and wait for Middark?"

Nicco nodded.

"Why not let me go early? I won't betray the Secession—their interests are my interests. Like them, I want the Pox stopped."

Nicco sat in silence for a long moment before answering. "Will you agree to let me place a geas on you that will magically seal your oath?"

Arvin hesitated, uncomfortable with the thought of a compulsion spell being placed on him. A geas was dangerous—if you broke its conditions, it could kill you. Was it worth it, just to be on his way a little sooner? Middark wasn't all that far away. But what if Gonthril changed his mind about Arvin's usefulness in the meantime, or if Chorl returned?

"Do it," he said.

Smiling, Nicco rose to his feet. He placed three fingers on Arvin's mouth and whispered a quick prayer. Arvin felt magic tingle against his lips where Nicco's fingertips touched them.

Nicco stared into Arvin's eyes. "You will not reveal any information about the Secession."

So far, so good. This was what Arvin had expected.

"You will not reveal the names of any members of the Secession," Nicco continued. "Or provide any description of their appearance, or...."

The terms of the geas were surprisingly thorough—

too thorough. Arvin winced as he heard the final part of the oath.

" . . . or speak the name Osran Extaminos."

How in the Nine Hells was Arvin going to make his report to Zelia?

24 Kythorn, Evening

The Terrace was busy this time of night. After a hot, humid summer day, Hlondeth's wealthier citizens were at last relaxing and enjoying themselves in the more bearable temperatures that evening brought. Seated at tables under softly glowing lights, they had a view across the city, with its towers and arches shimmering a faint green, down to the harbor below, where ships crowded together so closely their masts looked like a forest. Beyond them was the Churning Bay.

Arvin, flush with energy after having performed the *asana* he'd learned from Zelia, watched the slaves who bustled between the tables, trays balanced on one hand above their heads, serving tea and sweets. At last he spotted the slave he wanted to speak to—a young woman with a slight limp. He slipped into a seat at one of the tables she was serving. When she approached, she showed no sign of recognizing him, even though he'd ordered two of Drin's "special teas" from her just yesterday. She set a small glass on the table in front of him. Inside it was a chunk of honeycomb. Then she asked which of the teas he'd like her to pour.

Arvin glanced over the collection of teapots on her tray and shook his head. "None of those," he said. "I want a special blend." He pretended to wave the tray away, but as he did, his fingers added a word, in silent speech: *magic.*

The slave was good; her expression never changed. "What flavor, sir?"

Arvin dropped his hand to the table, drumming it with his fingers to call her attention to his hand. "Let's see," he mused. *Need*—"Perhaps some mint"—*speak*—"and chamomile"—*Drin*—"and a peel of cinnamon."—*now*.

"That's an expensive blend," the slave countered. "And it will take time to fetch the ingredients."

"I'm prepared to pay," Arvin said, tossing a silver piece onto her tray. "And I'm happy to wait. Give me some black tea to sip in the meantime. And I'll take two of those poppy seed cakes. I'm famished."

The slave set a teapot and two cakes down on his table and limped away. Arvin sat, sipping the honey-sweet tea. Despite his hunger, he found himself doing little more than nibbling at the cakes. Their taste was every bit as good as always, but somehow they seemed flat and lifeless in his mouth. He had to wash each mouthful down with a hefty gulp of tea.

Waiting in the warm night air was making Arvin lethargic. He closed his eyes, listening to the hum of conversation around him and drinking in the scent from the flower baskets that lined the Terrace. It was a welcome change from the sewer stink he'd been floundering around in lately. He dozed.

A chair scuffed. Arvin opened his eyes to find Drin sitting across the table from him. The potion seller looked worried, as always. His narrow face with its deep vertical grooves between his eyebrows gave him a perpetual frown. His wrists were narrow and his fingers long—that and the slight point to his ears suggested that there might be a wood elf hiding in the branches of his family tree. He smiled at Arvin—a quick twitch of his lips—and leaned forward. "You wanted to speak to me?"

Arvin nodded and spoke in a low voice. "Do you have anything that can undo mind-influencing magic?"

"Clerical magic or wizardry?"

"Neither," Arvin answered.

Drin's eyebrows raised. "Then what—"

"Do you know what a psion is?"

Drin gave him a guarded look. "I've heard of them. They cast 'mind magic.'"

"That's right. I want something that will block a psionic power."

Drin thought a moment. "There's no 'tea' that does that. None that I know of," he said. He glanced around then dropped his voice to a whisper. "But I think there might be a ring that blocks such spells."

"Would it work against one that's already been cast?"

"I'm not sure. It's not my area of expertise."

Arvin wet his lips. "Could you obtain a ring like that for me?"

Drin shrugged. "Maybe. But it would take time to find out. The . . . merchant I need to speak to won't be back in Hlondeth for at least a month." He dropped his voice to a whisper. "The druids have been busy."

Arvin drummed his fingers on the table in frustration. Coming to Drin had been a long shot—a gamble that hadn't paid off. But perhaps Drin could tell him something about the potion the Pox were using—something that might help Naulg. Assuming Arvin was able to find him again, that was.

"One other thing," Arvin said. "There's a 'tea' that I'm trying to find out more about. A very rare blend. It comes in an unusual container—a small metal flask that's shaped like the rattle of a snake. Do you know anything about it?"

"I'm sorry, but I can't help you," Drin said. "I've never heard of a tea like that."

The guarded look was back in Drin's eyes; the potion seller was lying. "Listen, Drin," Arvin said, dropping his voice to a whisper. "A friend of mine *drank* some of that tea, and it's had an . . . unpleasant effect on him. I'm trying to help him." Focusing on the potion seller, silently willing him not to leave, Arvin felt the prickle of his psionics coming into play. "All I want is information," he pleaded. "Just some friendly advice—anything you think might help. I'm willing to pay for it." He placed ten gold pieces on the table.

The wary look in Drin's eyes softened. He leaned forward and scooped up the coins. "Let's move to a quieter table," he said. "One where we won't be overheard."

Arvin smiled.

They moved to a table at the back of the Terrace, well away from the other customers. When they settled into their chairs, Drin continued. "I can't tell you much," he said. "I've only seen a flask like that once before, in a 'teashop' in Skullport, a few months ago. The man behind the counter said it came from the Serpent Hills."

Arvin hissed softly to himself. The Serpent Hills lay far to the northeast, up near the great desert. Once the area had been the seat of a mighty kingdom, but now the yuan-ti who lived in those desolate hills were forced to ally with lesser reptilian races just to survive. The yuan-ti kept vowing to retake what had once been the capital of their kingdom, but the humans who had unwittingly encamped upon the ruins stood in their....

Arvin shivered, suddenly uneasy. Once again, the information had come from nowhere; it had just popped into his mind. He had never traveled beyond Hlondeth, yet he was able to picture the hills, the river that wound its way between them, and the enormous stone arch that spanned it—part of a coil that reached from one bank to the other....

He wrenched his mind back to the present. "How much do you know about the potion the flask contained?" he asked Drin.

"Only what the seller told me. That whoever drank it would be able to perform 'mind magic' that would duplicate a yuan-ti's innate magical abilities." He paused, and the creases in his brow deepened still further. "I sensed that there was something he wasn't telling me, but I was still interested in buying."

"Did you?" Arvin asked.

Drin shook his head. "I was outbid by another buyer, a yuan-ti slaver by the name of Ssarmn. Apparently he's someone big in Skullport—someone you don't refuse. The seller told me I shouldn't be angry at being cut out of the deal, because the potion had an additional, undesirable effect on humans. It turned them into yuan-ti. Permanently. And there was more. Once the potion took effect, anyone who was transformed by it would unquestioningly obey any true yuan-ti who happened to give orders."

Drin sat back in his chair and shrugged. "I thought the seller was trying to pacify me, so he wouldn't lose my business; we've had dealings with each other for years. But maybe he was telling the truth. Is that what happened to your friend? Did he sprout a tail and grow scales?"

"Nothing so obvious as that," Arvin said. "At least, not yet. His saliva turned venomous, but otherwise he appears human."

Drin stared at Arvin then nodded. "Where did he get the potion?"

"He was forced to drink it. By a cleric."

"One of Sseth's?"

Arvin shook his head. "No. The cleric was human."

"Why did he force your friend to drink it, then? Did he think it would make your friend obey him?"

"I'm not sure," Arvin said. He thought back to what Kayla had said about the old sailor—about him instantly obeying the cultist's command to attack. That compulsion could equally have been produced by a clerical spell. If what Drin had just said was true—if the potion in the rattle-shaped flasks compelled its victims to obey yuan-ti, but not humans—Naulg wouldn't necessarily be a mindless servant of the Pox. Arvin just might be able to free him, even with the potion in Naulg's system.

Unless a yuan-ti showed up at an inopportune moment.

Arvin was starting to have a clearer picture of what was going on—and why Osran Extaminos was involved. He was tricking the Pox into transforming the humans of Hlondeth into his willing servants. With an army of thousands at his disposal, Osran could easily snatch the throne away from his sister and would wind up ruling a city filled with complacent citizens.

A city of slaves.

"Did the seller in Skullport say whether there was a countermeasure that could negate the potion?" Arvin asked. "A counter-potion, for example?"

Drin shook his head. "If there is, I don't know of it."

Arvin sat back, disappointed. He wet his lips. "Thanks for the information," he told Drin.

The potion seller rose to his feet. "Glad to give it," he said, giving Arvin a knowing wink. "I hope it helps your 'friend.'"

CHAPTER 12

24 Kythorn, Evening

Arvin walked through the night with his hands thrust into his trouser pockets, oblivious to the people who passed him on the narrow streets. At long last he had the information Zelia wanted, but he couldn't give it to her, thanks to the geas Nicco had placed on him. Nor was he any closer to finding Naulg. None of his contacts in the Guild had seen the Pox, or heard any word of them—or smelled them.

In a short time—it was fast approaching Middark—the rebels would be making their assassination attempt on Osran Extaminos. Arvin toyed briefly with the idea of trying to reach Osran first, to see if he could charm information about the Pox out of the yuan-ti prince. But trying to sneak into the palace on the same night as an assassination attempt would be nothing short of suicidal.

No, there had to be another way to find the Pox, something Arvin hadn't thought of yet. If only Tymora would smile upon Arvin and cause him to cross paths with another of the cultists, he might be able to learn where they were hiding. He wouldn't make the same mistake as last time. This time he'd follow the cultist rather than try to question him. Asking questions had only caused him to lose his warehouse. Someone was sure to have noticed the stench of the corpse by now and called in the clerics to....

Arvin slowed, suddenly realizing something. He'd questioned the cultist, but he hadn't searched him. There hadn't been time. For all Arvin knew, there might have been something on the body that would lead Arvin straight to the cultists. And thanks to Zelia, Arvin had a tool he could use to search the body from a safe distance.

Arvin hurried to his warehouse. It didn't take him long to get there—the streets were emptying of people as Middark approached. He passed the public fountain and turned into the intersection his warehouse fronted. He saw that the front door was still shut—and unmarked. He bypassed it, holding his breath as soon as he caught the rotten odor coming from behind the door, and made for one of the barred windows, instead. Leaping up, he grabbed the bars, supporting himself, and peered in. The corpse—or rather, what was left of it—was still tangled in the magical rope. It lay on the floor just inside the door. The cultist's tunic was disheveled, but Arvin could see that it had at least one pocket.

He concentrated, drawing psionic energy up into his "third eye." He sent it out and saw a streak of silver light flash toward the corpse. As soon as it touched the pocket Arvin gave it a mental yank and heard the fabric tear. Three items spilled out: a leather sling, a lumpy-looking pouch that probably contained sling stones—and a key.

Immediately, Arvin coiled his mental energy around the key. He yanked, and the key lifted in the air and sailed toward the window. Springing back from the wall, Arvin landed on the street below, pulling the key out between the bars. It landed with a dull clink on the cobblestones at his feet.

Arvin stared at it, his heart racing. This was no ordinary key, intended to fit the door of an inn or warehouse. It was made from a peculiar reddish metal, was as long as Arvin's index finger, and had teeth that were an odd shape. They were jagged and triangular, instead of square. It probably opened a lock that was equally unusual. Possibly the door to whatever building the Pox had chosen for their hiding place.

Arvin carefully picked it up—with his gloved hand—and spoke the glove's command word, sending the key into extra-dimensional space. Then he set out for the artisan's section of the city. That was where Lorin, the Guild member he'd purchased his belt buckle from, had his workshop. Lorin was a master locksmith; if anyone knew what lock this key fit into, he would.

24 Kythorn, Middark

Arvin banged at the shutters of the Lorin's workshop. After a few moments they opened. Lorin's apprentice—a slender boy in his teens with mouse-brown hair as fuzzy as frayed rope—stared out at Arvin, yawning.

"Is Lorin here?" Arvin asked. Silently, his fingers added, *I'm Guild.*

The apprentice shook his head. "He's out on business." He stressed the last word, adding a wink to it, then yawned again.

"When will he be back?" Arvin asked, irritation rising in him.

"I dunno. Maybe tomorrow morning. Maybe the next day."

Arvin hissed in frustration. Tymora wasn't with him tonight, it seemed. Should he wait—or try to find another locksmith? The trouble was, Lorin was the only one he knew for certain was Guild. "Fetch him," he demanded. "At once or I'll—"

Only at the last moment did Arvin realize what was happening. It was the mind seed again, intruding upon his thoughts, stirring up his emotions like a nest of spitting vipers. With an effort, Arvin forced himself to calm down. "Sorry," he apologized, rubbing his temple. "But it's important. Can I leave something here for Lorin?"

"What?" the apprentice asked.

"A key—one I'd like him to identify, if he can. I'll pay well for whatever information he can provide." To back up his words, he passed the apprentice a gold piece.

The apprentice suddenly wasn't sleepy any more. He pocketed the gold piece and held out a hand. "Leave the key with me."

Arvin shook his head. "You mustn't touch it," he cautioned. "It came from the pocket of a dead man—a man who died of plague."

The apprentice's face paled. He drew back from the window, and for a moment Arvin worried that he'd slam the shutter in Arvin's face. But after a moment's fumbling inside the workshop, he reappeared. "Plague," he said with a shudder. "No wonder you're so edgy." He held out a ceramic jar, which he uncorked. "Put the key in this."

"Good idea." Arvin summoned the key into his gloved hand and dropped it inside the jar, which the apprentice hurriedly corked.

"Tell Lorin I need the information as soon as possible," Arvin instructed. "It's urgent. The life of a Guild member is at stake."

The apprentice nodded, his eyes serious. "I'll tell Lorin about it as soon as he gets back," he promised.

"Thanks." Turning away from the window, Arvin set off down the street, seething with barely subdued frustration at the delay. It was unacceptable, intolerable....

He'd walked some distance before he realized that he was hissing—and that worried him. The mind seed's hold was intensifying. Arvin was thinking more and more like a yuan-ti—reacting like one, too. His dreams, crowded with Zelia's memories, were no longer his own. Even in his waking moments it was difficult to hold on to *himself*. He never knew when he was going to lose control, when the mind seed was going to twist his thoughts and emotions in a direction that frightened him. His mind was like a tiny mouse half-swallowed by a snake. Squeal though the mouse might, it was only a matter of time before its head disappeared down the serpent's throat.

Arvin wet his lips nervously then grimaced as he realized what he'd just done. At least he was still noticing the odd mannerisms.

He wandered the streets with no clear destination in mind. What he really needed was someone to talk to—someone in whom to confide. He had dozens of associates among the Guild, but that was all they were—customers and contacts. Naulg was the only one Arvin could call a friend. There weren't any woman to whom Arvin could turn. Wary of ever getting too close to anyone, he'd never formed a permanent bond with a member of the opposite sex. He'd rarely slept with the same woman twice, let alone become a lover and confidant to one.

Yet he needed help—that much was clear.

Nothing, it seemed, could dislodge the mind seed.

Wizardry had failed, prayers had failed, and there was no known potion that would work against it. Then his footsteps slowed as he realized there was one form of magic he'd not yet tried.

Psionics.

From childhood, he dimly remembered his mother once mentioning that psionic powers could be "negated." Presumably, this was a process akin to a wizard or cleric dispelling a spell. If Arvin could find a psion—one who was willing to help him and who was powerful enough to counter the mind seed—perhaps he could free himself from it. But where was he going to find a psion? In his twenty-six years in Hlondeth, Arvin had only met one, other than his mother. Zelia. Was there really no one else, or had Arvin just not recognized the subtle signs?

The secondary displays, for example. Zelia and Nicco had both recognized Arvin as a psion by the ringing sound they'd heard when Arvin had manifested his charms. Zelia had attributed the secondary display to the fact that Arvin was untrained, implying that more powerful psions didn't produce any such telltale traces. But what if she'd been lying? On several occasions, Arvin had noticed her eyes flashing silver as they "reflected" the light—even when the light was behind her. Was that a secondary display, too?

As Arvin thought about it, he realized there was someone else who had produced something that might have been a secondary display when working his "magic"—Tanju, the militia tracker. When Tanju had tried to view the inside of the enormous pot Arvin had fallen into, Arvin had heard a low humming similar to the drone that Arvin's distract power produced. He'd assumed Tanju had been humming to himself, but the noise might have, in fact, been an involuntary secondary display. And there was the bundle of crystals Tanju had been carrying. . . .

With a start, Arvin realized he knew what they were: a "crystal capacitor," a device for storing psionic energy. The capacitor was charged using a complex series of *asanas*, which directed energy from the *mu-ladhara* up into. . . .

Arvin shook his head. He was doing it again. Linking, thanks to the mind seed, with Zelia's memories and drawing information from them.

He saw that his wanderings had carried him to the vicinity of Zelia's rooftop garden. He could see the tower between the buildings up ahead. How in the Nine Hells had he allowed himself to wander so near to it?

He turned abruptly, intending to stride away in the direction from which he'd just come and nearly collided with a man who had been walking a few steps behind him. The fellow had his neck craned to look up at the buildings ahead of him and saw Arvin only at the last moment. He gave an irritated hiss—which made Arvin take a second glance at the fellow. All Arvin needed was to run afoul of a yuan-ti. But this fellow appeared wholly human—and he had four chevrons branded into his arm. Yuan-ti were never called for militia service.

Muttering his apologies, Arvin walked on. He'd gotten no more than a few paces before a hand reached out of the shadow of a ramp to grasp his arm.

A hand covered in fine green scales.

"Zelia!" Arvin gulped as she stepped out into the street. "What a coincidence. I was just heading back to the tower to look for you."

Her lips crooked in a smile. "I can see that," she said. "Obviously you have something to report, something important enough to have come in person, rather than using a sending." She stared unblinkingly at him. "What have you learned?"

Arvin thought furiously. What *could* he tell Zelia? "You were wrong about the flasks," he began. "They don't contain plague."

Zelia merely stared at him. "No?"

"They contain a potion."

"What kind?"

"One that transforms humans into yuan-ti. It comes from the Serpent Hills, possibly by way of Skullport. A contact of mine saw a flask similar to the ones the Pox carry, a few months ago in a potion seller's shop. He tried to buy it, but before he could, it was purchased by a slaver."

"What was the slaver's name?" Zelia hissed.

"Ssarmn."

Zelia hissed thoughtfully. Apparently she recognized the name.

"That's all I've been able to learn so far," Arvin concluded.

"Is it?" Zelia asked.

"Yes," Arvin answered evenly. He stared at Zelia. The last thing he needed was for her to question him, to force him to tell her about the Extaminos connection to the Pox. If he did, he'd be a dead man. Deliberately, he forced Osran's name out of his mind—but not quickly enough.

Zelia's eyes suddenly flashed silver. She gave a long, slow hiss. "Osran? I suspected there was a bad egg in the brood."

As she spoke the name aloud, Arvin felt a stabbing pain in his throat. Doubling over, he began to cough. Dark droplets flecked the ground; when he swallowed, he tasted blood. He felt a chill of fear course through him as he realized what was happening. The geas was taking hold, even though he hadn't spoken the name aloud—hadn't even intended for it to be overheard. He swallowed again, his throat raw. Hoar, he pleaded silently. I didn't mean to. Please don't kill me.

Zelia didn't even ask what was wrong with him. She just stood, smiling like a snake that had swallowed a mouse. Arvin, meanwhile, felt the pain in his throat ease—just a little. Then his coughing stopped. Hoar, it seemed, had heard his plea and spared him.

Arvin touched the bead at his throat. "Nine lives," he whispered. He followed it with a silent thank-you to Hoar.

At least it was Middark. Tymora willing, the assassination would already have taken place and the Secession would be on their way out of the palace.

"Zelia," Arvin said, finding his voice again as the raw ache in his throat at last subsided. "I've given you what you wanted. Remove the mind seed. Get out of my head."

Zelia's eyes blazed. "You dare make demands?" she hissed. "The seed will remain in place—at the very least, until I've had a chance to put a few questions to Osran."

Unbidden, an image flashed into Arvin's mind. Of just what Zelia meant by "putting a few questions" to Osran. First she'd place a lock on his higher mind, causing a mental paralysis that would render him unable to take any physical actions. Then she'd slither into his mind. She'd poke and prod into the darkest crevices of his thoughts, finding his weaknesses and fears. One by one, she'd bring these into the light of full awareness. She'd nudge his helpless mind this way and that, forcing him to dwell upon that which most demoralized him, filling him to the brim with fear. Then, when she'd forced her victim to retreat into a tight coil of despair, she'd beat the last of his will down with her questions. What did it matter, she'd say, if he revealed his secrets to her? All was lost, hopeless, bleak. He was doomed. *She* was in control, not him.

Arvin dwelled upon the image, gloating. It felt good to be the one in command. To savor the raw, weeping anguish of another that he so thoroughly dominated. He remembered the first time he'd ever used his psionic powers to reduce someone to sniveling helplessness—

his former master. The master whose psionic powers Arvin had so easily surpassed. The human had proved as fragile as an egg when Arvin at last tired of toying with him....

Arvin felt sweat trickle down his temples. He shivered, despite the warmth of the night air. He wrenched his mind back to the present, away from Zelia's memory, and glanced around.

Zelia was gone. Having gotten what she wanted from him, she'd slithered away into the night without another word.

Arvin pressed his forehead against the stone wall next to him, savoring its coolness. It helped ease the throbbing of his headache. Through half-closed eyes, he saw the pale-green shimmer of residual magical energy the stones contained. The color matched the scales on Zelia's skin—and reminded him that he could no more shed her than the stone could shed its luminescent glow. Nicco had been right. Arvin *was* doomed.

No. He was thinking like one of Zelia's victims. There was still hope if Tanju could be persuaded to help him. But how to make contact with the tracker? Tanju might be quartered at the militia barracks, or he might not. Being an auxiliary, rather than a regular member of the militia, might have its privileges. If Arvin tried to ask one of the militia where Tanju was, he would probably be mistaken for Gonthril again, and the chase would be on.

And Tanju would be summoned to help track him.

And if, in his flight to "escape," Arvin swung through the section of the city that contained the palace, he might just draw enough of the militia away from it to enable Gonthril and the others to make their escape after the assassination attempt. And in the process, make amends to them for having let Osran's name slip.

Grinning, Arvin set off in the direction of the palace.

Arvin clung, panting from his rapid climb, to the underside of a viaduct. In the street below, three members of the militia pounded past, never once thinking to glance up as they ran directly beneath his hiding spot. Escaping them had been too easy, he thought. Despite the hue and cry they'd raised after spotting "Gonthril," they hadn't called out their tracker. Tanju was nowhere in sight.

This was getting ridiculous. Arvin had allowed himself to be seen in at least a dozen different locations, without success, and it was almost dawn. He'd have to find some other way to flush out Tanju.

Climbing back down the pillar that supported the viaduct, Arvin jogged in the opposite direction the three militiamen had just taken. As he made his way up the winding street, he caught glimpses of the tower that rose high above the central courtyard of the royal palace. The tower was capped with an enormous statue of a cobra, its flared hood covered in overlapping scales that were said to be slabs of solid gold. The eyes of the statue—which flashed red in daylight, but which by night looked like dark, brooding pits in the golden head—were rumored to be chunks of ruby as large as a human heart. No rogue had ever climbed the tower to find out if that was true, however. Just getting into the palace compound was problem enough. The walls were protected by magical glyphs far more powerful—and deadly—than the one Arvin had fallen victim to in the Secession's hiding place, and the grounds were patrolled by officers from the human militia. Assuming the rogue actually made it inside the palace, he would have to run a gauntlet of its yuan-ti guard: high-ranking clerics from the Cathedral of Emerald Scales.

Arvin shook his head, wondering how Gonthril and the Secession had ever hoped to get that far. But even if they had failed in their mission, it wouldn't matter. Zelia knew that Osran Extaminos was the backer behind the Pox. When she was finished with Osran, the cultists' supply of transformative potion would be cut off, and Hlondeth's citizens would be saved.

Saved, of course, with the notable exception of Naulg, and the other poor wretches the Pox had already used for their experiments.

Arvin, thanks to the mind seed, was equally doomed—unless he could find Tanju.

If only Arvin had access to Zelia's powers—and not just her emotions and memories—he might be able to search for Tanju using psionics. That would certainly improve his odds of finding the tracker. A simple sending would do. . . .

Slowing to a walk, Arvin hissed an oath. He reached into his pocket and pulled the lapis lazuli from its hiding place. Had he the means to find Tanju in his hands all this time—or rather, in his pocket? When Zelia had told him the lapis lazuli would allow him to manifest a sending, he'd assumed she meant that it would only allow him to contact her. But perhaps that was an incorrect assumption.

He stared at the stone, trying to will the answer from the seed that was buried deep within his mind. It only took a moment before the answer bubbled to the surface: the stone could be used to manifest a sending . . . to anyone.

Smiling, Arvin slipped into the shadow of a ramp then touched the flat of the stone to his forehead. *"Atmiya,"* he said, speaking its command word out loud.

The stone grew warm against his skin. His forehead tickled as if tiny stitches were being sewn into his flesh, securing the lapis lazuli in place. He tried picking at the edge of the stone with a fingernail but could find no edge; it was embedded in his forehead. Suddenly worried, he thought the command word.

Instantly the tickling sensation was gone. The stone fell from his forehead and he caught it in his hand. He rubbed his forehead, expecting to find a hole, but his skin was smooth, not even dented.

Once his heart had stopped racing, he returned the stone to his forehead and repeated the command word, locking it in place. Then he closed his eyes and concentrated, calling to mind Tanju's face. Gray hair, strangely slanted eyes....

After a few moments, he felt a familiar prickling of psionic energy at the base of his scalp. The image of Tanju he held in his mind seemed to solidify; it was almost as if Arvin were staring at him in the flesh. The tracker lay on his side with eyes closed and head cradled on one arm, his face bathed in the dim glow of either a lantern or a low-burning fire. *Tanju*, Arvin thought. As he gave mental voice to his words, the lapis lazuli began to vibrate softly against the skin of his forehead. It was as if the stone were a fingertip, rapidly tapping the head of a drum. *This is Gonthril. I'm in Hlondeth. I want to meet with you. Tell me where to find you.*

Tanju sat up, a startled look on his face. Surprise muted into a thoughtful expression, and he mumbled something—to someone else, since Arvin couldn't hear what was said. Fortunately, Tanju was equally unable to hear Arvin's chuckle. Arvin had baited his sending with something the tracker found irresistible: "Gonthril." And Tanju had just swallowed the hook.

I'm on the road to Mount Ugruth, Tanju answered. *Camped at the top of the first pass. I'll wait until Evening for you, but no longer.*

The vibrations faded as the sending ended.

Arvin smiled. Perfect. Even allowing for a brief nap—which he badly needed—he could reach the pass by Sunset. That would still give him four full days until the mind seed took over. He started to speak the command word that would cause the lapis lazuli to drop from his forehead when he realized something. Zelia had told him that the stone could be used to manifest a sending just once a day, but this was only partially true. The stone could be used several times per day—if a different person was contacted each time. If Naulg was still alive....

Arvin summoned the familiar prickle of psionic energy back to the base of his scalp. Then he concentrated on Naulg's face: his easy grin, his dark hair, his distinctive eyebrows....

Just as the image of Tanju had done, the mental picture of Naulg suddenly solidified in Arvin's mind. It was as if Arvin were staring at the rogue from a point somewhere behind Naulg. He was sitting, arms wrapped around his drawn-up legs, his head hanging down dejectedly, chin on chest.

Alive! Naulg was still alive!

Elated, Arvin tried to see more, hoping for some clue as to Naulg's whereabouts. But it was no use. All he could see was Naulg himself.

Naulg, he thought urgently. *It's Arvin. Answer me. Tell me where you are so I can rescue you.*

Abruptly, Naulg's head lifted. He whirled around, still in a seated position, searching for the source of the voice he'd just heard. Arvin, still linked by the sending, gasped as he saw the rogue's face. Naulg's cheeks were as sunken as those of a corpse, and his eyes were hollow pits under a scalp that was dotted with bald patches. Horrified by the change in his friend's appearance, Arvin nearly lost the connection. Then Naulg's reply came whispering back at him.

I am . . . unclean, he answered, his eyes gleaming with madness. A shiver passed through his body, and he wrapped his arms around his legs once more. *My body must . . . burn.*

"Unclean?" Arvin echoed. He wet his lips nervously.

Naulg, as if mimicking Arvin, wet his own lips. Arvin felt his face pale as he saw Naulg's tongue. The tip of it was forked, just like a yuan-ti's.

The rogue was still speaking telepathically to Arvin, still linked to him by the sending. He shook his head violently, and his eyes seemed to clear for just a moment. *Arvin?* he asked. *You escaped?*

"Yes, Naulg, I escaped. Where *are* you?" Arvin spoke out loud, despite the fact that Naulg wouldn't hear him. That was how a sending worked: the psion sent a brief message, and received one in return. Then it ended.

Fortunately, Naulg was still answering—though his eyes had resumed a wild, darting look. *The walls. . . . It's hot. They're burning.* The rogue paused, and his eyes cleared a little—though they were glazed with pain. *It hurts. Oh gods, my stomach feels like it's—*

Abruptly, the sending ended.

Arvin stood, shaken by what he'd just seen and heard. His friend was in the grip of a hideous transformation that seemed to be sapping both his strength and his sanity. And he was counting on Arvin to rescue him.

Arvin spoke the command word and the lapis lazuli fell from his forehead. As he tucked it back inside the false seam of his shirt pocket, he debated what to do. Tanju was well to the north of the city—it would take Arvin a full day to reach him and another to get back to the city. Could Naulg wait that long for rescue?

If Naulg had been able to say where he was, Arvin wouldn't be asking that question. But his reply to the sending had been baffling. Burning walls? The Pox could be hiding inside a foundry, or a pottery factory . . . or next to a building that was being cleansed of plague.

With a sinking heart, Arvin decided that Naulg would have to come second. Tanju would only wait one day for Arvin; Arvin couldn't let his only chance at dislodging the mind seed just walk away.

"Hang on, Naulg," Arvin whispered. "I'll come for you. Just hang on."

CHAPTER 13

25 Kythorn, Sunset

Arvin trudged onward, weary and footsore after a full day of walking in the hot sun along the road that wound its way into the foothills north of Hlondeth. Built centuries ago when the aqueduct was constructed, the road was little more than a track, its flagstones all but lost among the weeds. The aqueduct itself was still sound; Arvin could hear water gurgling through the enormous stone troughs overhead. Here and there water spurted out through a crack where two of the troughs joined, providing a cooling shower for the travelers trudging below.

Arvin had expected to be the only one on the road; summer was a grueling time to be undertaking a climb into the mountains north of the city. He was surprised by the number of people who were heading in the same direction that he was. They turned out to be devotees of Talos the Destroyer, on their way to Mount Ugruth to view the most recent venting of the volcano. Every so often—whenever they caught sight of the plume of smoke rising from the peak of the mountain—the pilgrims would fall to their knees, tear their shirts, and claw at the earth until their fingers bled. A few even went so far as to claw at their faces, opening bloody wounds they displayed proudly to one another, bragging that this would speed the flow of lava down the mountain's sides and the destruction of all in its path.

Arvin, reminded of the excesses of the priests who had run the orphanage, kept well away from these fanatics. What point was there in worshiping a god who offered only death and destruction as rewards for faithful service? Surely that was madness.

Yet it was madness that offered the perfect cover. As he drew nearer to the top of the first pass, Arvin stepped into the trees, out of sight from the road. When he emerged again, his shirt hung in tatters, his trouser knees were dirty and his hair and face were streaked with blood from a cut he'd opened on one finger. Raising his hands to the distant volcano, he continued up the road.

Up ahead on the left was a blocky cliff that had been cut into the forested hillside—one of the quarries that had provided the stone used to build the aqueduct. Chunks of partially squared stone littered the ground; travelers in years gone by had used these to create rough, unmortared shelters. Their crude walls were roofed with tree branches, hacked from the nearby forest. Many of the shelters had fallen to pieces, but at least two or three were currently in use, judging by the thin wavers of smoke that rose from them into the summer sky.

Arvin entered the old quarry and began going

from one shelter to the next, mumbling nonsense about death and ashes under his breath. But every shelter that he looked inside held only pilgrims. They beamed at Arvin, waving him inside, then shrugged as he turned and stumbled away.

After peering inside the last of the shelters, Arvin slowed. Had Tanju already gone? The tracker had promised to wait until Evening, but perhaps Sunset had marked the end of his patience.

Arvin turned and stared back in the direction from which he'd come. Hlondeth lay far below, a dark spot at the edge of the vast expanse of blue that was the Vilhon Reach. Far away across the water, Arvin could just make out the opposite shore, where the Barony of Sespech lay. Clouds were gathering above the Reach, indicating that the muggy heat would soon break.

Wiping the sweat from his forehead with the back of a sleeve, Arvin wet his lips. He certainly could use a drink of water. Then again, he was equally drawn by the heat he could feel rising from the sun-warmed stone on which he stood. Exhausted after a full day of walking, he yearned to curl up on it and soak up the last few rays of the setting sun. Perhaps if he drowsed, the headache that had been plaguing him would finally ebb. Tilting his face up to the sun, he closed his eyes and stretched....

He heard a faint tinkling, like the sound of chimes being stirred by the wind. An instant later pain lanced through his skull, staggering him. Gasping, he clutched his head. The pain was unbearable; it pierced his skull from temple to temple. He heard the familiar *thunk* of a crossbow shot. Something wrapped itself around his ankles, lashing them together. In that same instant, a second mental agony was added to the first. This time it slammed into the spot between his eyes and out through the base of his skull. Arvin would have screamed, but found himself unable to force a sound out through his gritted teeth. Opening his eyes seemed equally impossible, as was anything other than toppling over onto his side. A third bolt of agony pierced the crown of his head as he fell. This one seemed to explode within his mind, sparking out in all directions like a shattered coal and burning everything in its path. As it sizzled inside his skull, Arvin felt his mind dulling. Coherent thought was a struggle, and yet somehow a part of what remained of his consciousness—the part that held the mind seed—recognized the attack for what it was. A series of crippling mental thrusts.

Tanju was still at the quarry, after all.

He ... dares ... attack ... me? thought the part of Arvin's mind that had been seeded.

Then he crumpled to the ground.

25 Kythorn, Evening

Arvin came to his senses suddenly, sputtering from the cold water that had just been dashed on his face. Blinking it out of his eyes, he saw that he was inside one of the crude shelters in the old quarry. Moonlight shone in through the loose lacing of branches that constituted the roof, revealing a shadowed form sitting cross-legged on the opposite side of the shelter: Tanju. The tracker stared silently at Arvin, his hands raised above his head and palms pressed together, his hairless chest visible through rips in his shirt. His eyes were filled with shifting points of colored light; it was as if hundreds of tiny candle flames of differing hues were flickering in their depths.

Standing next to Tanju was a young man with pale, close-cropped hair who held a dripping leather bucket in one hand. His shirt was also torn like those of the pilgrims; through the rents in his sleeve Arvin could see three chevrons on his left forearm. That, and the peculiarly rigged crossbow that hung from his belt, marked him as a militiaman. Arvin's backpack lay near his feet.

Arvin tried to rise but found that he was unable to move. Cool, wet tendrils of what looked like white mist encased his body from head to foot, leaving only his eyes and nose uncovered. They shifted back and forth across his body like drifting clouds, but though they left a damp film on Arvin's hair and skin, he was unable to slip out of them. When he strained against them, they held firm, as solid as any rope. The knowledge of what they were came to him out of one of Zelia's memories. They were strands of ectoplasm, drawn from the astral plane by force of will and twined around the victim with a quick twist of thought. The resulting "ectoplasmic cocoon" was almost impossible to escape. If cut, the strands would just regenerate.

Much like a length of trollgut, Arvin thought, his mind still groggy.

The flickering points of light disappeared from Tanju's eyes. He lowered his hands. "This isn't Gonthril," he told the other man. "His aura is wrong. Very wrong."

The militiaman frowned. "He looks like Gonthril."

"Gonthril wouldn't have allowed himself to be captured like this."

Arvin tried to speak, but the strands of ectoplasm pressed against his lips and held his jaw firmly shut. All he could manage was a muffled exhalation that sounded like a hiss.

Tanju waved a hand in front of Arvin's face, as if fanning a candle flame, and the strands shifted away from Arvin's mouth. "Who are you?" he asked.

Arvin wet his lips nervously. "My name's Arvin," he said. "I'm a rope maker from Hlondeth. Unfortunately, I look like this Gonthril fellow you're searching for. You mistook me for him in the Mortal Coil two mornings ago."

"That was you?" Tanju asked.

"Yes."

"Why did you flee?"

Arvin tried to gesture with his head, but could not. "Take a look at my left forearm," he suggested. "The militia were rounding up men for a galley. The thought of four years of pulling an oar didn't appeal to me."

"I see," Tanju said. He didn't bother to inspect Arvin's arm. "How do you know Gonthril's name?"

"I overheard one of the militia mention it when I was hiding in the pottery factory," Arvin said. "'There's a ten thousand gold piece bounty coming to the man who captures Gonthril,' he said. I figured that was the name of the person you were looking for."

"Why did you claim to be him?" Tanju asked.

"I didn't think you'd agree to meet with me otherwise." Arvin was uncomfortable inside the cocoon of ectoplasm. The slippery feel of the strands reminded him of the unpleasant cling of sewer muck. His clothes and hair were growing damper by the moment. At least the ectoplasm was odorless, the gods be thanked for small mercies.

The militiaman standing beside Tanju snorted as he placed the bucket back on the ground. "It's a trick, Tanju," he said. "The stormlord is trying to stall us—and we fell for it. We've already lost an entire day."

Tanju gave the militiaman a sharp look, as if the other man had just said something he shouldn't have. "Our quarry knows nothing about the rebels, least of all what their leader looks like."

"What if we were wrong?" the militiaman suggested. "Maybe the rogues were, in fact, rebels and the theft nothing more than a plot to draw you out of the city."

"The theft was real enough," Tanju said grimly. "And they *weren't* rebels. I know that much already."

The militiaman frowned. "But how does this man fit in?"

"I don't," Arvin interrupted, exasperated by their endless speculations about rogues and rebels and stormlords—whoever they were. "I'm here because I need Tanju's help. I need him to negate a psionic power that's been manifested on me."

Tanju tilted his head. "Why should I do this for you?"

"I can pay," Arvin continued. "Look in my backpack and you'll find a magical rope. It's yours, if you'll help."

The militiaman began to pick up Arvin's backpack, but Tanju held up a hand, cautioning him. Then Tanju waved his hand over the backpack and a faintly sweet smell filled the air. The scent was a little like the burnsticks Arvin's mother had burned when she was meditating—flower-sweet, with sharp undertones of resin.

Tanju lowered his hand. "You can open it now," he told the militiaman.

The militiaman undid the buckles on the backpack and tipped it open. Arvin's clothes, extra pair of boots, blanket, and food spilled out, together with a neat coil of rope. Tanju stared at them, his eyes sparkling with multicolored fire a second time.

"It's braided from trollgut," Arvin explained. "I made it myself. A command word causes it to expand. The extra fifty paces worth of rope will eventually rot away, but it can be grown back over and over again. The rope is quite valuable; you can sell it for three thousand gold pieces or more to the right buyer." He paused then, when the tingle arose at the base of his scalp, used his most persuasive voice. "Will you do it? Will you use your psionics to negate the power that's been manifested on me? If you do, I'll tell you the command word; the rope is useless without it."

Tanju fingered the rope, squeezing its rubbery strands between his fingers. He cocked his head as if listening to a distant sound—the secondary display of the charm Arvin was manifesting. When he turned back toward Arvin, he was smiling. Arvin peered at the psion, uncertain whether his charm had worked on the man or not. "Well, friend?" he ventured. "Will you help me?"

"I need to know what power has been manifested," Tanju said.

Arvin wet his lips. "A mind seed."

Tanju's eyes widened. He placed his hands on his knees then nodded. "That explains the aura."

"What aura?"

"The one that surrounds you. It was a strange mix. Dominated by yang—male energy—but streaked with yin. Mostly good but tainted with evil. It contained elements of both power and weakness, human and reptile. I assumed you were trying to alter your own aura . . . and not quite succeeding. But I see now that it must be the mind seed."

"Can you negate it?" Arvin asked.

"Excise it, you mean," Tanju said. He shook his head. "You really are a novice, aren't you? Despite the fact that you used a sending to contact me, you didn't mount even the simplest of defenses against my mind thrusts."

Arvin glanced down at the ectoplasm that held him. "If I'm so harmless, how about releasing me?"

Tanju considered Arvin for a moment, as if weighing the danger he posed. He took a deep breath then blew it out like a man extinguishing a lamp. The tendrils of ectoplasm vanished.

Arvin sat up, working the kinks out of his muscles. He ignored the militiaman, who had scooped up his crossbow and was aiming it at him. Pretending to stretch, he saw with satisfaction that his glove was still on his left hand, his braided leather bracelet still on his right wrist. So far, so good. The slick wetness the tendrils had left disappeared rapidly in the warm night air. Within the space of a few heartbeats, Arvin's hair and clothes were dry. He turned to Tanju. "I know the name of the power, but not much about it. Tell me what a mind seed is."

"It's a psionic power that can be manifested only by the most powerful telepaths," Tanju answered. "It inserts a sliver of the psion's mental and spiritual essence in the mind of another—a seed. As it germinates, it slowly replaces the victim's own mind with that of the psion who manifested the seed. When it at last blooms, the victim is no longer himself, but an exact duplicate of the psion. In mind, but not in body. His thoughts, his emotions, his dreams—"

"I get the point," Arvin said, shuddering. He massaged his temples, which were throbbing again. "How do I get rid of it?"

"Your head aches?" Tanju asked. "That's to be expected. It's the seed, setting in roots. The pain will get worse each day, as the roots expand and—"

"Gods curse you!" Arvin shouted, shaking his fist at Tanju. This human was toying with him, being coy. Gloating as he withheld the very thing Arvin most needed. "I haven't got much time. Don't just sit there—*excise* it, you stupid, insolent—"

The *click-whiz* of a weighted wire from the crossbow cut off the rest of Arvin's shout. One of the paired lead weights slammed into his cheek, making him gasp with pain as the other yanked the wire tight, pinning his wrist against his neck. Almost unable to breathe with the wire around his throat, Arvin felt the amulet his mother had given him pressing into his throat. "Nine lives," he whispered to himself—a plea, this time. He raised his free hand, palm out, in a gesture of surrender. "I'm sorry," he gasped. "That wasn't me. I didn't mean to. . . ."

"I could see that," Tanju said, rising to a kneeling position. He carefully began to unwind the wire from Arvin's neck and wrist. He spoke over his shoulder to the militiaman. "That was unnecessary. Please wait outside."

The militiaman grumbled but did as he was told, flipping aside the blanket that served as the shelter's door and stalking out into the night. Tanju, meanwhile, coiled the weighted wire into a tight ball and placed it in a pocket. He must have realized it would make an ideal garrote.

"Who planted the mind seed?" Tanju asked.

Arvin hesitated. "Why do you want to know?"

"I'm curious," Tanju answered. "Judging by your mannerisms—and your aura—it was a yuan-ti. I didn't know that any of them were trained in psionics."

Arvin stared at Tanju; the tracker's curiosity seemed to be genuine. Arvin decided that he might as well answer. "Her name's Zelia."

Tanju's expression didn't change. Either he didn't know Zelia—or he was a master at hiding his emotions.

"Will you help me?" Arvin asked.

"To excise a mind seed, one must know how to perform psychic chirurgery," Tanju said. "Unfortunately, that is a power I have yet to acquire." He paused. "You asked if I could negate it. There is a chance—a very slim one, mind you—that a negation might work. I'll attempt it now, if only for my own peace of mind while we speak further. Sit quietly, and look into my eyes."

Arvin did as instructed. Tanju stared intently at him, his eyes once more glinting with sparks of multicolored light. An unusual secondary display, a part of Arvin's mind noted—the part that had access to Zelia's memories. Tanju must have trained in the East....

The motes of color suddenly erupted out of Tanju's

eyes like sparks leaping from a fire. They shot into the spot between Arvin's eyes, penetrating his third eye and spinning there for a brief instant, then rushed through the rest of his body, leaving swirls of tingles at the base of his scalp, his throat, his chest, and his naval. The tingling coiled for a moment around the base of his spine then erupted out through his arms and legs, leaving his fingers and toes numb.

"Did it work?" Arvin asked, flexing his fingers.

"Try to think of a question that you don't know the answer to—something only Zelia would be able to answer," Tanju suggested.

Arvin stared at the rough walls of the shelter. Zelia seemed to know a lot about gems and stones. Presumably, she would know what type of stone had gone into the making of these rough walls. It was a reddish color, the same as the stone used in the oldest buildings in Hlondeth. . . .

Marble. Rosy marble, a crystalline rock capable of taking a high polish. Useful in the creation of power stones that conveyed the power to dream travel.

Arvin hissed in alarm. "It didn't work," he told Tanju in a tense voice.

Tanju sighed. "I didn't think it would. The mind seed is too powerful a manifestation. I can't uproot it." He gestured at Arvin's backpack. "You can keep your rope."

Arvin felt panic rise in his chest. "Is there nothing else you can try?"

Tanju shook his head.

"The mind seed was planted around Middark on the twenty-second of Kythorn," Arvin said, wetting his lips. "If it blooms after seven days, that means I've only got four days left—until Middark of the twenty-ninth."

"Possibly."

Arvin caught his breath. "What do you mean?"

"It could bloom sooner than Middark," Tanju said. "Any time on the twenty-ninth, in fact."

"But Zelia said it would take seven days to—"

"A mind seed is not like an hourglass," Tanju said. "It doesn't keep precise time. The seven-day period is somewhat ... arbitrary."

Arvin swallowed nervously. "So I've really only got three days," he muttered. He shook his head. "Will I ... be myself until then?"

"As much as you are now," Tanju said. "Not that this is much comfort to you, I'm sure."

"When will I be able to start manifesting the powers that Zelia knows?"

Tanju shook his head. "You won't. Not until it's her mind, not yours, in your body. If it worked any other way, the victim would be able to use the psion's talents against him."

"Is there *nothing* that can be done to stop it?" Arvin moaned.

"Nothing. Unless...."

Arvin tensed. "Unless what?"

Tanju shrugged. "There is a prayer that I once saw a cleric use to cure a woman who had been driven insane by a wizard's spell. He called it a 'restorative blessing.' I asked him if it was a divine form of psychic chirurgery. He had never heard the term before, but his answer confirmed that the prayer was indeed similar. He said a restorative blessing could cure all forms of insanity, confusion, and similar mental ailments—that it could dispel the effects of any spell that affected the mind, whether the source of the spell was clerical magic or wizardry. Presumably, that included psionic powers, as well. If you could find a cleric with such a spell, perhaps he could—"

"I don't know any clerics," Arvin said in exasperation. "At least, I don't know any that would—" Here he paused. Nicco. Did Nicco know such a prayer? He'd known what a psion was. Perhaps he knew more about "mind magic" than he'd let on. But if Nicco did know the restorative prayer, would he agree to use it?

Thinking of Nicco put Arvin in mind of the promise he'd made to the cleric: to attempt vengeance upon Zelia. If Arvin actually succeeded—if he was somehow able to defeat Zelia—perhaps she could be forced to remove the mind seed. The only trouble was she was a powerful psion, and he, a mere novice.

But a master was sitting just across the room from him.

Zelia had taught Arvin, in a single evening, to uncoil the energy in his *muladhara* and reach out with it to snatch his glove from the air. Perhaps there was something that Tanju could teach him, too. Some power that would help him confront Zelia—or at the very least, to defend himself against whatever else she might throw at him.

"That 'mind thrust' you used on me when I first arrived," Arvin said. "Could you teach it to me?"

"I'm surprised you don't know it already," Tanju said. "The five attack forms—and their defenses—are among the first things a psion learns. What lamasery did you train at?"

"I didn't," Arvin said. "My mother was going to send me to the one she trained at—the Shou-zin Lamasery in Kara Tur. Unfortunately, she didn't live long enough to—"

Tanju's eyebrows lifted. "Your mother trained at Shou-zin?"

Arvin paused. "You've heard of it?"

Tanju chuckled. "I spent six years there."

Arvin's mouth dropped open. "Did you know my mother? Her name was Sassan. She was a seer."

Tanju shook his head. "She must have trained there after my time." He paused. "How old were you when she died?"

"Six," Arvin said, dropping his gaze to the floor. He didn't want to discuss the orphanage, or what had followed.

Tanju seemed to sense that. "And those who cared for you after her death never thought to send you to a lamasery," he said. He pressed his palms together and touched his fingertips to his forehead then lowered his hands again. "Yet you know how to manifest a charm."

Alvin's cheeks flushed. "It didn't work, did it?"

Tanju shook his head.

"Did it anger you?"

"No."

Arvin glanced up eagerly. "Will you teach me the attacks and defenses?" As he spoke, he stifled a yawn. The long walk had left him weary and exhausted; he was barely able to keep his eyes open.

"Tonight?" Tanju chuckled. "It's late—and I'm as tired as you are. And I have an ... assignment I need to attend to. Perhaps in a tenday, when I return to Hlondeth."

Arvin hissed in frustration. "I haven't got that much time. The mind seed—"

"Ah, yes," Tanju said, his expression serious again, "the mind seed."

"I'll pay you," Arvin said. "The trollgut rope is yours, regardless of whether I learn anything or not."

Tanju stared at the rope. "For what you ask, it is hardly enough. The secrets of Shou-zin are living treasures and do not come cheaply."

"I know how to make other magical ropes. If you wanted one that could—"

"Your ropes are of less interest to me than your eyes," Tanju said. "You're Guild, aren't you?"

Arvin hesitated. "What if I am?"

"I may need a pair of eyes within that organization, some day," Tanju said. "If I agree to help you, can I call upon you for a favor in the future?"

Arvin paused. If he agreed, Tanju would be yet another person to whom he'd be beholden. Then again, in four days' time the promise might not matter, anyway. At last he nodded. "Agreed."

Tanju smiled. "Then in honor of your mother—may the gods send peace to her soul—I'll teach you what little I can. But not until tomorrow morning, when you're rested and your mind is clear."

"In the morning? But—"

Tanju folded his arms across his chest.

Grudgingly, Arvin nodded. He'd hoped to begin his walk back to the city at dawn's light. But Naulg had survived this long. An additional morning probably wouldn't make much difference. "All right. In the morning, then."

Tanju turned toward the doorway.

"Where are you going?" Arvin asked.

"To join my companion," Tanju answered. He paused, his palm against the blanket that was the shelter's doorway. "I'm reluctant to sleep in here with you. The mind seed...." He shrugged.

Arvin hissed in frustration, but held his temper.

"Sleep well," Tanju said. He stepped out into the night, letting the blanket fall shut behind him.

CHAPTER 14

26 Kythorn, Sunrise

In his dream, Arvin gasped as the mental blast slammed against the shield he had thrown up, shattering it. The shield exploded into a bright nova of individual motes of thought, which swiftly vanished. Immediately, before he could manifest a fresh shield, a second mental blast slammed into him. The psionic attack targeted his mind, rather than his body, but even so it sent him staggering backward. The backs of his legs struck something—the low wall around the fountain—and he flailed backward into its pond.

Leaping to his feet, he was dimly aware of water streaming from his hair and the sodden fabric of his dress clinging to his breasts and thighs. But the vast majority of his awareness—which had lessened, thanks to that last blast of energy, which had stripped away several layers of his painstakingly constructed self-control—was focused on his attack. Summoning energy up from his *muladhara*, he formed it into a long, thin, deadly whip of thought and sent this lashing out at his opponent.

He heard a low thrumming noise—a sound like an enormous, low-timbral drum still vibrating long after it has been struck—and cursed, knowing his master had raised a defense just in time. Arvin's mental whip struck harmlessly against a barrier then vanished.

His master, standing several paces away, his bare feet hidden by the flowering bush he'd stumbled into, shook his bald head. His face was deeply lined, almost haggard looking. He'd aged—greatly—during the years in which he'd served as Arvin's tutor.

In one dark hand he held two thumb-sized crystals, bound together with silver wire, his capacitor. The golden glow that once blazed brightly in it was dimmer than it had been a moment ago, almost gone.

"Enough!" the master cried. "You've proved your point. You surpass me."

Arvin hissed with satisfaction, but sweet as his master's admission of defeat was, there was something more Arvin wanted. His tongue flickered out of his mouth, tasting defeat in the wind.

Then power surged, coiling and furious, into the spot at the base of his skull. Arvin lashed out with it, wrapping it tightly around his master's will. But in that same instant, his master's eyes flared, emitting a bright green light as pale as a new-grown leaf. One final blast of energy crashed into Arvin, shredding his confidence like a once-proud flag frayed by the wind. A shred of his mental fabric, however, held. Control, Arvin told himself, repeating the favorite motto of his master—this human who had been foolish enough to share his secrets.

His psychic crush held.

Arvin squeezed with it—and his master crumpled. First his face, which sagged into a look of utter despair, then his shoulders and his torso. His legs buckled under him and he folded to the ground. The crystal capacitor, drained by his last, feeble attempt at defense, fell to the ground beside him, darkened, drained of energy.

Swiftly, Arvin manifested one of his favorite powers—one that locked away the victim's higher mind, leaving him paralyzed and unable to react. As the flash of silver light died away from Arvin's vision, he saw that his manifestation had been successful. From the crown of his bald head to the pink soles of his feet, his master was covered in a thin sheen of ectoplasmic slime.

As the human lay there, unable to move, Arvin strode across the garden. He bent low over his defeated opponent and tasted the sweat on the man's brow. "Surpassing you wasn't enough," he whispered in his master's ear. "But this will be."

He reared back, opening his mouth wide, and sank his teeth into the old man's throat. . . .

Arvin gasped and sat up, heart pounding, horrified by what he'd just done. He'd just killed a man. By *biting* him. And the taste of the old man's blood had been so *sweet*.

For several moments all he could do was look wildly around. Where was he? Still in the garden of his family compound?

With an effort, he shook off the dream-memory. He saw that he was inside one of the crude huts in the ancient quarry. Early-morning sunlight was streaming in through its open doorway. He stared at it for several moments before realizing that the blanket that had served as its door was gone.

Tanju! Had the psion crept away in the night?

Leaping to his feet, Arvin scrambled outside, only to nearly run into the psion as he was coming in through the doorway.

Tanju chuckled. "Eager to begin, I see. Good. Once you've relieved yourself and washed, we can start."

A short time later, Arvin sat cross-legged in the crude stone shelter, hands resting on his knees and eyes closed, in the position he'd seen his mother adopt each morning at Sunrise. He'd always assumed her morning meditations to be a form of dozing, but now he understood what she'd really been doing. The mental exercises Tanju was putting him through were every bit as strenuous as the *asanas* Zelia performed. They were not a flexing of muscle, though, but a flexing of mind.

Following Tanju's instructions, he relaxed his body, concentrating on letting his muscles loosen, starting with his forehead, his eyes, his jaw—and thus on down through his entire body. That done, he concentrated on his breathing, drawing air in through his nose, out through his mouth, in through his nose, out through his mouth....

He was supposed to be aware only of his breathing—to clear his mind of all other thoughts—but this was a much more difficult task than it sounded. Like a small child running zigzags across an open field, spiting its parents' attempts to make it stand in one place and be still, Arvin's mind kept darting this way and that. To Zelia and the mind seed—if Tanju didn't help, whatever was Arvin going to do next? To the rebels—were Gonthril and the others still alive, or had they died in the assassination attempt? To the horrible rotted-flesh *thing*, and Kayla, and the sewers, and the Pox, and the flasks shaped like snake rattles, and the—

"Maintain your focus," Tanju snapped. "Concentrate! Clear your mind of stray thoughts."

With an effort, Arvin wrenched his mind back to the current moment. He breathed in through the nose, out through the mouth, in through his nose.... Dimly, he was aware of Tanju, seated beside him in the shelter. The psion's breathing matched his own. Slowly, Arvin's mind stilled.

"Better," Tanju said. "We can begin now."

Tanju took a deep breath and began his instruction. "Before he can master a power, a psion must master his own mind," he told Arvin. "He must explore every corner, every crevice. Especially those that he would rather remain in darkness. He must seek out the desires, fears, and memories that lie in darkness and bring them out into the light, one by one. Until you can prove yourself capable of doing this, it is pointless for me to try to teach you."

Arvin nodded, determined to try.

"In order for you to attempt to gain mastery over your fears, it will be necessary for me to guide you," Tanju continued. "To do this, I must join my mind with yours."

As he realized what Tanju was asking, Arvin's breath caught. Zelia had already trampled through his mind and left her deadly seed. Did he really want another person crowding in there, too? "Is there any other way?" he asked.

"Without my guidance, what you're about to attempt could take a tenday or more to master. It's your choice."

After a few moments, Arvin realized that's just what he didn't have: a choice. This might be his only chance to learn more about psionics before.... Shrugging the thought aside, he concentrated and found the breathing pattern again. In through the nose, out through the mouth; in through the nose.... "All right," he sighed. "Do it. Join."

Suddenly, Arvin's skin felt wet. A thin, slippery

coating of ectoplasm coated his body. Then it was gone.

Good, Tanju said, his words slipping into Arvin's mind like a whisper. *Now we can begin.*

Tanju guided him, instructing Arvin to come up with a mental picture that represented his mind. Some object that Arvin could visualize—a network of roads, perhaps, or a system of streams and rivers down which his thoughts journeyed.

Arvin considered these examples and decided to visualize his thoughts like a flowing river. It proved to be a mistake. The river swiftly shifted into an image of snakes, slithering through his mind, trying to find each other so they could form a mating ball. Recognizing them as the tendrils of the mind seed, Arvin recoiled, his heart pounding.

What is it? Tanju asked.

The mind seed.

You fear it.

Yes. Arvin hesitated. *Must I . . . overcome this fear . . . before you will train me?*

Arvin felt rather than saw Tanju shake his head. *This fear is too great, and it is justified. We will choose something else, instead. But first you need to picture your mind—your mind, rather than the portion the mind seed has already claimed. Choose another image, one that has a resonance for you alone.*

Arvin, still struggling to keep his breathing even, considered. What could he picture his mind as that wouldn't trigger a sharper image from the mind seed? Then it came to him. *A net?* he ventured. His mind indeed felt like that: a series of strands of thought, knotted together by memory.

A net that Zelia was trying to unravel.

Tanju gave a mental nod. *A net. Good. Now explore that image. Send your mind ranging over the net and show me what you see.*

Arvin did as instructed. The net he visualized was made up of strands of every fiber he had ever worked with, from coarse hemp twine to silken threads woven from individual magical hairs, from leather cord to rubbery trollgut. A handful of these strands were green and scaly and writhing with life—the strands of the mind seed, gradually snaking their way into the weave. But the center of the net was still intact, still Arvin's own. The knots that held it together ranged from simple square knots to the most complicated knot he knew how to tie—the triple rose. The latter—a large, multilooped flowering of twine—was at the very center of his imaginary net, lurking like an ornate spider at the middle of its web.

That one, Tanju said, *The largest knot, the memory you've tied the tightest. Ease it open, just a little, and look inside.*

Arvin did as instructed, teasing one of the strands back ... and saw his mother's face. She was smiling at him, leaning forward to tie a leather thong around his neck—the one that held the bead he'd worn since that day. "Nine lives," she said with a wink and tousled his hair.

With the memory came an emotion—one of overwhelming grief and loss. "Mother," he moaned aloud. The strands of thought that led to this memory seemed thin, frayed, ready to snap and recoil.

Tanju gave Arvin's hand a mental squeeze, steadying him. *Go deeper,* he urged, *As deep as you can. Learn to look upon your mother's death and not be afraid.*

Arvin shuddered. *I can't,* he thought back. *Not with you watching.*

But I need to guide—

No!

Very well.

All at once, Arvin felt Tanju withdraw. Relieved, Arvin steadied his breathing and returned to his task. He could do this on his own. He could confront this fear and master it. He loosened the memory knot a little more, forcing himself to revisit the day he'd learned that his mother was dead. Arvin continued reluctantly, like a man probing with his tongue at an aching tooth.

He remembered the words his uncle had spoken when breaking the news of his mother's death—how he'd callously answered Arvin's tearful questions about whether her body would be brought back to the city for cremation. "Are you mad, boy?" his uncle had asked scornfully. "She died of plague. Her body will have to be left where it lies. Nobody would be stupid enough to touch it. Besides, you wouldn't want to see it. She died of the Mussum plague. She'll be covered in abscesses."

Arvin hadn't known what an abscess was. He'd imagined his mother's skin erupting with maggots. That night, he'd had a nightmare—of his mother's face, her eyes replaced with two fat, white, squirming things.

It had been more than a tenday before he was able to sleep without the lantern illuminated. Every time his uncle had stormed in and angrily blown it out, Arvin had lain awake in darkness, imagining "abscesses" wiggling under his own skin. He sent his mind deep into that memory, remembering how he had felt to be a small boy lying awake all night long, too terrified to touch his own skin. It was just a nightmare, he told himself. Mother didn't actually look that way when she died.

No, she would have looked far worse. According to what Arvin had learned over the years since then, the Mussum plague turned the skin green and covered it in terrible boils.

He imagined her covered in pockmarks, like the Pox.

He immediately wrenched his mind away from the image. But after a moment, he forced himself to return to it. His mother was dead—she'd been dead twenty years. By now the marks of plague would be long gone. She'd be a skeleton . . .

A skeleton lying alone and forgotten, on the plains outside Mussum. . . .

Once again, his mind recoiled. He forced it to return to the thought, to make himself acknowledge the fact that his mother was indeed a corpse. Or perhaps, not even that—her body would have been consumed by time and the elements long ago.

She is dust, he told himself.

The thought comforted him. In his mind, he held the dust that was his mother close to his heart then extended his hand and let it trickle through his fingers to be borne away by the wind. His mother was at peace.

And so, he realized with some surprise, was he.

Tanju must have heard the change in Arvin's breathing. "Well done," he said, a hint of awe in his voice. "Perhaps I will be able to teach you something, after all. Are you ready to continue?"

Arvin gave a satisfied smile. "Yes."

"Good. Then, open your eyes."

Tanju rose to his feet and gestured for Arvin to do the same. "It's unlikely that you can learn a form in so short a space of time as a single morning, but I can introduce you to the concept of psionic combat," Tanju began. "We will begin with the defenses," he said. "There are five of them, each designed to counter a specific psionic attack but still useful, to a lesser extent, against the other attack forms. It is useful to picture each as a physical posture. This gives the mind something to visualize as it manifests the defense.

"The first form is Empty Mind," Tanju continued. "It is most useful against a psychic crush. It can be visualized like this." Raising his hands, Tanju held them on either side of his face, palms toward himself. For a moment he stood utterly still, eyes closed and face turned slightly up to the sunlight that shone down on him through gaps in the ceiling above. Then his hands began to move, sweeping through the air in front of his face as if he were washing it clean.

"The empty mind leaves the opponent with nothing to grip," Tanju continued. "The mind slips through the fingers of the psychic crush like an eel sliding through the hands of a fisher."

"Or a rat slipping out of the coils of a snake," Arvin said as a memory came to him—one of Zelia's, not his own. Of coiling her thoughts around the mind of a priest who had threatened her, of squeezing his mind until it was limp. When she was finished with him, the priest had been unable to understand even the simplest of symbols for several days. The snake-headed staff that was in his hand had seemed no more than a carved piece of wood. . . .

Arvin shuddered. "Zelia knows the psychic crush attack," he told Tanju.

The psion lowered his hands. "I suspected that she would. Empty Mind is also the most useful defense against a mind thrust—the attack I used to render you helpless—and against insinuation."

"What's insinuation?" Arvin asked.

"An attack form that forces tendrils of destructive energy into the opponent's mind," Tanju answered, raising a hand and wiggling his fingers. "They worm their way in deep and sap the mind's vitality—and with it, the body's strength. If the insinuation is repeated enough times, the opponent will be debilitated to the point where he cannot lift himself off the floor, let alone mount an attack."

Tanju settled into a stance like that of a bare-handed brawler, feet firmly on the ground and hands balled into fists. "The second defense form is Shield, which can be visualized like this." He raised his left arm to forehead level, as if shielding his face from a blow and lifted his left leg, twisting it so his shin was parallel with the ground. He stood like this for a moment, perfectly balanced on one foot. Then he spun in place—whipping his body around to present the shield to imaginary opponents closing in from all sides.

"Shield is most useful against a mental lash," he told Arvin, returning to an easy standing position. "The lash cracks harmlessly against it and is unable to tear apart the energies that bind mind and body together. Without the shield, the opponent would become weak and unsteady, unable to coordinate his limbs."

Once again a memory bubbled unbidden to the surface of Arvin's mind. Zelia lashed out again and again with her mind, reveling in each strike. It was better than sinking your teeth into flesh—better because the mental lash didn't use up its venom, but could go on and on....

Arvin shuddered. "Zelia knows that attack, too."

Tanju nodded. "The third form, Fortress, is also an effective defense against a mental lash," he continued. "Visualize a tower, erected by your own will." He dropped into a wide, crouching stance and raised his hands to head level, bending his elbows at right angles. His hands were stiff, fingers tight together, palms facing inward toward his head.

After a moment, he relaxed. "The Barrier form is similar," he continued, "but circular. Like so." Leaning to the side, he lifted his left leg until it was parallel with the floor, presenting the sole of his foot to Arvin. He drew his hands in tight against his chest, palms facing outward, then suddenly spun in a circle. Returning to an easy balance, he stood on both feet again. "Think of it as a wall. An impenetrable barrier constructed from determination, and strong as stone."

Arvin nodded, trying to imagine what that would feel like. It might be a second skin, perhaps, one with the toughness of scale mail. One that could be quickly donned then shed as soon as it had—

No. He was thinking like Zelia again. He massaged his temples, trying to ignore the ache that throbbed through his mind. He hissed angrily, wishing it would just go away.

Tanju paused, a wary look on his face.

"I'm fine," Arvin reassured him, lowering his hand. "Please go on. What is the fifth form? Did you save the best defense for last?"

Tanju's lips quirked into a brief smile. "The fifth form is known as the Tower of Iron Will. It can be used not only to protect oneself, but also one's allies—providing they are standing close by."

"Show me," Arvin said.

Tanju held his right hand out in front of him, palm up and fingers curled. "The will," he pronounced, staring at it. Then he clenched his fist. Slowly, he raised it above his head, turning his face to stare up at it as his hand ascended. He extended his left hand to the side, as if reaching for the hand of a companion, then clenched it, as well. "Walled inside the tower, the will can weather the stormy blasts of the opponent's mental attack. Imagine it as a secure place, as a home."

Arvin imagined his workshop, hidden at the top of the tower in his warehouse. It had been secure, safe . . .

Until Zelia had breached it. She hadn't come in with the fury of a storm, but instead had slithered in, silent as a snake. Any psionic attack she mounted would likely be the same, sneaky—and intimate.

From the brief taste he'd just had of her memories of psionic combat, Arvin knew which attack form was Zelia's favorite. It was the one that allowed her to wrap herself around her opponents mentally and savor their agonies face to face, or rather, mind to mind.

The psychic crush.

"Empty Mind," he told Tanju. "That's the form I want to learn."

Tanju inclined his head. "An interesting choice. Let us see if you are capable of learning it."

They worked together for some time, Arvin slowly learning how to "empty" his mind and at the same time maintain his focus and awareness. Under Tanju's guidance, he began by using the motions that Tanju had, "washing" his face with his hands as he visualized himself erasing his features. Slowly, he learned to imagine replacing his face—*himself*—with vacant space, hiding his mind from sight in shifting clouds of mist. He felt himself getting closer, closer . . . and a tingling began in his throat. Suddenly the shelter was filled with a low, droning noise—the same deep, bass tone that had accompanied his manifestation of the distract power. Arvin laughed out loud, realizing he'd done it—and was surprised to hear his laughter overlapping the droning noise. Abruptly, the droning stopped.

"I did it!" Arvin exclaimed. Then he noticed the expression on Tanju's face. The psion was nodding, as if in encouragement, but there was a wary look in his eyes.

"You learn remarkably fast," Tanju said, "quicker than any pupil I've ever taught—quicker than you should. Under the guidance of the right master. . . ."

Arvin waited for Tanju to finish the thought, but instead the psion turned and picked up the trollgut rope. "That's enough for now," he said, undoing the buckles of his backpack. "I must be going. What is the rope's command word?"

Arvin frowned. "But we only just—"

Tanju stared at him, the rope in his hands. "The command word?"

The lesson was definitely over. Sighing, Arvin told him.

As Tanju tucked the coil of rope into his pack, Arvin saw a glint inside the pack—a shiny surface that reflected the sunlight. It was the three finger-length quartz crystals—one a smoky gray, one clear, and one rosy—bound together with silver wire.

"That's a crystal capacitor, isn't it?" Arvin asked, pulling the words from Zelia's memories. As he stared at it, his upper lip lifted disdainfully, baring his teeth. The human who had tutored Zelia had used one of those to augment his abilities. It had allowed him to continue manifesting psionic powers long after his own internal supply of energy was depleted. Over time, the crystal capacitor had become a crutch—one that gave the tutor a false sense of security. It had been easy, once that crutch was kicked away, to defeat him. . . .

Arvin shook his head to clear it and realized that Tanju was staring warily at him.

"My mother carried a crystal with her," Arvin said. "Until . . . recently I didn't realize what it was."

"A single crystal?" Tanju asked, buckling his pack shut.

Arvin nodded, remembering. "An amethyst."

"How large was it?"

Arvin held his hands about three palm's widths apart.

"A dorje, then," Tanju said. "And not a power stone."

"What's the difference?"

Tanju rebuckled his backpack. "A dorje is like a wizard's wand. It contains a single power, and enough psionic energy to manifest that power up to fifty times. A power stone can contain more than one power—I've heard of some with as many as six inside them. But each power can be manifested only once."

"So a dorje is more valuable," Arvin guessed.

Tanju shook his head. "A dorje can hold only low-level powers," he said. "A power stone, on the other hand, can hold powers that could normally be manifested only by a master psion. Using a power stone, however, is dangerous. If the psion makes the slightest error during the manifestation, the result can be brain burn."

Arvin nodded. Whatever brain burn was, it didn't sound healthy.

"A power stone is smaller than a dorje, then?" he asked.

"Typically, about half the length of a finger," Tanju answered, slinging his backpack over one shoulder.

Arvin thought of the lapis lazuli in his pocket, wondering if it might be a variant on a power stone. If so, perhaps it would allow him to do more than merely manifest a sending. "How do you know what powers a stone contains?"

"The psion must hail it," Tanju said. "He must send his mind deep into the stone, address it by name, and link with it. Only then will the stone give up its secrets."

"But how—"

Tanju held up a hand. "I've taught you enough for this morning," he said. "And I must go. I've already tarried here too long. Look me up again, when I get back to Hlondeth, and I'll tell you more." He paused. "Unless. . . ."

"Yes," Arvin said softly. "The mind seed."

"Tymora's luck to you," Tanju said. "I hope you find a cleric who can help."

26 Kythorn, Highsun

Arvin stood and watched the psion and the militia-man trudge up the road, wondering if he'd see Tanju again. The pilgrims had departed from the quarry at dawn; Arvin would be the last to leave the crude stone huts baking under the intense, midday sun. Stepping back inside the hut in which he'd spent the night, Arvin touched a hand to his breast pocket, reassuring himself that the lapis lazuli was still there. He'd already decided what he'd do next. He would use it to send a message to Nicco, to ask the cleric if he did indeed know the restorative prayer that Tanju had mentioned. But first Arvin wanted to try something. If the lapis lazuli really was a power stone, perhaps it might hold other, even more useful powers.

Arvin pulled the lapis lazuli out of his pocket and stared at it, trying to penetrate its gold-flecked surface. Meanwhile, the morning grew hotter. Arvin hooked a finger under the collar of his shirt, fanning himself with it. For just an instant, his mind brushed against something cool and smooth—and multifaceted, like a crystal. But though he tried for some time to connect with it, he was unable to get beyond this point. Eventually, thirst—and the knowledge that time was sliding past—made him put an end to the experiment.

He touched the lapis lazuli to his forehead. *Atmiya*, he thought, and felt it adhere. Then he imagined Nicco's face. It took even less time to contact the cleric than it had to contact Naulg or Tanju—within heartbeats, Arvin felt a tingle of psionic energy at the base of his scalp as his visualization of Nicco solidified. Arvin was surprised to see the cleric's face twisted in a mixture of grief and barely controlled rage. Nicco was staring at something Arvin couldn't see. Whatever it was, it didn't seem to be an opportune time for Arvin to be asking a favor. Quickly, he amended the message he'd been about to send.

Nicco, it's Arvin. I'm a day's journey from Hlondeth. I need to meet with you—tonight. Where will you be at Sunset? And . . . what's wrong?

Nicco startled. A moment later, however, his reply came back—terse and angry. *You want to meet? Then be at the execution pits at Sunset—if you dare.*

Abruptly, the connection was broken.

"*Atmiya,*" Arvin whispered. The lapis lazuli fell into his palm.

The execution pits? Arvin shuddered. That was what Nicco had been staring at with such a look of grief and loathing on his face. Someone was being publicly executed—and Arvin could guess who.

CHAPTER 15

26 Kythorn, Fullday

Hot, footsore, and thirsty, Arvin hurried through the city. Hlondeth lay under a muggy torpor; the storm clouds that were gathering over the Reach had yet to break. The public fountains he passed tempted him with their cool, splashing water, but he passed them by, wary of drinking from them. Instead he wiped the sweat from his brow and trudged on.

Though Arvin had returned to the city as quickly as he could, it was almost Sunset. But before he met Nicco, there were two stops Arvin had to make. The first was the bakery up the street from his warehouse.

As he drew near the warehouse, he noticed a half-dozen militia standing guard outside. At first, he thought they were looking for him—then he saw the yellow hand painted on the door. Someone had finally reported the stench of the dead cultist. A crowd of people stood across the street from the warehouse, murmuring fearfully to each other in low voices. From inside the building came the sound of a chanted prayer. Arvin found himself making an undulating motion with his right hand—the sign of Sseth. He jerked his hand back and thrust it in his pocket.

He circled around the block to the bakery. Kolim stood on the sidewalk, crumbling a stale loaf of bread for a cluster of tiny brown birds at his feet. They took flight as Arvin approached. The boy looked up, and a wary expression came over his face. He tossed the bread aside and backed up a pace.

"Hi, Kolim," Arvin said, halting a short distance from the boy. "What's wrong?"

"They found a dead guy in your warehouse."

"Really?" Arvin asked, rubbing his aching forehead.

"They say he died of plague."

Arvin looked suitably grim and glanced up the street. "That's bad. That means I can't go back to my warehouse. I wonder what he was doing in there." His breath caught as the militia turned in his direction. When they glanced away again, he hissed in relief.

Kolim stared up at him. "Why are you breathing funny?"

"It's nothing," Arvin hissed angrily. Then, seeing Kolim flinch, he hurriedly added, "I'm fine, Kolim, really. I'm just having trouble catching my breath. I've been walking all day. I'm hot and tired—and I'm sorry I snapped at you."

Kolim nodded, uncertain. "There's a cleric inside your warehouse," he continued. "They say everything in it has got to be burned."

Arvin nodded. He'd expected that. Fortunately he had cached his valuables well away from the warehouse—one of them, at this bakery. "Kolim, remember the 'monkey fist' I asked you to keep for me?"

Kolim nodded.

"I need it. Can you go and—"

"Kolim!" a shrill voice cried from within the bakery. "Get inside this instant!"

Kolim's mother, a dark-haired woman with a chin as sharp as a knife blade, stepped out of the bakery and grabbed Kolim by the ear, yanking him inside. Then she rounded on Arvin. "How dare you come here? Get away from my son." She glanced up the street and waved, trying to catch the eye of the militia.

Arvin took a step forward, wetting his lips. "I knew nothing about the dead man until just now, when Kolim told me about him," he said, holding up his hands. "I haven't been inside my warehouse in days. There's no danger of—"

Kolim's mother didn't wait to hear the rest. Abruptly stepping back inside the bakery, she slammed the door shut. A moment later, however, Arvin heard a noise from one of the windows above as a shutter opened. Kolim leaned out of the window, waved, and dropped a ball-shaped knot attached to a short length of twine. Arvin caught the monkey's fist and signed his thanks to Kolim in finger speech.

Easy going, Kolim signed back. The sound of his mother's harangue came from somewhere behind the boy, and Kolim ducked back inside.

Arvin hefted the monkey's fist. It looked identical to a nonmagical monkey's fist—a round knot, trailing a short length of line, used to weight the end of a ship's heaving line. But instead of having a lead ball at its center, this monkey's fist contained a surprise—a compressed ball of powder taken from the gland of a gloomwing. To release it, the correct command word had to be spoken as the monkey's fist was thrown. When it landed, the knot would immediately unravel, releasing the gloomwing's powerful scent.

Arvin tucked the monkey's fist into his pocket and glanced up at the sun, which was slowly sinking behind Hlondeth's towers. There was one more stop he had to make before meeting Nicco. Fortunately, Lorin's workshop was on the way to the execution pits. He hurried in that direction.

As he approached the locksmith's workshop, he heard the sound of a file rasping against metal. Entering the shop, he found Lorin hunched over a bench, filing the pin mechanism of a brass padlock. The locksmith was a tall, skinny man with a wide forehead from which his short dark hair was combed straight back. The hair was tarred flat against his scalp, like that of a sailor, to keep it out of his eyes. Faded chevrons marked Lorin's left forearm; he'd done his time in the militia years ago, serving as a guard in Hlondeth's prisons. Rumor had it that he'd been working for the Guild even then, slipping lockpicks to prisoners the Guild wanted freed.

Lorin looked up as Arvin entered the workshop. He immediately set the file aside and rose, but held up a warning hand as Arvin strode forward. "Stop right there," he said. "I heard about your warehouse. I'd rather not take any chances."

Arvin halted. "Word travels fast. Did you have a chance to look at the key?"

"Yes."

"And?" Arvin pulled ten gold pieces from his pocket and set them on the end of the workbench. Lorin made no move to pick them up.

"It was very interesting ... but I don't appreciate objects tainted with plague being brought to my workshop."

Arvin placed ten more gold pieces on the bench. "Interesting in what way?"

"When I tossed it into the fire to cleanse the plague from it, an inscription appeared on the key." He folded his arms across his chest and eyed the coins Arvin had set out, waiting.

"I didn't know you could read," Arvin said.

"I can't. But there's those in the Guild who can. And their services cost. The lorekeeper I consulted was equally as expensive."

Arvin pulled his last eight gold pieces from his pocket and placed them with the others. "That's all the coin I have—aside from three silver pieces."

"It'll do," Lorin said. "With a consideration: a discount on the next thief catcher I buy from you of fifty gold pieces."

Arvin hissed in frustration. "That's an expensive rope," he protested. "Cave fisher filament isn't easy to come by—or to work with—and I go through at least a gallon of brandy stripping the stickiness from the ends. Then there's the spell that has to be cast on the middle third of the rope, to hide the sticky residue...."

"Do you want to know what the inscription on the key said, or not?" Lorin asked.

Arvin sighed. "You'll get your discount. But with my warehouse currently being ... cleansed I'm not sure when I'll be back in business."

Lorin waved the protest aside. "You'll manage." Left unspoken was an implied threat. If Arvin didn't supply a thief catcher in a reasonable amount of time, something unpleasant would happen. The Guild took a dim view of tardy deliveries.

Lorin turned and picked up a wooden tray that was slotted into several compartments, each holding a key. He pulled out the key Arvin had found in the cultist's pocket and laid it on the workbench then wiped soot from his fingers. "What's interesting is that you found this in the pocket of someone who died of plague," he began. "The inscription on it reads 'Keepers of the Flame.' That's a religious order—one that was active during the plague of '17."

"What god did they worship?" Arvin asked, certain the answer would be Talona.

Lorin laughed. "What god didn't they worship? They were clerics of Chauntea, of Ilmater, of Helm, even of Talos...."

"So the key would have belonged to one of those clerics?"

Lorin nodded. "One of the duties the Keepers of the Flame were charged with was collecting and disposing of the corpses of those who died in the plague. They set up crematoriums all over the Reach."

Arvin smiled grimly. It all fit. The cultists were attracted to places associated with disease—their use of the slaughterhouse and sewers were prime examples. Naulg had said he was in a building with burning walls, and the cultist had bragged about Talona's faithful "rising from the ashes"—a boast he'd meant literally. No wonder he'd been smug. A crematorium, intended to put a stop to one plague, would serve as the starting point for another.

"Was one of those crematoriums in Hlondeth?" Arvin asked.

"Yes—and anyone who was living in the city in '17 can tell you where it is. But that key is probably for a crematorium in another city. The one in Hlondeth had walls of solid stone, without a door or window anywhere in them."

"Why would they build it like that?"

Lorin shook his head. "Nobody knows for sure, but the loremaster I consulted heard that the building contained a gate that opened onto the Plane of Fire. I suppose the clerics didn't want anyone messing with that."

"How did the clerics get inside?"

"They teleported—together with the corpses they were going to burn." He snapped his fingers. "Just like that. It eliminated the problem of having to haul bodies through the city in carts—and spreading the disease."

Arvin frowned at the key. The Hlondeth crematorium must have had a door—possibly one cloaked in illusion. That no one had sought this door in fifty-six years was no surprise. Only a madman would want to break into a building in which plague victims had been housed, however briefly.

A madman—or someone with a mind seed in his head.

Lorin nodded at the key. "If I were you, I wouldn't use it."

Arvin picked up the key and slipped it into his pocket. "Don't worry," he told Lorin. "If I do enter the crematorium, I'll be sure to take a cleric along."

26 Kythorn, Sunset

The Plaza of Justice was a wide, cobblestoned expanse, large enough to accommodate several thousand people and encircled by a viaduct supported by serpent-shaped columns. From his vantage point on a rooftop just above the viaduct, Arvin could see down into the execution pits—two circular holes, each as wide as a large building. Inside each pit was an enormous serpent, its body so thick that a man would barely be able to encircle it with his arms. One was an adder, its venomous fangs capable of imparting a swift death. To this serpent were thrown the condemned deemed worthy of "mercy." The other was a yellowish green constrictor, which squeezed the life out of its victims slowly. On rare occasions, it would skip this step and swallow its victims while they were still alive and thrashing.

Arching over each of the pits was a short stone ramp. Up these, the condemned were forced to march. Their final step was off the end of the ramp and into the pit below.

Both of the snakes had eaten recently. Arvin counted one bulge inside the adder, three inside the constrictor. He shuddered, wondering which of the rebels they were. Only one of the rebels had been shown "mercy," which made Arvin's choice easier. Nicco would show no mercy, either. He'd choose the punishment the majority of the Secession's raiders had suffered.

Slaves were still sweeping up the litter dropped by the crowd who had come to watch this morning's executions. The yuan-ti spectators were long gone from the viaduct that encircled the plaza, but a couple of dozen humans still lingered below—those who had been mesmerized by the serpents. They stood, staring into the pits and swaying slightly, as mindless as grass blown by a malodorous wind. The slaves swept around them.

One man stood, alone and rigid as an oak, at the western edge of the plaza. Nicco. He stared at the pits, scowling, arms folded across his chest. His shadow was a long column of black that slowly crept toward the pits as the sun sank. So unmoving and determined did he appear that Arvin wondered for a moment if Nicco had stood there since morning, plotting divine vengeance against the executioners.

And against Arvin.

Arvin waited, watching the cleric. Nicco finally turned and glanced at the setting sun, as if gauging the time of day, then stared out toward the Reach and the clouds that were building there. While he was thus occupied, Arvin rose to his knees and whirled the monkey's fist in a tight circle over his head. He spoke its command word as he let it fly—and hissed in satisfaction as it landed inside the constrictor's pit. The enormous snake didn't react to the sudden movement. Eating three condemned people in a single day must have sated it.

As Nicco returned his attention to the pits, Arvin climbed down onto the viaduct. He strode around it to the spot where Nicco stood. Only when he was directly above the cleric did Nicco look up. Nicco squinted and raised a gloved hand to shield his eyes from the sun; Arvin had the sun behind his back and would be no more than a silhouette. Then Nicco pointed an accusing finger. "Four people died this morning," he rumbled in a voice as low and threatening as thunder. "Their blood is on your lips. You betrayed them."

Arvin shook his head in protest. "I didn't say anything that—"

"You must have! How else do you explain the yuan-ti who surprised them just outside Osran's door—a yuan-ti with powers far beyond those normally manifested by her race—a psion. Deny that you serve her, if you dare!"

"I don't serve her. Not willingly. She—"

Nicco jerked his hand. A bolt of lightning erupted from his fingertip. It blasted into the viaduct at Arvin's feet, sending splinters of stone flying into the air. Several of them stung Arvin's legs. The edge of the viaduct abruptly crumbled and Arvin found himself falling. He managed to land on his feet and immediately let his knees buckle to turn the landing into a roll, but scraped his ungloved hand badly in the process. Blood began to seep from it as he stood, and from the numerous nicks in his legs that had been caused by the flying stone.

As the startled slaves fled the plaza—together with those spectators whose trances had been broken by the thunderclap—Arvin turned to face Nicco. Arvin was careful not to make any threatening moves. The cleric was angry enough already.

But at least he was still talking. All Arvin had to do was get him to listen—and to believe him.

"I didn't tell the yuan-ti psion anything," Arvin protested. "If I had, your geas would have killed me. She reached into my mind—she *violated* it—and plucked out Osran's name."

"You gave it to her willingly," Nicco accused. "That's why you fled the city. You feared Hoar's wrath."

"Then why would I have come back? Why would I seek you out? I needed help—I left the city to find it. But the person who tried to negate what Zelia had done to me wasn't able to—"

"Zelia." Nicco's eyes narrowed. "So that's the name of your master."

Arvin opened his mouth to explain further, but in that same moment Nicco barked out a quick prayer. "Walk," he commanded, the lightning bolts in his earring tinkling as he thrust out a hand, pointing at the execution pits.

Arvin felt the compulsion of the prayer grip him—and found himself turning smartly on his heel. Like a puppet, he marched toward the pits, guided by Nicco's pointing finger as the cleric strode along behind him. Arvin had an anxious moment when they passed the pit with the adder. He hissed with relief as Nicco directed him to the constrictor's pit, instead.

"Halt," Nicco ordered.

Arvin did. Stealing a glance down, he saw a strand of cord peeking out from under the serpent's body—the unraveled monkey's fist. A faint, powder-sweet odor rose from the pit, just detectable over the stink of the snake—the last of the gloomwing scent. Arvin took care not to inhale too deeply.

Nicco stared at him from the edge of the pit. "Any last words, condemned man?"

"Just this," Arvin answered. "If I'm guilty, then may Hoar punish me by allowing the serpent to crush and consume me. If I'm innocent, may Hoar let me survive unharmed."

"So be it," Nicco said. Then he gave a third command: "Walk."

Arvin did, not even bothering to try to fight the compulsion. He fell onto the serpent's back and tumbled to the floor of the pit. The constrictor had been placid about the monkey's fist landing beside it earlier, but at the touch of a large, living creature, it immediately responded. It whipped a coil around Arvin's upper chest and flexed, driving the air from Arvin's lungs. Another coil immediately fastened around Arvin's legs.

For one terrible moment, Arvin thought he had miscalculated. As the serpent squeezed, his vision went gray and stars began to swim before his eyes. . . .

Then he felt its coils loosening. The one around his legs slackened and fell away, followed by the one around his chest. Gasping his relief, Arvin staggered away from the constrictor. The gloomwing scent had done its work. The serpent had just expended what remained of its strength.

From above, he heard a sharp intake of breath. Glancing up, he saw Nicco staring down at him, a troubled expression on his face. "It seems that I accused you unjustly," he said. He reached down into the pit. "Take my hand. Climb."

Arvin did.

From the east side of the plaza came the sound of running footsteps. Looking in that direction, Arvin saw a dozen militia hurrying down one of the side streets toward the plaza. From one of them came a shout: "There he is!"

Arvin thought it was Nicco they were pointing at; then he realized it was him.

Nicco began murmuring a prayer that Arvin had heard once before and recognized. It was the one that would teleport him away. Realizing he was being left behind, Arvin spoke quickly. "I know where the Pox are hiding!" he cried. "Take me with you!"

A weighted line, fired from a crossbow, whizzed overhead.

Nicco smiled. "What makes you think I was going to leave you here?" Then he touched Arvin's shoulder. Arvin felt himself wrenched through the dimensions by a teleportation spell. The Plaza of Justice—and the militia who were raising their crossbows—all disappeared from sight.

26 Kythorn, Evening

Arvin and Nicco stood together in the alley the cleric had teleported them to, talking in low voices. A few paces away, the alley opened onto the courtyard of the Nesting Tower, an enormous pillar honeycombed with niches in which flying serpents made their nests. Every now and then, their dark shapes flitted across the moonlit sky toward the faintly glowing tower.

"Zelia's not my master," Arvin explained to Nicco. "I met her for the first time four nights ago. She negated the poison the Pox made me drink and tried to hire me to spy on them. She needed a human who would pretend to join their cult—someone who had survived one of their sacrifices. When I refused, she told me I was going to wind up working for her, like it or not. She'd planted a mind seed in my head."

Nicco's eyebrows rose.

"It's a psionic power," Arvin said. "In seven days, it—"

"I know what a mind seed is," Nicco answered.

Hope surged through Arvin. "Do you know the restorative prayer that will get rid of it?"

Instead of answering, Nicco stared into the distance. "Whether you meant to betray them or not, four members of the Secession are dead: Kiffen, Thrond, Nyls . . . and Kayla."

"Kayla?" Seeing the ache in Nicco's eyes, Arvin dropped his voice to a sympathetic murmur. "But she was so young. . . ."

"She died swiftly—and bravely. Her father would have been proud of her. Ironically, by now he will have turned into the very thing he fought against—one of the foul creatures who condemned his daughter to die—a yuan-ti."

"Kayla's father was among those handed over to Osran Extaminos by the Pox?" Arvin asked.

Nicco nodded sadly. "Kayla hoped to save him. In that endeavor, she failed. But she did succeed in exacting Hoar's retribution for what was done to her father. It was she who dispatched Osran with her knife."

"Osran's dead, then?" Arvin asked.

"Gonthril saw him die."

Arvin wet his lips nervously as Nicco continued his story. Zelia had surprised the assassins as they were preparing to leave Osran's chambers. Only Gonthril, thanks to one of his magical rings, had been able to escape. Hearing this, Arvin realized that Zelia had arrived too late to question Osran. She wouldn't have been able to learn if additional yuan-ti were involved with the cultists. Without this information, she wasn't going to remove the mind seed from Arvin's head any time soon . . .

If she had ever planned to at all.

Nicco stared at Arvin, his face dimly illuminated by the glow from the wall beside him. "You said you knew where Talona's clerics were hiding."

Arvin reached into his pocket with his left hand, at the same time whispering his glove's command word, and felt the key appear between his fingers. "Not only do I know what building they're in," he told Nicco, pulling his hand from his pocket. "I have a key that will get us inside." He held it up where Nicco could see it. "So what do you say? Is a chance at vengeance against the Pox worth a restorative prayer?" He held his breath, waiting for Nicco's answer.

Nicco stood in silence for several moments before answering. "It is . . ."

Arvin let out a hiss of relief. Nicco was going to save him, after all.

" . . . if that key leads where you say it does," Nicco concluded. "Shall we find out?"

"Now?"

Nicco scowled. "Have you given up on rescuing your friend?"

Arvin shook his head. "Not at all. I just thought that maybe you could say the restorative prayer first."

Nicco shook his head. "After," he said firmly.

Arvin hissed in frustration, but managed to hold his temper. At least the solution to his problem was in sight. He and Nicco would sneak into the crematorium, make certain the Pox were indeed there, and sneak out again. Then Nicco would remove the mind seed and Arvin could go on his way, leaving it up to the Secession to deal with the cultists.

Arvin reached for the bead at his throat for reassurance. "Nine—," He stopped abruptly as his fingertips brushed the bead. The clay he'd used to repair the crack was crumbling, falling out. The bead felt as if it was ready to break in two. Was it an omen that he'd used up the last of its luck?

He didn't want to think about that just then. Not when every moment that passed brought him closer to his doom. The throbbing ache of the mind seed was slowly, inexorably spreading throughout his head. The sooner they explored the crematorium, the better.

"Let's go," he told Nicco.

CHAPTER 16

26 Kythorn, Middark

Arvin and Nicco stood in a doorway across the
street from the crematorium, staring at what
appeared to be a blank stone wall. Earlier,
Nicco had whispered a prayer, one that allowed
him to see through the illusion that had been
placed on the building. He'd assured Arvin that
there was, indeed, a door—one with a lock. But
instead of trying the key in it right away, Nicco
had insisted upon waiting. And so they had
stood, and waited, and watched, hoping to see
one of the cultists enter or leave the building.

None had.

Nor had anyone walked down the street.
And no wonder—all of the buildings in the
area, including the one behind Arvin and
Nicco, bore a faded yellow hand on their
doors.

Arvin was getting impatient. The throbbing in his head wasn't helping. "This is useless," he griped. "We've got the key; let's use it."

Nicco nodded. "It looks as though we'll have to. But first, a precaution."

The cleric began a soft chant. When it ended, he vanished from sight. The only way Arvin could tell that Nicco was still standing beside him was by the sound of his breathing and the rustle of Nicco's kilt as the cleric shifted position.

"Your turn," Nicco said. "Ready?"

When Arvin nodded, Nicco repeated his prayer. Arvin felt a light touch on his shoulder—and suddenly couldn't see his body. It was an odd sensation. Being unable to see his own feet made Arvin feel as if he were floating in the air. He touched a hand to his chest, reassuring himself he was still corporeal.

"Is the key in your hand?" Nicco asked.

Arvin held it up. "Right here."

Instead of taking it, Nicco grasped Arvin's arm and steered him across the street. When they reached the crematorium, Nicco guided the jagged-toothed key up to what, to Arvin, appeared to be solid stone, and Arvin felt the key enter a keyhole. Nicco let go of his arm. The cleric was obviously wary about whatever traps might protect the door. Wetting his lips, Arvin turned the key in the lock and heard a faint click. With a hiss of relief—the poisoned needle he'd half-expected to emerge from the lock mechanism hadn't—he eased the door open. Then, pocketing the key, he whispered the command that materialized the dagger from his glove.

"You first, this time," he told Nicco. He waited until he had felt Nicco brush past him then closed the door behind them.

They stood in a round, empty room as large as the building itself. At its center was a circular platform, about ankle high. Around its circumference were dozens of tiny, finger-sized flames that filled the room with a flickering light. They burned with a faint hissing noise and seemed to be jetting out of holes in the platform.

Arvin hadn't known what to expect a crematorium to look like, but this certainly wasn't it.

Beside him, Nicco murmured the prayer that would allow him to see things as they truly were.

"Is there a way out of this room?" Arvin breathed.

The tinkling of Nicco's earring told Arvin the cleric was shaking his head. "My prayer would have revealed any hidden doors. It found none," he whispered. "I'm going to search the platform."

"Be careful," Arvin warned. "It might teleport you to the Plane of Fire."

"That would require a teleportation circle— something only a wizard can create," Nicco answered, his voice moving toward the platform. "We clerics must rely upon phase doors, which merely open an ethereal passage through stone."

Arvin saw the flames flicker as the cleric walked around the platform. "Are you certain the cultists use this place?" Nicco asked.

Arvin was starting to wonder the same thing. He fingered the key in his pocket. Then his eye fell on something—a small leather pouch that lay on the other side of the platform. He strode over to it and picked it up, and felt something inside it twitch. He raised the now-invisible pouch to his nose and caught a faint leafy smell he recognized at once—assassin vine.

"Nicco," he whispered. "The Pox were here—or at least, they kept their victims here. I've just found my friend's pouch."

There was no reply.

"Nicco?"

Worried that the cleric might have stepped onto the platform and been teleported away, Arvin tucked the pouch in a pocket and crossed the room. He stood beside the platform, listening, and heard what sounded like snoring over the hiss of the flames. It seemed to be coming from the center of the platform.

Wary of the flames, Arvin leaned across the platform. His hand brushed against tassels—one end of Nicco's sash. The cleric must have fallen victim to a spell that sent him into a magical slumber. Arvin grabbed the sash and tried to pull Nicco toward him, but when he yanked, the sash suddenly came free, sending him stumbling backward. Dropping it, Arvin made a circuit of the platform. He leaned over it as much as he dared, but his questing hands encountered only air. He could hear Nicco snoring but couldn't reach him. The platform was simply too wide. Nicco must be lying directly at its center.

Arvin paused, thinking. Whatever laid Nicco low hadn't taken effect immediately. Maybe if Arvin didn't venture too close to the center of the platform, he'd be safe. He couldn't just let the cleric lie there. If he did, Nicco might never wake up.

Arvin stepped up onto the platform.

As soon as he did, he felt a rush of vertigo. It was as if someone had grabbed hold of his trousers at the hip and yanked, sending him tumbling forward. Too late, he realized what had happened. The key in his trouser pocket must have triggered something—one of the phase doors that Nicco had spoken about. Like an anchor chained to Arvin, the key pulled him down into a patch of blurry, queasy nothingness.

Arvin landed facedown on a hard stone floor, knocking the air from his lungs. He felt a throbbing in his lip and tasted blood; his lip was split. Hissing with pain, he sat up and looked around and found that he was in utter darkness. He wet his lips and found them coated with a damp, gritty substance that tasted of ashes.

The remains of the cremated dead.

He spat several times, not stopping until his mouth was clean. Then he rose to his feet. Somewhere in the distance, he could hear a faint chanting—the voices of the cultists, raised in prayer to their loathsome god. As his eyes adjusted to the darkness, he saw, in the direction the chanting was coming from, a patch of faint reddish light, rectangular in shape—a hallway. As he stared at it, something small scurried across the floor nearby, making him hiss in alarm.

It's just a rat, he admonished himself angrily, embarrassed at having startled. Where's your self-control?

He raised a hand and found that the ceiling was just overhead. Its stonework felt solid. He tried prodding it with the key, but nothing happened. Whatever doorway Arvin had just passed through appeared to work only in one direction.

Somewhere above, Nicco lay in magical slumber. The cleric might as well have been in another city, for all the good he was going to be.

Arvin worked his way around the room, feeling the walls. He didn't find any other exits; there was only one way out.

Toward the chanting voices.

He shuddered at the thought of facing the cultists alone and raised a hand to touch the bead at his throat. "Nine—"

The bead wasn't there.

Hissing in alarm, Arvin dropped to his knees and scuffed around in the ash. Dust rose to his nostrils and he choked back a sneeze. Then he spotted something near the middle of the room—a faint blue glow. Brushing the ash away from it, he saw that it was coming from his bead. It was no longer smooth and round; fully half of the clay had crumbled away and something was protruding out of it—a slim length of crystal that glowed with a faint blue light.

A power stone.

Suddenly, his mother's last goodbye made sense. "Don't lose this bead," she'd told him as she tied the thong around his neck. "I made it myself. I had intended to give it to you when you're older but...." She paused, eyes glistening, then stood. "One day, that bead may grant you nine lives, just like a cat. Remember that—and keep it safe. Don't ever take it off."

"Nine lives," Arvin repeated in an anguished whisper as he stared at the power stone. "And you gave them to me. Why didn't you use them to save yourself instead?" He knew the answer, of course. That his mother must have foreseen her death in the dream she had the night before—and, contrary to her assurances, believed it to be inevitable.

A tear trickled, unheeded, down Arvin's cheek.

Grasping what remained of the bead in both hands, he crumbled it apart. The crystal came away clean, unmarred by its years inside the bead. Holding it between his thumb and finger, he peered into its depths. The faint blue light inside it was the color of the summer sky and seemed equally as limitless. His mother had created this power stone. Somewhere, deep inside it, was a tiny piece of her soul. It whispered to Arvin in a voice just at the edge of hearing, as if calling his name. Allowing his mind to fall into the cool blue depths of the stone, he tried to answer.

Mother?

There was no reply—just a soft sighing, as impossible to grasp as the wind.

Staring at the power stone, Arvin drifted in that vast expanse of blue, no longer aware of his physical surroundings. What was it that Tanju had said? In order to hail a power stone, one had to know the proper name to use. If a stranger had created the stone, Arvin might guess for a thousand years and never come up with the right name. But it wasn't just anyone who had crafted this power stone. It was Arvin's mother.

This time, he used his mother's name: *Sassan?*

Still nothing, just an empty sighing.

Arvin drifted, trying to think what his mother might have named the stone. It would almost certainly be a name Arvin was familiar with—one his mother knew he would eventually guess. She wouldn't have given him the power stone if there were no hope of him ever using it.

He tried again, using the name of the lamasery: *Shou-zin?*

Nothing.

He thought back, again, to his mother's final words to him, wondering if they might have held a clue. But she hadn't said anything, really, after the cryptic message about the bead granting "nine lives." She'd simply given him one of her brief, formal hugs then turned to go, stopping only to shoo the cat away from the door so she could open it.

Suddenly Arvin realized the answer.

Cinders? Arvin tried, using the childish name he'd given the stray cat that had taken up residence with them, despite his mother's protests.

Who hails me?

The voice that answered sounded female—and slightly feline. It was braided together from several different voices, each with a different timbre and pitch. Though they all spoke at once, Arvin knew instantly how many they were—six. The maximum number of powers a power stone could hold.

Arvin hails you, he answered. *Show yourselves.*

Six twinkling stars suddenly appeared in the pale blue sky. They hung like ripe gems just waiting to be plucked, each burning with a light either bright or faint according to the amount of energy that fueled it. Arvin brushed his mental fingers against the closest of these stars—a medium-bright mote of light—drinking in the knowledge of the power it contained. By manifesting this power, he would be able to teleport, just as Nicco did, to any destination he could clearly visualize—the chamber above, for example.

Laughing, he touched another of the motes of light, its glow approximately equal to the first. This second power also conveyed the ability to teleport but was intended for use on another person or creature, rather than on the manifester himself. Strange, Arvin thought, that his mother had included a power that would only affect others. The ability to teleport someone else wasn't exactly a life-saving power. Giving a mental shrug, he moved on to the next.

He touched another of the gemlike stars and discovered it to be a power that would allow him to dominate another person, forcing him to do whatever he bid. He gave a mental hiss of satisfaction—then realized that was the mind seed, reacting to the extremes to which this power could be put. Even so, a part of him savored the idea of using it on Zelia. With it, he could force her to obey his—

Wrenching his thoughts off that path, he shifted his awareness to the next power, which had the brightest glow of any of them. It was also an offensive power, designed for use against other psions. By manifesting it, Arvin could strip a single power from another psion's mind. Permanently.

The fifth power would allow Arvin to produce, from one or both hands, sweat even more acidic than a yuanti's. It was a useful weapon—and one that would have the element of complete surprise.

The sixth and final power was an odd one: it would allow him to plant a false memory in someone's mind—

but that "memory" could be only a few moments long. What good was that, he wondered. Surely, in order to be convincing, the false memory would have to span a period of days, or even tendays.

It was a strange mix of powers to have chosen. Arvin shrugged, wondering what his mother had been thinking. Perhaps she had been shown, in one of her visions, what Arvin would one day find useful. The teleport power, for example, was just what he needed at the moment. He'd use it to teleport to a spot *beside* the platform where Nicco lay then use the cleric's sash to drag Nicco from the platform. He hoped Nicco would then wake up, and Arvin wouldn't have to face the cultists alone.

Visualizing the chamber above, Arvin grasped the mote of light with his mind. He felt its energy rush into the third eye at the center of his forehead, filling his vision with bright sparkles of silver light. It started to paint the scene he held in his mind, limning it in silver, making it more solid and real. . . .

Then the motes of silver light came rushing back at Arvin, slamming into his mind. Pain exploded throughout his head then arced through the rest of his body, at last erupting out of his fingers and feet. The part of Arvin's mind still capable of coherent thought noted the power crystal slipping from numbed fingers, his legs buckling. Arvin's mind felt hot and ready to burst, like a melon left too long in the sun.

Brain burn.

Slowly, he sat up and shook his head then stared at the power stone that lay, glowing, in the ashes. He felt weak, shaky. He wasn't going to try *that* again any time soon.

Picking up the stone, he thrust it into his trouser pocket. Then he stood and contemplated his options. There was only one way out toward the chanting voices.

Moving quietly, he crept down the hallway. It was arrow-straight, with a ceiling that was square, instead of curved—built by humans, rather than yuan-ti. It led to a heavy metal door with a palm-sized sliding panel, set at about eye level. The panel was open. Through it came a flickering red light—and the chanting.

After first making sure he was still invisible, Arvin tiptoed up to the door and peeked through the opening. In the room beyond the door were nearly two dozen people—men and women, judging by the blend of voices, though most had faces so heavily pockmarked it was difficult to recognize which were which. All wore the same shapeless, grayish green robes—and all stank of old, sour sweat. They stood in a loose circle around the wooden statue of Talona that stood, buried to its ankles, in the ashes and crumbled bone that covered the floor. Kneeling next to the statue was a naked man with unblemished skin, save for the chevrons on his arm. His arms were outstretched as if he were about to embrace the pitted stump of wood. For a moment, Arvin thought he must be captive—then he discarded this idea. The man was chanting along with the rest.

Glancing up, Arvin saw a dozen fist-sized balls of flame hovering just below the ceiling, next to the walls. They must have been magical, since there were no visible torches or lamps supplying them with fuel. They burned with a dull, red light, as if close to being extinguished. Something was climbing the wall directly beneath one of them—a rat with ash-gray fur and glowing orange eyes. It paused just below one ball of flame and thrust its head inside it. Withdrawing its head a moment later, it scurried down the wall and disappeared into the ash that covered the floor.

Arvin dropped his gaze back down to the cultists. They blocked his view of the far wall, but by leaning to the left and right, he was able to see the side walls.

The one to the right had a door. Like the one he was peering through, it was made of thick metal, with a small panel in it at eye level. The inner surface of the door was blackened, as if by fire.

It seemed to be the only way out.

It would be suicide, however, to make a move at this point—even invisible, Arvin couldn't hope to sneak past the cultists. The instant he opened the door, they'd be alerted to the presence of an intruder. All he could do was wait and hope that they would finish their ritual and exit through the second door.

One of the cultists stepped into the center of the circle. He was a large man with hair that grew only in patches. Arvin hissed in anger as he recognized him as the cultist who had forced him to drink the poisoned potion. As the man reached for a pouch on his belt and began untying its fastenings, Arvin held his breath, expecting to see one of the potion flasks. Instead the fellow pulled out two miniature silver daggers, each about the length of a finger and nearly black with tarnish. The tiny weapons were a type of dagger known to rogues as a "snaketooth." Their hollow stiletto blades usually held poison.

Was this some new kind of sacrifice? As the patch-haired cultist raised the daggers above his head—one in either fist—over the kneeling man, Arvin tensed.

The chanting stopped. The patch-haired man's arms swept down—but instead of stabbing the kneeling man, he presented the daggers to him, hilt first.

"Embrace Talona," the patch-haired cultist droned. "Endure her. Prove yourself worthy of the all-consuming love of the Mother of Death."

The kneeling man reached up and took the daggers. "Lady of Poison, Mistress of Disease, take me, torment me, teach me." Then he stabbed the tiny daggers into his flesh. Once, twice, three times . . . over and over again, he jabbed them into his arms, chest, thighs—even into his face—leaving his body riddled with a series of tiny punctures. Meanwhile, the cultists surrounding him chanted.

"Take him . . . torment him . . . teach him. Embrace him . . . enfold him . . . endure him."

The man continued to stab himself, though with each thrust of the daggers, he was visibly weakening. Rivulets of blood ran down his chest, arms, and face, dripping onto his wounded thighs. Even as Arvin watched, the punctures puckered and turned a sickly yellow-green. Soon the blood that ran down his body was streaked with pus. At last the man dropped the daggers and fell forward into the ash. He clutched weakly at the image of Talona for a moment then his hand fell away, leaving a smear of blood on the pitted wood.

Sickened, Arvin looked away. The kneeling man had been healthy, handsome—but after this ritual, assuming he survived it, the fellow would be as disfigured as the rest of the misguided souls who served the goddess of plague. He was ruined in body, as he must have been in mind.

Arvin was glad that he'd refused Zelia's demand that he pose as an initiate. This would have been the result. This was why Zelia had sown the mind seed—no sane man would ever willingly go through the initiation rite Arvin had just witnessed. To infiltrate the Pox, what was needed was not just a human, but a human whose mind was not his own—a mere shell of a man, controlled by a yuan-ti who was as ruthless as she was determined. Or she could have used a man whose life was measured in days, desperate for a reprieve.

Rusted hinges squealed, breaking Arvin's train of thought. Peering into the room, he saw that the door in the wall to the right—which was indeed the only other exit from the room—was open. The cultists filed out through it. None so much as glanced at the man who lay trembling in the ashes beside the statue of Talona. As the last of them left, the door squealed again and grated shut.

Arvin waited, his eyes firmly on the other door. When he was certain the cultists weren't returning, he slowly eased open the door behind which he stood. Like the other, its hinges were rusted. Each time they began to squeal, Arvin paused, waited for several heartbeats, and resumed his task even more slowly than before. Eventually, the gap was wide enough for him to slip through it.

Hugging the wall, not daring to come any closer to the newly pockmarked man than he absolutely had to—those punctures were fresh, and weeping—Arvin made his way to the other door. The floor felt uneven under his feet; curious, he scuffed the ashes away and saw that it was made from a thick metal mesh. More ashes lay below this grate; he wondered how deep they went. As he stared at the floor, his legs and feet suddenly appeared. Nicco's prayer had at last worn off. The fact that he was visible again was going to make his escape more difficult—assuming the second door really did offer a way out.

As he reached for the handle of the door, he heard a voice behind him.

"You're not . . . one of them," it gasped. "Who—"

Whirling around, Arvin saw that the new convert had risen to his knees. He stared at Arvin, pressing a hand to his temple. His face was ghastly with streaks of ash, yet something about it was familiar.

"Did you bring . . . the potion?" the man asked, his eyes gleaming with hope.

Arvin had no idea what the man was talking about. As the fellow crawled toward him, he shrank against the door. "No," he answered. "And stay away from me."

The fellow sank back down into the ash, the hope in his eyes fading. "But I thought Zelia—"

"Zelia?" Arvin echoed. He stared at the fellow more closely, suddenly realizing where he'd seen him before—on the street near Zelia's tower, two nights ago. Suddenly he realized why the fellow had been holding a hand to his head.

"She did it to you, too, didn't she?" Arvin whispered. "She planted a mind seed in you."

The man nodded weakly. "Three . . . nights ago."

"Abyss take her," Arvin swore softly.

"Yes." The latter was no more than a faint sigh; the blood-streaked man was fading fast. A tremble coursed through his body and sweat beaded his forehead. Arvin stared at him, wondering what to do. If this fellow provided Zelia with the information she wanted, Arvin would become superfluous. Would Zelia remove the mind seed—or simply dispose of him? He fingered his dagger, wondering whether to use it. Would killing this man be a mercy—or a selfish act? It looked like a moot point, however. The fellow had his eyes closed and was lying prone in the ash, his body still except for the occasional tremor.

He was dying.

Of plague.

As quickly as he dared, Arvin eased the second door open. He was relieved to see only an empty hallway beyond it. The hallway ran a short distance, meeting up at a right angle with another, wider hallway.

As Arvin slipped through the door, something under the layer of ash brushed against his boot—another rat. Within heartbeats, his foot grew unbearably hot. The rat—as hot as an ember fresh out of the fire—was burning through the leather of his boot! Arvin kicked it away from him. The rat sailed down the hallway and thudded into the far wall. It shook itself, sat up—and stared at Arvin with its glowing orange eyes. Then it opened its mouth and squealed, shooting a gout of flame from its mouth that licked at Arvin's trousers, scorching them.

"By the gods," Arvin muttered. He'd never seen a creature anything like this. He whipped his dagger out of its sheath, but even as he prepared to throw, squeals immediately sounded from the room where the initiate lay. The layer of ash began to hump and move as dozens of rats scurried up through the grated floor and moved in a wave toward the door. Worried now, Arvin whirled and kicked the door. It slammed shut with a groan of rusted hinges. In that same moment, the first rat attacked. This time its gout of flame struck Arvin's chest, setting his shirt on fire. Tearing at the burning fabric with his free hand, Arvin simultaneously threw his dagger. He grunted in satisfaction as it sank into the rat's chest. The rat fell onto its side, twitched twice—then erupted into a ball of bright orange flame. An instant later, it crumbled into ash and the dagger clinked to the floor.

Summoning the hot dagger back into his hand, Arvin hurried down the corridor, slapping at the smoldering remains of his shirt. He peered quickly down the wider hallway in both directions. Behind him, the other rats scrabbled at the closed door. The wider hallway was completely dark; Arvin wished he'd thought to bring another of Drin's darkvision potions along. From the left came the sound of voices, raised in what sounded like anxious conference—no doubt the cultists, wondering what had caused the noise. From the right came only silence. Arvin hurried in that direction, his gloved hand tracing the wall, fearing that he'd tumble down an unseen flight of stairs at any moment. Behind him, he heard a door open. Clutching his dagger—and wincing as the heated metal blistered his palm and fingers—he hurried on.

The hallway turned a corner just in time to hide Arvin from the lantern light that suddenly filled the hallway behind him. The voices of the cultists grew louder. He heard one of them direct another to check on the initiate and the creak of hinges as the heavy metal door was opened. Meanwhile, the hallway Arvin was hurrying along brightened as whoever was holding the lantern drew nearer to the bend he'd just rounded. Two choices presented themselves: a flight of stairs, leading up, and a doorway in the wall to the left. Arvin immediately sprang for the stairs—then whirled and bolted down them again at the sound of footsteps rapidly descending. Hissing with fear, he rushed to the door instead. It was locked—but the key he still had in his pocket opened it. He wrenched the door open and hurried into the dimly lit room beyond. Closing the door as quickly and quietly as he could behind him, he locked it.

"Nine lives," he whispered, touching the place at his throat where the bead had hung.

He turned, trying to make out details of the room into which he'd blundered. The light was poor; the single oil lamp that hung against one wall had its wick trimmed so low that it cast only a dim red glow that left the corners in darkness. The air smelled bad—a mix of urine, sickness, and sweat. Arvin saw that, aside from the door behind him, the room had no exit. Worse yet, there was a body lying on the floor, next to the far wall. Another initiate—one who didn't survive whatever disease was in the poisoned fangs? No, this "body" was stirring.

Strike swiftly! a voice inside his mind shouted.

Arvin lifted his dagger, ready to throw it, but something made him pause. The creature that rose from its slump to stare at him was horrifying. Its eyes were sunken and bloodshot, its body misshapen and gaunt, its skin a diseased-looking yellow-green with the hair falling out in clumps . . . except for the heavy eyebrows, which met above the nose.

"Naulg?" Arvin whispered, lowering his dagger.

The creature wet its lips with a forked tongue. "Ar ... vin?" it croaked.

The voices in the hallway drew level with the door. There were two of them—a man and a woman, arguing about whether the initiate had been the one to open the door of the "chamber of ashes," then slam it shut. "Something stirred up the ash rats," the woman insisted. The man at last concurred.

"Search the upper chamber," he shouted at someone down the hall.

Hearing that, Arvin prayed that Nicco wasn't slumbering there still. He reached for his breast pocket. Perhaps the lapis lazuli would allow him to contact Nicco before—

The pocket was gone—he must have torn it away with the rest of his burning shirtfront—and so was the lapis lazuli. Arvin cursed softly as he realized the stone must be lying in the hallway where he'd killed the rat.

Another voice joined the two outside the door. "What's happened?" It was male, and sibilant, the inflection that of a yuan-ti. The voice sounded vaguely familiar, but Arvin couldn't place where he might have heard it before.

Naulg, meanwhile, shuffled across the room to Arvin, his arms wrapped tightly around his stomach, his eyes glazed. "It hurts," he groaned, letting go of his stomach to pluck imploringly at Arvin's sleeve. His fingernails were long and yellow, almost claws. The stench that preceded him made Arvin's eyes water, but Arvin kept his face neutral. He remembered, from his days at the orphanage, how it felt to have a stench spell cast on him—how the children would pinch their noses and make faces as they passed. The crueler ones would throw stones.

Arvin might have lost the lapis lazuli, but he still had his power stone. He thrust a hand into his pocket, trying to decide whether he should teleport Naulg out of here. The rogue was obviously unstable; if Arvin tried to sneak him out, he'd probably give them both away. But brain burn wasn't something Arvin was willing to risk, not with a yuan-ti just outside the door.

Naulg's voice rose to a thin childlike wail. "It *hurts*. Help me, Ar . . . vin. Please?"

Arvin winced. Naulg's plea reminded him of how he'd felt during those long months in the orphanage before he'd finally found a friend: lost and alone—and frightened. He pressed a hand against the rogue's lips. "Quiet, Naulg," he whispered. "I'm going to get you out of here, but you have to be—"

The clicking of the lock's bolt was Arvin's only warning. He whirled as the door opened, whipping up his dagger. As the patch-haired cultist leaned in through the door with an oil lamp, flooding the room with light, Arvin hurled his dagger. The weapon whistled through the air and buried itself in the cultist's throat. The cultist fell, gurgling and clutching at his bloody neck, his lamp shattering on the floor. Arvin spoke the dagger's command word and his dagger flew back to his hand. He caught it easily, despite Naulg tugging on his sleeve.

"*Why?*" Naulg wailed. "Why did they—"

Arvin shook him off. "Not now!" From the hallway came the female cultist's voice, raised in rapid prayer. Arvin sprang toward the doorway, trying to line up a throw at her, but the yuan-ti whose voice Arvin had heard a moment ago stepped into the doorway, blocking it. He was a half blood with a human body and head, but with a snake growing out of each shoulder where his arms should have been. The lamp wick—still burning, feeding off the puddle of spilled oil—threw shadows that obscured the yuan-ti's face, but Arvin could see his snake arms clearly. They were banded with red, white, and black. The snake heads that were his hands were hissing, their fangs dripping venom. If either of them succeeded in striking Arvin, he'd be lucky to feel the sting of the puncture; a banded snake's venom was that swift.

Arvin took a quick step back. The yuan-ti followed him, his head weaving back and forth, his snake arms thrashing and hissing. Arvin wet his lips. Hitting a vital spot with his dagger was going to be difficult.

"Ar . . . vin!" Naulg wailed.

Arvin elbowed the rogue aside.

In that instant, the yuan-ti attacked—not with his venomous hands but with magic. A wave of fear as chilling as ice water crashed into Arvin's mind and sent shivers through his entire body. Gasping, Arvin staggered backward. Irrational fear gripped him, made him fling away his dagger, turn his back to the yuan-ti and scrabble at the wall like a rat. The yuan-ti was too powerful; Arvin would never defeat it. Crumpling to his knees, he began to sob.

A small portion of his mind, however, remembered the pouch he'd stuffed into his pocket—the one that held the assassin vine he'd sold to Naulg—and realized that this could be a weapon. But the main part of Arvin's mind was consumed with the magical fear that engulfed him as water does a drowning man.

Hissing, slit eyes gleaming, the yuan-ti walked slowly and deliberately toward him.

The fear increased, making it difficult even to sob. Arvin was going to die—he knew it. He . . . could . . . never—

Control. The word echoed faintly in Arvin's mind: a thin, distant cry. Then again, louder this time, a shout that throbbed through his mind, pounding like a fist against the fear. *Control! Master the fear. Move!*

Arvin screamed then—a scream of defiance, rather than fear. He yanked the pouch out of his pocket,

ripped it open, and hurled the twine at the yuan-ti.
The yuan-ti tried to slap the writhing twine aside,
but it immediately wrapped itself around his wrist
and swarmed up his arm. A heartbeat later it had
coiled around his throat. The yuan-ti staggered
backward, his snake hands trying to get a grip on the
twine around his neck but only succeeding in tearing
slashes in his throat with their fangs.

The fear that had nearly paralyzed Arvin fell away
from him like an unpinned cloak.

Arvin scooped up his dagger and leaped to his feet.
"Naulg!" he shouted, shoving the rogue toward the
door. "Let's go!"

The yuan-ti had at last managed to grab the twine
with one of his snake-headed hands and was pulling it
away from his throat. He glanced wildly at Naulg then
gestured at Arvin with his free arm.

"Kill him!" he cried.

Before Arvin could react, Naulg spun and leaped
on him. Together, they tumbled to the floor. Naulg
was weaker than Arvin, and slower, and Arvin had
a dagger in his hand—but he was loath to use it, even
though Naulg's eyes gleamed with crazed rage. Arvin
vanished it into his glove instead. Seizing the oppor-
tunity, Naulg grabbed Arvin by the neck. Arvin was
able to wrench one of Naulg's hands free, but the rogue
continued to cling to Arvin. He snapped with his teeth
at Arvin's shoulder, his neck, his arm. Only by writhing violently was Arvin able to avoid Naulg's furious
attacks. Locked together, they rolled back and forth
across the floor.

Out of the corner of his eye, Arvin saw the yuan-ti
at last succeed in tearing the twine from his neck.

That brief glance was Arvin's undoing. Naulg
reared up, lifting Arvin with him, then slammed
Arvin's head into the floor.

Bright points of light danced before Arvin's eyes.

They cleared just in time for him to see Naulg swoop down, mouth open wide. Arvin felt Naulg's teeth stab into his shoulder—and a hot numbness flashed through him.

Poison.

Naulg's spittle had turned poisonous, just as the old sailor's had.

Arvin tried to draw air into his lungs, but could not. His body was rigid; he was dying. His mind, however, was whirling. He was stupid to have tried to rescue Naulg. He should have listened to the mind seed's warning and killed the rogue the instant he saw him. Instead, the faint hope of aiding an old friend had been his undoing.

Arvin let out a final, hissing sigh. The room, the snake-armed yuan-ti, and Naulg all spun around him as he spiraled down into darkness.

CHAPTER 17

Arvin heard a soft hissing and felt breath
stir the hair near his left ear. Someone was
bending over him, touching his cheek with
something as soft as a feather. It tickled
against beard stubble then was gone.

He opened his eyes and saw he was lying on
the cold stone floor of the chamber in which
he'd discovered Naulg. The transformed rogue
was nowhere to be seen, but the yuan-ti was
still there. The half blood was kneeling beside
Arvin, one of his snake hands hovering just
above Arvin's face. Its flickering tongue was
what had brushed against Arvin's cheek a moment ago. Arvin wet his lips nervously. The
eyes of the banded serpent were small, slit—
and held just as much intelligence as the half
blood's human eyes. Those serpent hands—like

the yuan-ti's voice—seemed vaguely familiar to Arvin, yet he knew he'd never met this yuan-ti before. He decided that the sense of familiarity must have come from one of Zelia's memories.

The yuan-ti's face was illuminated by what was left of the lamp the patch-haired cultist had dropped. The wick was still burning, fueling itself from the patch of spilled oil. Arvin could feel the oil seeping into his hair. Instinctively he turned his head away from it and felt a sharp pain in his shoulder—the one Naulg had bitten. The venom in his spittle had come close to killing Arvin.

He stared up at the yuan-ti. "You neutralized the poison, didn't you?" He didn't bother to ask why; that much was obvious as soon as the yuan-ti spoke.

"Did you come here alone or with others?" it hissed.

"I. . . ." Arvin let his words trail off, pretending to be mesmerized by the venom beading at the tips of the snake-hand's fangs and the head's slight swaying motion. All the while, he was thinking furiously. The yuan-ti must have heard Arvin and Naulg use each other's names and realized Arvin had been making a rescue attempt. If Arvin could convince the yuanti he was on his own, it might protect Nicco—but he'd doom himself. He needed to convince the yuan-ti that it was more than a rescue mission, that there was vital information only he could provide.

Which, fortunately, there was.

"Rescuing my friend was only one of my goals in coming here," Arvin answered. "I also wanted to learn more about the Pox. I was ordered to spy on them by a yuan-ti who goes by the name of Zelia." As he dropped the name, he searched the yuan-ti's eyes for a sign of recognition.

The yuan-ti's expression remained unchanged. "Describe her," it ordered.

"She looks human, but with green scales. There's nothing else, really, to distinguish her."

"Her scales had no pattern?"

Arvin shrugged. "Not that I noticed. They were just ... green."

The yuan-ti considered this. Fortunately, it didn't ask about Zelia's one distinguishing feature—her hair. Hair color and length was something the scaly folk generally took no notice of; all human hair looked alike, to them. Even so, Arvin wasn't going to volunteer the information that Zelia was a redhead. Nor was he going to reveal that she was a psion. She'd be all too easy to track down if he did, and Arvin would become ... superfluous. But he could whet the yuan-ti's appetite a little.

"I think Zelia works for House Extaminos," Arvin continued.

A sharp hiss from the yuan-ti told him he'd struck a nerve.

"Though that's just a guess on my part," Arvin continued quickly. "Zelia only engaged my services a few days ago. And she did it in a fashion that hardly endeared me to her. She placed a ... geas upon me. If I don't return with the information she wants in two days' time, I'll die."

"She's a cleric?"

Arvin nodded.

"Of Sseth?"

"I suppose," Arvin demurred. As he answered, a part of his mind was focused deep within himself, drawing energy up his spine and coiling it at the base of his skull. When he felt the familiar prickle in his scalp, he narrowed his eyes in what he hoped was a suitably sly expression. "If you remove the geas, I'll help you kill Zelia or capture her, whichever you prefer. Do we have a deal?"

The yuan-ti cocked his head as if listening to something then gave a thin-lipped smile. Arvin's hopes rose. His charm must have worked. Then he realized the yuan-ti had heard footsteps in the hall. Arvin heard a rustling in the doorway and turned his head. Slowly—he didn't want to give the snake-hand an excuse to bite him.

The female cultist who had fled earlier entered the room. She held a flask in one hand. It was metal, and shaped like the rattle of a snake. She started to remove the cork that sealed it then glanced at the yuan-ti, as if seeking his permission.

Arvin wet his lips nervously. "The Pox have already made me drink from one of those flasks," he told the yuan-ti. "The potion didn't work on me. As you can see, I wasn't transformed into a—"

"Silence!" the yuan-ti hissed.

The cultist lowered the flask, a puzzled expression on her face. Seeing it, Arvin realized that the Pox still believed the flasks to contain poison or plague—and he had just come within a word of destroying that fiction. Had he just proved himself too dangerous to be allowed to live? He wet his lips nervously. His dagger was still inside his glove. There was a chance—a very slim chance—that he could kill the yuan-ti before the snake-hand sank its venomous teeth into Arvin's throat.

The yuan-ti nodded at Arvin. "This man is dangerous," he hissed. "Why don't you let me feed him the plague, instead?" He held up his free hand, the jaws of its snake-head open, imploring.

The cultist hesitated. "It should be a cleric who. . . ." Then her eyes softened, and she held out the flask.

Quicker than the blink of an eye, the yuan-ti's free hand shot out. The cultist gasped as fangs sank into her hand then she immediately stiffened. Unable to breathe, she purpled. Then she toppled sideways, crashing onto the floor like a felled free.

The yuan-ti picked up the flask with one of its snake

hands then turned its unblinking stare on Arvin. "You must be tired—why don't you sleep?" it hissed. "I have no reason to harm you. I *need* you. Sleep."

Arvin felt his eyelids begin to close. He mounted the only defense he could think of—the Empty Mind Tanju had taught him—pouring his awareness out in a flood. But it was no use. The suggestion felt as though it came from deep within; it wasn't something that grasped the mind from without. What the yuan-ti was saying just seemed so *reasonable*. Arvin was safe enough; the yuan-ti wasn't finished with him yet. And Arvin was exhausted, after all. . . .

His heavy eyelids closed as the last shred of his resistance fluttered away like a snake's discarded skin.

27 Kythorn, Fullday

In his dream, Arvin slithered across the floor of the cathedral between its forest of columns, each of which was carved into the form of two vipers twining around each other, one with its head up, the other with its head down. The columns supported an enormous domed ceiling of translucent green stone through which sunlight slanted, bathing everything in a cool light reminiscent of a shaded jungle. Water from the fountain that topped the cathedral dripped through holes in the roof, pattering onto the floor like rain.

Just ahead was one of the Stations of the Serpent—an enormous bronze statue of the god in winged serpent form, his body banded with glittering emeralds and his mouth open wide to reveal curved fangs of solid gold. The base of the statue was wreathed in writhing jets of orange-red fire, symbolic of Sseth's descent into the Peaks of Flame.

One day, Sseth would rise from them again.

A dozen other yuan-ti were weaving in prayer before the station, mesmerized from by the slit eyes of Sseth. Arvin slithered closer, welcoming the warmth of the oil-fueled fire on his scales. Twisting himself into a coil, he raised his upper body and swayed before the statue then opened his mouth wide in a silent hiss. Feeling a drop of venom bead at the tip of each of his fangs, he lashed forward in a mock strike, spitting the venom forward onto the tray that stood just in front of the statue. The venom landed on the fire-warmed bronze and immediately sizzled as it boiled away.

Hearing the hiss of scales against stone behind him, Arvin turned and saw the priest he had come here to meet. The priest's serpent form was long and slender and narrow-nosed, with black and white and red stripes running the length of his body. The part of Arvin's mind that was his own—the part that was observing the dream from a distance, like a spectator watching a dance and unable to resist swaying in time with the music—recognized the priest as the one he—no Zelia—would eventually reduce to a broken-minded heap. But that memory was months in the future.

The priest flickered a tongue in greeting and gestured with a weaving motion. "This way," he hissed.

Arvin followed him down a side corridor. The priest led him to one of the binding rooms. Inside it, on a low slab of stone, lay the body of a young man—a yuan-ti half blood. The head was that of a snake, with yellow-green scales and slit eyes, and each of the legs ended in snakelike tails, rather than feet. The body was naked. Arvin could see that a number of its bones were broken; one jagged bit of white protruded through the skin just below the shoulder. The left side of the face was crushed, caved in like a broken egg.

Two yuan-ti were working on the corpse, binding it in strips of linen. Both were male and both wore tunics that bore the Extaminos crest. They appeared human at first glance, save for slit eyes and brown scales that speckled their arms and legs. They worked quietly and efficiently—but carefully, giving the corpse the respect it was due as they wound the linen around it. When finished, the binding would be egg-shaped, a symbol of the spirit's return to the cloaca of the World Serpent.

"Leave us," the priest said. The two servants exited the room, bowing.

The priest slithered up to the corpse and raised himself above it. Arvin slid around to the other side of the slab. He didn't recognize the dead man, but he knew who he was—a younger cousin of Lady Dediana. Arvin let his eyes range over the body. The corpse reminded him of prey that had been constricted then rejected as unfit to swallow.

"Keep your questions simple," the priest said. "The dead are easily confused. And remember, you may ask only a limited number of questions. No more than five."

Arvin nodded. The information he wanted was very specific. Five questions should do nicely.

The priest swayed above the body in a complicated pattern, tongue flickering in and out of his mouth as he hissed a prayer in Draconic. As the prayer concluded, the mouth of the corpse parted slightly, like that of a man about to speak. "Ask your questions," the priest told Arvin.

Arvin addressed the body. "Urshas Extaminos, how did you die?"

"I fell from a great height." Urshas's voice was a creaking echo, his words sounding as if they were rising out of a dark, distant tomb. Broken bones grated as his smashed jaw opened and closed.

Interesting. Urshas's body had been found late last night, lying on a road near the House Gestin compound. The tallest of the viaducts that spanned that road was only two stories above street level—and was three buildings distant from the spot where the body lay. "How did you reach that height?" Arvin asked.

"Sseth's avatar carried me. We flew."

The priest gave a surprised hiss. "How do you know it was Sseth's avatar?" he asked.

Arvin's head snapped around angrily. "*I* am asking the questions."

Urshas, however, was compelled to answer: "She told me so."

"She?" Arvin said aloud—then realized his error. His inflection had turned the word into a question.

"Sibyl," Urshas answered.

"Sibyl who?" Arvin asked.

"She has no house name," Urshas croaked. "She is just . . . Sibyl."

"Sibyl," a different voice—one that wasn't part of his dream—hissed from somewhere close at hand.

Roused to partial wakefulness, Arvin contemplated the dream. At the time of the memory he was reliving, the name Sibyl had meant nothing to Zelia. But it would, in the months to come. Arvin tried to cast his mind into Zelia's more recent memories, to conjure up an image of Sibyl, but he could not. Instead he made a momentary connection with one of his own memories—of the way Sibyl's name had popped into his head while Gonthril was questioning him. With it came a realization. It was desperately important that Zelia find out if Sibyl was involved in all of this. If she was, it would give Lady Dediana the excuse she needed to—

"Sibyl," the voice hissed again.

Fully awake at last, Arvin opened his eyes the merest of slits. He was lying, bound hand and foot, in a different room than the one in which he'd fallen asleep. Its walls were round, not square, and were made of green stone. By the hot, humid feel of the air, the room was above ground, and it was day. The floor was covered in a plush green carpet, on which stood a low table. A yuan-ti half blood—the one from the crematorium—was seated at the table, his back to Arvin. He stared at a wrought-iron statuette of a serpent that held in its upturned mouth a large crystal sphere. Sitting next to it on the table was the lamp that illuminated the room.

"Sibyl," the yuan-ti hissed again. "It is your servant, Karshis."

Silently, Arvin took stock. His glove was still on his left hand, but the restraints that held him made it impossible to tell if his magical bracelet was still on his wrist. His wrists were bound together behind his back by something cold and hard; his ankles were similarly restrained. A length of what felt like a thin rod of metal connected these restraints. Glancing down, he saw that his ankles were bound by a coil of what looked like rope but felt like stone. He was hard-pressed to suppress a grin. He'd braided the cord himself from the thin, fine strands of humanlike hair that grow between a medusa's snaky tresses. The Guild and Secession weren't Arvin's only customers, it would seem.

Nine lives, he thought to himself, adding a silent prayer of thanks to Tymora.

The yuan-ti's attention was fully focused on the sphere, which was filled with what looked like a twisting filament of smoke. This slowly resolved into a solid form—a black serpent with the face of a woman, four humanlike arms and enormous wings folded against her back. As the winged serpent peered this way and that with eyes the color of dark-red flame, tasting the air with her tongue, Arvin made sure he remained utterly still, his eyes open only to slits. Then the winged serpent turned her head toward Karshis, as if she'd suddenly spotted him. Her voice, sounding far away and thin, rose from the sphere. "Speak," she hissed.

Karshis wet his lips. "A problem has arisen," he said. "A human spy has discovered the hiding place of the clerics. Fortunately, we captured him."

"A human?" the black serpent asked scornfully. Her wings shifted, as if in irritation.

"He says he was sent by a yuan-ti who calls herself Zelia. She may be a *serphidian* of House Extaminos."

Though the word was foreign, Arvin recognized it as one of the titles used by the priests of Sseth. He suddenly realized that the entire conversation between Karshis and Sibyl was being conducted in Draconic—a language he didn't speak. Zelia spoke it, however. And the mind seed—a familiar throbbing behind Arvin's temples—allowed Arvin to understand it.

"Shall we abandon our plan?" Karshis asked.

The winged serpent inside the sphere fell silent for several moments. "No," she said at last. "We will move more swiftly. Tell the clerics to abandon the crematorium—"

"It has already been done. They have scattered into the sewers."

"—And to prepare to receive the potion tomorrow night."

"That soon?" Karshis exclaimed. "But surely it will take more time than that to replace Osran. We haven't—"

"You dare question your god?" the winged serpent spat, her voice low and menacing.

"Most assuredly not, oh Sibilant Death," Karshis groveled. Both of his secondary heads hissed as he twined his arms together. "This humble member of your blessed ones simply expresses aloud the confusion and uncertainty that inhabits his own worthless skin. Forgive me."

"Foolish one," she hissed back. "Sseth never forgives. But your soul will be spared a descent into the

Abyss—for now. There's still work ahead. See that it is done well. The barrel will be delivered to the rotting field at Middark. When it arrives, be sure the Pox save a little of the 'plague' for themselves. After tomorrow night, we'll have no further use for them."

"What of the spy?" Karshis asked.

"Kill it."

Arvin's heart thudded in his chest.

"But find the *serphidian* first," Sibyl continued. "If she has disappeared into some hole, use the human as bait to lure her out again."

"Yes, Great Serpent," Karshis answered, bending his flexible upper torso into a convoluted bow. "I will set our spies in motion. She will be found."

The image inside the sphere dissolved into a coil of dark mist then was gone.

As Karshis rose from the table and lifted the sphere out of the statuette's mouth, Arvin closed his eyes fully and made sure his breathing was even, slow, and deep. Soft footsteps approached. Karshis prodded him in the ribs with a foot then continued across the room. Arvin heard a key rattle in a lock, the groan of hinges as a door opened and closed, and a click as the door was locked again.

He waited for several moments then opened his eyes. He spoke a command word and the stone coils that bound his wrists and ankles turned back into braided hair and fell to the carpet. Arvin sat up, quickly coiled it, and stuffed it into a pocket.

Tymora willing, he would get out of here—wherever *here* was.

Crossing to the door, Arvin inspected it carefully. He didn't want to fall victim to another glyph like the one Nicco had used. This door, however, appeared unmarked. Reaching for his belt buckle, Arvin bent down and fitted its pick into the keyhole. One pin clicked into place, a second—

The door suddenly smashed into his face, sending him crashing to the floor. Blinking away the pain of a bloodied nose, Arvin realized Karshis had returned. The yuan-ti was trying to force the partially open door, which was blocked by Arvin's body.

One of Karshis's arms snaked in through the opening, its snake-hand trying to sink its fangs into Arvin. He flung himself to the side, barely avoiding the bite. *"Shivis!"* he cried, summoning his dagger to his glove. He leaped to his feet in the same instant that Karshis lunged into the room. As the yuan-ti's snake-hand lashed forward a second time, Arvin met it with his dagger, slicing cleanly through the snake-hand's neck. The head dangled from a thread of flesh, its eyes glazing as blood pumped from the wound.

Karshis staggered back, hissing with pain, and grabbed at the door with his other snake-hand to steady himself. Seizing his chance, Arvin leaped forward and slammed the door shut, crushing the second snake-hand between the door and its frame. All that remained was the yuan-ti's main head—which, unfortunately, also had venomous fangs.

The yuan-ti writhed in pain then rallied. Suddenly, the room was plunged into darkness. Unable to see anything, surrounded by a darkness through which not even the faintest pinprick of light penetrated, Arvin backed up warily, his dagger at the ready. He could still hear the yuan-ti's labored breathing; Karshis was standing somewhere just ahead of him. Could the yuan-ti see in the dark? Would he use it as a screen for a retreat—or an attack? Taking aim by ear, Arvin readied his dagger for a throw.

Karshis slammed into Arvin, knocking him sprawling, facefirst, onto the carpet. Arvin slashed wildly with his dagger—only to feel a snake-arm coil around his wrist, trapping it. A second snake-arm coiled around Arvin's other wrist, but this snake-arm was slippery with blood. Arvin wrenched one hand free and scrambled to his feet. He tried to leap away, but Karshis's grip on his other arm was too strong. Held fast, like an unwilling dance partner, all Arvin could do was flail in a circle around Karshis, blindly dodging the yuan-ti's attempts to bite him. Venom sprayed him each time the yuan-ti lunged and missed.

The dagger was still in Arvin's gloved hand, but that was the arm Karshis held. Despite the wounds Arvin had inflicted upon him, Karshis was still swift and strong; even if Arvin was somehow able to wrench his arm free, a dagger might not be enough to stop the yuan-ti.

The power stone, however, might.

If it didn't knock Arvin flat with brain burn.

Swiftly—between one desperate dodge and the next—Arvin cast his mind into the crystal. Linking with it took only a fraction of a heartbeat; finding the power he wanted among the five glittering gem-stars that remained took only an instant more. Arvin felt its energies flow into his third eye, as before, and also into a spot on his spine directly behind his navel. Silver motes of light danced in his vision—and this time coalesced into a line of bright silver light that lanced out at Karshis through the magical darkness. In that same instant, Arvin felt Karshis's dry, scaly skin suddenly become slippery and wet with ectoplasm and knew that, this time, his manifestation had been a success. Strangely, though, he was unable to lock his mind on the spot to which he wanted to teleport Karshis. His mind remained unfocused, blank, *scattered*.

Karshis's body suddenly flexed, bringing his venomous fangs within a hair of Arvin's throat. Then it exploded. One moment Karshis was lunging at Arvin—the next, a fine spray of mist erupted from him, soaking Arvin, his clothes, and the carpet around him. What remained of the yuan-ti fell to the floor with a thump.

Hissing with relief, Arvin dragged the body out of the pool of darkness and stared at Karshis's corpse. Its flesh was dotted with thousands of tiny tunnels from which blood was starting to seep; it seemed as if miniscule portions of the yuan-ti had been teleported in all directions. Arvin shook his head in disgust and spat until the bloody, scale-flecked mist was gone from his lips. He wiped his face with a trembling arm then reached into his pocket and pulled out the power stone. The second teleport power had seemed so benign—had he used it improperly? Somehow, he didn't think so. He hadn't suffered brain burn, this time. He hissed in relief, glad he hadn't tried to use it to teleport Naulg.

Out of long habit, he raised a hand to his throat to touch his bead then remembered it wasn't there. "Nine lives," he whispered, shoving the stone back into his pocket.

Then he picked up his dagger and rose to his feet. The door was unlocked and open—and the hallway it opened onto was silent. No one, it seemed, had heard the sounds of the fight.

Arvin whispered a prayer of thanks to Tymora. He'd really have to fill her cup this time. But there was much he had to do, first. He had to rescue Naulg . . . and find Nicco.

But not necessarily in that order.

CHAPTER 18

In his dream, Arvin stared at the wemic who stood before him, flexing his muscles. The creature was magnificent, his body that of a lion and covered in lustrous golden fur, his upper torso that of a human. The wemic's face was a blend of both: human in overall appearance, but framed by a mane of coal-black hair and with pupils that were vertical slits. His long tail swished back and forth behind him, fanning the grass that stretched in an unbroken plain to the distant mountains.

"How does it feel," Arvin asked, his forked tongue flickering in and out of his mouth as he spoke, "to occupy that body?"

In answer, the wemic threw back his head and roared then flexed his forepaws, rending the earth with his claws. "Powerful," he replied, throwing a low growl into the word.

"And your psionics?" Arvin asked.

The wemic squatted, placing his human hands on the ground, then slowly bent his human torso backward. He held the pose for a time then balanced awkwardly on his front paws and raised his hindquarters into the air, tail lashing wildly as he sought to maintain the *asana*. He went through the entire series of *asanas*—slowly and clumsily, making up in brute strength what he lacked in balance and flexibility—and was panting by the time he had finished.

"I've lost some of the powers you had when you created me," the wemic answered at last. "The more powerful ones are gone."

Arvin gave a soft hiss of satisfaction. "Keep that in mind," he told the wemic. "And remember what happened to the seed who tried to defy me with what she retained."

The wemic, which shared the memory of the first seed—the dwarf whose mind Arvin had squeezed into a pulp by a psychic crush—nodded slowly.

"Events have progressed swiftly over the past seven days," Arvin told the wemic. "Garrnau has been padding about, insisting that she be the delegate to the Three Cities. She felt that you have been too ... preoccupied over the past few days to present the Ten-Paw tribe's case clearly. She will need to be dealt with. And there has been a communication from Lady Dediana. She thought it might be amusing if you were to be caught in the act of devouring one of Lord Quwen's horses—especially if it was the racing stallion she sent him two days ago, as a truce offering."

The wemic threw back his head and gave a roaring laugh. It was followed, incongruously enough, with a satisfied hiss. "All of Ormath will spring for their saddles and swords," he said. "To protect their precious herds from—"

"Yes," Arvin said. "And Hlondeth will have one less bothersome neighbor."

The wemic leveled a stare at Arvin. "And what of me ... afterward?"

Arvin smiled. "Cast your memory back to the elf-seed in Xorhun, and the lizardman-seed in Surkh. Did I abandon them?"

The wemic shook his head. "No." A guarded look crept into his eyes. "As of seven days ago, you had not."

Arvin laid a palm against the wemic's broad chest and let his fingers slide seductively through the downy chest hair. "In fact," Arvin murmured, his flickering tongue tasting the lionlike musk that hung heavy in the air, "in the case of the elf-seed, I continue to visit—frequently."

The wemic mirrored Arvin's lascivious smile. He wrapped muscular arms around Arvin, drawing him to his chest. Arvin felt claw tips poke with delicious pain into his back as the wemic lowered his head to kiss him. Surrounded by the wemic's mane and musky scent, Arvin met the kiss with a hunger of his own—

Suddenly, Arvin was awake—and gasping for air. He didn't know which was more disturbing, the image of Zelia twining herself about a creature that was half lion—or the thought of her making love to herself. A part of him, however, insisted on lingering on the memory. Zelia was a beautiful woman, after all....

Shaking his head, Arvin pushed the thought from his mind. Control, he told himself.

Rising from his bed, he crossed the rented room and splashed lukewarm water on his face from a ceramic bowl that stood on a low table. Sunlight streamed in through the shutters on the room's only window; it was going to be another hot, humid day.

If he didn't find Nicco, it might also be his last.

Suddenly furious, he hurled the bowl across the room. It hit the far wall and shattered, leaving a spray of water on the wall. He manifested his dagger into his glove and stared at it. Maybe he should just end it, he told himself. Death was one way to prevent Zelia from claiming him, from *winning*. One quick stab and it would all be over....

No. He was thinking like her again. It was doing him no good to rage. What he had to do was stay calm, try to find a way out of this mess. There was still time—though not much. He rubbed his temples and squeezed his eyes shut, forcing the anger aside. Then he disappeared the dagger back into his glove.

He sank into a cross-legged position on the floor and slowed his breathing then ran through the series of mental exercises Tanju had taught him. When he had finished, he assumed the *bhujanga asana*. It came even easier to him than it had before; his body seemed to adopt the pose of its own accord. As he held the *asana*, muscles straining, he cast his mind back over the events of the evening before.

After escaping from Karshis, he'd hurried back to the crematorium to search for Nicco and Naulg. He no longer had the key—Karshis must have taken it from him—but by fumbling at the blank stone wall, he'd found the door and its keyhole by feel and managed to pick the lock. He'd crept in, half expecting to find the Pox inside, but the room had been empty. So, too, was the platform where Nicco had fallen into magical slumber. Arvin had tossed a loop of rope onto the platform and pulled it back again and again, hoping that, by some miracle, Nicco might still be lying there, invisible. But the cleric was gone. Whether the cultists had found him or he had simply woken up and teleported away, Arvin had no idea.

Arvin had searched the room again—thoroughly—but the results were the same as before. The only way into the crematorium proper, it seemed, was through the platform. Without the key, Arvin was only going to wind up in magical slumber, as Nicco had. If Arvin was going to get in, he'd need Nicco's help.

Slipping out of the building again, Arvin had once more turned, reluctantly, to his Guild contacts. He put out the word that he was looking for a man of Nicco's description—or a man matching Gonthril's description, or even Chorl's. Someone, somewhere, had to have seen one of them. But without coin to pry open their lips, the Guild members weren't saying anything. "No," was the usual reply, "haven't seen anyone like that."

At last, exhausted, Arvin had rented a room above a tavern near the waterfront. The bed still stank of the tarred hair of the sailor who'd occupied it last, and the room was stiflingly hot, despite the window. Arvin had lain awake long into Darkmorning, listening to the sounds of laughter and ribald singing from the tavern below. He'd tossed and turned, hissing with frustration at having come so close to salvation—only to lose Nicco. If only he knew where the rebels had holed up after abandoning the chambers under the garden. . . .

Ending the *asana*, Arvin rose to his feet and rubbed his forehead. The ache of the mind seed had grown worse, and was now a constant throbbing behind his eyes that filled the front of his head from temple to temple. Frustrated, he banged his hand against the shutters, sending them flying open. No wonder the room was so hot; the window faced north, away from the breeze that blew off the harbor.

Arvin stared up at the city. Though his room occupied the fifth floor of the tower, its window was barely level with the foundations of the buildings farther up the hill, those of the yuan-ti section of the city. Only by craning his neck could Arvin see the snake-shaped fountain that topped the cathedral dome, or the spires of the palace, or the Nesting Tower....

Arvin frowned as he stared at the distant, flitting specks of flying snakes. It was odd that Nicco had chosen that location to teleport them to when they had fled from the Plaza of Justice. Why teleport into an area frequented by yuan-ti nobles? Arvin would have thought the cleric would have teleported them somewhere that, to Nicco, represented safety.

Maybe, Arvin mused, he had. What was it Kayla had said about Gonthril's choice of hiding places for the Secession? The rebel leader liked to use spots Lady Dediana would least suspect—a private garden of the Extaminos family, for example.

And perhaps, also, the Nesting Tower that housed many of the royal family's flying snakes.

Arvin nodded; it made sense. Gonthril had been so certain he and his fellow rebels would be able to slip into the royal palace undetected. What was it he'd told them? Closing his eyes, Arvin tried to recall the words he'd overheard, just before Nicco's glyph had frozen him in place. "One sip of this," Gonthril had said, and something about the royal family mistaking the rebels for "his little pets, out for a Middark soar."

Arvin realized what he'd been talking about—a potion of polymorphing that would turn the rebels into flying snakes. And not just any flying snakes, but ones that Osran Extaminos would recognize: his pets. In order to polymorph that precisely, the drinker of the potion had to have seen the creature he wanted to polymorph into firsthand. That much Arvin knew from his conversations with Drin.

The rebels were using the Nesting Tower as one of the Secession's hiding places. Arvin was certain of it.

Tymora willing, they would be there.

And Nicco would be with them.

Arvin stood at the base of the Nesting Tower, resisting the urge to pinch his nose against the smell of snake feces. The slave who tended the flying serpents was mucking out the holes, sluicing them out with water. It ran in stained torrents down the sides of the tower into drains in the courtyard below—which was unoccupied at the moment, due to the filthy spray. The flying snakes, meanwhile, wheeled in elegant circles overhead, their wings flashing green, red, and gold in the sun.

Stepping warily to avoid a rain of murky, stinking water, Arvin waved at the slave who was floating above. He was an older man with a shaved head, clad only in sandals and a filthy pair of trousers. His skin was as brown as a cobra.

"Slave!" Arvin shouted through cupped hands. "Descend. At once!"

The slave glanced down, hesitated, and hung the bucket he'd been holding on a hook on his belt. Slowly he began his descent. He halted several paces above Arvin and eyed him suspiciously—and for good reason. Flying snakes were expensive pets and there had been attempts to steal them in the past. For this reason, the outer walls of the tower had been bespelled with a magical grease to discourage climbing; it glistened in the sunlight. With a magical rope—like the one Chorl had used to help Arvin and Kayla climb down into the garden—Arvin might have bypassed the greased wall under cover of darkness. But he didn't have another climbing rope, and it was broad daylight. The only way up was via whatever magical item the slave was using to levitate.

"Yes?" the slave asked.

Arvin stood with hands on hips, swaying impatiently. Deliberately, he let his tongue flicker in and out of his mouth as he stared up at the slave. "A yuan-ti died three nights ago," Arvin told him. "He was killed by a flying snake—one with venom powerful enough to fell a yuan-ti. That snake is to be dispatched."

"Which one is it?" the slave asked. "I'll—"

"No you won't," Arvin said. "I will."

"But it's Highsun," the slave protested. "The snakes are all away from the—"

"Don't question me, *slave*," Arvin spat, easily imitating Zelia's imperious tone. The throbbing in his head helped; it gave an edge to his impatience. "Come down here at once, or you will be punished." Arvin twitched his upper lip, as if about to bare his fangs. "I'll see to it myself."

The slave's face paled and he sank to the ground. As he landed, Arvin eyed his sandals. They were made from unblemished white leather—pegasus hide.

The slave stood, eyes obediently on the ground but with a wary look on his face. It was clear he didn't believe Arvin's story, yet at the same time he was frightened of disobeying a yuan-ti. Seeing this, Arvin drew upon his psionic talent. The base of his scalp prickling with energy, he spoke softly to the slave. "You've served the Extaminos family for many years, slave. You can be trusted to keep a secret. It wasn't just any yuan-ti that was killed, but Osran Extaminos, tenth in line for the throne."

The slave had been standing with his head tilted, as if listening not just to Arvin but also to a distant sound—the charm's secondary display. "I heard the palace slaves whispering about Osran," he confided. "I didn't believe it was true."

"I assure you, it is," Arvin said gravely, steering the slave into the shade of a nearby building. "We suspect the snake that killed him was a polymorphed assassin. I'm here to lay a trap for him. I need to take your place for the day. Give me your clothes and bucket . . . and those sandals."

The slave looked at him warily. "I can't. I'll be punished if they find out."

"They won't," Arvin snapped—a little more testily than he'd intended. "Nobody will know." He reached into his pocket, pulled out his last three silver pieces, and pressed them into the slave's hand. "Take the day off. Treat yourself to a bath—a long one. Don't come back until Sunset. I'll leave the sandals in the bucket, under here." He gestured at the base of a nearby ramp. The shadowed hollow under it would make an excellent hiding place.

The slave stood, staring uncertainly at the silver coins on his palm. "I don't know. . . ."

Arvin rubbed his throbbing temples. The midday heat was making them pound worse than ever. "You don't know *what?*" he snapped, hissing angrily.

The human swallowed nervously. "Maybe we should speak to my master, first, before. . . ."

Arvin couldn't stand it any longer. Humans weren't supposed to question—they were meant to obey. His whole plan was about to come undone. He couldn't permit that to happen. His angry hiss turned into a whisper. *"Shivis!"*

Quick as thought, the dagger was in his gloved hand. He thrust forward and the blade bit deep into the slave's stomach. "You're not"—*stab*—"speaking"—*stab*—"to your master!" Arvin hissed.

The slave sank to the street, eyes wide and mouth making faint gasping sounds. His bucket clattered to the ground beside him, spilling its last dribble of water. Something warm and sticky coated Arvin's hand; he licked his fingers and was rewarded with the sweet taste of blood. "Insolent human," he muttered, the last word twisting his lips.

Only then did he realize what he'd done.

He stared down at the slave, horrified. Then he realized the man's blood was still on his lips. He spat and nearly threw up. He slammed his fist into the wall. "Gods curse you, Zelia."

Realizing he might be in trouble—big trouble—if any of the militia were nearby, Arvin looked wildly around. No one was in sight. Disappearing the dagger into his glove—he'd clean it later—he shoved the body under the ramp. He crouched for a moment in the cool shadow, and closed his eyes against the throbbing in his head, saying a prayer for the slave's soul. Then, hands shaking, he unfastened the man's sandals. He glanced at the bright red drops of blood on the white leather then at the body. "I didn't mean to ... " he started to say. Then he sighed. What did it matter what he meant to do? The man was dead.

Arvin pulled off his boots and fastened the sandals to his feet then crawled out from under the ramp. The three silver pieces lay on the street, next to a smear of blood. He left them where they'd fallen. Picking up the empty bucket, he walked toward the tower.

The magical sandals proved surprisingly easy to use. Arvin merely visualized himself rising and up he went. The tower was six stories high, but fortunately, he had no fear of heights. He stared, unconcerned, as the ground seemed to fall away below him. He landed easily on the rooftop, which was bare aside from a single tap whose pipe rose out of the ceiling like an erect snake.

A trapdoor at the center was closed with a padlock. Using the picks in his belt buckle, Arvin quickly opened it. He lifted the trapdoor and saw a stone staircase that spiraled down. Sunlight slanted into it through holes that gave access to the niches in which the flying snakes nested. The air in the narrow stairway was dry, dusty, and hot—and stank of snake.

Arvin stepped down into the stairway then sat and pulled off the sandals. They were valuable, and he might need them to get out of the tower, but he didn't care. He didn't want them on his feet a moment longer than was absolutely necessary. He placed them, together with the padlock, inside the bucket and set it aside. Then he closed the trapdoor and tiptoed down the stairs, barefoot.

The stairs seemed to spiral down endlessly. After a while the air grew cooler as Arvin descended below the last of the beams of sunlight—and below ground level. At last, after several more turnings, they ended. The light at the bottom of the stairs was extremely poor, but Arvin had a sense that the staircase opened onto a large room. A new odor filled the air—rodent droppings. As his eyes adjusted to the gloom, Arvin saw that the walls of the room were lined with cages. Rats scrabbled within them, filling the air with their soft scurrying. Remembering the rat that had burst into flames, Arvin shuddered. But at the same time he wet his lips in anticipation and strained forward, half expecting to sense the rat's body warmth through the pits in his—

No. He was thinking like Zelia again. The rats were *not* food.

Not for him, at any rate.

He made a circuit of the room, inspecting the floor in front of the cages. Had he gone to all this trouble—even killed a man—for nothing? Then he spotted something that gave him hope—faint scrapes in the layer of grime that covered the floor. The cages had been moved recently. Peering at the wall behind them, he saw a faint line: a hidden doorway. Warily, he grasped the top cage and began to move it aside.

Pain exploded in his head as something smacked into the back of it. Staggered by the blow—and the jolt of magical energy it unleashed—Arvin fell against the cages, which crashed down on top of him. The rats inside them squealed furiously and nipped at his hands as he scrambled to knock the cages aside, to see who had attacked him.

"Wait!" Arvin gasped, flailing under the cages. "I'm a friend. I'm—"

"Arvin!" a harsh voice said, completing the sentence for him.

Chorl stood looking down at him. The balding rebel must have been invisible until his attack. He held the end of his staff level with Arvin's chest, ready to thrust it at him. Its tip crackled with magical energy, filling Arvin's nostrils with a sharp, burnt odor. With a sinking feeling, Arvin saw that it was poised over his heart. All that was holding Chorl back was righteous anger—and the need to tell Arvin off. "You dare come back here, you scaly bastard?" he spat. "This time, I'll see to it that—"

"Get Nicco," Arvin said. "He'll vouch for me."

"Nicco's busy."

Relief washed through Arvin. "He escaped?" He started to let out a slow hiss but abruptly covered it with a whispered prayer. "Tymora be praised. Tell him I've learned more about what the Pox are up to. They're taking delivery of the transformative potion tonight—a whole barrel of the stuff. It's going to be delivered to the cultists in a field, and I can tell you which one. Your people will need to move quickly, if you want to prevent them from tainting the public wells. They—"

"You want Gonthril to rush everyone out to some field," Chorl guessed. "Tonight."

Arvin nodded. "It will be your one chance to stop the cultists," he said then quickly added, "and to stop the yuan-ti who are really behind this."

"And you, of course, will lead us to this field."

"No. All I promised was information—which I've just delivered—in return for a . . . healing from Nicco. Saving Hlondeth—preventing its humans from being transformed into yuan-ti—is in the Secession's hands now."

Chorl scowled. "You yuan-ti," he growled. "You think you're so superior. Did you really think we'd fall for—"

Seeing what was coming, Arvin attacked—not with his dagger, but with the power stone. Linking with it was a matter of mere thought; manifesting the power he wanted came almost as swiftly. Even as Chorl thrust his staff at Arvin's chest, a rush of energy filled Arvin's third eye. He caught the head of the staff with his bare palm just before it struck his chest and heard it begin to sizzle. The staff's magical energies flared—then were snuffed out as the acid in Arvin's palm ate away at the staff. The wood crumbled back like a candle being melted by a blast of flame.

Shoving what remained of the staff—a mere stub that Chorl held in one hand—Arvin sent the rebel staggering backward. Arvin followed him, sending a stinging flick of acid at Chorl from his dripping hand. The rebel winced as it struck his cheek.

"Be thankful I chose to dissolve your staff," Arvin hissed angrily. "I could have chosen your hand—or your face."

Chorl gaped at the stub he held in his hand then threw it aside. "I *knew* you were a yuan-ti," he snarled.

Too late, Arvin realized he'd manifested a power that "proved," in Chorl's mind, that Arvin was a yuan-ti. As Chorl drew a dagger and moved forward, holding it low and ready, Arvin manifested his own dagger into his glove. He heard the scrape of stone—the hidden door behind him was opening. So filled with fury was he, that he ignored it. Hissing with rage, he drew back his arm for a throw at Chorl's throat even as Chorl tensed for a charge.

"Peace!" a man's voice shouted.

Calm flowed into Arvin, filling him with a warm, slow languor. Part of his mind recognized it as a magical effect, but he couldn't seem to find the energy to fight it. As his anger drained away, he lowered his dagger. His free hand rubbed his temple and he stared at Chorl, who stood, staring at his own weapon. Why had Arvin wanted to hurt the rebel? Oh yes, because they were fighting. He'd been angry about . . . something.

Nicco stepped forward, plucked the dagger from Arvin's hand, and shoved it into the sheath on Arvin's belt. "Arvin," he said, wrapping an arm around his shoulder. "I've been looking for you. Come with me." He turned. "You too, Chorl."

Feeling relaxed and content, Arvin walked with the cleric through the hidden door—not even caring that his back was to Chorl—and down a short corridor. It led to a wine cellar. Enormous barrels, split with age, lined the walls. A staircase that used to lead up to ground level was nearly buried under rubble from the Nesting Tower's construction. A dozen or so rebels were in the cellar, some sitting and conversing in low tones, others drowsing on blankets spread on the floor. They turned to stare at Nicco and Arvin as they entered the room. Several leaped to their feet, drawing swords. One of them—Gonthril—held up a hand, halting them. His intense blue eyes took Arvin's measure for a long time before he spoke.

"Four rebels are dead," he said, toying with one of the rings he wore. "Explain to me why we should let you live."

Wetting his lips nervously, Arvin glanced at Nicco. The cleric gave a nod that Arvin hoped was meant to be encouragement.

"Osran wasn't the only yuan-ti involved with the Pox," Arvin began. "There are at least two more. Karshis, who I killed—"

This brought a murmur of surprise from the rebels.

"—and the yuan-ti who is Karshis's superior: an

abomination named Sibyl. She's delivering the transformative potion to the cultists tonight, and I know
where that delivery is going to take place. All of the
cultists will be together in one place. If you want to
finish what you started, tonight may be your only
chance."

Gonthril reached into his pocket and withdrew a
silver ring—the one that compelled the truth. "Tell me
how you know this," he said, handing it to Arvin.

Arvin put on the ring then recapped what had
happened in the crematorium, reciting from memory
the conversation he'd overheard between Karshis and
Sibyl. "It took me a while to figure out which field they
must have been talking about," he said. "The Pox like
to use places associated with disease: the sewers, the
closed slaughterhouse, the crematorium. The 'rotting'
field is the one that lies trampled and burned. The
field used for last year's Rotting Dance."

Chorl, standing beside Gonthril, listened with narrowed eyes. "An open field," he grumbled, "with no
place to hide. If this is an ambush, we'll be cut down
like ripe wheat."

The rebels muttered; Gonthril silenced them with
a curt gesture. "Arvin has told us the truth," he told
them. "Tonight may be our only chance to save our
people. It's worth the risk; we'll send someone ahead
to scout the field, and the rest of us will wait here until
just before Middark. In order to prevent information
from . . . slipping out again, Arvin will remain here
with us, under guard." He turned to Arvin. "Agreed?"

Arvin wet his lips. "Agreed," he said.

Gonthril held out a hand and the ring was suddenly
loose on Arvin's finger. Arvin took it off and passed it
back to him.

As the rebels clustered around Gonthril, talking,
Nicco led Arvin aside. Arvin dropped his voice to a
whisper, and spoke urgently to the cleric. "I've given

the rebels what they need," he reminded Nicco. "Now how about that restorative prayer?"

Nicco shook his head. "I'm going to need all of the blessings Hoar has bestowed upon me for tonight's work. There are more than a dozen people who must be rendered invisible—not to mention bestowed with protective blessings—and other prayers will be needed. Once we have dealt with the cultists—"

"But that won't be until Middark!" Arvin protested. "And tomorrow will be the seventh day since the mind seed was planted. It could blossom as soon as Middark turns. By making me wait, you're condemning me to—"

"I condemn you to nothing," Nicco flared. "I have promised you a restorative prayer, and you shall receive it—when I am ready. Until then, you are in Hoar's hands. If it is his will that the mind seed blossom at the turn of Middark, it may blossom. But I think that it will not. Hoar showed you mercy once, already, in the pit. He will surely continue to do so."

Arvin nodded glumly. His own clever trick was working against him. Nicco might be convinced that Hoar favored Arvin, but Arvin himself knew otherwise. He reached to touch the bead at his throat then remembered it wasn't there any more. He thrust a hand into his pocket instead, clenching the power stone in his fist.

"Nine lives," he muttered.

Then he stood and watched—and waited and fretted—as Nicco, Gonthril, and the rebels conferred with each other, laying plans for tonight's ambush.

28 Kythorn, Evening

Arvin squatted next to a low stone wall, staring at the field it enclosed. The Rotting Dance had been held eight months ago, at Highharvestide, but the field still had a ripe, rotten odor. Low, mushy mounds of what had once been piles of rotten fruit and vegetables dotted the ground, and a large patch of blackened earth near the center of the field marked the spot where the bonfire had raged. The field was fallow and tangled with weeds.

Like Arvin, Gonthril and the other rebels had been rendered invisible by Nicco's prayers. Nearly two dozen of them were waiting, positioned around the field, for the cultists to appear. Unlike Arvin, though, they were free to move about. At Chorl's insistence, Gonthril had ordered Nicco to use an additional prayer on Arvin, one that prevented him from moving. All Arvin could do was breathe and blink.

Was it Middark yet? He had no idea. His temples pounded like drums. For the moment, however, his mind was still his own.

Sweat trickled down his sides as he waited in the darkness. Even though the sun had set long ago, the air was still muggy and hot. The heavy gray clouds that had been building over the Reach had at last moved inland over Hlondeth, and, judging by the low rumbles of thunder in the distance, would soon break. In the meantime, they obliterated the moon, throwing the vineyards and fields outside the city into utter darkness. Out of the corner of his eye, Arvin could see the green glow of Hlondeth's walls, several fields distant.

The rumble of wheels announced the approach of a cart. Though he strained to turn his head, he still could not move; he was only able to see the cart after it turned into the rotting field. It was being driven by a yuan-ti who sat balanced on a coiled serpent's tail. A cask the size of a wine barrel was lashed in the back. It was too dark to make out details of the yuan-ti's face, but Arvin could see his head snaking this way and that as he scanned the field. While the yuan-ti seemed at ease, his horse did not; it kept tossing its head and whickering, as if it had sensed the invisible rebels. When the yuan-ti reined it to a halt, the horse pawed at the ground with a hoof, digging a furrow into the stinking soil.

The yuan-ti glanced up at the sky, as if trying to tell what segment of the evening it was, then continued glancing around the field. As his head turned toward the spot where Arvin crouched, Arvin would have tensed—if he had been capable of it. Instead he let out a low hiss of relief as the yuan-ti's glance continued past him.

A moment later, the yuan-ti's head whipped around as something materialized on the far side of the cart. It happened in the blink of an eye. One moment the burned patch near the center of the field was bare of all but ashes, the next, a dozen cultists were standing there, holding hands. Their gray-green robes made them almost invisible in the darkness. Their pale, pox-spotted faces were faint white ovals.

Arvin felt something brush against him and heard the faint tinkle of Nicco's earring.

"At the signal, use your dagger," the cleric breathed, touching his arm. "Aim for the yuan-ti."

Suddenly, Arvin could move. Wary of making any noise, he rose slowly to his feet—only to find that his legs were numb from having remained in a crouch for so long. He winced at the hot tingling of blood returning to his feet, and nearly stumbled.

The attack began without him.

A shrill whistle sounded. A heartbeat later, from several points around the field, came the *thwap, thwap, thwap-thwap* of crossbow strings releasing. Several of the cultists staggered, clutching at the bolts that had suddenly appeared in their bodies. In that same instant, the rebels became visible. Arvin saw Gonthril, running at the cultists with his sword raised, and other rebels closing with spears and swords. Nicco had not yet become visible, but Arvin could hear him praying. The cleric's voice came from a spot near the cart.

The yuan-ti also heard the prayer. Hissing with anger, he turned to face the spot where Nicco must have been standing. A tangle of weeds next to the cart came alive and began wrapping themselves around an invisible form.

Belatedly, Arvin threw his dagger, but in that same moment, the yuan-ti reared up. The dagger plunged not into his throat but into his coiled body, well below any vital organs. Hissing in frustration, Arvin threw up his bare hand, summoning his dagger, which yanked free of the yuan-ti's scaly body. Arvin caught it—but the yuan-ti had seen him. The yuan-ti stared at Arvin, turning the full force of his magical fear on him.

Arvin staggered backward under a wave of magical fear. He had to flee, to get out of here, to *run*. The dagger forgotten in his fist, he whirled to look for an escape—

Something jerked him to a halt: the mind seed. The pain of it was excruciating. *No*, an inner voice shouted. Zelia's voice. *The driver must be captured. He's the proof I need that Sibyl is—*

"Get ... out of ... my ... head!" Arvin raged.

Whatever else the mind seed might be saying, he didn't hear it. The compulsion to flee was gone—but his head felt as though it were about to explode from within. Each thought was a slow, sluggish step, like wading through tar.

Only dimly aware of the battle that was raging in the field, Arvin caught no more than brief glimpses of it. Despite the fact that they were outnumbered two to one, the cultists had magic on their side. One of them waved his hand in a circle, causing a greasy, roiling darkness to rise from the field and engulf the four rebels closest to him. Three staggered away, retching, while the fourth sank to his knees and disappeared from sight under the black cloud. Another rebel, trying to spear a cultist from a safe distance, was swarmed by a cloud of insects summoned by a cultist; the rebel dropped his spear and staggered away, screaming and slapping at the thousands of black dots that covered every bit of exposed skin. Chorl managed to take one of the clerics down with a well-thrown dagger, but then one of the Pox grabbed him from behind and drew a finger across Chorl's throat. The bare-handed attack opened a gushing wound; when the cultist released Chorl, the rebel fell to the ground.

Gonthril accounted for two of the Pox in quick succession, lopping the head off one and disemboweling the other. Then one of the cultists lunged past his sword and slapped a hand on the rebel leader's chest. Gonthril ran the cultist through, but the damage had been done. The rebel leader staggered, his arms shaking so violently that he nearly dropped his sword. A hideous cough that sounded like hiccupping laughter burst from his lips as he doubled over, chortling and gasping.

"Cackle fever!" one of the rebels closest to him shrieked—then turned and ran away.

Nicco, visible now, was frantically dodging as the yuan-ti lashed down at him from his seat on the cart, trying to sink his fangs into Nicco's neck. Unable to move, his feet entangled by the weeds, Nicco prayed loudly, one hand raised imploringly to the heavens. A glowing shield of magical energy sprang up in front of his hand, but even as Nicco swept it down between him and the yuan-ti, the driver lunged past it and sank his fangs into Nicco's shoulder. The cleric sagged to his knees as venom coursed through his blood.

"No!" Arvin cried.

Thunder boomed overhead once, twice, a third time—Hoar's death knell for his fallen cleric?

One hand clutching his pounding head, Arvin raised his dagger. The yuan-ti was still sitting on his cart, no more than a dozen paces away. An easy target, in daylight—but rain was falling in thick, splattering drops, further obscuring his aim. Arvin threw—and hissed in satisfaction as he saw the driver thrash once then crumple in a loose coil.

The rebels were faltering, more than one of them turning to run, but somehow Gonthril managed to pick up his sword and rise to his feet. "Finish them," he croaked, staggering weakly forward.

Amazingly, the rebels rallied. Weapons raised, they moved grimly forward.

The Pox seemed to have had enough. They stared, stricken, at the dead yuan-ti. Then one of the cultists leaped up onto the cart. "Form a circle!" she shouted. "Join hands with me."

They did and, a moment later, were gone.

So, too, was the barrel. It had been teleported away—right out of the straps that had bound it to the cart.

Arvin, nearly blinded by the falling rain that soaked him to the skin, staggered forward to the place where Nicco had fallen. The cleric, he saw to his infinite relief, was still alive. One of Nicco's hands gripped a deep puncture in his shoulder, which closed, healing itself, as he completed his prayer. As Nicco tore his feet out of the weeds that had entangled them, Gonthril staggered up to him, a stricken look on his face.

"We have . . . failed," the rebel leader gasped. "They took . . . the potion."

"Yes—Hoar be praised," Nicco said, a gleam in his eye.

Seeing Gonthril's mute question, Nicco explained. "Not only did I dispel the potion's magic and negate its poison; I also placed a blessing upon it. The 'potion' is harmless—to anyone but the Pox. When they drink what is now holy water, Hoar's vengeance will be complete."

Gonthril laughed then—a genuine laugh, if weak. Then a violent trembling shook his limbs and he sagged weakly.

As Nicco moved toward Gonthril, Arvin clutched at the cleric's rain-soaked shirt. Arvin didn't have much time left. He could feel the mind seed unfolding within his head, pushing aside his awareness, crowding out his thoughts with a fierce, gloating joy.

"The mind seed," Arvin gasped. "It's blossoming. Nicco, *please*, pray for me."

Nicco glanced at him, sympathy in his eyes, then turned away. "Gonthril first," the cleric said over his shoulder. "His need is more urgent."

"No!" Arvin wailed.

Too late. Nicco had already slipped out of Arvin's grasp. As the cleric prayed over Gonthril, healing him, Arvin sank to his knees under the weight of the crushing pain that filled his head. Moaning, he felt the mind seed expand and start to push his awareness aside. He saw Nicco finish his prayer and turn toward him, but then his vision dimmed. What remained of his consciousness began to slough away like a torn and tattered skin.

CHAPTER 19

29 Kythorn, Darkmorning

*Z*elia cast her awareness ahead to the tavern where the human-seed waited. He sat at a table near the far wall of the room, at the same table where she herself had been seated seven nights ago. As she watched, he paid for a mug of ale then tipped it back, swallowing whole the small egg it contained. That—and his loose, swaying body posture—convinced her. He had succumbed.

Her tongue flickered in anticipation. How delicious he looked.

Her lapis lazuli was affixed to his forehead. He must have used it to manifest the sending Zelia had just received. The wording of his brief message had been tantalizing. At long last she would have the proof she needed that Sibyl was moving against House Extaminos.

She walked down the ramp and into the tavern, pausing to give the half-dozen sailors who were drinking there a quick scan. Silver flashed in her eyes as her power manifested, but it revealed nothing—all of the sailors were exactly what they seemed. She crossed the room and joined the human-seed at the table. He rose and greeted her with a passionate kiss that sent a fire through her, but she pushed him away and indicated that he should resume his seat. There would be plenty of time for pleasure, once this bit of business was concluded.

"Tell me what happened," she said.

"I found myself lying in a field," the human-seed told her. "The signs of a recent battle were all around me. There were seven bodies—six clerics of Talona and one yuan-ti."

"Describe him."

"He was a half blood with a human upper torso. His scales were black, banded with purple. The bands had a faint diamond pattern within them."

Zelia nodded. The pattern was typical of the yuan-ti of the Serpent Hills. Interesting.

"There was no sign of whoever attacked the clerics. They must have hauled their dead and wounded away. I must have been fighting on the side of the clerics, since I was left for dead."

"The attackers were probably the humans who killed Osran," Zelia mused.

The human-seed stared at her. "Osran is dead?"

Zelia smiled. "A lot has happened in the past seven days." She stared at the human-seed, noting its strong resemblance to the one human who had escaped after Osran was assassinated—Gonthril, the rebel leader. The faction he led was little more than an annoyance, but perhaps it could be manipulated into providing a distraction, should Lady Dediana choose to move against Sibyl. All that would be required would be to replace Gonthril with the human-seed.

Or perhaps, she mused, to seed Gonthril himself.

The barman approached with a mug of ale. Zelia glared at him, sending him scurrying away, then turned to the human-seed. "You said you found proof that Sibyl is backing the Pox?"

The human-seed nodded. "That's why I asked you to come here. I found a letter in a scroll tube the yuan-ti was carrying. It's addressed to Karshis, from Ssarmn. It makes reference to Talona's clerics—and to Sibyl." He placed a scroll tube on the table and pushed it toward Zelia. "It should prove quite . . . enlightening."

Zelia stared at the tube. "Read it to me."

The human-seed showed no hesitation as he tipped the document out of the tube; perhaps her suspicions were unfounded. Unrolling the document, he began to read in a low voice. "'Karshis,' it begins, 'Please relay, to Sibyl, a warning about the potion. If the clerics drink it and survive—and are not transformed—an unforeseen result may occur. Any psionic talents they have will be greatly enhanced. You may inadvertently produce an opponent capable of—'"

"Give me that," Zelia said, thrusting out a hand. Anticipation filled her. Perhaps the letter would also contain proof that Sibyl was not the avatar she claimed to be, but mortal, like every other yuan-ti.

The human-seed passed her the letter. She avidly began to read.

The letter flared with a sudden brilliance that left her blinking and unable to see. Too late, she realized it had been a trick, after all. The letter had contained a magical glyph—one that had blinded her. She could still hear the human-seed, however, and could still pinpoint his position by his body heat. Immediately, she attacked. Wrapping mental coils around him, she flexed her mind, squeezing with crushing force—only to feel her target slip away. Suddenly his mind was gone—empty—and her coils were passing through insubstantial, vacuous emptiness. The human-seed's mind had retreated into the distance, leaving her with nothing to grasp.

Expecting an attack in return, she threw up her own defense, raising a mental shield and interposing it between them. From behind it she lashed out with a mental whip—and hissed aloud, a vocalization that overlapped the hissing of her secondary display, as she felt it lash the human-seed's ego. Surprisingly, he had maintained the same defense, instead of switching to a more effective one. Of course, he had only half of her powers. Gloating, Zelia drew back her mental whip to strike again.

She heard a sound that startled her: a faint tinkling, like the sound of distant bells. She recognized it in an instant as a secondary display and knew that it was coming from the human-seed across the table from her, but something was somehow *wrong* about it. Then she realized what it was. The tone of the sound was subtly off. It wasn't *her* secondary display.

It wasn't a human-seed who sat across the table from her, but Arvin.

She almost laughed aloud at the notion of a novice psion—a mere *human*—daring to attack her. Arvin, with his pathetic roster of powers, what was he trying to do, charm her? He didn't stand a chance of—

Her arrogance was nearly her undoing. Arvin's mind thrust into hers like a needle into flesh, forcing a link between them. Into this breach quested mental strings, seeking to knot themselves into the part of Zelia's mind that controlled her physical body. She recognized the power he was using at once. He was hoping to dominate her, to make her his puppet. Where had he learned to manifest that power? It should have been well beyond him.

No matter. Unwittingly, he'd played right into her hands. She'd half expected her seed to go rogue—it happened with disturbing regularity when she seeded a human. And so she'd manifested a turning upon herself. The strings of mental energy suddenly doubled back on themselves and needled their way into Arvin's mind instead.

There, they knotted.

"Stop fighting me," Zelia commanded.

Arvin did.

Zelia tasted the air with her tongue, savoring the odor of fearful sweat that clung to Arvin. This was going to be so much fun.

29 Kythorn, Highsun

Arvin trudged along the seawall, his footsteps as reluctant as a man going to the execution pits, with Zelia a step behind him. She was still blind, but it didn't matter. She had manifested a power that allowed her to "see" without eyes. She was taking a great delight in humiliating him; back at the Coil she'd forced him to order a second ale, and a third, and crack the eggs they contained over his head, much to the uproarious delight of sailors at a nearby table. The yolk was still in his hair and growing crustier by the moment in the Highsun heat. Then, when they began walking along the seawall, she'd forced him to deliberately bump into a burly sailor who had flattened Arvin's nose when Arvin "refused" to apologize. Arvin's nose was still stinging from the punch and blood was dribbling down his lips and dripping off his chin. But none of the people they passed—even those who spared Arvin a sympathetic look—dared to question what was going on. They took one look at Zelia, lowered their eyes, and hurried past.

Arvin had tried to fight the domination Zelia had turned back on him, but to no avail. She controlled his body completely. All he could look forward to, once she was done playing with him, was a swift death—preferably a bite to the neck, like she'd given her tutor.

Arvin had been stupid to think he could defeat her, even with Nicco's help. The glyph the cleric had provided hadn't even slowed Zelia down. So much for the "nine lives" Arvin's mother had promised. The power stone was still in his pocket—Zelia had been too confident in her domination to bother searching him—but the two powers that remained weren't going to be any help. He wished the teleportation power he'd used to kill Karshis were still available. He could have used it when they first embraced in the tavern.

In the end, Arvin thought, he'd gone in a circle. Despite all of his efforts, he'd only succeeded in replacing one form of control with another. Nicco had managed to purge the mind seed even as it blossomed, but at the end of it all, Arvin had wound up back under Zelia's thumb. She couldn't force him to do anything truly self-destructive—to stab himself, for example—or else the domination might be broken. But she could certainly think up numerous lesser torments.

Smelling a foul odor, he glanced at the waves that gently lapped against the base of the seawall and shook his head. The sewage outflow—in this spot, seven nights ago, the circle had begun.

"Stop," Zelia ordered.

Arvin jerked to a halt, wondering what new instrument of torment Zelia had just spotted. Perhaps she was going to order him to flagellate himself with the coil of line that lay on the seawall, next to a bollard. The monkey's fist at the end of it would inflict some fine bruises....

He glanced back at her and saw a malicious smile on her lips.

"Turn toward the harbor," she said.

Arvin did.

"Jump into the water."

Arvin's body tensed. No. He wouldn't. That was *sewage* down there—foul-smelling, filth-choked water, laden with disease. The stench of it brought back all of Arvin's worst memories of the orphanage and the cruel punishments Ilmater's priests had inflicted on him. Of being wrapped in magical stink that wouldn't wash off, that made him the subject of the other children's taunts and jeers, of—

"I said *jump!*" Zelia hissed.

Arvin couldn't. He *wouldn't*. . . .

Like a cloak falling from his shoulders, the domination fell away. In the split second that Arvin knew he was free of it, he realized something more. If he tried to attack Zelia directly, he wouldn't stand a chance. Zelia was swifter than he, more powerful. He needed a distraction.

He jumped.

Cold water engulfed him. He came up with his eyes and mouth screwed shut and heard Zelia's hissing laughter above him. Ignoring the disgusting slime on his lips, the feel of sewage on his skin and the sludge dripping from his hair, he forced his eyes open. Immediately, he spotted his weapon—the monkey's fist. Energy flowed up and into his third eye then streaked out in a flash of silver toward the monkey's fist, which rose into the air, spinning, as if twirled by an invisible hand.

Hissing in alarm, Zelia spun around—but too late. The monkey's fist shot through the air toward her, striking her temple with a loud thud. Eyelids fluttering, Zelia tried to turn back toward Arvin but only managed a half-turn before sagging at the knees—then suddenly collapsing.

Arvin, still treading water, was as surprised as Zelia by the result. Had he really felled a powerful psion with so simple a manifestation as a Far Hand?

Quickly, he scrambled up the seawall. He stood, dripping, over Zelia, hardly daring to believe his eyes. Her chest still rose and fell, but she was definitely unconscious. Already a large red welt was swelling at one side of her forehead.

Arvin flicked his sodden hair back out of his eyes and shook his head. "You shouldn't have taught me that power," he told her. Then, seeing the curious onlookers who were starting to collect—including a militiaman who was striding briskly up the seawall—he knelt beside Zelia and pretended to pat her cheek, as if trying to revive her.

The militiaman shoved his way through the spectators and glared down at Arvin through the slit-eyed visor of his cobra-hooded helmet, his crossbow leveled at Arvin's chest. "What's going on here?" he demanded.

Arvin glanced up at the militiaman. "Thieves," he said quickly. "They shoved me off the seawall and knocked my mistress unconscious. They stole her coin pouch." He felt the familiar tingle of energy at the base of his scalp.

The militiaman cocked his head, as if listening to a distant sound, succumbing to the charm. But Zelia was beginning to stir. Arvin prayed she wasn't going to regain consciousness just yet.

"I'm a healer," Arvin continued. "I just have to lay hands on my mistress, and she'll be all right. We don't need your help. Why don't you try to catch the thieves, instead? There was a bald man and a little guy." He pointed. "They went that way."

The militiaman nodded and jogged away. Arvin, meanwhile, flourished his hands then laid them on Zelia's forehead. He linked with his power stone. Seizing one of the two remaining "stars" in its sky, he delved deep into Zelia's mind. It was as he'd visualized it when he'd first explored the mind seed under Tanju's guidance—a twisted nest of snakes. Her powers lay within this writhing mass. They looked, to Arvin, like a cluster of glowing eggs, some large, some small. He hefted them one by one, getting a sense of what each one was. The largest proved to be the one he was looking for. Lifting it from the nest, he crushed it.

Somewhere in the distance, he thought he heard a faint cry. Ignoring it, he linked with his power stone once more and manifested its final power, the one that would allow him to tailor memories. Reaching out with mental fingers, he began rearranging the snakelike strands of thought, braiding them into lines of his choosing.

Zelia's eyes fluttered open. Someone was touching her temple—Arvin! He had just manifested a psionic power on her, had reached deep into her mind and removed something that had taken her nearly a year to learn—the mind seed power. He was still rummaging around inside her head, manifesting a second power on her. Immediately, before he could throw up a defense, she attacked. A loud hissing filled the air as she manifested a power. An instant later it was joined by a sharp exhalation as the air was forced from Arvin's lungs.

Wisely, the other humans fled.

Arvin attempted a gasp, but was unable to inhale; Zelia's power had squeezed his lungs shut. She rose to her feet as he crumpled to his knees and watched, smiling, as his face turned first red, then purple. His eyes were wide, pleading—she would have loved to have heard him beg for his life, but the crisis of breath he was experiencing prevented that. Instead, she leaned forward and let her lips brush his ear as she whispered into it.

"Which was worse," she asked. "The mind seed . . . or this?"

It took all of her self-control to resist sinking her teeth into his throat. Instead, she stepped back and watched him fall to the seawall. He twitched for a time, mouth opening and closing like a landed fish. Eventually, he lay still.

Zelia placed a foot against his back and shoved. Arvin's body flopped over and fell, landing with a splash where it belonged.

In the sewage.

As Zelia slowly regained consciousness, Arvin strode away down the road at a brisk pace, away from the harbor, pleased with the false memory he'd just planted. As he walked, he pulled the power stone from his pocket. Its powers spent, it had stopped glowing.

He tossed it into the air and caught it again then thrust it back into his pocket. "Nine lives," he chuckled.

29 Kythorn, Evening

Arvin paced back and forth across the room, unwilling to look at his friend. Naulg lay on the floor, writhing and gnashing his teeth, trying to strain his hands out of the twine that bound them. The twine—the same one Karshis had used to bind Arvin—was solid stone; Naulg didn't have a hope of slipping it. Even so, he'd continued to struggle long after his wrists were chafed and bloody.

Arvin turned to Nicco. "Isn't there anything we can do for him? There must be some way to reverse the effects of the potion, some healing prayer you could try."

Nicco's earring tinkled as he shook his head. "I've tried everything. Your friend is beyond help. Hoar grant that, one day, you'll find a way to avenge him. There is only one thing, now, to be done."

Arvin forced himself to stop pacing, to turn and look at Naulg. The rogue was barely recognizable. His body was emaciated and his skin was a yellowish green, like that of a plague victim. The last of his hair had fallen out and his distinctive eyebrows were gone. His eyes—which only days ago had still held a spark of sanity—were the eyes of a madman. Sensing that Arvin was looking at him, Naulg bared his teeth in an angry hiss. Venom dripped from his incisors.

Arvin squatted on the floor beside him. "Naulg," he said, touching the rogue's shoulder. "I'm sorry. If only I'd been less concerned with saving myself...."

Swift as a snake, Naulg twisted his body and snapped at Arvin's hand. Arvin jerked it away just in time to avoid the bite. Rising to his feet, he stared down at the creature Naulg had become. Once, this had been a friend. Now, it was nothing but a monster—a dangerous one.

Why, then, were Arvin's eyes stinging?

"Do it," he croaked, turning away.

Nicco nodded. Quickly—perhaps wanting to complete the act before Arvin changed his mind—he chanted a prayer. Arvin heard a rustle of clothing as Nicco bent over Naulg and touched him. There was a choked gasp—then silence.

A tear trickled down Arvin's cheek. He felt Nicco's hand gently touch his shoulder.

"Will you avenge him?" the cleric asked.

Arvin shrugged the hand from his shoulder and angrily wiped the tear from his cheek. "There's no one left to take vengeance on," he said. "The Pox will have consumed the holy water by now; I doubt if any of them are still alive. Osran, too, is dead."

"You're forgetting Sibyl."

Arvin turned to face Nicco. "We know nothing about her," he said. "Where she is, *who* she is. . . . What if she's an avatar, as she claims?"

Nicco's eyes blazed with grim determination. "Even avatars may be defeated," he said. He placed a hand on Arvin's shoulder. "You've proved your worth to Gonthril. And Chorl—may Hoar weigh his soul well—is no longer here to oppose you. It's time for you to take a stand, to join us. Throw in your lot with the Secession." His eyes softened as he smiled. "It wouldn't be the first time a member of the Guild had secretly joined our ranks."

Arvin sighed. The offer was tempting. The Secession just might be his way out of the Guild. But old habits died hard.

"I'm sorry," he told Nicco. "I prefer to work alone. And I need time to hone my talent."

Nicco nodded, dropping his hand. "Hoar be with you, then." He turned and left.

Arvin stared at the door for a long time after it closed. Then he turned to the body of his friend. At least he could give Naulg a proper cremation—something the rogue wouldn't have had if he'd died back in the sewers—or if he'd starved to death in the locked room of the crematorium, where the Pox had left him. Arvin spoke the command word and the stone binding Naulg's wrists turned back into twine. Arvin knelt and gently unwound it from Naulg's wrists.

Slowly coiling it, he paused. Maybe, he decided, Nicco was right.

"I'll make Sibyl pay for what she did to you, Naulg," Arvin promised. "If the gods grant me the chance, I'll avenge you."

Somewhere out over the Vilhon Reach, thunder rumbled.

CHECK OUT THESE NEW TITLES FROM THE AUTHORS OF R.A. SALVATORE'S WAR OF THE SPIDER QUEEN SERIES!

VENOM'S TASTE
House of Serpents, Book I
Lisa Smedman

Serpents. Poison. Psionics. And the occasional evil death cult. Business as usual in the Vilhon Reach. Lisa Smedman breathes life into the treacherous yuan-ti race.

March 2004

THE RAGE
The Year of Rogue Dragons, Book I
Richard Lee Byers

Every once in a while the dragons go mad. Without warning they darken the skies of Faerûn and kill and kill and kill. Richard Lee Byers, the new master of dragons, takes wing.

April 2004

FORSAKEN HOUSE
The Last Mythal, Book I
Richard Baker

The Retreat is at an end, and the elves of Faerûn find themselves at a turning point. In one direction lies peace and stagnation, in the other: war and destiny. *New York Times* best-selling author Richard Baker shows the elves their future.

August 2004

THE RUBY GUARDIAN
Scions of Arrabar, Book II
Thomas M. Reid

Life and death both come at a price in the mercenary city-states of the Vilhon Reach. Vambran thought he knew the cost of both, but he still has a lot to learn. Thomas M. Reid makes humans the most dangerous monsters in Faerûn.

November 2004

THE SAPPHIRE CRESCENT
Scions of Arrabar, Book I
Available Now

FORGOTTEN REALMS®

R.A. SALVATORE'S
WAR OF THE SPIDER QUEEN

THE EPIC SAGA OF THE DARK ELVES CONTINUES.

New in hardcover!

EXTINCTION
Book IV
Lisa Smedman

For even a small group of drow, trust is the rarest commodity of all. When the expedition prepar
for a return to the Abyss, what little trust there is crumbles under a rival goddess's hand.

January 2004

ANNIHILATION
Book V
Philip Athans

Old alliances have been broken, and new bonds have been formed. While some finally embark f
the Abyss itself, others stay behind to serve a new mistress—a goddess with plans of her own.

July 2004

RESURRECTION
Book VI

The Spider Queen has been asleep for a long time, leaving the Underdark to suffer war and rui
But if she finally returns, will things get better... or worse?

April 2005

The New York Times *best-seller now in paperback!*

CONDEMNATION
Book III
Richard Baker

The search for answers to Lolth's silence uncovers only more complex questions, allowing dou
and frustration to test the boundaries of already tenuous relationships. Sensing the holes in th
armor of Menzoberranzan, a new, dangerous threat steps in to test the resolve of the Jewel of
Underdark, and finds it lacking.

May 2004

Now in paperback!

DISSOLUTION, BOOK I
INSURRECTION, BOOK II

THERE ARE A HUNDRED GODS LOOKING
OVER FAERÛN, EACH WITH A THOUSAND
SERVANTS OR MORE. SERVANTS WE CALL ...
THE PRIESTS

LADY OF POISON
Bruce R. Cordell

Evil has the Great Dale in its venomous grip. Monsters crawl from
the shadows, disease and poison ravage the townsfolk, and dark
cults gather in the night. Not all religions, after all, work for good.

July 2004

MISTRESS OF NIGHT
Dave Gross

Fighting a goddess of secrets can be a dangerous game. Werewolves
stalk the moonlit night, goddesses clash in the heavens, and a lone
priestess will sacrifice everything to stop them.

September 2004

QUEEN OF THE DEPTHS
Voronica Whitney-Robinson

Far below the waves, evil swims. The ocean goddess is a fickle
mistress who toys with man and ship alike. How can she be
trusted when the seas run red with blood?

May 2005

MAIDEN OF PAIN
Kameron M. Franklin

The book that **Forgotten Realms®** novel fans have been waiting
for—the result of an exhaustive international talent search. The
newest star in the skies of Faerûn tells a story of torture, sacrifice,
and betrayal.

July 2005

FATHER AND DAUGHTER COME FACE-TO-FACE IN THE STREETS OF WATERDEEP.

New in hardcover!

ELMINSTER'S DAUGHTER
The Elminster Series

Ed Greenwood

Like a silken shadow, the thief Narnra Shalace flits through the dank streets and dark corners of Waterdeep. Little does she know that she's about to come face-to-face with the most dangerous man in all Faerûn: her father. And amidst a vast conspiracy to overthrow all order in the Realms, she'll have to learn to trust again—and to love.

May 2004

ELMINSTER: THE MAKING OF A MAGE

ELMINSTER IN MYTH DRANNOR

THE TEMPTATION OF ELMINSTER

ELMINSTER IN HELL

Available Now!

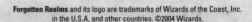